WITH
A FRIEND
LIKE YOU

Also by Fanny Blake

What Women Want
Women of a Dangerous Age
The Secrets Women Keep

WITH
A FRIEND
LIKE YOU

Fanny Blake

First published in Great Britain in 2014 by Orion Books,
an imprint of The Orion Publishing Group Ltd
Orion House, 5 Upper Saint Martin's Lane
London WC2H 9EA

An Hachette UK Company

1 3 5 7 9 10 8 6 4 2

A CIP catalogue record for this book is
available from the British Library.

ISBN (Hardback) 978 1 4091 2850 2
ISBN (Trade Paperback) 978 1 4091 2849 6
ISBN (Ebook) 978 1 4091 2848 9

Typeset at The Spartan Press Ltd,
Lymington, Hants

Printed and bound by the CPI Group (UK) Ltd,
Croydon, CRO 4YY

The Orion Publishing Group's policy is to use papers that are natural,
renewable and recyclable products and made from wood grown in sustainable
forests. The logging and manufacturing processes are expected to
conform to the environmental regulations of the country of origin.

For Lizy, with love and gratitude

I

'Pregnant?!' Beth put down the jug of water and stared at her eighteen-year-old daughter, hoping she had misheard. From habit, her hand flew to the thin gold chain around her neck, twisting it round her forefinger.

Ella was opposite her, glaring at her glass, turning it slowly on the table, waiting for her parents' reaction. Her fair hair was scraped back into a ponytail, so Beth could see the vulnerability and uncertainty chasing across her face. She turned to Jon, who sat speechless, his mouth slightly open, eyes wide. In front of them, the steaming salmon and vegetables were forgotten.

She had not misheard.

She took a deep breath, and glanced around the kitchen as if looking for help. The door of one of the duck-egg-blue cupboards was ajar, the span of oak worktop reassuringly empty, but for the coffee-maker and kettle. The huge framed photograph of Vietnamese paddy fields, taken by Jon on their first holiday without the girls, took up most of the empty wall. Nothing was out of place.

The three of them had just sat down together for an early supper. The judge presiding over the hearing in which Beth was representing the aggrieved wife had drawn proceedings to a close early in order to write up his judgment, so Beth had been home in good time. For once, she had had time to change out of her black work suit into jeans and a jumper. She had been planning to ask the others where they wanted to go that summer once the exams were over. As usual, they had proved impossible to pin down so far. Croatia? Turkey? Greece? All hot, relaxed places that would have something to offer each of them. Now that Ella was about to leave home for university, this might be the last family holiday they'd ever take together. The thought had struck Beth with sadness.

Then Amy had rung to say that after the school hockey match she was going round to her best friend Hannah's house to revise – whatever that really meant. Beth was under no illusions when it came to Amy's less than enthusiastic academic leanings. Ella had come down from her bedroom and helped lay the table as usual, then waited till they were all sitting down before blindsiding them with her announcement. There had been no preamble, just a straightforward 'I've got something to tell you.' And then she did.

'Are you sure?' Beth asked. Her instinct was to play for time, uncertain how she should react. She straightened the blue place mat in front of her, aligned her knives and fork. Order.

Ella gave a little nod, still turning her glass. 'Yes,' she whispered, looking up, her face drawn but set, her eyes shiny. 'I've done a test.'

Beth sprang up and went around the table to sit by her, hugging her tight, feeling Ella's tension as she leaned into her for support. Pregnant! For a moment, Beth's shock stopped any thought, only allowing her to feel Ella's anxiety and her dread of their reaction as if they were her own. She held her closer. 'Those tests have never been one hundred per cent reliable. It could be wrong.' But she knew she was really only clinging to a fragment of wreckage as they were washed out into choppy waters.

Ella shook her head wordlessly, scrabbled for a tissue in her pocket and blew her nose. Beneath the sloppy jumper, Beth could feel her daughter's slim frame trembling. She reached out with her spare hand to stroke the stray wisps of hair back from Ella's face.

'I've done more than one test,' Ella choked out, as she regained some control of herself. 'They were all positive, so they must be right.'

'Oh, Ella.' Beth kissed her cheek. 'How many weeks, do you think?' She blinked back the tears that stung her eyes, and swallowed hard. This couldn't be happening. Not to Ella. A dart of fear shot through her: fear of the unknown, of what would happen to their daughter. Until now, Ella's path through life had been virtually obstacle-free. She'd done everything expected of her, all the boxes ticked. But this! They'd never expected anything like this to rock their world.

Ella looked at her. 'Seven or eight, I suppose. I'm not sure.'

Beth concentrated on maintaining an outward appearance of calm, while inside her thoughts were whirling, one unanswered question tripping over another. How could this be happening? How could Ella not be sure? What had she been doing two months ago? Around Christmas? As far as Beth knew, she didn't have a boyfriend. So who ...?

'I don't know what to do,' Ella said.

'You must do what you think is right,' said Jon, speaking slowly at first, as if he was making up his mind. 'We'll support you whatever you decide.'

Whatever you decide. The words ricocheted around Beth's head as their dual significance sank in. Her hand rose to her gold chain again, twisting it once, twice around her finger.

'Who's the father?' Jon asked quietly. 'Does he know?'

He had asked the question burning on the tip of Beth's tongue. She watched his expression, which showed nothing but love and concern. He was keeping anything else well hidden. He had always been so protective of Ella and Amy. When they were tiny, he'd joke about how, in the future, he'd insist on right of veto over any potential boyfriends. Even if he had been serious, there hadn't been any for him to approve or disapprove of. Too late now. The thought flitted through Beth's head.

Ella had always been a model daughter. Everyone said so.

Unlike her wayward younger sister, she had never done anything to make them worry. She was polite, kind and a hard worker at school, always focused, determined to get the outcome she wanted from whatever she was doing. Yes, she could dig her heels in, but where was the harm in that?

A baby. Nobody had said the word yet. But they were all thinking it.

If Ella really was pregnant, what would happen to her plans for the future? The predicted star-graded A levels, the place to study medicine at Cambridge. These were what she had worked for, what she had wanted and, therefore, what they had wanted for her. But if she had a baby … Beth tried to leave the thought unfinished, but she couldn't stop herself racing through the possible repercussions. She felt tears stinging her eyes again, but she wouldn't let them fall. Crying wouldn't help. Her first instinct was to protect, her second to guide and advise. After all, sorting out other people's problems was what she did for a living.

'You've never mentioned a boyfriend.' The words were out before Beth could stop them. They hung in the air, more accusatory than she had intended. 'Or have I forgotten?' she finished, gentle again, not wanting to reprimand Ella. Guilt that she hadn't talked to her more, didn't know what was going on in her life, niggled at her.

Ella shook her head, blowing her nose again. 'He's not exactly.' Her words were so quiet that her parents barely heard them.

Oh, God! Had she been sleeping around? Having unprotected sex? A new set of circumstances and their consequences entered the equation. Beth pulled back so she could see Ella clearly. Her daughter straightened up, her face blotchy but more determined now. Beth recognised that look. She drew in a shuddery breath. 'What is he, then?' she asked.

'I don't want to talk about him until I've told him. Until we've decided what to do.' Ella sniffed, back in control of herself again as she folded her arms across her chest and shifted out of her mother's embrace.

'What do you mean?' Beth hadn't meant to sound so anxious. Dealing with problems was one thing when they were someone else's, but this was different. 'Are you really not going to tell us who he is?'

'Being angry isn't going to help,' Jon intervened, ever the family peacemaker.

'I'm not. Really I'm not.' He was right, of course. Beth squeezed Ella's shoulder, reassuring her, before returning to her place at the other side of the table. Was this really happening to them? If she pinched her wrist, perhaps she would wake up. She didn't.

'I just want to talk to him first.' The damp tissue twisted between Ella's fingers and tore. 'I should have done it before telling you, but I couldn't keep it to myself...'

Jon ran a hand through his curly hair, his expression both puzzled and concerned. 'Of course, Lulu.' He used her childhood nickname, the one she always responded to.

Beth glared at him, then looked away. She didn't want to argue with him in front of Ella, especially not now, but surely they should insist that she told them. Whoever the boy was, he shared the responsibility. He would have his own views about what should happen.

'Tell us when you're ready, and then we can work out what to do together.' Jon reached across the table and clasped both of Ella's hands. She looked up at him, grateful.

As she witnessed their exchange, Beth was beginning to appreciate the strong young woman her daughter had become. When had that happened? It was no time since they had been collecting her from school, taking her to piano lessons, helping her with homework, applauding her at prizegivings and school plays, driving her to and from parties. So many snapshots from her past flicked by. Now tall and leggy in her black skinny jeans and baggy jumper, with a purposeful expression, she had grown up almost without Beth realising. She suffered a familiar pang of guilt for all those hours spent at work that might have been spent at home; all those opportunities to discover what really made her daughter tick that she would never get back. The truth was, of course, that Beth had no idea who her daughter spent her time with when she wasn't at home. She had made assumptions about her being with her girlfriends, hanging out, sleeping over. She should have involved herself more.

But, she justified to herself, she and Jon had always agreed that she could never have been a stay-at-home mother. When they'd met, she was already well on the way to becoming a successful lawyer. She adored her family, but her job was what made her get up in the morning. She relished the challenge, the difference she could make to people's lives, the intellectual rigour. No, she had wanted to have it all – career and family – and had tried her best to make it work. She couldn't have done more than that.

'I'm sorry,' she said. 'Of course that's what you must do. It's just such a shock. Shall we start again?'

Jon shifted in his seat, crossing his legs, clearly relieved that she wasn't going to make a scene. She started to serve the supper, not that she would be able to stomach a mouthful.

Ella pushed her plate away. 'Sorry, Mum, I'm just not hungry. I've been dreading telling you. I knew how hard it would be. Dad's right, though. This is my decision.'

'We only want what's best for you,' said Jon, toying with a bit of salmon.

Beth stared at her plate. 'Have you thought about—'

'Mum, don't.' Ella stopped her from saying any more. 'I know what you're thinking.' She scraped back her chair and stood up, taking her plate over to the dishwasher, her huge monkey-faced slippers shushing over the limestone tiles.

'I'm not thinking anything,' Beth lied. 'But I don't want to see everything you've worked for thrown away. You shouldn't make any decision lightly. You must look at all the possibilities.'

Ella's resigned expression was reflected in the glass splashback in the second before she squatted down to pet Jock, their grey schnauzer, who had come in to investigate the possibility of food. Then she straightened up and walked towards the door, shoulders hunched. Jock followed her, tail wagging, hoping this was the preamble to a walk.

Oh, God, thought Beth. This is so like what happened to me. The one thing I hoped the girls would never have to go through. At that moment, she wanted nothing more than to go over and hug her daughter again, but something in Ella's bearing prevented her. And then the moment had passed.

'Where are you going?' she asked instead, desperate to prolong the conversation, to reach some kind of resolution. 'We can't leave it at that.'

Ella looked back at them, biting her bottom lip hard before letting it slide away from under her teeth. 'I'm going upstairs. I've got to finish last year's physics paper for tomorrow. Not that I can concentrate, but I've got to try. Of course I'm not going to decide anything lightly or on my own, but there's no point in talking about it any more. Not at the moment. I just wanted you to know, that's all.'

'But ...' Beth felt the weight of Jon's foot on hers, warning her that she was in danger of saying too much.

'Not now,' he whispered.

Ella shut the door behind her.

'But if not now, when?' Beth hissed back.

He shook his head.

They sat together listening to the thump of Ella's footsteps on the stairs. The kitchen was silent except for the sound of the rain beating on the glass roof of the extension. After a moment, Jon let out a deep sigh.

'How could this have happened?'

7

'We know *how*.' Trying to get on top of her own confusion, Beth spoke sharply. She took a mouthful of her salmon, but almost gagged on the taste. Swallowing, she put down her fork. 'What we don't know is *who*.'

'I can't eat a thing either.' He stacked the plates, sweeping her leftover food on to his. 'If she's kept him secret till now, she's not going to tell us until she's ready. Even with this. You know what she's like.' He stood to pick up the plates and heap some of the leftovers into Jock's bowl. 'I can't believe we haven't noticed.'

Beth hesitated. 'But she can't have a baby.' Her voice broke. Jon passed her a bit of kitchen roll as she began to cry. 'What about all her plans?'

'Sometimes plans have to change.' He sounded stern, as if he had to make her understand. 'You of all people should know that.'

She ignored the dig. 'She doesn't have to have it, you know. There is another way.' She hesitated to say more, because she knew how strongly he felt about the issue. He'd made that crystal clear when she had told him about the abortion she'd had long before they met. He'd been sympathetic, but he hadn't hidden his feelings. 'If only I'd known you then,' he'd said, looking into her eyes. 'I would never have let you go through with it.' She'd been so touched; she had never forgotten his reaction. 'I'd have looked after you and made sure everything worked out for the best. You can't get rid of a life just because it's inconvenient.' Put like that, how could she argue?

At the same time, she had never regretted her decision. She couldn't help thinking that now. Having a baby at sixteen – only two years younger than Ella – in the household in which she had been brought up had been unthinkable. She would never have got away from there. Or if she had, she would never have survived. Usually she and Jon agreed about everything. But not about this, and maybe not when it came to their own daughter, whose career was mapped out, beckoning. All her teachers said the same thing.

'You're not seriously suggesting …?' He stopped, his head cocked to one side.

She didn't reply immediately. She needed to think the situation through, tread with care. 'I just think we should consider all the options, that's all. She's only just eighteen. What about her A levels, Cambridge, her life?' Did he not see how much those things mattered, how much a baby would disrupt everything?

'Why couldn't a baby be factored in? It wouldn't be the first time someone's done it.' He looked directly at her, challenging her, his dark eyes glittering. The silvering in the hair over his ears, the lines that deepened when he smiled and the slight pouches under his eyes gave him a lived-in look that she loved. If anything, age had improved him.

She was shocked to realise that he was quite serious. She recalled her own anguish when she had realised she was pregnant as if it was yesterday. However necessary it might have been, the decision to have an abortion had not been easy.

'Seriously, how could she possibly study medicine and look after a baby?' She heard the ghost of her young self talking. This was the girl who had wept with fear but hung, white-knuckled, on to the idea of a future, one she could never have had with a baby in tow. Surely the question was a reasonable one, something they should debate. When she had been studying law, there had certainly been no room for anything other than her career. Her family had come much later.

'Beth, listen to yourself. This is your grandchild you're talking about.' Jon straightened up from the dishwasher, shut the door and leaned against the run of units. The set of his face said he was not going to be easily budged. 'I know it's difficult, but we can't get rid of it just like that.'

She tried to sound reasonable. 'I'm playing devil's advocate here. We're not really talking about a baby at this stage, are we?

It's just a few cells that are frantically dividing. That's all. They don't amount to anything yet. Plenty of young girls take the other route without coming to any harm. I did.' The more she spoke, the more she began to see this alternative as a possible answer.

He shook his head. 'I can't agree with you. Think of it this way. If we'd done what you're suggesting, we wouldn't have had Ella, and think how empty our lives would be without her. The *only* way I would ever go along with her having an abortion is if that's what she decides she wants. Then I'll support her, not because I approve, but because she's my daughter and I'd do anything for her. But I won't encourage her.' He twisted his wedding ring around his finger, but didn't take his eyes off Beth. 'I'm sorry.'

How could he be so infuriatingly calm? So closed? So wrong? Beth didn't want to be the bad guy, but didn't someone have to consider every option? She wouldn't let herself think of it as a baby. If she did, she wouldn't have the strength to argue. She would think only of Ella, the life ahead of her, and what was best for that.

Before she could say anything else, the front door slammed. Footsteps sounded in the hallway, followed by the thud of a bag being dumped on the floor, before the kitchen door was thrown wide. Amy stood there, her pleated grey school skirt disappearing under a huge green hoodie with the school logo emblazoned on the back. Her eyes, peering out from under her side-swept fringe, were rimmed with black liner and thick mascara, presumably lashed on the moment the school bell rang at the end of the day. She certainly hadn't left the house looking like that in the morning.

'Hey, peeps. Why the serious faces? Looks like someone's died.' She headed for the fridge, opened the door and grabbed a carton of apple juice. Once the straw was in, the other end in her mouth, she looked up at them.

'Do you want some supper?' Beth asked.

'Good game?' Jon spoke at the same time.

Beth knew instinctively that he felt, as she did, that there was no need to involve Amy in Ella's situation. They would have to continue their discussion later.

'Rubbish.' Her daughter slouched across the room and flung herself at a chair. 'We lost thanks to that effing bitch Suzy Featherstone. Like she missed two goals. Can you believe it?'

'Amy, please. Language.' Beth observed Amy's sunny mood cloud over in an instant. Beneath the too-long fringe that never quite fell enough to one side, a sullen expression took shape.

'Well, she is. She's an utter cow. You don't know.'

'Salmon?' Jon pointed to the congealing remains of roast fish and wilted vegetables.

Amy shook her head, at the same time pulling at her skirt, which certainly did not meet the not-more-than-eight-inches-from-the-knee-when-kneeling rule that Beth remembered from her own school days. 'Nah! We had pizza at Hannah's.'

'But—'

'It was home-made,' Amy protested before Beth could object to pizza as a school-night meal.

A sudden blast of unidentifiable tinny music interrupted them. Amy reached into her hoodie pocket for her phone and held it to her ear, glaring at them all the while. Her face lit up. 'Yeah. You're joking. He's dope. No, I'll text her now. Yeah, thanks. Laters.' As soon as she cut the call off, she was texting, thumbs going at a million miles a minute, head bowed as she concentrated, a small smile on her lips.

Jon raised his eyebrows at Beth. They knew perfectly well the impossibility of imposing their opinions or lifestyle on their younger daughter, although they hadn't given up trying. She was a law unto herself. They had to choose their moments carefully, and perhaps they'd had enough upset for one evening.

'I'm going up,' Amy announced, scraping her chair across the floor. She swept her fringe towards her left ear, where it stayed for a nanosecond before flopping back over her face.

'Homework?' ventured Beth tentatively.

'Maybe. I've got stuff to do, though.'

Beth could imagine. In the jumble that passed for Amy's bedroom, the still small centre was the area of desk reserved for her laptop and the chair in front of it. Hers was the one room in the house where disorder prevailed, as her clothes were pulled out or taken off and dumped unceremoniously on the floor or the bed. Occasionally Beth ventured in there. Since her own disordered childhood, chaos of any kind was anathema to her. But if she said anything, or tried to impose some sort of order herself, she was shouted at. Apart from that, she had lost count of the number of family rows that had stemmed from their daughter's unyielding preference for social media over her schoolwork. She couldn't face another one right now.

As Amy left the room, Jon went over and pulled a bottle of red wine from the wine rack. 'A drink, I think,' he said, as he opened a drawer to find the corkscrew.

Beth fetched two wine glasses from a cupboard. The more she thought about it, the more she leaned towards the arguments for Ella not keeping the baby. She felt an urgent need to talk to Megan. But this wasn't the moment to call her – not when she and Jon were recovering together from the shock. Her closest friend would understand where Beth was coming from. Megan would understand how torn she was feeling. Megan loved Ella and Amy as if they were her own daughters, having known them and often looked after them since they were babies. And Beth loved Jake and Hannah likewise, although her work had stopped her from getting to know them in quite the same way. She and Megan had spent hours discussing their children; their hopes and fears for them. They had been equally proud of Ella's achievements, particularly given the lack of academic prowess shown so far by the other three.

Ever since Ella was born, Megan had been there for Beth as a constant source of advice and friendship. Beth liked order. She'd been reassured by a schedule, feeding every four hours, knowing when Ella was due to go down or get up. Except of course Ella didn't always oblige. And that provoked flurries of panic, of diving into the manuals, reading and rereading them as if an answer to a sleepless or food-refusing baby would come rearing out of the pages. When it didn't, Beth would consult Megan, who had endured all this and survived to tell the tale. With three years of motherhood, albeit of a rather undisciplined nature, under her belt, Megan was considered by Beth as the fount of wisdom. Unlike Beth, she had binned the baby books after those initial weeks of barely suppressed panic and adopted a more laissez-faire approach. She ignored scheduled feeding, scheduled naps and scheduled bath- and bedtimes. Jake ate when he was hungry. Megan was completely relaxed about when he spoke, crawled or walked. She wasn't looking for any signals that he was more or less advanced than other babies the same age. He was who he was. Beth envied her approach and tried to emulate it – without much success, but without any harm done to Ella, who became as obliging a toddler as Jake had been before her.

From those early days, they had debated motherhood, marriage, life, the universe and everything over countless cups of coffee and bottles of wine. They made each other laugh. They calmed each other's worries. They had become part of each other's story. Mothers-in-arms. That was what they were. Bonded by motherhood. Friends for ever.

They were due to meet for supper the following evening. Less than twenty-four hours away. Together they would work through the situation, through Beth's and Jon's reactions, and what the best course of action might be. Without having to contend with Jon's emotions as well as her own, Beth would be able to consider the situation more objectively. Megan would be that valuable sounding board they so often were for one another.

2

Instead of doing her physics, Ella was lying on her bed, face to the ceiling, eyes shut, surrounded by the patterned cushions she'd once made in a burst of sewing mania when Beth gave her a sewing machine for her birthday. Needless to say, said machine was now gathering dust in a cupboard downstairs. Having inherited her mother's fierce sense of order, everything around her was in its place: clothes in the cupboard and chest of drawers, bed made, desk orderly with pens lined up, notebooks piled on top of one another, treasures stashed in small boxes. Nothing could look more different from her sister's room. Beth straightened one of the myriad shades of nail varnish lined up on the regimented bookshelves. On the dressing table, a row of brightly coloured African baskets held the rest of Ella's make-up, hair-ties, belts and scarves.

Beth was about to tiptoe away when she spotted the white earphones and the cable linking them to Ella's iPhone on the bed beside her. The middle finger of her right hand was moving just enough to mark a rhythm. In her other arm was the manky pink elephant that had accompanied her to bed every night since she was tiny: a third birthday present from Jon.

'Ella,' whispered Beth, to absolutely no effect whatsoever. She stood at the end of the bed. Ella was quite beautiful. Her skin was almost translucent, with a few light freckles dropped on to the bridge of her nose. Wasn't a straight nose said to be a mark of success? The dimple on her chin that she had so hated as a child was less noticeable now. When she was little, Beth used to touch it with a finger and tell her that the good fairy had done the same when she was born, marking her out as hers.

Under the poster-boy gaze of some half-naked heart-throb, Beth leaned over and touched her daughter's arm.

Ella's eyes flew open. The iPod slipped off the bed, taking the earphones with it. 'God, Mum. Don't do that!' She sat up, crossing her legs, making room for Beth to sit in front of her. 'I had a feeling you'd come up.'

'Am I that obvious?' Beth asked, smiling.

'Mm-hm.' Ella nodded, her hair falling forward, curtaining her face.

'I'm not angry, if that's what you're worried about.' After all, her daughter had only replicated her own mistake. She was hardly in a position to be cross. 'I want to talk this through with you, calmly. Just the two of us.' She paused. How best to begin? 'We're so proud of you. You know that.'

'You mean you're not any more.' Ella took off her lucky charm bracelet, laden with gifts from friends and family, and laid it next to her jewellery boxes. An unfamiliar edge had entered her voice, a defiance that Beth hadn't heard before.

'Of course I don't mean that,' she protested, taken aback. 'All I mean is that you don't have to have this baby. There are other options. Your life and your future is what matters.'

She looked up at the outsize noticeboard packed with photos of Ella and her friends pulling silly faces, pissed at parties, crammed into photo booths, happy on holiday. Interleaved with them were postcards, favourite birthday cards and bits of stationery that she'd saved. If Ella were really to have a baby, her friends would carry on with their young lives, forgetting the one of them left at home knee-high in nappies. Her eyes strayed over the maxims her daughter had printed out and pinned to the wall:

Life is too short to waste a single second with anyone who doesn't appreciate or value you.

Friendship isn't about who you've known longest. It's about who came and never left your side.

Give up. That's too simple. Fight. Now that takes strength.

How she had grown up. If only Beth could work out what was going on in her head.

Ella didn't respond. She lifted the elephant and nuzzled it just as she had when she was little. Seeing the familiar gesture put a lump in Beth's throat.

'If you told us who the father was, perhaps we could talk to him.' She paused. Newspaper stories about Internet grooming and inappropriate liaisons with schoolteachers ran through her head. She dismissed them. No. Ella was far too smart and discerning for anything like that. Wasn't she?

Ella was concentrating on tracing around the flowers on her duvet with a finger.

'Not yet. I told you what I'm going to do.'

'At least go and see the doctor. Please,' Beth pressed her. 'If you won't talk to us, talk to her. I'll support you every step of the way, I promise. I want to help you, Lulu. I'll come with you.'

Ella shook her head. 'I'll go on my own.' She looked up, her blue eyes fixed on Beth. 'I'd rather, I promise. I'll be fine. Then I'll decide.'

'But I don't understand.' Beth hesitated, anxious to say the right thing. 'I mean, I know you love kids and working with Megan at ArtOfficial in the holidays, but looking after other people's children is a whole different thing from looking after your own. Think of what it would involve. And not just for a few months, but for years to come. Don't throw away everything you've worked so hard for. Please. You've got the rest of your life to have children. Wait until you're in a stable, loving relationship.' She was beginning to sound like something out of a family planning pamphlet. But how else could she make Ella listen?

Ella's eyes grew big. 'I can't believe you're actually encouraging

16

me to have an abortion. You're my mum!' If the matter hadn't been so serious, her outrage would have made Beth laugh.

Megan would know what to say, said her inner voice. She tried again. 'All I'm doing is offering my support if you're not sure. Go to the doctor tomorrow and talk it over with someone who isn't emotionally involved. It might help.'

Ella's finger stopped moving over the duvet. 'If it'll make you happy.' She looked at her mother, and Beth could read the confusion and anxiety in her eyes. After a moment, she started to trace another flower. 'Maybe you're right.' She sounded unsure. 'Perhaps that is what I should do. But I'm going on my own. OK?'

Beth began to protest but Ella cut her short. 'Mum! That's the deal. I want to make up my own mind, not be pressurised by you.'

Beth sighed as she hugged her daughter, floored by her stubbornness – though not for the first time. However, going over and over the same ground would not get them anywhere. She had made her point as clearly as she knew how. Ella had taken it on board. Her only hope was that her argument would take root somewhere inside her daughter's brain and bear fruit.

The journey between home and her office usually put a distance between whatever Beth had left behind and whatever lay ahead. However, the following morning, as she walked along the canal towpath to the tube, she couldn't shake off her family. Instead of concentrating on the increasingly messy and complex divorce proceedings she would be discussing later that day, she kept on returning to Ella.

She had left Jon at the kitchen table, poring over the morning paper. Amy had been late, stomping downstairs, her face creased from sleep. She'd grabbed a piece of toast, swearing about the stupid homework that she'd have to finish on the bus, and slammed out of the house, throwing a 'See ya' over her shoulder.

Moments later, Ella had appeared, looking as if she hadn't slept at all. She poured herself a glass of orange juice, took a yoghurt from the fridge and sat down, opening the book she'd brought with her, making it quite clear that she didn't want to talk. Despite the familiar routine, the atmosphere was freighted with tension. Both Jon and Beth knew better than to press their arguments this early in the day. Ella ate quickly before disappearing to her room.

Despite Beth's best attempts at persuasion, Jon had refused to come round to her point of view. While getting dressed that morning, they'd had a terse exchange in which Jon had promised he would make sure Ella made and kept a doctor's appointment – if that was what she wanted to do. The proviso made Beth nervous.

Seeing a cyclist pelting down the towpath at breakneck speed, she stepped on to the scrappy bit of verge, bumping into a dog-walker, plastic bag in hand. She pulled away.

Jon had looked anxious as she left the kitchen. 'What time will we see you this evening?'

'I'm going to have supper with Megan, but I'll come home first just to see how Ella is.' Megan could be relied on not to bring the emotional baggage to the debate that Jon and Beth inevitably did, nor would she judge. Having sixteen-year-old Hannah meant she would grasp the situation as another mother. If Beth asked, she might even talk to Jon for her. Megan had been friends with Jon when Beth first met him, and they had remained close, although not as close as she and Beth had become. Women's friendship was different – that was a fact.

These thoughts were still circling Beth's mind when she reached the offices of Watson, Threadwell and Standish. Whenever she saw her name on the door plate, she felt a small surge of pride. Being a partner in a well-respected family law firm had been the culmination of her professional ambitions. This was where a huge chunk of her heart lay, where she spent so much of her time wrestling with problems that were not her own, sorting them out, working alongside colleagues she liked and who liked her.

Behind the Dickensian exterior of the building was a hymn to glass and steel. She crossed the shiny lobby to take the lift to the second floor. Joanne was already behind the reception desk on a call. Beth smiled at her, admiring the new flowers – clashing anemones, freesias, lisianthus and tulips – the only splashes of colour in a symphony of Farrow & Ball off-whites. She walked down the corridor towards her office, noting that Martin, the paralegal, was late again.

David, one of her partners, called out as she went past. 'Morning.'

Beth backtracked and stopped by his door. Typically, his desk had disappeared under a mound of paperwork. 'Morning. What've you got today?'

'Meeting Mrs Jonas in half an hour. The husband's a bloody nightmare. He lives like a king, but he's claiming he's broke and can't afford the child support. He's done a brilliant job of hiding his resources, but he's got four kids, for Christ's sake. Then court.'

'So just another day at the coalface.'

They both laughed.

In her office, Beth dumped her briefcase beside her chair and hung her coat on the back of the door before removing her trainers and slipping on a pair of black heels. On the shelves behind her desk were rows of bundles, court documents kept in red, blue and eau-de-Nil ring binders. On the floor were regimented boxes for files due to be returned to storage that day, and a small pile of green folders tied with flamingo-pink ribbon. She sat down and checked her diary, making sure she hadn't forgotten anything, although her mind refused to let her family go.

How much easier life had been when the girls were tiny. Back then, there were gregarious South African and Australian girls to help look after them. And Megan, when all else failed. Jon had been in the process of building up a modest portfolio of small businesses and was often at home, or could be at short notice, so Beth had never had to worry too much. But as Amy and Ella got older, more independent, the problems seemed to increase rather than lessen, becoming ones she felt less and less equipped to deal with.

With twenty minutes before she was due to meet her three assistants, she had begun catching up with her emails when the phone rang.

'I've a Mr Malik on the line. He needs to see a solicitor urgently. He's been given your name. Will you talk to him? He thinks his daughter's been abducted.' Joanne was completely calm. However frantic a client, however desperate they might be to speak to one of the solicitors, she could be relied on to remain unrattled while taking their details and passing them through to the right person.

'That's fine,' said Beth. 'Put him through.' The sniff of a challenge excited her. This was why she was here.

There was a click.

'Beth Standish.' She sat up a little straighter and swivelled her chair towards the window, frosted so that she could only make out the outlines of the neighbouring building.

'Anwar Malik speaking. Janice Weatherall suggested I call you.'

Beth heard the tremor of panic in his voice, while recognising the name of a client she had helped through a difficult divorce.

'I need advice urgently, Mrs Standish. My wife Shazia and I divorced two years ago. I have custody of our two children, although of course she has regular access to them.'

Not of course at all, but Beth let that pass.

'Kamran stayed with me this weekend for a party but Aiysha went to her mother as usual. But Shazia didn't bring her back on Sunday afternoon as she should have. She hasn't been answering my calls. I've been round to her flat but there's no one there. A neighbour said she saw them leaving with a couple of suitcases.'

There was a pause as he caught his breath. Then: 'I don't know what to do.' His distress was obvious.

'Are you sure they haven't just gone away for a few days? To friends or relatives?'

'No, I'm not.' He sounded angry, frustrated by the question. 'But however badly we get on, she always rings if there's a problem. I'm frightened she's taken Aiysha home to Pakistan.'

'How likely is that?' Alarm bells started to ring. Pakistan was one of the countries yet to subscribe to the Hague Convention, so if the mother really had abducted the child, they'd have a tough job on their hands to get her back. There were plenty of similar cases that had seen parents fighting for years to find, let alone see, their children again.

'Her immediate family are all in Pakistan. She's got an uncle and aunt and some cousins here, but she's been homesick for a long time. She wouldn't tell me if she was planning to take the children, even for a holiday. She'd know I'd never agree.'

'Have you spoken to anyone who knows her? Her family? Friends? Her employer?' All Beth's professional instincts were kicking in. However uneasy she might feel, her job was to keep calm and act decisively.

'Everybody says she's gone on holiday for a couple of weeks. But, if that is the case, why didn't she tell me? And why didn't she take Kamran? She always has before. This is so out of character.'

'The police?'

'They weren't interested. As far as they're concerned, Aiysha's on holiday with her mother. What's wrong with that? I've no evidence that they've left the country, but I know something's wrong. You've got to help me. Please. Aiysha is only four.'

Beth glanced at her diary again. 'I think you should come to my office as soon as you can. We'll apply for a Prohibited Steps Order and a Residence Order. If it turns out that she's just on holiday in the UK, then you can rest easy should something like this happen again. We'll have to alert your local police, properly this time, and you'll need to make a statement. They'll issue a port alert. If you're right, and your wife has already left the country for home, then we'll need to make an application to the Pakistani authorities for Aiysha's return.'

'I can be with you in about an hour.'

'I'll be tied up with another client then, but I'll have one of my assistants help you with the necessary paperwork until I'm free.'

'Will you be able to get Aiysha back for me?'

She knew what he wanted to hear, but her job was to be realistic and not give him false expectations.

'If you're right – and I hope you're not – there's a protocol that should help us, but you'll have to consult a lawyer in Pakistan to start court proceedings there. And of course without legal aid you'll need to be prepared for the expense of the proceedings. I have to warn you that they may take some time.'

Even if the courts decided in his favour, one of the great problems could be discovering the child's whereabouts, never mind getting her back through the welter of red tape.

As soon as they ended their conversation, Beth went to brief her assistant to deal with the initial form-filling. When Mr Malik arrived, she would be completing a pre-nup between a couple in their fifties – a romantic story of teenage sweethearts reunited after their marriages to other people had ended through death (his) and divorce (hers). All they wanted to do was preserve their individual assets for their children. How far removed was their experience from that of Anwar Malik? And how far removed was hers? Marriage and its endless variety of repercussions never failed to intrigue her. Her days were filled with people who managed to tie themselves up into terrible knots, and she was grateful that in her own home life she hadn't had to deal with any of the problems that visited her office. She was too aware that these rifts and break-ups could happen to anyone. No one was immune.

But she had seen the distress and heartbreak that visited separating couples and was determined that she and Jon would never be among their number.

3

Friday night. Megan was late. Again. She had tried to be on time, but she hadn't been able to find her ankle boots, the lace-up maroon suede ones. Eventually she had located them under a chair in the sitting room. Where else? Then she'd had to dash back because she had forgotten to feed the cats. Then she forgot where she had left her front door key. At the bottom of her bag. Then the bus didn't come, and when it did, it kept stopping to 'regulate the service', until Megan was hopping with frustration. She sent Beth a text warning her she was running late, but only mentioning the bus.

The normally quiet restaurant-bar where Beth had suggested they meet was packed with braying estate agents and office types throwing back cocktails as if their lives depended on it. Standing still for a second to catch her breath after her half-run down the street, Megan glimpsed Beth sitting at the back at a small table, head bowed over her BlackBerry, an untouched bottle of wine and two glasses in front of her. She pushed her way through the young crowd, who moved aside like the Red Sea, or as if she had an infectious disease. Beside the brashness of their youth, Megan felt about as ancient as Moses. At least she hadn't come out in her tatty school clothes, but had changed into her black skirt and long maroon jacket with the green silk lining.

'Hello, miss. A'right?' A shiny, familiar-looking young man in a pinstriped suit barred her way.

She stared at him, her memory racing through the thousands of children who had passed through the gates of St Columbus

Primary School, where she was deputy head. She prided herself on remembering the majority of them. And then, yes, in the nick of time she got there. 'Darren! How nice to see you. What are you doing now?'

'Working for Curton Estate Agents. It's a good job. I'm married, too. Baby on the way.' He beamed at his roll-call of achievements.

His pride was touching. 'A baby. Congratulations.' She was fleetingly reminded of Ben Fletton, the worst of the tearaways in year five. Darren was another boy from the Meadow Estate who hadn't had the best start in life. He could so easily have gone to the bad with his two older brothers, one of whom she had heard was doing time. Perhaps the teachers at St Columbus could be credited with a little of his success. Believing that they could help make a difference was one of the things that made the job worth doing. She needed to remember that. 'Good to see you.'

'Nice to see you too, miss.' He melted back into the scrum, leaving Megan to forge her way through to her destination.

Beth looked up as she approached, gave a weary smile and put away her phone before standing up so they could kiss each other hello. As Megan removed her jacket, Beth poured them both a glass of red. She looked exhausted, even allowing for the black of her suit, which drained the colour from her face. Her eyes were tired, with dark shadows underneath them, her hair pulled back in the severest of styles.

'Is something wrong?' For the first time that day, Megan's consuming preoccupation with St Columbus dropped away. Into the gap slipped the troubling memory of a ten-day-old conversation with Ella that she had tried to pretend hadn't happened. Because of it, she had half hoped Beth would cancel their meeting. Sometimes that happened when her workload got the better of her. Understanding the pressures her friend was under, Megan had never minded. She sought strength in her wine glass, taking a larger than necessary sip. To hell with her weekly unit intake.

Beth followed suit, then leaned forward, cradling her glass. 'It's Ella.'

Megan braced herself. Ten days ago, Ella had come over, certain she was pregnant, wanting Megan's advice and swearing her to secrecy. Megan had hated agreeing. How could Ella demand that she keep such a secret from her closest friend? Equally, how could Megan admit to Beth that Ella had confided in her first? As a mother herself, she understood exactly how crushed Beth would be. Since nothing more had been said, Megan had begun to hope that Ella had made a mistake, got her dates wrong. An invisible hand clutched her stomach and twisted.

Beth didn't go on, but sat as if she was shouldering the weight of the world. She was not usually one for public displays of emotion, but now she opened her handbag, took out a tissue and blew her nose as she recovered herself.

Megan helped herself to a few peanuts. She didn't want them, but she had to do something. 'What about her?' Under the table, she crossed her fingers in a childish attempt to stave off the subject she feared.

'She's pregnant.' Beth shook her head as if she couldn't believe what she was saying. 'She told us last night. She won't say who the father is. And she doesn't know whether to have it or not.'

Megan stared at her. Her stomach twisted tighter.

Beth went on. 'She agreed to go to the doctor this morning and came back persuaded she should have a termination. She's referred her for one. I suppose I'm relieved.' But she spoke as if it was a question. 'At eighteen,' she went on, balling the tissue in her hands. 'Everything she's worked so hard for ...'

Megan reached out to hold Beth's wrist as she listened to her relate the previous evening's events. Without thinking, she tossed the nuts into her mouth. Within seconds, her eyes widened as a flame-thrower blasted up the back of her nose, the heat rushing from her chest to her face. Wasabi peanuts! She hadn't noticed in the dim lighting. She groped for her wine, trying to control her coughing so that she didn't interrupt Beth as she described her and Jon's differences.

'Are you OK?' Beth broke off on seeing her friend choking on the other side of the table.

Megan shook her head. 'Water,' she gasped, waving a hand towards the jug on the counter. Before Beth had a chance to do anything, a passing waitress came to the rescue. Megan recovered herself, wiping her eyes, blowing her nose and removing most of her make-up at a stroke. She cleared her throat and pushed the offending nuts on to the next table. 'You can't exactly blame Jon for not condoning abortion. Some people feel very strongly about it.'

'I know that, of course. But what's best for Ella?' Beth waved away a hovering waiter, who was anxious for the table, or another order.

'He's only thinking about the family.' Megan poured another glass of water, her nose still burning. Jon was one of the most hands-on fathers among their friends. He had involved himself in his children's lives where many other men would have run an office-bound mile. 'His grandchild.'

'That's what he said.' Beth's elbows were on the table, her hands clasped. 'But the family's my priority too. Of course I want what's best for them. I can't bear that Ella's going through this, having to make such a choice.' Her voice rose.

'Of course,' Megan reassured her. 'But he's got a right to an opinion.' Her long friendship with Jon wouldn't let her hear anything bad about him. Once, in the early days, before Beth came on the scene, she had even wondered whether the two of them might make a go of things … if it hadn't been for Pete. Silly, really, but they'd all been young then, and, if nothing else, she still felt protective towards him.

'Whose side are you on?' Beth topped up their glasses, but her half-smile showed she wasn't serious.

'I'm not taking sides. I'm just saying I can see where you're both coming from.'

'I know, but if it were Hannah, what would you do?' Beth looked at her over the top of her glass.

Megan hesitated, finding it hard to imagine the situation. 'I'd probably be the same as you,' she eventually conceded, wanting to support Beth. 'They've absolutely no idea what having a baby involves. How could they?'

'But I'm so torn. My heart says one thing, yet my head is telling me different.' Beth lifted her hands as if to illustrate the point.

'And do you always listen to your head?' Although Beth was a woman very much in charge of her life, there had been times, in the early days of her relationship with Jon, when Megan had seen her act impulsively. They would never have tried paragliding in the Alps that summer if it hadn't been for Beth egging them on, daring them, inspired by the coloured sails gliding against the backdrop of the mountains. 'I want to fly,' she had shouted, arms out, wheeling round in front of them. 'Don't you?' Laughing, the others had agreed. Megan had thought she'd die from fear as she ran towards the edge of the mountain, the sail and an instructor strapped behind her, but the others were thrilled by the whole experience.

'Not always when it comes to me. But this is her.'

Megan smiled.

'At least she's gone to the doctor. That's the first step. The sooner it's over, the better now. Oh, God, that sounds awful.' Beth picked up her glass. 'Perhaps you could talk to her, let her know she's doing the right thing. I know how much she listens to you.'

Megan froze. Was there the smallest hint of resentment in Beth's voice? She hoped not. 'Thanks for the vote of confidence, but I'm not sure I'd make much difference. She's a girl who knows her own mind.'

'Of course you would. Thank God I can talk to you.' Beth's

shoulders sagged with relief. 'You're the only person I really trust. I've no idea what's going on in her head.'

Megan opened her mouth to speak, then hesitated. Should she tell Beth about her conversation with Ella after all? Would it help?

'Just say what you think,' Beth urged. 'I can take it. I know I haven't always been as involved with my kids as some mums, but it can't be that, can it? You know us all so well and we understand each other. I really need your help here.'

Yes, they did understand each other, and Megan could see how desperate Beth was. In that moment, she made the snap decision to come clean.

'Well, when we talked about it, she said—' She stopped as Beth's face changed, immediately realising her misjudgement. Sometimes, whatever they said, people only wanted to hear what they wanted to hear. They didn't want the truth at all.

'When you talked?' Beth looked puzzled. 'When you talked about what?'

'Oh, this and that. You know.' Megan tried to dismiss her conversation with Ella, at the same time wishing a sinkhole would open and swallow both her and the wine. She tried a quick change of subject. 'I've had the most God-awful afternoon.'

But Beth was leaning forward, studying Megan with the for-ensic deliberation of a prosecuting barrister. 'Did you know? Did she come and talk to you first?' Her expression was glacial. She was clearly not about to let Megan off the hook.

'Not exactly.' Why say that? Why not lie? Save yourself. But too late.

'What do you mean, "not exactly"?'

Although the music had been turned up and the pair of tables beside them pushed together for a rowdy gaggle of girls, Megan heard every word.

'Well, she did come round the week before last and say she thought she might be—'

'Two weeks ago!' Beth's face was changing as she pieced together

29

the truth of the matter. Megan could see that her relief at being able to confide was vanishing, replaced by anger. 'She told you she thought she was pregnant.' Each word was pronounced slowly and distinctly, as if she couldn't believe what she was saying. A couple of the girls on the next table turned to stare, but Beth didn't care who was listening. 'And you didn't think to tell me?' She glared at Megan, who wilted.

'She asked me not to.' How feeble that sounded. A fifty-year-old woman in thrall to an eighteen-year-old. There must be a way of explaining without making this worse for any of them. 'I couldn't betray her trust. Surely you can understand that?' But judging by the way Beth was looking at her as if she was something she had picked up on the sole of her shoe, she clearly did not understand at all.

'I thought your first loyalty would be to me.' She sounded confused, lost. 'You're my closest friend. Or I thought you were. Of course you should have told me. If Hannah came to me with a problem, the first person I'd tell would be you.'

'I'm sorry.' Megan tried to salvage the situation. 'To be honest, when I didn't hear from her again, I thought she must have made a mistake and there was nothing to say.'

But Beth wasn't to be appeased so easily. Her eyes flashed with a fierce anger. 'I can't believe you did that. Did she tell you who the father is too?'

'No.'

'So she didn't tell you everything, then.'

Megan flinched at the dislike in her voice. 'No.'

Ella had hedged around the subject and Megan had not pressed her. She suspected he was either new on the scene, or unsuitable – much older, perhaps, or someone of whom Beth and Jon would disapprove. She assumed she would tell them when she was ready, or when she had to.

Beth pushed her glass away from her as if she had drunk enough. 'What did you say to her?'

Caught in the hostility radiating from her, Megan hesitated again. 'I said I thought she should think very carefully, but that if she really wanted to go ahead, it wouldn't be impossible. I didn't think she should feel pressured. I told her that if she decided to keep it, of course we'd all rally round to help.'

'You said that?' Beth looked as if she had been slapped. She leaned back in her chair as the gulf between them widened.

'I didn't say whether she should do one thing or the other.' Megan floundered. 'I didn't think it was up to me to tell her what to do.' In fact, she hadn't been able to bear the idea of Ella getting rid of the baby, but she hadn't gone as far as saying so.

'Well that's something, I suppose.'

'Beth, don't be like this. She came to me. I could hardly turn her away. I said she should tell you, of course I did, and I still think it's better you heard from her than me.'

'I'm not sure you're the best judge of what's better any more.' Beth started to knot her scarf around her neck.

'You're not going? We've still got so much to talk about.' Megan reached out as if she was going to pull her back, then dropped her hand.

'I don't want to talk to you right now. I can't believe Ella told you before me. Why would she do that? Or that you gave her advice on something so important without bothering to find out what we thought.'

'Don't be angry with her,' pleaded Megan, wishing she could take back what she'd said.

'I'm not angry. I'm hurt. After all these years, I thought we told each other everything.' She straightened her scarf.

'We did. We do,' protested Megan. 'I didn't know what to do. I was torn between the two of you. Surely you can see that? It was impossible.'

The young women on the next table were quite clearly finding their neighbours' conversation intriguing. Two of them were making no pretence about listening to every word.

Beth took no notice of them and shrugged. 'I should really be with Ella.' She pushed the table out so she could stand up. 'I'll call you.' She didn't sound as though that would happen any time soon.

'But, the book group dinner? What are you taking?' Megan grasped at the one random straw that occurred to her. The themed dinner, this time Indian, had been a source of amused discussion since it was announced weeks ago.

Beth edged out. 'No idea. I haven't given it a thought.'

There was nothing Megan could do except watch Beth shrug herself into her coat, sling her bag over her shoulder and leave the bar without a backward glance. She felt profoundly uneasy. Falling out was not something they did. They overcame the occasional ups and downs with an apology, an explanation or a laugh. The last time she could remember was when Beth had identified cat hairs in a Victoria sponge Megan had made for her. She had picked them out and held them up in front of her face, before laying them on her plate and separating them with a teaspoon, her face a picture of disgust. Megan had taken the accusation of being unhygienic to heart. They'd only begun to see the funny side a couple of weeks later. But this was in a different league altogether. Furious with herself for the way she'd handled things, Megan decided to stay on and finish the wine.

Eventually the waiter returned, hovering again. Megan asked for the bill. She was angry with Beth too: angry that she hadn't even tried to see things from her point of view. Blaming her for what had happened was totally out of order. Megan had always made sure her working hours fitted as much as possible around the kids' schooling, so that she was there when needed. Just as she had been for Beth's and Jon's daughters. When they were working, or when their childcare arrangements failed, Megan's door had always been open, with the result that Ella and Amy were almost like daughters to her.

Instead of sharing her evening with Beth, she would go home

and make supper for Hannah. They could have a rare girls' night in, watch a film uninterrupted and finish that box of chocolate truffles someone had brought over when they'd come to supper the previous week. They could make the most of the time they had together while Jake was touring in Germany with his band for a couple of weeks in towns Megan had never heard of, and Pete was living it up in Oman on yet another press trip.

Opening the front door, Megan was greeted by their two tabby cats, Diva, a particularly well-upholstered prima donna of the species, and String, a leaner, meaner beast altogether. They wound themselves around her legs, purring like traction engines, until she picked up Diva and went into the kitchen to feed them, String in hot pursuit. She had got them years ago as kittens from the RSPCA, when Hannah was tiny. A combination of them being the last two in the litter and Hannah's constant badgering for a pet had swayed her.

Leaving the cats to the unappetising anti-allergenic dry food that cost almost the equivalent of the national debt, she went upstairs to change, picking up the piles of folded laundry she'd left waiting at the bottom of the stairs.

As she slipped into her blue and red plaid pyjamas and fleecy red dressing gown, a Christmas gift from the kids, and yanked on her sheepskin slippers, she caught sight of herself in the bedroom mirror. Oh, well. Beth, on the other hand, was always so enviably elegant. They had tried shopping together, but, quickly bored, Megan usually redirected their hunt towards the nearest coffee shop. What was the Internet for, if not for shopping? If it weren't for the friendship between their husbands, which pre-dated both her and Beth, she sometimes wondered whether they would ever have discovered how much they had in common. She might have shied away from someone so apparently high-maintenance and high-achieving in every area of their life.

The ice between them had been broken on a trip to Kew

Gardens. Beth and Jon had only met a couple of weeks earlier, so they were all still treading carefully. Megan had noticed Beth's discomfort when Pete rolled a joint, so she suggested they went for a stroll together, leaving Pete and Jon sprawled on the grass. However, Beth's unease only increased when Megan whipped out a pair of nail scissors from the pocket of her jeans and started snipping at a shrub by the path.

'What are you doing?' she asked, astonished, looking around nervously.

'Cuttings for the garden. I'll take them home and grow them. Don't you love that one? *Sophora*,' she read. 'Aren't these flowers gorgeous? And this clematis. I've never seen one like that before. Don't let anyone spot me.'

She leaped into the middle of the flower bed, brandishing her scissors, just as a gardener turned the corner. As if she'd rehearsed the move for years, Beth stepped straight into his path and got him chatting, asking about the plants behind him, and the tea room, and the pagoda, forcing him to turn around so he was effectively deflected from Megan. Whether her instincts had kicked in to protect herself or Megan, they had never been able to decide. Megan appeared at her shoulder just as the gardener was asking Beth if she fancied a drink when he finished at six. There was a decent pub not far from the main gate. He could meet her there. Flushed with embarrassment, she refused. The two of them had run back to the others and collapsed, bent double with laughter. 'Don't you ever do anything like that again,' Beth had warned through her giggles. 'I'll lose my licence to practise.'

'Oh, bollocks!' retorted Megan, stuffing her cuttings into a plastic bag brought specially for the purpose. 'You're too cautious. They're not going to care about something as minor as that.'

'You could be capable of anything, as far as I know. That could just be the beginning.' Beth stretched herself out in the sun, resting her head on Jon, just below his ribcage, reaching up to link fingers with him, her spare hand pulling at the grass.

'Anyway, you were brilliant,' Megan said. 'He didn't even look in my direction. You're appointed as my wingman from now on.'

'Can I refuse the appointment?' Beth lifted her head, shading her eyes with her hand as Megan flopped down beside Pete.

'Not if you know what's good for you.'

Since then, their friendship had only got stronger. With husbands who were inseparable friends, and then their children, they had grown to depend on one another. Megan got Beth in a way others didn't. She heard her stories of growing up in the back streets of Nottingham, and how she'd struggled to make a better life for herself, and admired her determination and drive. She was unfazed by the occasional abrasive or dogmatic remark that could send other people spinning off into dislike. She understood that they were rooted in the insecurity that, despite appearances, had governed most of Beth's life. When all was said and done, the two of them accepted their differences and enjoyed each other's company. Besides that, Beth was a warm and generous friend. Birthdays never went forgotten. Her presents were never over-elaborate, but always thoughtful; Megan still used the extra-long rolling pin she was given when Beth realised her love of baking. And Beth was ready with advice or a shoulder whenever necessary. They had shared so much, including the sourdough starter that Megan once gave to Beth to encourage her to bake. But baking didn't come naturally, and the starter was soon returned.

In the bathroom, she picked up her skirt from the floor, catching sight of herself in the mirror again. That woman she didn't recognise was there, looking back at her, confounding her expectations. At a certain angle, gravity was winning the battle for her face. She pressed it back with her fingers for a moment. How could she feel so different, so much more youthful on the inside? She gave a wry laugh. How you approached life was what mattered. She studied her reflection. Her curls, still auburn thanks to a bit of chemical assistance these days, were more ungovernable than ever. Beth would have the right product to tame them, but

Megan couldn't be bothered with any of that. Years of riding her bike to school and back probably hadn't helped her skin. Her eyes remained her best feature, the wide-set deep blue that had snared Pete all those years ago. He'd said they reminded him of Elizabeth Taylor's. Ridiculous, of course; no two women had ever been less alike, but she fell for it all the same. She ran her finger over the crows' feet that branched out from their corners and the lines that bracketed her mouth. A lot of laughter had gone into making those. Much of it shared with Pete, Jon, Beth and the kids.

She heard the front door slam just as she started downstairs.

'Anyone home?' Hannah's voice rose to greet her. 'What's for supper? I'm starving.'

'And it's lovely to see you too.' Megan reached the bottom just as Hannah threw her coat over a peg. As she turned her back on it, the coat slid to the floor, bringing the one underneath down with it.

They kissed before Megan – of course – picked up the coats. 'I'm going to make us something to eat.'

'You're in your pyjamas!'

'And your point is? I can still cook, whatever I'm wearing.' She retied the belt of her dressing gown.

'I'd better do my English first.' Hannah's voice conveyed all the enthusiasm of a dead kitten. She took out her books and spread them across the kitchen table before docking her iPod and flooding the room with music.

As Megan scoured the fridge for something she could knock together easily, shoving brown paper packets of seeds to one side, she tried to put Beth to the back of her mind. She extricated a tub of hummus and the dolmades that were sporting a particularly attractive blue shade of mould, and emptied them into the bin. She dug out a red and a yellow pepper, went through her garlic to find a few cloves that hadn't dried out and took some eggs from a bowl.

Once the pepper and garlic frittata was cooking, she opened

the door of the larder to get a piece of Camembert from the cheese safe Pete had bought her in France, and some biscuits from the tin. She looked around at the empty jam jars stacked on the top shelf, the melee of tins, many of which must be past their sell-by date, and the jumble of spice jars: how many of them had sat there well beyond their time? She quickly shut the door on them.

As she arranged everything on a tray, nine-year-old Ben Fletton flipped into her mind again. She could picture his expression as he'd sauntered out of her room that afternoon. She might as well not have bothered with her lecture about not fighting in the playground, the importance of friendship. He'd turned as he reached the corridor to give her a look that could only be interpreted as a smirk. Cocky little sod. Clearly nothing she had said had penetrated his thick skull. Threatened punishments and the real thing slid like water off a duck's back. He simply didn't care. The kid was a persistent offender with scant regard for authority, who fought his way in and out of confrontations, driving the teachers to the end of their collective tether.

No, her day had not been one of the best.

4

After being back home for a couple of hours, the prospect of a hot bath was the only thing keeping Beth going. Ella was in the girls' bathroom, while Amy had installed herself in Beth and Jon's, where she was standing in front of the mirror squeezing a spot on her chin to the accompaniment of some strident but unidentifiable music. The bath was running, foam billowing off the surface. The scent wafting on to the landing told Beth that her younger daughter had, yet again, helped herself to liberal quantities of her favourite tuberose bath gel. How many times did she have to tell her? Whenever she attempted to point out that the concept of borrowing didn't hold if you didn't return the thing you'd taken, even if it was only a couple of fingertips' worth of the most expensive moisturiser on the planet, Amy would stare at her as if she'd lost her mind.

'What about your revision?' Beth moved swiftly to turn down the volume on the iPod dock. She itched to pick up the towels Amy had knocked on to the tiled floor.

'Hey! I was listening to that,' Amy objected as she gave a particularly vicious squeeze to a pimple on her forehead before reaching out to turn up the volume again. 'What about it?'

'I thought you agreed you were going to do some tonight.' Beth turned down the volume again.

'So?' Another squeeze, before adjusting the sound to a level she thought might be acceptable.

'It's ten o'clock,' Beth pointed out, the music reverberating around the room. Unbearable. As Amy redirected her attention back to her chin, Beth noticed the unopened mink-coloured nail varnish balanced on the lip of the basin, bought especially to go with her new dress. She reached over and rescued the bottle.

'What're you doing?' Outrage.

'My new varnish. Hands off.' She opened the bathroom cabinet. Amy had clearly been rifling through her carefully organised lotions and potions, bought to keep the advancing years at bay. She began to straighten them up. 'Your revision?'

'I'm busy. Can't you see?' Amy swung round to turn off the bath taps. 'Why can't you leave me alone? I'll do it when I'm ready.' She stood in front of Beth, hands on her hips. 'Mu-um. Please.'

Astonished by the unexpected 'please', Beth took a step backwards out of the room. The door shut in her face before she had a chance to say any more, and the lock clicked into place.

Exhaustion made her lean against the wall for support. Why was Amy so difficult? She had obviously failed miserably somewhere along the line, despite her efforts to follow those parenting guides that claimed foolproof solutions. She had tried to follow their rules, but all she had discovered was that what worked for one child didn't always work for another.

She summoned up the energy to return downstairs. In the sitting room, she sank into one of the two white sofas, leaning back against the cushions, hands behind her head, eyes shut. Having come home expressly to see Ella, Beth had found her elder daughter upstairs in her room involved in a seemingly endless phone conversation with a girlfriend. In the few minutes they had together in between that and the next call, Ella made it clear that she didn't want to discuss the doctor's appointment or the possible termination. At least not with her mother. Not then.

When Beth went up again to check that Ella was all right, perhaps to talk to her, her daughter's voice could be heard inside, still chatting, even laughing on her phone. Beth had popped her head round the door, but Ella had waved her away, saying she'd be down later. Jon had been engrossed in something on TV so all Beth could do was make herself beans on toast and sit alone in the kitchen, thinking.

Megan was everything Beth was not, and Beth knew it. She was gregarious, demonstrative and loud. She didn't care what people thought of her – not really. Beth longed to be more like her, but, try as she might, she could never wear her feelings on her sleeve in the same way. Her childhood had encouraged her to keep secrets. A lifetime in the law had trained her to hold her emotions in check, not to be horrified or upset by what went on in other people's lives, to appear impassive and non-judgemental. Next to her own well-ordered home, Megan's was warm and chaotic (and that was being kind). Beth envied the way the smell of baking drew the children towards Megan's kitchen as surely if they were following the Pied Piper of Hamelin. There, they were guaranteed to find tins reliably stocked with home-made cakes and biscuits. Beth recalled her one attempt at making Megan a birthday carrot cake. She cooked it for hours, and presented it with pride, only to find it was still raw inside. In Megan's kitchen, there was always a cat curled in a chair or patrolling the worktop, leaving the odd pawprint in the flour or hair in the cakes. Megan seemed not to notice. But Beth had so little time, and she hated mess. And cat hair. However, she had long ago learned to appreciate their differences, realising how lucky they were that Amy and Ella thought of Megan as a second mum. In an unexpected way, she even quite liked that. But this ... this was too much.

She opened her eyes, focusing on the two outsize canvases that dominated the wall opposite her: enlarged black-and-white photos of each of their smiling, windswept daughters. Not so much family mementos as artworks. Jon had taken them years ago, when they were all on holiday in Majorca. There were no other photographs in the room, no clutter or ornaments. This minimalist approach was balm to Beth's soul, offering nothing to distract or trouble her. The girls could make their mess in their own rooms, but not in here.

She yawned. The noise from upstairs suggested that Amy had finished in the bathroom at last. Beth decided to skip the bath after all. Instead she would talk to Jon. They always reserved this special time. However tired they were, once the house was quiet and they had gone to bed, they would exchange news, talk about what needed to be done the following day. If only for five or ten minutes, this was when they had the rare privacy to discuss whatever they wanted and remember how close they were.

She went up and knocked on the girls' doors to say good night. Ella must be asleep, but Beth could hear the sound of music and the occasional low-level shriek from Amy's darkened room. Did she really think her mother wouldn't realise that she was watching something on her laptop, and would be until the early hours? She would be tired and grouchy tomorrow, and her schoolwork would be left undone – again. Beth was tempted to march in and yank the plug from the wall. But she couldn't face another row.

Jon was already propped up against the pillows, deep in a book about the D-Day landings. He looked up when she came in, staring at her over the half-moon reading glasses perched on the end of his nose, hair on end, rather like a benign owl.

'I made you a tea, but it'll be cold now.' He nodded towards the mug left at her side of the bed. 'Are you OK?'

'Not really.' She slipped off her clothes, putting them away or in the laundry basket before fishing out her folded nightie from under her pillow. 'Don't go to sleep yet.'

'I won't.' He turned the page of his book and carried on reading while she went to the bathroom.

Amy had left her signature mess behind. The mirror was steamed over, a clear patch scrawled in the centre. Damp towels were screwed up over the radiator; wet footprints circled the bathmat. Beth leaned over the bath and pulled a knot of hair from the plughole before showering off the remnants of foam from the sides. As she brushed her teeth, she noticed a wodge of chewing gum stuck behind the used baby buds swimming in the soap dish. She sighed and threw the lot away, then switched off the light and went back into the bedroom.

'What's up?' Jon had thrown back her corner of the duvet and now patted her pillow. 'Still worried about Ella? Work bad?'

She slid into the bed and over into the curve of his arm, her head resting in the hollow just beneath his collarbone. 'No worse than normal: a child abduction, a couple intent on revenge and the usual frantic phone calls and meetings. But I'm used to all that.' She gave a wry laugh. 'No, it's Megan.'

Her tone caught his attention immediately. He tightened his arm around her, and she relaxed against him, enjoying their closeness. At least they still had that.

'She knew about Ella.' She felt a tear run down her cheek, whether from anger or hurt she wasn't sure. 'She's known for days.'

'Not that sixth-sense thing again?'

Beth didn't join in with his laughter at the old joke about how Megan was always ahead of the curve with her sense of what was about to happen. Not this time, clearly. 'Ella told her she thought she was pregnant before she came and talked to us. She actually told Megan! Can you imagine how that makes me feel? One big fat failure as a mother, that's how.'

'Oh, Beth.' He dropped his book on to the floor and turned towards her, kissing her nose. 'That's one thing you're absolutely not. The girls are just bolshie teenagers, that's all.'

'And Megan actually told her we'd all rally round if she decided to have the baby. Who the hell does she think she is to give advice like that to our daughter? Especially when it's not what we might have said.' She felt him tense beside her.

After a minute or two, Jon broke the silence. 'But put yourself in Lulu's shoes. Being pregnant at eighteen must be bloody scary. Telling your parents is difficult enough, especially when we've got so many expectations. And she's heard us argue about the whole abortion thing before. Remember when Jane's daughter had one?' He shook his head. 'She knows we don't see eye to eye. That must have made it harder.'

'Of course I understand that.' She wrenched herself out of his embrace. 'But that doesn't mean that my daughter turning to someone other than me doesn't hurt like hell, because it does.'

'But Megan isn't exactly "someone else". She and Pete are as good as family.' He obviously didn't understand her point at all.

'Ella should have talked to me,' Beth insisted. 'I'd have listened.'

'Would you have told me, if she had?' He sat up before turning to straighten his pillows. Then he looked at her, his face serious.

She was shocked. 'Of course.'

'Even though you'd have known how I'd react?' There was a warning in his expression.

'Of course,' she protested, at the same time wondering whether she really would have. 'But Megan should have said something to us.' She looked down at her hands, one ring on each, her contemporary wedding band contrasting with her mother-in-law's slim Victorian ring.

'Ella probably asked her not to.'

'Of course she did, but that's not the point!' Why was he always so bloody reasonable, so able to see everyone else's point of view? 'Megan's supposed to be my closest friend. We tell each other everything. If she'd told me, we could have dealt with it sooner.' She ignored Jon's raised eyebrows, the twist of disagreement in his mouth.

'You've got to keep this in perspective,' he insisted. 'I'm sure neither of them meant to hurt you. They just didn't think. After all, this isn't about you.'

'What do you mean?' Beth threw off the duvet, which was now suffocating her with its heat, and got out of bed. His sudden change of heart maddened her.

He studied her, his eyes following her as she walked around the bed. 'You know perfectly well. This should be about Ella and her future, about what she wants, not about you and Megan. Come on. Get back into bed.' He took off his glasses. 'So she went to Megan rather than one of us. So what?'

He was right, of course. What more had she hoped for from him? He would never understand the depth of her friendship with Megan and why this hurt so much. He and Pete might have been best mates since they were at school and university together, but she'd bet they didn't scratch below the surface to discover what really mattered to either of them. Did Pete talk to Jon about the fact that Megan used his snoring as an excuse to sleep in the spare room sometimes; that sex didn't always seems as appealing to Megan as it used to? She doubted it. Did they laugh about ageing and discuss what they wanted to achieve in the life they had left, whether it was too late for a new start? She guessed not. How much did they know about each other's children? Not much. Jon would probably never know the value of being able to share with someone else the secrets, the worries, the misplaced thoughts that he couldn't share with her. If he even questioned them at all.

She got back into bed, lay on her side with her back to him. As she reached out to switch off the light, she felt him roll over behind her into spoons. His hand rested on the curve of her waist. Conciliatory? Expectant? Hopeful? It slid upwards and over to cup her right breast, brushing her nipple with his fingertips. She wriggled into her side of the bed, dislodging his touch, letting him know that sex was not on the agenda that night, not even sympathy sex. She heard his resigned sigh as he moved back to his side of the bed and leaned over the edge to pick up his book. Perhaps she should turn over after all so that they could make up in the way they knew best. But, with so much on her mind, she wasn't in the mood. She lay beside him, unable to sleep, hearing him turn the pages. Eventually he switched off his light. As his breathing deepened into a slight occasional snore, Beth lay staring into the dark.

Saturday started badly. After a monosyllabic breakfast, Jon disappeared into his study saying he wanted to go through the accounts of Scents and Sensibility, a high-end perfumery that he was considering adding to his portfolio. Beth made a cup of tea and took it up to Ella. There was no point in doing the same for Amy, who slept like the dead at the weekend and would make known her displeasure at being woken in no uncertain terms.

'Ella,' Beth whispered, peering round her door. 'Ella. Wake up. I've brought you some tea.' She crossed the room, put the mug by the bed and opened the curtains a fraction.

'Mum, nooo!' The heap in the bed moved as the bedding was pulled up against the light. 'I don't need to get up now. I'm not meeting Charlie and Emma till lunchtime. Let me sleep.'

'But we need to talk.' Last night's conversation was not enough. She had to know why Ella hadn't come to her first.

A long groan rumbled somewhere within the duvet. 'No we don't.' Ella's head appeared, eyes bleary, hair tangled. 'I've told you what the doctor said. We don't need to say anything else. It's happening, just like you wanted. Happy?' With a flounce, she curled herself round, invisible under the bedclothes.

'It's not what I want, Lulu … That's not what this is about.' Beth rested her hand on what she guessed was Ella's shoulder. *If only you knew how much I wish this wasn't happening.* But Ella didn't emerge, and Beth had little choice but to withdraw.

The sound of music floated from Jon's study. She wouldn't see him for the rest of the day. Buried in work, he could ignore what was going on in the real world for a while. Instead, she went to tidy up the kitchen and finish her shopping list. Sainsbury's and those long Saturday queues beckoned. The day ahead weighed heavy.

It was late afternoon when she heard the front door shut and footsteps on the stairs. She was reading in the sitting room to the faint accompaniment of the piano concerto drifting from Jon's room. The girls must have gone out earlier without her hearing them. She shut her novel and put her tapestry and wools back in their bag. She had been able to settle to neither.

She went into the hall, straightened the mirror, and shouted to whoever was listening, 'Tea, anyone? I'm just putting the kettle on.'

'Great. I'll be down in a sec,' Amy yelled from her room.

Beth had her back to the door when Amy entered the kitchen. She swung round, a plate of biscuits in her hand, and felt the smile slide off her face.

'Your hair!' She stood frozen to the spot. 'Amy! What've you done?' A chocolate bourbon slipped to the floor and broke on the tiles.

'Sick, isn't it?' The fringe of Amy's brand-new pillar-box-red hair swung out as she gave a twirl.

It was hard to think of a better way to describe the transformation. 'But ...' Beth was lost for words. 'What will school say?'

'Oh, nothing. They don't mind. Jacks went blue last week and no one said a thing. Don't you like it?'

This was all about Amy expressing her individuality, Beth reminded herself. Something to be encouraged. But there must be other, less dramatic ways she could do it? If she didn't object, Amy might just tire of the colour and revert to normal sooner than if she were rebelling against her mother's wishes.

'It's ... er ... different. I just need to get used to it.' Beth picked up the bits of broken biscuit. They should have sent the girls somewhere stricter than the lax secondary school that was just a bus ride away; somewhere where there were rules about hair colour and skirt length.

'Oh, you will. Hannah's had hers done too. 'Cept hers is pink, sort of candyflossy.' Amy went over to the mirror by the door, styling her hair with her fingers, turning from side to side to inspect it from different angles, obviously pleased with what she saw. When the phone rang, she picked it up.

'Megan, hi! Do you like Hannah's hair? ... I told her you would ... Mine's red.'

Beth bit the inside of her lip to prevent herself saying anything. If Megan was going to approve, she could hardly object without coming across as the tyrant she was trying not to be. She left the room, knowing what would come next. Sure enough ...

'You wanna talk to Mum? ... Yeah! ... Well, she was, but I'll see if I can find her. Mum!' Amy was following Beth into the hall.

Beth shook her head, waving her hand to indicate that she wasn't really there. Megan was the last person she wanted to speak to right now. Amy made a face and held out the phone. Beth's gestures grew more frantic, her eyes wide, as she tried to convey what she wanted to say without speaking. Amy put the phone back to her ear.

'Sorry, Megan. She's on her mobile. I'll get her to call you back.' She hung up, staring at her mother, eyes wide. 'You actually made me lie for you! After everything you say about how we must always tell the truth. I don't get it. Normally you practically snatch the phone from our hands if Megan's on the other end.'

'I'm just not in the mood to speak to anyone right now.' Beth changed the subject. 'Won't you have to get some new clothes to go with the hair?' She poured out their tea, and passed a mug to Amy.

'God, no. Even if I could afford it, I wouldn't. Confusion is cool.'

With that, Amy left the room again, taking her tea with her. Beth stared at the phone. Should she call Megan back? She picked up a biscuit and nibbled off one layer before binning the rest. No, that phone call could wait until she was ready.

5

Baking bread was one of Megan's favourite occupations. Sunday mornings were set aside for just that. She shooshed Diva down from the pine table, checked for hairs and wiped it with disinfectant (yet again), before oiling the board she kept for bread-making. It fitted neatly among the Sunday papers and mail-order catalogues that she'd shoved to one end of the table, and the butter dish and jam pots left over from breakfast that she'd moved to the other. She sipped at her mug of coffee, the second that morning. In the background, *The Archers* competed with the hum and rattle of the second-hand American-style fridge – her pride and joy – and the rhythmic tick of the circular school clock that she had liberated from her last job.

She oiled her hands, then eased the wholemeal dough from the bowl. After giving it a punch for Ben Fletton, and another for Pete, who was doubtless having a high old time in Oman without her, she began to work it rhythmically – fold and push, fold and push – just the way her mother had taught her.

Megan had grown up an only child with an indulgent (when she was allowed to be) mother and a formidably strict father who she suspected would rather have had a son with whom to share his obsessive interest in sport and birdwatching. She was a poor alternative, though she did her best and to this day could explain the offside rule, the rugby points-scoring system or the laws of cricket to anyone who cared to listen. As a young child, she'd relied on the company of Mrs Poopsgogs, her imaginary friend who went wherever she did. Growing older, she made up for the

48

absence of siblings with her school friends. She dreamed of Enid Blyton's boarding schools, of living in a chaotic house in the country, being part of a gang with a dog. As she entered adulthood, she yearned to be a mother to a large family, surrounded by children playing safely in the surrounding fields and woods before coming home to a menagerie of pets and the warmth of their comfortable and shambolic family home. But, apart from the latter, life had dealt her a different set of cards. Ella and Amy had helped swell their family, though, and she loved them as if they were her own.

She felt String rub against her legs before he uttered a plaintive miaow.

'No,' she said firmly. 'You've had breakfast. Go away!'

The cat looked up at her with an expression of mild reproof and stayed exactly where he was, back arched, tail at full mast.

'Well you're not getting anything,' Megan warned, pushing the heel of her hand into the dough.

He got the message and sprang on to the comfy maroon armchair in the corner, needling the cushions with his claws, circling, then lying down.

A final fold and push and the dough was ready to rise. She returned it to the bowl before pulling out a faded tea towel from the drawer to drape over it.

Beth still hadn't returned her call. In normal circumstances, the moment she saw Amy's hair she would have rung in a panic, just as she had when Amy and Hannah had their noses pierced. But this time, silence. However, Wednesday night was book group night. They would have to speak then. Megan had let Beth persuade her to join the group a couple of years ago. The only reasons she kept going were a) Beth and b) because it was one of those things she thought must be good for her. Like going to the gym. Except she didn't do that at all. Or drinking less. She didn't do that either. This month the plan was to accompany their discussion of *Life of Pi* with an Indian-themed supper. Megan had already cheated and watched the film, hoping that that would be enough to get her through the initial chat before it devolved into gossip and their sex lives – the bit she enjoyed most. She had read the first chapter, but time and concentration were not on her side. Beth would have read the novel from cover to cover, even making the odd note.

Abandoning the bread board dusted with flour and all the ingredients she needed for her two multi-seed and honey loaves, she picked up the phone and keyed in Beth's number. Eventually, and unexpectedly, Jon answered. Megan asked to speak to Beth.

'She's tied up at the moment.'

He was a terrible liar. 'What's she doing?' She couldn't resist putting him on the spot.

'Er, she's upstairs somewhere ...'

Megan knew him too well. 'She's told you what happened?'

A silence, which she took as a yes. Of course Beth had told him. They told each other everything, unlike her and Pete, who often forgot or didn't think.

'Look, Meg, this is tricky. If only you'd said something about Ella coming to see you ...'

'Don't you think I wish I had? But if we don't speak, how are we ever going to get over this?' She straightened the rag rug in front of the Aga with her foot.

'Give her a few days. At the moment, she's upset – you can im-agine. You know her better than anyone. But things will change.'

Of course he was supporting Beth – when did he not? – but Megan had expected a bit more sympathy from him. 'I didn't know Ella was definitely pregnant,' she defended herself, bending the truth to the conversation. 'She was worried she might be. That's all. We talked about what she might do *if* she was. But when I didn't hear any more, I assumed she'd made a mistake.' That didn't sound so unreasonable, did it?

She lifted a corner of the tea towel to see if the dough had risen.

'You should have told us, whatever Ella made you promise. She's only eighteen, for God's sake.'

'Exactly. Old enough to know her own mind.' Megan spoke more sharply than she meant. 'I'm sorry if you think it was the wrong thing, but I did what I thought was best.'

There was a doubting grunt from the other end of the phone. For heaven's sake! He should know her better than that.

'Well if Beth won't speak to me, perhaps you could tell her I called and that I'll see her on Wednesday.'

When she had hung up, Megan stood staring at the phone. She couldn't bear the idea of losing him too. They had known each other since she and Pete had met while working on the same free newssheet. The two men had shared a run-down flat and she had fitted into their lives from the beginning. They'd just clicked. After a time, Beth had joined the gang.

She picked up the unused plates on the table and returned them to the huge glass-fronted china cabinet that must once have graced some stately home. She and Pete had found it in an auction, and over the years they had filled it with china accumulated from all over the place – odd tea sets, parts of dinner services, her favourite blue Ovaltine mugs, pieces from the phase when they collected anything associated with Guinness. Megan used everything in there, and everything came with its own memory attached.

In the days BC (before children), when the four of them occasionally went away for weekends, Jon and Pete refused to miss Saturday afternoon football, so she and Beth would explore. It was Beth who had spotted the blue and white Burleigh fish plates in a junk shop in Norfolk, and together they had fallen on the complete Carlton Ware foxglove tea set in a car boot sale in Somerset. Beth would die rather than have any of this stuff cluttering up her house, but she enjoyed the hunt, the triumph of discovery and a bargain struck almost as much as Megan.

And then they became parents – first Pete and Megan, then

Jon and Beth – and weekends took a different shape, as they juggled work and parenthood. Jon and Beth had been happy for Amy and Ella to spend time at Megan's when they were at work during the school holidays, and Megan hadn't minded at all, not really. They had got on perfectly with Jake and Hannah, making the gang she had so envied as a child herself. Only within the last couple of years had Jake and Ella, the two oldest, begun to go their own ways and the little band had fractured.

She began to tidy up, putting the used bowls in the sink with the porridge pan. Pete had promised he would get the dishwasher looked at. Obviously that was another chore she would have to transfer to her list. She lifted one of the Aga lids and slid the kettle on to the hot plate.

Jake had left school first, refusing the university place he was offered at Manchester in favour of concentrating on his band, Heavy Feather. She and Pete (well, she) had pointed out the risks he was taking, the benefits of an education. All that. But he had never been remotely academic. He had an answer to each of their arguments. What would have been the point of objecting any more? They couldn't have stopped him even if they had really wanted to. They agreed to support him in whatever he wanted to do with his life (provided it was legal) and hoped that he made a success of it. That was the way Megan saw it. If things didn't work out, they'd deal with that as and when. She didn't believe in favourites, but she couldn't help nursing a secret special affection for her boy. Unlike his raucous younger sister, Jake always had a quiet air of vulnerability that made her worry about him, whatever he was doing.

Ella in contrast was about to leave school with a raft of good grades, a university place and her heart set on a solid career: things for a parent to be grateful for in these days of multiple-dip recession and rocketing living costs. Beneath her diffidence was a still, strong centre, a determination that had got her where she wanted to go in life so far. She was like her mother in that way. But that wasn't why Megan loved her.

During the school holidays, Ella sometimes worked at Art-Official, the art club that Megan ran for under-tens who were dumped there by deep-pocketed parents anxious to salve their consciences. While they escaped to work, their child was looked after, having fun and learning something: a win/win childcare situation. She had started the club about five years ago, when Pete had been made redundant by the *Mail* and they needed some extra income. Since then, during the Easter and summer holidays, she had had a ball, painting, making collages and papier mâché, cutting things out and constructing sculptures from loo rolls, cereal packets, glue and poster paints.

Ella shared Megan's natural talent with the kids who came there. She adored them, was patient, thoughtful and kind. She had a gift for bringing the quieter ones out of their shells. Over those five years, Megan had watched her transform from an introverted girl to a confident young woman, buoyed up by the affection and trust that the children gave her. Of course Beth had been pleased that she was constructively occupied for a good stretch of the holidays. One less daughter to worry about.

'String! Go away!' Megan brushed him off the worktop. As she crossed the kitchen, through the conservatory at its back to the garden door, Diva rose from the chair and followed them. When she opened the door, the two cats strolled out together, tails up. She wouldn't see them for a while.

Embarking on the multi-seed loaves she hadn't tried before, she went over the evening Ella had come round, for once bewildered, frightened and unsure of her future. All Megan had wanted to do was help and protect her. Given time to cool down, Beth would come to understand. Yes, time was all that was needed. And meanwhile, Megan was not going to try phoning her again.

*

Walking into the teeth of a force nine gale with a bowl of dal makhani in one hand and an umbrella in the other was no mean feat. Megan only drove when she had to, usually when someone asked her. She loathed being behind the wheel, middle-aged anxiety making her terrified of the hazards rushing towards her: schoolchildren darting into the road, buses only centimetres from the side of the car, stray animals. Disaster was always just a moment away. Instead, Pete would give her a lift, or she'd walk or resort to her trusty bike. If Pete hadn't already been halfway down a bottle of Merlot when she was ready to leave, Megan would have asked him to drive her this evening. He'd have agreed, too, heedless of the drink-drive laws. Should she be worried about his drinking? she wondered, remembering the latest scare story she had read about the wine-sodden middle-aged middle classes. Should she be worried about her own? Another reason for not driving tonight. There was always wine laid on to ease the flow of conversation.

At that moment, a particularly fierce gust of wind blew her collapsible umbrella inside out and sent the tin foil whirling off the top of the dish on to the pavement and her skirt halfway up towards her waist. All her concentration was needed to untangle herself and get through Fran's gate and up the steps to her front door.

The chimes rang once. Loudly. Fran flung open the door, her dress billowing around her like a scarlet galleon in full sail. 'Oh, good,' she breathed, as a cloud of floral perfume enveloped Megan. 'I wasn't sure when you'd get here.'

'I'm not last, am I?' Megan asked as she followed Fran down the hallway, avoiding knocking against the table or any of the extensive collection of dog portraits that covered the walls. Fran lived alone and poured her civil servant's salary into her collections. Every available wall space, every shelf was crowded with dog-related knick-knacks, just like a monstrous antique market stall. Megan's own hoarding was modest by comparison. One of

Fran's five miniature dogs, all bichon something or Pomeranian something else, danced round Megan's legs so that she almost tripped over.

'Fifi, don't.' Fran herded a ball of fluff towards the kitchen. 'Don't worry. The others have only been here for about twenty minutes.'

That rap over the knuckles stung, but Megan said nothing.

Once she'd handed over her contribution to supper (in the bright light of Fran's kitchen, it looked distinctly unappetising) and hung up her coat, Megan joined the others in the sitting room. Beth was noticeable by her absence. Everyone else was ready, a glass of wine and the book under discussion at the ready. Megan wished she'd at least broken the spine of her copy so that it would look as if she'd read the damn thing. She gratefully accepted the glass that Fran pressed into her hand, and prepared to bluff. She should have watched the film again. This was worse than being underprepared for an exam. Why did she put herself through it?

'Beth not coming?' she asked, as casually as she knew how. Beth was never late.

'She called to say she was held up.' Peggy, an overweight librarian from the local secondary school, generally dressed in a wild combination of loose neutrals, and tonight was no exception. She took her role as leader of the group extremely seriously, was intolerant of latecomers and dismissive if she sniffed out a member who had failed to do their proper homework. Megan had so far escaped reproof by the skin of her teeth. 'She said to start without her, but we were waiting for you.'

Megan refused once more to rise to the bait. She pulled *Life of Pi* from her bag, keeping her hand over its pristine spine, simultaneously fending off a small dog intent on mating with her leg. Mistaking her swattings for a game, the black bichon kept jumping back at her for more, yapping with excitement. Megan sat down in the only vacant chair, realising as she sank into its unsprung depths why it had been avoided by everybody else. From her uncomfortable position, she kicked at the persistent dog as surreptitiously as she could. At last, Fran picked up her attacker with a glare in her direction. Keen to make up, Megan straightened her skirt and leaned forward to ask her killer question. 'Does anybody understand why Pi tried so hard to save Richard Parker's life? I'd have wanted to get a tiger out of my lifeboat as soon as I could.'

The others looked at each other. Definitely time to turn up her intellectual firepower.

'But perhaps the situation's really a metaphor for how we deal with our own challenges in life? I'm not sure. What do you think?' She thanked the Lord for the online reading guide that she'd skipped through in the guilty minutes before she left home.

Peggy shot her a somewhat startled look. She was unused to such thoughtful contributions. Megan turned her gaze on the others. She'd neatly avoided having to give much of an opinion of her own and could just let them take over. Those old tricks were always the best.

The group had been talking for twenty intense minutes, glasses topped up, with Megan just about holding her own thanks to the flimsy knowledge she'd gleaned from the film and the reading guide, and contributing a series of 'Interesting' or 'Yes, absolutely' or 'Of course', when the doorbell rang.

'I'll go.' She hoisted herself out of her chair, relieved at being able to abandon the discussion before she was found out. This was a chance to speak to Beth. A couple of dogs raced ahead of her barking shrilly, ignoring Fran's commands to 'Come!'

On the doorstep, Beth looked less than overwhelmed to see her, even taking a small but noticeable step backwards. Megan considered shutting the door in her face but instead kissed both of Beth's cheeks and ignored the chill emanating from her.

'I'm so glad you've come.' She stepped back to let Beth in. A small white bundle of dog dashed through her legs, overbalancing her. Attempting to avoid crushing the animal, Megan tried to hop clear, but with no room to manoeuvre, she collided with the hall table. The two ceramic pugs that sat at its centre slid soundlessly towards the waxed oak floorboards. Beth and Megan watched as the head of one of them detached with a crack and the front legs of the other smashed into smithereens. Megan bent to pick up the largest pieces and stood with them in her hands. 'Oh, God. I should have taken that fasting diet more seriously!' Was that a flicker of a smile from Beth?

'I've got to put these in the kitchen first.' Beth spoke loudly enough for the others to hear, then beckoned Megan to follow her.

In the kitchen, she placed her casserole on the butcher's block table. 'Butter chicken.' She registered Megan's surprise that her culinary skills had been pressed into use on a weekday. 'Eat-In's finest.' Beth was a regular customer of the company that delivered home-cooked frozen meals to the door. 'But no one needs to know that.'

Once they would have laughed in agreement. Now, they merely exchanged a wary half-smile.

'What am I going to do with these?' Megan held up the broken ornaments. 'Fran's going to go ape.' She looked around for a hiding place. 'I hope they're not valuable.'

'You'll have to confess.' Beth took off her coat and slung it over the back of a chair.

'What to?' Fran sailed into the room. 'Red or white, Beth?'

'I'd love a glass of white.' She was obviously not going to come to Megan's rescue.

Fran opened the fridge, took out a bottle and turned to see Megan holding the broken bits of china. 'Oh.'

'I'm so sorry. I ...' Megan began, feeling heat rising up her chest and neck and into her cheeks. She fanned herself with her free hand. 'I'm afraid I couldn't pick up the leg of this one – too many pieces.'

Fran put down the bottle and relieved Megan of the fragments, staring sadly at the little head with its tiny button eyes. 'These were my grandmother's.'

For an awful second, Megan thought she was going to giggle. Instead she said, 'Can I replace them?'

Fran put the pieces on the worktop. 'I shouldn't have kept them there. I just liked the idea of them guarding the door, the same as they did in her house. Dear old Gran. I pestered her for them when I was tiny.' She sniffed.

Beth put her arm around Fran's shoulders and led her out of the room. 'Typical Meg,' she said, with a dismissive glance that left Megan smouldering.

By supper time, those embers of rage had been fanned into a conflagration. Just before they sat down to eat, the conversation turned to the ending of the book.

'I loved that bit when Richard Parker jumps overboard to chase the fish,' Megan commented, without thinking.

Beth looked at her. 'Have you actually read the book? Or just seen the film?'

Megan, exposed, felt the eyes of the earnest readers turn on her. 'Er, yes ... well, I had to rush the end a bit, and I'd heard so much about the film,' she improvised.

Beth raised an eyebrow.

'You must at least finish the book, or it's not fair on those of us who have,' offered Fran quite kindly, fanning her faintly perspiring brow with a paper fan decorated with poodles.

'I know, I know. I usually do, of course.' Megan couldn't look at Beth, aware that her friend knew full well that she usually didn't. 'I've had a lot on my plate.'

No more was said as the discussion picked up again, but Megan was left simmering, humiliated. After a short while, they all moved to the dining table for supper. Everyone's contributions were brought in to be tried, and were oohed and aahed over. Competitive cookery was something Megan hated. She sat with her temperature rising, listening to the accolades heaped on Beth's butter chicken. Beth smiled and took the compliments as if she were Rick Stein fresh back from a recipe-sourcing trip to India. She didn't look at Megan, who, at last, couldn't bear the situation a moment longer. She took a forkful. It was good: mild and creamy, with hints of ginger, chilli and spices. 'Mmm. Delicious,' she pronounced.

Beth gave her a tight warning smile. But nothing would stop Megan now.

'Where did you get the recipe?' she asked. 'I'd love to try this at home.'

All eyes turned to Beth, a couple of heads nodding in agreement.

As Beth embarked on a lengthy self-justifying confession, Megan allowed herself a small smile of satisfaction.

Checkmate.

6

As far as Megan was concerned, the evening was anything but an unmitigated success. The group must have noticed Beth's increased (if that were possible) coolness towards her after she'd made her confess. When they'd continued their discussion of the book, she had taken a back seat, having exhausted her limited insights into the story and received her slap on the wrist. Beth, on the other hand, was in her element. She was keen to discuss the novel in detail, ensuring that her reading made up for her cheating on the cooking front. If the conversation ever threatened to veer towards everyday life, Beth and Peggy had wrenched it back on track.

Eventually the party splintered into those few who wanted to continue discussing the book and those who drifted back to the sofa and chairs to discuss the upcoming wedding of Ruth's daughter. Ruth, another librarian, and her husband were being bulldozed into spending far more than they could reasonably afford on a church wedding. 'She's not been inside a church since her christening, and now she wants the full works. A hen weekend in Berlin, six bridesmaids, a string quartet and a couture dress! She's been on a diet for weeks. So have I, without losing a pound!' Ruth helped herself to a chocolate from the bowls Fran had put out. 'And worse, I'm not allowed to wear the dress I'd chosen because it's not part of the colour palette she wants for the photos.' The others laughed with a twinge of superiority, as they pictured themselves in the same position, confident that they wouldn't give in to any daughter of theirs in the same way.

'I know what you're thinking. But you'll cave in in the end,' moaned Ruth. 'You will. You just want them to be happy.'

At the end of the evening, Megan found herself in the hall beside Beth. Once the dogs had been shooed into the kitchen, they passed the table, its emptiness a glaring reminder of Megan's accident, and stepped out into the night together. The wind had dropped. As the others headed towards their cars, Beth held the gate open and looked along the garden railings.

'No bike?'

'I walked. Easier with the dal.' This was Megan's chance to put things right between them. She adjusted her scarf and pulled on her gloves as they fell into step. 'Look, what happened in there was silly. We must talk.'

'I don't think we've much to say to each other at the moment.' Beth was staring straight ahead. Her hair was pulled off her face and hidden under her cream knitted hat. In profile, her nose was a perfect straight line, and her chin jutted forward, determined. At that moment, she looked so like Ella.

A fox darted out from between two cars and stood in the middle of the road, staring at them, before disappearing into the darkness of a garden.

Before Megan had a chance to say anything more, Beth had turned down the road that took her home. Megan watched her, dumbfounded, hardly noticing that the rain had started to fall more heavily.

Beth could feel Megan's eyes on her back as she walked away. The rain was visible on the surface of the puddles. She pulled her coat around her against the cold, still smarting from the way Megan had got one up on her.

Beth understood about keeping confidences. That was what she did every day of her life, as one woman after another poured out her problems to her. What was tormenting her was more primal. However irrational and extreme her reaction, she hated Megan for being the person Ella had turned to first. She couldn't escape that feeling that stemmed from deep within. She had left home meaning to be friendly, to build bridges, but when Megan had opened Fran's door to her, something had locked off inside her, stopping her from responding. Then those ugly china dogs had broken and the evening had deteriorated from there.

She paused for a moment, turning round at last. But Megan had gone.

She started walking again, empty inside. A man was coming towards her. His dog strained at its lead, tail wagging, jumping towards her. Jon was giving Jock his late-night walk. She smiled and bent to scratch the dog's chin, making sure his wet paws didn't land on her coat.

'I thought we might meet you if we came this way.' A dog-walker's trophy bag swung from Jon's hand. Beth walked around to his other side.

'You've just missed Megan.'

'How was it?' She heard the hope in his voice. He didn't want them to fall out.

'Terrible.' She slipped her arm through his as he turned back towards home. 'I talked like a maniac about the book so no one could get a word in edgeways – except Peggy, of course. She's always got something to say.' They laughed. Peggy's reputation for being a book bully had remained untarnished through all the meetings they had held.

'Didn't you talk to Megan at all? Jock! Here!' He yanked the straining dog away from the wing of a car, where a black cat was motionless, hackles up, hissing in the shadow.

'Not really. She even made me admit that I hadn't made the damn chicken!' She omitted to mention her own public disloyalty.

'But you've been friends for years. You can't let this get to you, especially not now that Ella's decided to follow your advice.' His voice gave away exactly his feelings on the matter. He had kept his promise and was supporting Ella's decision, although his weighty silence during the one lengthy discussion they'd had with her since she'd been to the doctor had again said everything about what he really felt.

'But you do agree it's the right thing for her?' She tightened her grip on his arm, willing him to say yes.

'You know the answer to that.' He took his hand from his pocket as he pulled Jock away from a tree. Her arm fell from his. 'I'm going along with it because of both of you. I know I'm in the minority, but I can't bear the idea of her going through this.'

'Neither can I. It's the last thing I want for her, but ... I really do think it's best for everyone.'

He quickened his pace so he was walking slightly ahead of her. 'So long as you believe that ...'

She caught up with him. 'This is as hard for me as it is for you, you know.'

Jon just grunted.

'Once it's over, we can move on.'

But would moving on be that easy? The lid had been eased off Pandora's box. Who knew what else was hiding in there, eager to be let out?

As they neared their house in silence, they saw a young couple come around the corner ahead of them. Despite the rain, they stopped by their gate and engaged in a long and intense kiss while they fumbled around under each other's clothes. Jock was all interest, pulling ahead, keen to get home. The girl's hood fell back. There was a flash of red.

'Amy!' Beth's voice was loud in the otherwise empty street.

The young woman turned, a look of alarm on her face. 'Oh, shit, it's the parents.'

The boy removed his hands from underneath her top and stood beside her, awkward in his black jeans and long black coat, one incredibly thin leg bent back against the wall. Heroin chic? Beth's mind was whirring. That was all she needed: one daughter pregnant, the other involved with drug dealers and addicts.

'What are you doing?'

Jon squeezed her arm hard, warning her not to be unnecessarily confrontational. 'Have you had a good evening?' he asked them.

'Yeah,' the boy said uncertainly. 'Thanks.' He and Amy exchanged a shifty glance.

'Where've you been?' They had drawn level now, Jon's hand on the gate, Jock jumping up at Amy, who gave him some half-hearted attention. There was a clang as Jon threw away the plastic bag and replaced the dustbin lid.

'Oh, please. Disgusting,' Amy muttered under her breath, but the words were audible nonetheless. 'Hope and Anchor,' she admitted grumpily.

Beth knew just where she meant. Known locally as the Grope and Wanker, it was the grungy pub on the main road where the Goths hung out, intimidating with their heavy make-up and piercings, their extraordinary-coloured hair extensions and black clothes. It was exactly the sort of place she'd prefer her daughters to avoid. She took in Amy's heavy-soled black shoes, black tights and pleated red tartan skirt that left little to the imagination. And her red hair. And her eyes, smudged with dark make-up.

'Good night,' she said firmly but politely to Amy's friend, who murmured something and slunk off into the night, obviously grateful to be let go. 'Inside.' She stood back to let Amy past her, following her to the door.

As soon as she was indoors, Amy raced upstairs to her room. 'Hang on a minute,' Beth called after her. But she was answered only by the slam of a bedroom door. Jon's hand on her arm prevented her from going up in pursuit.

'Not now. This isn't the time to say anything. Let's do it tomorrow, when it's not so late and we're not so tired.'

'But … when did she start dressing like that?' Beth was at a loss, certain that those clothes hadn't found their way into Amy's wardrobe until very recently. One daughter pregnant and the other … Oh, God.

She sat on the bottom stair and put her head in her hands. 'Why did you let her go out on a school night?'

'Beth! Stop this!' He hit the banister with his fist and left it there. 'I don't question your decisions about how we run our lives. You have to trust me. She said she'd done her revision at school and would be back by ten thirty, which she is. Well, just about.'

Ten thirty? On a school night? What was he thinking? And why hadn't he quizzed her about where she was going? Or said something about what she was wearing?

She groaned. 'Now what have we done? You always said you'd veto their boyfriends. What happened?'

He moved his hand to her shoulder. 'That was when they were little. We can't lock her away. This is just a phase. Like all the others. She'll be experimenting with something else before we know where we are.'

But what else? How could he be so calm? Shouldn't he be upstairs remonstrating with her? But then, he could never say no to either of the girls. He drove Beth mad by bending the rules she thought they had agreed if doing so made Ella or Amy happy. She pictured Amy and the boy groping each other against the railings. She was only sixteen. Just. And that skirt! Had Beth talked to her enough about birth control? She couldn't remember saying anything recently. Had she said anything at all? She had obviously failed along the line when it came to Ella. That boy's hands … She couldn't bear to think where they had been. Hadn't Jon noticed? Didn't he mind?

She followed him into the kitchen, where he was already opening cupboards for mugs and tea, putting on the kettle. 'I think I need something stronger.'

'After the group?' He sounded surprised. 'What would do the trick? Brandy?'

'Yep, why not? Just a tiny one.' She pulled out one of the chairs and sat down, leaning her elbows on the empty table while Jon reached for the brandy from a cupboard. He poured her a slug and pushed the glass in front of her. She cradled it in her hands. 'When did she start dressing like that? How could I not have noticed?'

'Because we see her in her school uniform most of the time, and then she dives in and out of the house without our registering. But she's not going to turn into a Goth, not our Amy.' The idea obviously amused him. 'There's no point in aggravating things by talking to her now, but I will find out about that boy.' He managed to sound faintly threatening.

That was the Jon she knew and loved. 'As if we haven't got enough on our plate,' she groaned.

'It's another reason to make up with Megan, darling. One thing less to worry about.'

If only it were that easy.

Jon went on, not noticing Beth's grimace. 'She'll know what to do. What about your spa weekend? Isn't that coming up in a month or two?'

Beth didn't need the reminder. She and Meg had been going to the Haven together once a year for too many years to count – ever since that terrible child custody case that had taken so much out of her. The eight-year-old girl had been passed like a chattel between the two parents and their assorted nannies. Beth suspected that neither of them really wanted her except as a trophy in the case. She had represented the father, who barely knew his daughter's name, let alone her exact age. But he had money, and his wife did not. Beth would have been wholly unprofessional if she had shown her upset or her dislike to him, so she had offloaded on Megan, confessing how haunted she was by the child's bewilderment. She had been privately appalled by the judge's decision to award residence to the father, to the accompaniment of the heart-rending screams of both mother and child. Megan had suggested a stay at the Haven to help her unwind and regroup. It had been such a success that ever since, they had holed themselves up there for one long weekend a year – no work, no children, no husbands. But she couldn't go with Megan now, especially not when Ella might need her.

'I'll have to cancel.' She spun the brandy in her glass.

'Isn't that a bit drastic? Wouldn't it be the perfect opportunity to patch things up properly?'

'Maybe.' Beth felt herself closing up again. She took a swift sip and felt the burn of the brandy in her throat. Why did Jon assume that Megan would know what to do, and that she didn't? Perhaps it was naïve of them not to have expected Amy to be hooked up with some boy or other by now. She had been Amy's age when she had her abortion. Time concertinaed so quickly.

'It feels like only yesterday that Amy was a baby,' she said, remembering their daughter when she was only months old, often cross, always sleepless, with a mop of black hair. 'Where's it all gone?'

'Poor old you. You're tired.' He came up behind her, bent to kiss the top of her head. 'Shall I run you a bath?'

She nodded. 'I'd love that.'

'It'll all look different after a night's sleep.' He left the room.

Being treated like something precious reassured her, making her feel secure in their marriage. Jon was the glue that kept their family together, always thoughtful, rarely getting riled unless one of them stepped right out of line.

By the time he came back down, exhaustion was making every bone in her body ache. Being up late after a day in court was a lethal combination. And tomorrow would be another tough day. She had finally established that Shazia Malik had left the country with little Aiysha and had entered Pakistan. The child's father was devastated, desperate to travel out there to bring her back, but had been unable to track down her whereabouts. All the necessary preparations were being made to obtain a hearing in the High Court in Islamabad. Beth consoled herself with the thought that she might be going through a bad patch with her girls, but at least she hadn't lost them.

'Your bath gel's run out.' He took her glass and went over to the sink to wash it up. 'Amy, I suppose?'

'I suppose,' she said, resigned, reaching for the drying-up cloth.

'Don't bother. I'll do this. You go up before the bath overflows.'

She kissed his cheek and passed the cloth to him. 'Or Amy gets into it.'

They both laughed. For a brief moment, harmony was restored.

7

Beth had cancelled her Monday-morning appointments to take Ella to the clinic. She remembered how she herself had felt when she was sixteen; how much she would have loved to be able to tell her mother what was going on and be looked after by her. She wanted to make sure Ella had everything she hadn't had, whenever it was needed.

That Sunday night, the two of them were curled together on the sofa in front of the TV, gripped by some gruesome Nordic detective serial. The curtains were drawn, they had stoked up the fire, and on the table their mugs of hot chocolate sat beside Ella's discarded revision notes. Amy had gone upstairs to shut herself away with her social network – God knows what she did that took up so much of her time – while Jon was in his room reading.

'You'll need someone with you when you come home. I want to be there,' Beth insisted when the ads came on, lifting her feet and tucking them underneath her.

'Mum, I really won't. I can get a cab.' Ella bit at the skin of one of her cuticles. Beth winced and automatically reached out to stop her. Ella snatched her hand away. 'Anyway, I've asked Carly to come with me now.'

'You have?' Beth tried to keep the hurt out of her voice. She had to let Ella deal with this in whatever way made it easiest for her. As Jon had pointed out, it wasn't about Beth. The termination was what was important now, not who went with her.

'I thought you'd be at work. You usually are,' said Ella, needling at Beth's maternal guilt.

'Of course I won't be,' she protested. 'Not for something like this.'

Among a host of absentee occasions, two had gone down in family lore. Ella was probably remembering them, too. Perhaps worst was the time Beth burst through the doors of the school hall just as Ella was taking her curtain call. Heads turned at the commotion as the audience's attention transferred from the stage and her daughter to her. Ella had been both furious and mortified. Almost as bad was when Amy broke her arm. Beth had been unable to extract herself from a meeting, so their au pair had had to go to hospital with her. There were plenty more she preferred not to dwell on. But it wasn't too late to make up for them.

A scream came from the TV, claiming Ella's attention.

'Lulu! Look at me. Let's go together. Please.'

Ella shot her a look. 'Mum, I've just told you. Carly's coming.'

'Are you sure?' Did she sound too desperate? She took a cushion and hugged it to her stomach. Her eyes strayed to the large photo of the young Ella, wild and carefree. 'Won't you tell us who the father is? Why isn't he going with you?'

The look intensified. 'Mum, don't go on! No, I won't.'

'But why not?'

'Because I don't want to. I don't even know if we're together, so just leave it. Please.' She turned her attention back to the screen, bringing any conversation to a full stop.

Despite a week of tactful questioning, Ella had remained resolutely silent on the matter. If there wasn't going to be a baby, though, then perhaps a boyfriend didn't need a place in the picture. But why hadn't she told him? What kind of relationship did that imply?

'Are you sure you'll be all right with Carly?' Beth insisted. 'You can always change your mind.'

'Yes, really. Honestly, I'd rather go with her.' She picked up her mug, holding it in both hands, her sleeves covering most of her fingers, and peered at Beth over the top of it. 'Less fuss! I'll be fine. Honestly. I know what happens. I'll see you when I get back. When it's over.'

There was clearly no point in arguing.

On the TV, yet another mutilated corpse had been discovered. The body count in the remote Norwegian backwater was increasing, but Beth wasn't taking in much of the convoluted plot. Instead, she was busy going over the ways in which she should have been a better mother to her two girls, a particular torture she had been perfecting during the last couple of weeks. She had tried her best. She thought of the nights spent making fancy dress costumes. The Colgate tube and bottle of Guinness should definitely have won prizes but didn't because it was obvious a parent had made them. It wasn't her fault that she had forgotten her glasses when she went to the swimming gala and cheered for someone else's child. Megan had encouraged her to cook for a school fair, but her attempts were left unsold until she bought them herself. She hadn't been asked again. The list went on.

The following morning, Ella left the house without giving Beth an opportunity to talk more. She'd picked at her breakfast, saying little. Beth longed to comfort her, reassure her she was doing the right thing, but Ella brushed her concern aside. Jon had promised to be in all day, in case he was needed. If she changed her mind about the journey home, all Ella had to do was call and he'd collect her.

Once Ella had left, Jon disappeared into his room. His business partner was coming round later to go through the due diligence report on Scents and Sensibility. Although he was sticking to his word and saying nothing, his unhappiness was obvious. Beth couldn't stay at home in such an atmosphere, waiting for Ella's return. She'd be better off in the office, where she could fill her mind with other families' troubles.

She shouted her goodbye at Jon's closed door. He was unlikely to hear her over the music that made him oblivious to the outside world, removing him from what he didn't want to be part of. She opened his door and raised a hand. He barely looked up.

The rush-hour traffic was at its peak. Beth was about to cross the road on her way to the canal when she spotted Ella at the bus stop on the other side, talking to a frazzled-looking mother trying to cope with a screaming toddler and a crying baby. She must be one of the babysitting circle that regularly employed Ella. The toddler, in an oversized coat and a stripy bobble hat, was reaching up for something on the buggy. Ella squatted down to him, her hands on his waist, explaining something, while the mother tried to calm the baby. Beth started to cross the road. She had one foot off the kerb when the lights changed and a stream of traffic moved past, blocking her view. When she saw the tableau again, the situation had changed. Now the mother was bent over, pacifying the toddler, and Ella was holding the baby on her hip, rocking from side to side. Beth could hear its cries from where she stood.

Just then, a bus turned the corner and pulled in to the stop. Through its windows, Beth could see the four of them struggling on board. As the mother negotiated her buggy around a bunch of irritated, clock-watching commuters, someone got up to let Ella sit by the window with the baby on her knee. The mother passed Ella a bottle of milk and she slipped the teat into the baby's mouth, her face a picture of concentration. Then she looked up, saw Beth, and smiled.

Beth waved. She had a lump in her throat. This was exactly what she didn't want for her daughter, despite how happy Ella looked. She couldn't bear to think of her being tied down by a baby so young.

*

Beth's morning passed quickly. She used the unexpected free time to catch up with her assistants and prepare instructions and enclosures for a barrister representing a client in a hearing to decide with which parent the three children of the marriage should live. At lunch, she went out for a coffee and a sandwich, all the time thinking of Ella. She tried phoning her mobile, then Jon at home. But nobody picked up. She calmed herself with the thought that if something had happened, Jon would have rung her. Her afternoon sped past as she unpicked the unreasonable behaviour of a husband who had squirrelled away his earnings out of his wife's reach, making her subsist on a limited allowance and expecting her to account for how she spent every penny of it. A couple of meetings were scheduled with new clients, one wanting to initiate divorce proceedings on the grounds of her partner's violence, and another who wanted to apply to change his access arrangements to his three children. By the time she had written follow-up letters to the clients she'd seen that day, caught up with her paperwork and returned several phone calls, the working day was over.

Greeted by an ecstatic Jock as soon as she opened the door, she hung up her coat and went to the kitchen, following the sound of voices and the strong smell of burned cheese. She found Jon and Ella at the kitchen table. The worktop was a chaos of used pans, open packets and tins.

'Cauliflower cheese and bread and butter pudding,' said Jon in answer to Beth's look. Ella and Amy's childhood favourites and still the best family comfort food.

She went straight to Ella and hugged her, relieved to see she was all right. Not wanting to let her go, she brushed her daughter's hair off her face and kissed her forehead. 'How are you feeling, Lulu? Shouldn't you be in bed?' She looked over at Jon, surprised he hadn't encouraged her. 'If you want to go, I'll bring you up something to eat.'

'I'm fine, Mum. Honestly.' Ella grasped her hand, squeezed then let go.

The atmosphere in the room was unexpectedly charged. Jon and Ella looked uncomfortable. Neither of them was looking at her or each other. 'Is something wrong?' Beth asked.

Ella got up and went over to stand by the French door into the garden, staring out into the dark. Beth could see her reflection in the glass, trim in her leggings and red check shirt that hung open over a crop top, despite the near Arctic temperatures outside. Her face was unreadable.

'Are you going to tell her or am I?' There was something in Jon's voice that made Beth turn towards him. He was stirring sugar into his coffee, his attention focused on the task.

'What?' she asked, suddenly nervous. She picked up some of the mess they had made and headed to the bin. If she behaved normally, perhaps that would make everything else normal. 'What's happened?'

Ella still didn't say anything. The only noise was the clink of Jon's spoon in his mug. Round and round.

'What is it? You've got to tell me now.' Perhaps it wasn't as bad as she was imagining. 'Did something happen at the clinic?' God forbid that something had gone wrong. Suppose her encouraging the abortion meant Ella would never be able to have children. She wouldn't forgive herself if that was the case. No, they wouldn't be making cauliflower cheese if something terrible had happened. She looked from one to the other. 'Ella, please tell me.'

'Not wrong exactly.' Ella faced them as she struggled to find the right words. She bent over to shoehorn her heel back into her black ballet pump with a finger.

'Was your appointment postponed?' They should have gone private, then that would never have happened.

'Sort of.'

'What do you mean?'

'I didn't go.' Ella straightened up, her relief at having come clean obvious. 'I didn't go to the clinic. I couldn't. I'm sorry.'

'Why not?' She should have insisted on going with her.

'I couldn't do it, Mum. I want to keep the baby. I really do.'

Beth stared at Jon, willing him to say something, to support her view, but his eyes were glued to the table. This was between mother and daughter. 'You can't,' she managed.

'But, why not? Dad agrees with me. He thinks we can manage, and so do I.'

Jon still didn't look up, although his spoon was still.

'Ella, no!' Beth stood frozen, despite the desperate urge to shake sense into her daughter. 'I saw you with that baby this morning at the bus stop. That's what it'll be like day in day out.'

'I know. But I don't mind that. I didn't mean this to happen, but now that it has, everything's changed. I'll work it out, you'll see.'

'We can make another appointment when you've had more time to think,' Beth suggested. Her hand went to her necklace.

'I don't need more time. Really.'

Jon raised his head at last, his expression a confusion of impatience, determination and despair. If she didn't know him better, she might even have said dislike.

'No,' he said. 'We're not making another appointment. Ella has decided she wants this child. That's what it is, Beth. A child. Our grandchild.'

She shook her head, feeling the clutch of panic. 'That's not true. Not yet.'

But Jon went on. 'Listen. We've been talking, and if Ella gets her grades, she'll defer her university place. And we're going to give her all the support and help we can.'

The wind was punched out of her, as she thought of not just Ella's future, but theirs too. A baby in the house again. 'But ... you can't ... Jon, please ...'

'Mum, don't be like that.' Ella came and sat beside her. 'I've thought this through and it's what I want.'

'And what about the baby?' The words burst from Beth, unguarded. 'Who's going to look after it while you're studying? They don't look after themselves, you know. It's a full-time job.'

'I know that.' Ella spoke quietly. 'But there are crèches and child-minders. That's what you did, after all.'

Jon cleared his throat.

'And how are you going to pay for them? The two of you aren't thinking straight.'

'No, Beth. You're the one not thinking.' Jon dismissed her objections. 'This may not be what we planned, but think – a grandchild. Our grandchild.' His face had lit up. 'If Ella needs help, of course we'll support her financially until she can stand on her own two feet.'

'And what about Amy?' Beth could feel the situation running away from her, like sand through her fingers.

'What about her?'

'We can't give Ella all she'll need without giving Amy the equivalent.' They had always agreed on being scrupulously even-handed with their daughters.

'I don't mind, Mum. Really,' Ella interrupted. 'If you can't afford it, I won't go to university at all.'

'It's not about money, Lulu. We can work something out with Amy, I'm sure,' Jon said.

'I really want this baby. My baby.' She put her hand on her completely flat stomach.

Beth recognised that tone. Once Ella set her mind on something, she could be impossible to shift. Racing through the remaining possibilities open to her, Beth kept returning to the same answer. She baulked at the idea of including anyone else in this piece of family business, but Megan was the one person to whom Ella might listen. That she had gone to her in the first place showed how much she trusted her. Beth would institute a truce. There was still time. Then she had another thought.

'But this decision isn't just yours, Lulu. Is it?'

'What d'you mean?'

'*If* you're having this baby, the father and his family will have to be involved. That's only fair. You'll have to tell us who he is now, won't you?'

Ella shook her head, gnawing the side of her thumbnail. Tears were welling in her eyes. 'I don't want them to know yet.'

Beth put her arm around her. 'If he doesn't know now, he'll know in a few months, my love. So you might as well tell us.' She hesitated. 'It's not one of your teachers, is it?'

'Mum! How could you even think that? That's so gross.'

'What's not one of her teachers?' They hadn't heard Amy come in. She threw herself into a chair.

'We're just talking about Ella's boyfriend.'

'Her boyfriend?' Amy reached over to cut herself a piece of cheese.

If Ella's face was pale before, it was ashen now. 'Amy, shut up!'

Telling Amy to shut up was a red rag to a bull. 'Why should I? You've been drooling over him for years.'

'Oh, go away.' Ella snatched the plate of cheese from her. 'Haven't you got something better to do?'

Amy stuck out her tongue.

'Girls, stop it,' interrupted Jon, reacting at last. 'Can we have a civilised conversation for once. Please.'

'I don't know what all the fuss is about,' said Amy, going over to the cupboard where the biscuits were kept. 'He's not even here half the time.'

'Amy!' Ella's voice was low now, warning.

'Who are you talking about?' Beth was looking from one daughter to the other, not understanding.

Ella rushed at Amy, pushing her out of the door. 'Get out!'

As she was unceremoniously shunted from the room, Amy

shouted back over her shoulder, 'You must have noticed. It's Jake, of course.' Then a shriek as Ella aimed a slap at her and missed.

Beth froze. Jake. Amy had said the name as if it would mean something. But they only knew one Jake, and it couldn't be him. 'Come back, both of you!' she yelled. 'Now! I mean it.'

Ella stamped back into the room, her face red, eyes filled with tears. She tried to slam the door behind her, but Amy caught it and followed her in.

'Well?' asked Beth, dreading the answer.

'Just somebody I've met,' muttered Ella. She glared at Amy, warning her not to say any more.

At last, Amy seemed to grasp the gravity of the situation. She pulled out a chair and sat down, her eyes fixed on her sister, avid to find out what was going on.

'Lulu, you're going to have to come clean.' Jon looked as anxious as Beth felt.

Ella shook her head, pulling a tissue from her pocket to blow her nose. 'Why couldn't you keep your mouth shut?' she shot at Amy. 'You knew we didn't want anyone to know.'

Amy looked shamefaced. 'Sorry,' she muttered. 'I didn't know it was so important.'

'It wasn't up to you to judge.' Ella was only just controlling her temper. 'And now you've made everything a thousand times more difficult.'

'I don't understand why.' Amy had recovered herself already, eager for information, pleased that for once it was her sister who was the centre of a family drama, not her. 'Isn't anyone going to tell me what's happening?'

'Not right now,' said Beth firmly.

'Then I'm going out.' She stood up and went to the door.

'You're not doing anything of the sort.' Beth pictured her pinned against their front railing by the anonymous Goth.

'You can't stop me.' Amy opened the door and ran upstairs. 'Going to Hannah's. Won't be late.'

'Jon, please.' Beth's head was about to explode. 'Go after her.'

'OK. But you know what she's like.' With a sigh, he got to his feet, touching Ella's shoulder lightly as he passed her. 'I'll be right back.'

When they were finally alone, Beth and Ella sat quietly for a moment, both of them gathering themselves to face the coming storm. Eventually, Beth broke the silence. 'Come here.'

Ella pulled her chair closer and snuggled into her mother's arms, just as she used to when she was younger. Beth held her tight. However old they were, whatever they got up to, her daughters never stopped tugging at her heart. She patted Ella's back, breathing in her scent, making herself relax before she spoke. 'I'm not angry, you know. We can sort this out.'

'How are you going to do that?' Ella snapped as she sat up straight. 'Why did Amy have to say anything?'

'We'd have to know in the end,' Beth reminded her.

'Yes, but not first. Not before he knows.' She fiddled with a loose button on her shirt.

'He doesn't know?'

'How could he? He's on tour.'

'On tour,' Beth echoed. 'You don't really mean it's …'

'Yes.' Ella sounded defiant as she stuffed her tissue up her sleeve. 'It's that Jake.'

Jake Weston. Megan's son. Beth took a deep breath. He was practically Ella's brother, for God's sake. This was going to change everything. Ella and Jake. How had that happened under their noses? She had never suspected a thing.

'When did you start seeing him?' She paused. 'Romantically, I mean. Why didn't you say anything?'

'Because we didn't want any of you to know. We knew what a fuss everyone would make.'

Not as much as they would make now. Beth tried to take in the implications. Surely Jake would be horrified when he heard.

What twenty-one-year-old man wanted to be tied down by a family?

'Amy walked in on us at Christmas. She promised not to say anything.' Ella's eyes flashed with anger.

'You don't think he's bit young to be a dad?' Beth spoke cautiously, not wanting to trigger another argument. 'And what about his band? Won't he be away all the time?'

'I know what you're trying to say, but we'll work something out.' Ella smiled. 'I love him, Mum.'

What could her eighteen-year-old daughter know of love?

'Does Megan know?' She felt a little pinch of jealousy, followed by a surge of fury. Megan and Pete deserved some of the blame for this. Megan had always been too indulgent towards Jake, had let him get away with anything. Things might be different if they'd ... they'd what? She didn't know.

Ella shook her head again. 'I wanted to tell her. When I went to see her, I thought I would. Then I realised that if I didn't have the baby, I didn't want them to know. But now I've made up my mind, it's different.'

It certainly was. Beth looked at her daughter, eighteen going on twenty-eight. Where on earth would they go from here?

8

With the first flush of youth well behind her and her curls blown about (she refused to wear a helmet), Megan sat bolt upright on her battered sit-up-and-beg black bike, one hand at the ready to keep her skirt from blowing up. A big wicker basket attached to the front handlebars held her handbag, and a couple of panniers straddled the back wheel for anything else she needed to transport.

She had cycled home from school as fast as she could (which was not very) and had immediately shooed a reluctant Pete out of the door to get some nuts and white wine. He had only been home a couple of days and was exploiting his jet lag to the hilt, but she was having none of it. She had an hour before the others arrived. Jon hadn't said why they were coming, but he had sounded so peculiar when he phoned that she had been in a sweat of anxiety ever since.

'Something's happened,' he said. 'The four of us need to talk.' Never comfortable on the phone, he had been short even for him.

'Give me a clue,' she'd begged, half joking.

'We'll explain when we see you. This isn't something we can discuss over the phone.'

'How's Ella?' she tried.

But he ignored the question. 'Tomorrow night?' he asked. 'About seven OK?'

'Fine,' she said, totally mystified. 'Shall I do supper?'

'No, don't bother. We won't stay long.'

She had never heard him this brisk before. 'Jon. What is this? Is something wrong?'

'I can't discuss it now. Sorry, Meg. We'll talk about it to-morrow,' was all he said.

Something must have happened to Ella. No, he would have said. What else could it possibly be? Her mind went into over-drive. What if he and Beth needed to borrow money to get them out of a hole? But would they come to her and Pete to bail them out? Unlikely, given their more than precarious finances. Could Amy and Hannah have got up to something, she didn't know about? Not getting pissed again? Not the hair? She thought they had all recovered from that.

Wondering where to tidy first, she looked at her sitting room through a visitor's eyes. The warm red of the walls that she and Pete had picked years ago was now tatty and marked where Christmas cards and children's drawings had been stuck and pulled away. The reds, blues and browns of the Indian rugs were faded. The between-the-wars portraits they had fossicked for in house clearance auctions crowded the walls. Once, they had treasured them, but now they took them for granted and barely noticed their presence. She had meant to get the sofa and chairs re-covered years ago, but what with the children, their friends and the pets, the time had never been right. Their various covers sort of went together; their cushions were squashed and disorganised. Everywhere were trophies from her days of trawling junk shops and antique fairs: glass jugs, the Venetian mirrors she had once liked so much, the glass-fronted cabinet in the corner that contained the antique decanter collection, never used. From where she was standing, she could see how badly the windows of the conservatory at the back of the house needed cleaning. A spider's web drifted from one of the cross beams. She sighed. Housework had never been her strongest suit.

She plumped up the cushions and straightened the kelim-covered ottoman before getting the cobweb brush from the cupboard, surprised as always to find that she owned one at all. A present from her mother after a visit. She grabbed a duster at the same time. But, once in attack mode, she soon realised she was making things worse. Without picking everything up – and she didn't have time to do that – a clear line divided the dusted from the undusted. What was it Quentin Crisp once said? If you didn't dust for two years, it never got worse. Something like that. If it weren't for family embarrassment keeping her on the rails, she might seriously consider following suit.

Oh, sod it! It was only Jon and Beth. They'd been here umpteen times and knew what to expect. Megan abandoned the duster and brush in favour of wrapping some parcel tape, sticky side out, around her hand. She shooed Diva off the sofa, and attempted to remove the cat hair from where she'd been sitting. Accepting defeat when the tape wrinkled up, she sank into the floral chintz chair. Just a moment of peace before the others arrived.

Apart from the usual *Sturm und Drang* of regular school existence, today had featured a visit from Ben Fletton's mother – a day later than arranged, but demanding to be seen nonetheless. Not a pleasant experience. Josie Fletton was a mistress of passive aggression, making it quite clear that if Ben was misbehaving, she held the school responsible. Megan's head ached at the memory. Co-operation was not a word in Josie Fletton's lexicon. She had patted her bleached-white hair as she listened to what Megan had to say.

'So you saw 'im take the money then?'

'No. But the two playground monitors—'

'If you didn't see it, then how do you know 'e done it? 'E says 'e didn't.'

However hard Megan tried to make the woman appreciate what a monster-in-the-making her son was, Josie Fletton refused to listen. She protected Ben as a lioness would her cub. Megan admired that in her, but at the same time …

The cheese puffs! She had forgotten to make them. Beth might not touch them, but Jon had always loved them and they might ease things along. Abandoning the housework, she retreated to the kitchen and got out the ingredients. She was mid mix when she heard the click of Pete's key in the door.

'What *are* you doing?' Pete put an off-licence bag on the side before shedding his layers and half hanging them on the hooks by the back door. 'Won't they be here in a minute?' Last to go was his Russian hat with the furry ear flaps that made him look as if he'd just walked in from the Siberian steppes. Without it, he appeared more the mad professor. What was left of his once thick dark hair was all over the place, his bald patch gleaming, his cheeks flushed from the biting wind, his eyes glinting like chips of grey glass. He bent over to swap his shoes for slippers.

'I thought food might ease things along a bit. Jon sounded so peculiar. Are you sure you don't know why they're coming? Has he said anything to you? Is it something to do with Ella?' She kissed his nose and tried to rebutton his unevenly done-up grey cardigan across his paunch, showering him with flour. She turned her attention back to adding in the grated cheese.

'Not a clue. Think we should have a quick bracer before they arrive?' He brushed his belly, distributing the flour over his jeans.

'Let's wait till they're here.' She didn't think he should start drinking before that. She didn't want him pissed tonight.

'I'll have one on my own, then.' He went into the conservatory, where she could hear him getting some glasses from the cupboard. There was a pause. Just long enough for him to pour and down a shot. Then, 'Red or white?'

'Beth always has white,' she yelled back, wishing he wouldn't do this, hoping he wouldn't help himself to another.

'Then I'll open both.'

As she moulded the mixture into balls and arranged them on a baking tray, she heard the pop of a cork and the glug of something being poured. She resigned herself to whatever the evening might bring.

84

'Thought I'd better give it a try,' he said, returning to the kitchen with a glass of red in his hand. 'So what's all this about then?'

'No idea.' Megan dodged his hug to slide the tray of puffs into the oven.

At that moment the doorbell rang.

'I guess we're about to find out. I'll go.'

As Pete lurched towards the hall, Megan ripped off her apron and, in the tiny kitchen mirror, arranged her hair with her fingers. She grabbed her emergency lipstick from the weighing scales and slashed it on. Better. Her cheeks were flushed with the effort of getting the puffs ready on time. Instead of following Pete, she went via the conservatory into the sitting room, quickly plumping up the cushions she'd ignored earlier. She could hear Pete taking Beth and Jon's coats. The cobweb brush was leaning against the TV, where she'd abandoned it. Beth came into the room to find her standing to attention like an armed soldier, the brush in her hand.

Normally, they might have laughed. Megan's lax attention to housekeeping had long been a joke when set against Beth's shaming high standards. This time a smile that could best be described as cool was enough to tell Megan that she had yet to be forgiven. Her hackles rose as Beth took the sofa. She was damned if she was going to let this feud develop. She watched Beth get comfortable, struck by how tired she looked. The subtle make-up did nothing to disguise how thin and pinched her face had become.

'It's freezing tonight,' Beth commented, picking something from her black trousers.

'Glass of wine?' said Megan, at exactly the same time.

'Yes thanks. Love one.'

'Jon?' Jon had hung back in the hall with Pete – sports chat, no doubt – but now came in to join them. The difference between the two men was striking. Slim and impeccably groomed, Jon was clearly familiar with the inside of a gym. As far as Pete was concerned, fitness meant the odd amble to the pub or once round the garden, pulling at a few weeds. But appearances clearly didn't matter when it came to their friendship, which had continued through every stage of their life since secondary school.

'I'd love a glass of red, if it's open,' Jon said with a smile. Relieved that he at least was being friendly, Megan disappeared to get the drinks.

When she returned, Beth and Jon were patiently listening as Pete, still full of his most recent trip, regurgitated the one about the escapee goat in Niswa market. They exchanged glances once or twice, as if debating whether to interrupt and broach what they had come to say. But Jon would never cut Pete off in his stride. He was Pete's most appreciative audience. Megan plumped herself by Jon on the sofa, aware of his fidgeting, trying discreetly to signal to Pete that he should hurry up or shut up. At last, he drew to a close, beaming at all three of them, expecting them to laugh with him. Confused when they didn't, he took a sip of his wine, rallied and leaned back in his chair.

'So what's up? To what do we owe the honour?'

Megan heard Beth's sharp intake of breath, but Pete carried on undeterred. 'Come on, guys. Spit it out. Put us out of our misery.'

Jon inclined his head towards Beth, giving her the floor, just as Diva jumped on to Megan's lap.

Beth cleared her throat. 'The thing is ...' She stopped as her hand rose to her throat, stroking it up and down, her forefinger finally catching in the chain of her necklace. 'The thing ...'

'The thing is,' echoed Jon, 'Ella's pregnant, as you know.' He exchanged another glance with Beth. Pete looked puzzled, as if he had forgotten that Megan had told him.

Jon cleared his throat and looked at them both. 'She's decided to keep the baby.'

Beth was watching him, her eyes glassy. Her effort to remain in control was painful to watch. Her body language – crossed legs, arms wrapped round herself as she leaned forward – warned off Megan from trying to comfort her.

'Well!' puffed Pete, apparently oblivious to the mounting tension. 'How do you feel about that? What about all her plans?'

Megan kept stroking Diva, almost on automatic, the action soothing. But hadn't Beth been leaning towards Ella having an abortion when they last spoke? 'But I thought she … you said …'

'Yes,' said Beth, struggling to keep her voice level. 'She did arrange a termination, but she changed her mind.'

Megan could see that Pete was as puzzled as her as to what any of this had to do with them.

'And you're all right with that?' she ventured.

Beth sat straight, uncrossing her legs then clamping them together at the knee and ankle, angling them to one side. She put down her wine glass and clasped her hands on her lap, white-knuckled. 'I'm not really. No. But I've got to accept her decision, particularly since Jon agrees with her.'

Jon gave a small shake of his head but said nothing. He would never make public a rare disagreement between them. But this fundamental difference in opinion at least explained the strained atmosphere they'd brought with them.

'I'm sorry,' said Megan. Beth would feel rudderless not being in control. 'But I'm sure everything will work out for the best. Just think, a baby.' The envy she heard in her voice surprised her. But this was obviously not a moment for celebration.

'Yes,' said Pete, getting up to fetch more wine, even though he was the only one to have made an appreciable difference to the level in his glass. 'Things will look better in a few months.'

Beth made a sound like a kicked dog.

'I'm sorry if I'm being stupid,' said Megan, still puzzled. 'But I'm not sure what any of this has got to do with us. Is there something we can do to help?'

87

'You've done enough,' said Beth, her mouth tight with contained emotion.

'Beth! Don't make things worse.' Jon warned her.

'Megan's right,' said Pete, one of his feet searching for his plaid slipper, which had dropped on to the floor. 'Why don't you tell us why you're here, and then we can get on with the rest of the evening.'

Jon leaned towards Beth. 'Do you really want to do this? Or shall I?' He covered her hands with one of his. 'Let me.'

Beth nodded, staring at her lap, either upset or angry, hard to tell. Pete sprawled in his chair, topping up his own glass. The others shook their heads when he waved the bottle in their direction. Megan willed them to get on with it, whoever was going to speak.

'The one thing Ella wouldn't tell us, until she confirmed what we found out by accident, is who the father is.' Jon switched his focus from Megan to Pete.

Was that an appeal for help in Beth's eyes? Before Megan had time to be sure, Beth looked away.

The sudden knowledge of what was coming next hit Megan hard, driving the breath from her body. There was a rushing in her ears as she watched Jon's mouth moving, hearing the word 'Jake' as if it came from miles away. As he spoke, Beth looked as if she was about to erupt. Her jaw was clenched, mouth strained, eyes steely. She blinked just once.

Jake's name hung in the air for minutes as they took in the information. On the other side of the room, Pete sat up, shock registering on his flushed face, before he settled back and began to shake with laughter. 'You're having us on?' He looked around the assembled group for the reassurance that was not forthcoming. 'Jake and Ella?' he protested. 'They're like brother and sister. You're joking.'

'They're not joking, Pete,' Megan managed, although she

desperately wished they were. Beth and Jon wouldn't joke over something like this. 'I'm sorry. Excuse me for a moment.'

She had to get some air, even if it was a freezing winter night. She let herself out into the garden through the conservatory door, the eyes of the others burning into her back. The cold air gave her system the jolt it needed. She sat on her favourite garden bench by the pergola, comforted by the familiar silhouettes ahead of her: the shrubs leading down the left-hand side to the crab apple tree at the end, the unused wooden beehive, the stone winged gryphon by the pond; the right side of the garden emptier, waiting for everything to waken in the spring. Taking several deep breaths to compose her racing thoughts, she leaned forward, elbows on knees, and buried her head in her hands. How could this have happened? Pete was right. Having been virtually brought up together, Jake and Ella *were* like brother and sister. She had never dreamed that there would ever be more to their relationship than that. Of her two children, Jake was much the more straightforward, the more confiding. He had always told her everything. Or so she'd thought.

A quick calculation of dates took her back to Christmas. They had long ago abandoned those skiing trips on which the children overtook their timid efforts, leaving them on the green runs, aching in every joint and longing for the après-ski partying. Instead, Jon and Beth always had a Christmas Eve party then came round to theirs on Boxing Day for lunch. The children went back and forth between the houses as usual, just with more friends in tow as they got older. Jake and Ella must have got it together then. Bloody idiot! What about all those contraceptive lectures she'd doled out over the years – hadn't he been listening?

She jumped as a hand touched her shoulder.

'Are you OK?' No, not Pete, who was no doubt washing down the problem with another drink, but Jon. His words came wrapped in a white plume of breath. He sat beside her, close enough for her to feel the heat of his body.

89

'Yeah, I'm fine.' She sat straight, slipping her hands under her thighs for warmth, shivering slightly. 'It's too much to take in. Are you sure Ella's right?'

'What do you mean? That she's been sleeping around? Megan! You know her better than that. Don't ever let Beth hear you say that.' He rubbed his hands together against the cold. 'Of course we're not sure. But that's what she's told us.'

'Does Jake even know?' Wouldn't he have told her if he did?

'We don't think so. But Ella won't tell us anything until she's seen him. When's he going to be back?'

'I don't know exactly. After the weekend, I think.' He had told her, she was sure. How could she not remember when he was due back? She didn't even know where exactly in Germany he was at that moment. Another example of her lackadaisical parenting skills. But, of course, he didn't know. He would have said.

'How's Beth?' she asked. Perhaps this pregnancy might bring them together again after all.

'Not coping too well. She thinks it's going to blow all Ella's dreams of being a paediatrician out of the water. But Ella's adamant.'

'And you're torn between the two of them?' Still not at all sure what she felt herself, Megan was sympathetic to his predicament.

'Yes and no.' He tipped his head back to look up at the stars. 'I want to support Beth, of course I do. But I'm against abortion on principle. My heart and my head tell me that Ella's doing the right thing.'

Was that what Jake's heart would tell him? Somehow Megan doubted it. He was way too busy being a rock god, having a good time, enjoying the attention from his growing group of fans. The band were about to sign with a label and had big plans for the future. He wasn't ready to be tied down. A baby? If he was really going to be a father, things would look very different. Would he want that? She needed to talk to him. Together they would put their weight behind Beth. It wasn't too late. Ella would see sense.

Megan was all too aware that this was Jake's child; her and Pete's grandchild too. How could she even begin to think like this? But Jake had to come first. She would support him.

'I think we'd better go back to the others,' she said, pulling her hands from under her thighs and blowing hot breath on to her palms, feeling suddenly disloyal to Jon.

She reached the door just as Beth started to open it from inside. 'Something's burning,' she announced, her nose screwed up.

'Shit! I forgot all about the bloody puffs.' Megan dashed into the kitchen, knocking a plastic bottle of milk on to the floor as she grabbed the oven gloves and flung open the oven door. She pulled out the baking sheet, but the diminutive offerings were charred almost to extinction.

Jon slipped inside to find Pete, leaving Beth looking on as Megan slid her efforts into the bin. Megan glanced up, hoping to see a smile on Beth's face. Instead, her eyes were unforgiving. She leaned forward so that what she was about to say wouldn't be overheard.

'Don't think I've forgotten,' she said. 'Because I haven't.'

Their faces were so close, their noses were almost touching.

Megan recoiled. 'Don't you think that's the least of our worries now?' She took a step back. 'The fact that Ella came to me first and whether or not I should have told you doesn't really figure in the light of this.'

A cloud crossed Beth's face. 'You haven't a clue, have you? You've no idea how upset I've been.'

Was this really her old friend talking? Suddenly it was all too much for Megan. 'For Christ's sake, Beth,' she exploded. 'Don't be so bloody sanctimonious. Listen to yourself. Our children are going to be parents and that's all you can think about? Yes, Ella came to talk to me, but look at it another way. As your girls grew up, you used me time and again ... yes, used ...' She heard Beth's short intake of breath and knew she'd gone too far, but she wasn't going to stop now. 'Don't get me wrong. I never minded being your unpaid babysitter ...' Another gasp. A pursing of the lips and a narrowing of the eyes accompanied Beth's attempt to interrupt, but Megan was on a roll and wouldn't be stopped. 'I loved having them here. Still do. They're like family. But here's the thing: it was all very well when *you* needed me to be a mother to them, wasn't it? I helped you out. No problem. But when *they* need me to be one, you don't like it. But whose fault's that? If you'd been around more—'

'Easy, Meg,' Pete had returned to the kitchen, just catching the last of her words.

She whipped around towards him. 'Shut up, Pete. I'm just sorting out a few home truths.'

'If I'd known ...' Beth's cheeks were ablaze. Her hand rose to her face before she spun round to the door. 'Jon! I'll be in the car.' Without waiting for him, she marched into the hall, snatched her coat from its hook and left the house, slamming the door behind her.

The other three stared at each other, speechless.

9

Jon stayed just long enough for him and Pete to insist that Megan speak to Jake. Her suggestion that they should wait until he was back was discounted. Beth had already persuaded them that as soon as he was home they would hold a second family council with him and Ella. As Jon went down the path, wrestling with his coat in the wind, Megan could see Beth's silhouette bent forward in the passenger seat of their car.

'That went well,' said Pete, as soon as Jon had dashed out into the dark. 'Did you have to?' He slugged back his wine and returned to the sitting room, where she heard him help himself to more.

Jon's evident misery was already making Megan regret her outburst, without Pete adding to her guilt. But, too late now. What was said couldn't be unsaid. Besides, she reminded herself, it was true – even if saying so wasn't going to help.

So, the rules of engagement had changed. Megan knew that as far as Pete was concerned, what would be would be. The kids could sort themselves out. But without wanting to admit it, she had moved towards Beth's position. If only Beth had allowed her a chance to say so, instead of giving her the needle. Jake was not ready to be a father. She reassured herself that he would persuade Ella that continuing the pregnancy was a mistake. Eventually, and perhaps painfully, the status quo would reassert itself. This might not quite echo what she had said to Ella, but when it came to her own son … well, things were different.

The phone call was not one she would easily forget. When she finally got through to Germany, it was late. She could hear voices in the background, the clink of a glass and the hum of traffic.

'Hey, Mum. What's up?' At least Jake sounded pleased to hear from her. She pictured him leaning against a wall outside a bierkeller, looking like Pete in his much younger days. The two men in her life shared that same flop of dark hair, the same generous features under thick straight brows, the same engaged eyes. They were chipped from the same block, with the same deep mischievous streak running through. Both of them were always on the lookout for a good time. Jake would be wearing his awful skintight black jeans, ripped at the knee, some old T-shirt and plimsolls, enjoying the company of his mates in the band.

After the briefest of catch-ups about what he'd been up to since they'd last spoken, Megan came to the point.

His first reaction to hearing of Ella's pregnancy was a long-drawn-out whistle, then, 'Wo-ow! No way!'

'Beth and Jon have been round.' She hesitated, recalling their meeting. There was a noise in the background and someone laughed.

'Yeah? Why?' Someone spoke to him. 'Yeah, wha'ever, mate. I'll catch you in there.'

She could hear that she was already losing his interest, so she hurried on. 'Ella's told them you're the father.' She gave a short, nervous laugh, hoping … no, waiting for him to deny it. She wouldn't accept his involvement until he had confirmed it, a small part of her still certain that that wasn't going to happen.

After a moment during which she heard him thank someone, and then a sharp inhalation as he took a drag of something, he said, 'Yeah? You're joking, right?'

If only she had an equally obliging friend who would pass her a calming spliff. She had no illusions about what went on during these road trips. 'How I wish I was.'

She heard him take another drag, considering what she had said.

'But they wouldn't say it if they didn't believe it was true,' she went on, every ounce of her willing him to contradict them. 'They insisted I call you.'

'Well, I guess I could be.' He was hesitant, as if he didn't want to commit to the possibility.

'You could be!' Disappointment and panic collided in Megan. 'You slept with her?'

'Chill out, Mum. That's how these things happen.' He laughed in that affectionate but superior manner her children adopted when dealing with what they considered her less intelligent moments.

'We're going to have to sort this out as soon as you come home,' she said, sounding like the sort of mother she had never managed to be: both organised and organising. 'Beth's trying to persuade her to have an abortion, but Ella wants to have the baby.'

There was a second long whistle down the phone. 'Shit. No way.'

'When are you back?' This was hopeless. They needed a proper talk, not this unsatisfactory phone call where too much was left unsaid. If he was there in front of her, she would be able to read his reactions and get a better idea of what was going through his mind.

'You're not asking me to break the tour, are you? We've only got two days left. The lads ...' He sounded alarmed, despite knowing she would never tell him or Hannah what to do. She might advise firmly but never tell. They were old enough to make their own decisions and learn from their mistakes.

'No. Some bad shit at home,' she heard him say, his voice faint as he turned away to talk to someone.

'Then I'll tell them we can all meet on Friday night,' she said firmly.

'All of us? Must we?' She had his attention again.

'Now that everyone's involved, I think we must.' He wasn't alone in not wanting to, but she could hardly say that.

'Els should have told me instead of waiting for me to come back.' He sounded puzzled rather than angry. 'We could have decided what to do together, without all of you lot. This is totally weird.'

Did that mean he *was* against Ella having the baby, just as Megan had expected him to be? Was that regret she was feeling? Where had that come from? She had years ahead of her in which to be a grandmother. She cleared her throat.

'She's only eighteen,' she said, as if she needed to remind him. 'And this isn't part of the Standish grand plan. Ella's future was all mapped out. None of us knew you were even … together.' She said the last word as if it was a question. Perhaps they weren't. Perhaps it had just been a drunken one-night stand. Would that make it better or worse?

'Can you imagine if you had known?' She could tell he was drawing the conversation to a close. She wanted to prolong it, to find out what he was thinking and what she was thinking herself. But he, like she and Pete, needed time to absorb the news. 'The fuss,' he said. 'We didn't want anyone to find out till we were ready.'

'But, it hasn't been going on for long?' She wanted to reassure herself. Besides, what did he mean? Ready for what?

'Mmm, I don't know … on and off. You know.'

'No, I don't. Why didn't you say something?' How come neither she nor Beth had noticed that their children's relationship had changed? Should they have been watching out for this? The possibility had never entered her head, and she was meant to be good at sussing out what was going on. But they had become adults without her noticing.

'Because there wasn't anything to tell,' he protested. 'You guys practically threw us together all our lives so far, so what's the fuss about?'

'The fuss is about a baby.' Surely he wasn't so obtuse that she had to spell that out for him.

'Yeah, and I've said I'll talk to Els as soon as I'm home. I'll Skype her when I'm back at the hostel.'

For the first time Megan could remember, Jake was shutting her out. She had always imagined that she would be the first to know when he had a serious girlfriend. Even if he hadn't said anything, she had been confident she'd be able to tell.

She remembered the distraction that had come with Rick, her first serious boyfriend. Hours spun out for ever as she waited for him to phone, imagining where he was, what he might be doing, playing the music they listened to together on repeat until she drove her mother around the bend, leaving the washing-up half done, forgetting stuff. She had always assumed Jake would behave in the same dotty way when the time came. At the slightest hint, she'd have winkled the details out of him. But there hadn't been the slightest hint. Had there? Perhaps boys were different. Working with children for so long had taught her that they were past masters at hiding things, but she knew her own children better than that, didn't she? Had Hannah known all along? If so, the cards-on-the-table family that Megan had prided herself on having nurtured had become something else altogether.

'Where's Ella?' Beth shouted over the music emerging from Jon's study. She recognised Chopin's Nocturne No. 9, a piece he often played when he was thinking. 'Jon!'

He raised his voice above the piano. 'No idea. Haven't seen her. Why?'

'Megan and Pete will be here soon – with Jake.' The boy's name stuck in her throat like an unpleasant sweet.

During the days that had passed since they last saw Megan and Pete, Beth's feelings about the pregnancy hadn't changed. Emotion versus reason, and reason won. What had been right for her when she was a teenager would surely be right for her daughter.

Having an abortion was what had made everything possible for Beth. A baby would have made progress in her career so much more difficult, if not impossible. That was all she wanted for Ella – a future that held the greatest possible number of options. Babies could wait.

The morning when she herself had fled weeping from home to have the procedure was as clear in her mind as ever. She hadn't told her mother, had known the shame she would feel and what repercussions there might be from her mother's boyfriend, Barry. She hadn't told Neil, the boy she had slept with more out of curiosity than anything else. She certainly hadn't loved him. Fancied him, yes. The competition was stiff: all the girls fought for a place on the back seat of the bus with him, falling for his Mick Jagger mouth, long wavy hair, and deep blue eyes you could drown in. They dated a few more times afterwards, but he was too immature, too flaky for her. Her heart was set on university, achieving a first-class degree and finding her way as a lawyer. More than anything she wanted to escape the threadbare poverty of her mother's house, the scrabbling for every last penny, Barry. For Beth, boyfriends had been a pleasant distraction, but not ever to be put first. Only when Jon came along all those years later, when her career was established, had she allowed herself to fall in love.

Their marriage had been long and happy. Jon had proved to her what a remarkable man he was. They had triumphed together over difficulty before and become stronger as a result, and she was confident they would do so again.

She checked her watch. The Westons were due in ten minutes, and there was no sign of Ella. Furious about this family council foisted on her and Jake, she had gone out to meet a friend, promising to be back on time. Amy was out with friends too. For once she was not with Hannah, and that gave Beth some relief. They should keep the two families separate for a while – till things calmed down. Too much harm had been done.

Pete and Jon wouldn't like that, but she was past caring. Apart from everything else, Megan had been completely out of order. 'Used'! The word still rankled with Beth. That was unfair. Hadn't she helped Megan out in other ways over the years? Wasn't that what friendship was?

She was sitting deliberating, eyes shut, arms straight, hands resting on her thighs, trying to compose herself, when the doorbell startled her into awareness. Jon emerged from his study to answer it. She rose as he showed Pete and Megan into the sitting room, and the four of them stood awkwardly, looking at one another, uncertain how to behave. No one made a move towards the usual hugs and greetings.

'Did you see last night's match?' Pete turned to Jon, but was silenced by a look from Megan.

'Let's sit down.' Beth gestured towards the chairs. 'Where's Jake?' Megan had always let her children get away with murder. If they had allowed him to duck out of facing up to his responsibilities, she would be furious.

'He said he'd be here,' said Pete, as if that was all they needed to know. 'And Ella?' He sank into one of the two sofas with an 'oof', comfortably occupying over half of it. His paunch grew larger every time Beth saw him.

'She'll be back,' she said, taking the sofa on the other side of the coffee table. Megan sat next to Pete, leaving the space beside Beth for Jon. Battle lines were drawn.

No one was willing to break the embarrassed silence that fell between them. Megan fiddled with a broken nail. Pete shifted to get comfortable, crossing and uncrossing his legs. Beth stared at the vase of white tulips that had begun to droop.

'Drinks?' Jon crossed to the side table where the bottles stood.

'Thought you'd never ask.' But Pete's attempt at joviality fell flat.

Jon moved between them, dispensing glasses, and olives that no one but Pete touched. Beth found herself rather relishing the atmosphere. She was damned if she was going to make this easy for them. If they'd kept a tighter rein on their son, they wouldn't all be in this mess …

At the sound of the front door opening and shutting, all heads turned expectantly. They heard coats being removed and hung up, then footsteps, and Jake and Ella walked into the room.

Beth was immediately struck by the change in her daughter. Happiness radiated from her, replacing the gloom of recent weeks. She was standing so close to Jake you couldn't put a pin between them, her face turned up to his like a flower to sunshine. This was not what Beth had wanted or anticipated. She had been expecting Jake to freak out at the news of Ella's pregnancy and to want to put as much distance between them as possible. By the look of Megan, she was feeling much the same. As obvious as Ella's adoration of Jake was his of her. He draped a protective arm around her shoulders.

'Well, we're here,' he said, matter-of-fact. He looked older, more mature than Beth remembered him.

'Sorry we're a bit late,' echoed Ella. She, on the other hand, looked so young. Beside Jake, she was short, her legs skinny in their leggings, her hair down.

Beth stared at them, unable to say a word. Did Jake and his baby really mean so much to Ella that she was prepared to sacrifice everything she had worked so hard for?

Instead, Jon cleared his throat. 'Why don't you take a pew? Then we can discuss this sensibly. Together. Beer or wine, Jake?'

How could he talk as if this was a normal family get-together? Beth watched as Jon stepped to one side. Ella perched on the edge of the chair facing the fire while Jake sat on its arm. He accepted a beer. Beth leaned forward to offer a coaster so the glass coffee table wouldn't get marked. Ella raised her eyebrows at Jake, including him in a small rejection of her mother.

At last, they were ready. By now, Pete was looking faintly

bemused, his glass already half empty. Megan, on the other hand, seemed edgy with impatience.

'Well, we all know why we're here.' Jon sat beside Beth and opened proceedings. 'Ella has decided she wants to have Jake's baby.'

'Not *my* baby, Jon,' Jake corrected him. '*Our* baby.' They gazed at each other as he put his arm around her shoulders again. Beth looked away.

'Are you saying you're OK with it?' Megan spoke quietly.

So she was as excluded from their plans as Beth. The super-close family façade they presented wasn't as solid as it seemed. Beth took a crumb of comfort from that.

He nodded. 'That's what I mean. We've talked for a long time and we've worked out how we can do this.'

'You have?' All Beth could do was close her eyes and regroup, as what little wind there was in her sails disappeared. When she opened them again, nobody had moved. 'That's extremely sweet and kind of you, Jake. But, Ella …' Her appeal was halted in its tracks by her daughter's expression. The resentment and determination she read there warned her off. But she had to go on. The two of them were only children themselves, for heaven's sake. 'Ella. Your future. Please, think. I know I've said it before, but you won't be able to do everything you wanted if you have a baby.'

'Then I'll do something else.' Ella shook her hair back over her shoulders so they could all see how set her face was, how steady her gaze.

'Jake,' began Megan. 'Are you telling us you want to have the baby?' There was no mistaking the genuine surprise in her voice. 'What about the band?'

'He can still be in the band. I don't mind.' Ella seemed to have gained new strength from Jake's presence.

'But he could be away for months at a time, if they make it big,' Megan objected.

'And your exams?' asked Beth simultaneously.

'I'll manage, I'm sure.' How calm and collected she was.

'And where will you both live?'

'I thought I'd stay at home … if that's OK. Well, at first, anyway.' Her eyes darted towards her lap for a second.

Nobody spoke.

Ella seemed momentarily taken aback, then rallied. 'Don't worry. It won't be for ever. I'm going to do my A levels but I'll defer my university application for a year and then put the baby in a crèche while I'm working. I won't be the first.' She didn't show a smidgeon of doubt about her plans.

'And what will you be doing, Jake?' Jon spoke for the first time. Beth was probably the only one to notice the hostility in his voice.

'I'll be going ahead with the band. Neither of us wants to change our plans. Do we?' He looked at Ella, who shook her head firmly before resting her arm on his thigh. 'But that doesn't mean we won't see each other or be together.'

'While you're on the road?' Megan sounded astonished. 'You really think you can do that?'

'Of course we can,' he countered, squeezing Ella's hand. 'I know what it's like. Whenever I'm home we'll be together. And Ella and the baby can join me sometimes.'

'That's absurd.' Jon's face was set, flushed with rage. 'We're talking about a child here, another life, not some sort of toy that you can put down when you're bored.'

'Steady on,' Pete weighed in. 'He knows that.'

Ella laughed. 'Dad, calm down. We're not living in the dark ages. Of course the baby will come first. But if we say we can make this work, we will.'

'Ella, you're only a child yourself,' Beth appealed. 'Do listen to what we're saying. Please.'

'We have listened. I've always known what you'd say. But times have changed. People my age do have babies, and they survive.

'I'll survive too, especially now that I know Jake's behind me. I didn't know that before for sure.' They exchanged a smile that excluded everyone else in the room.

'Jon, please...' This was Beth's last chance to appeal to her husband. Perhaps his unhappiness with the proposed arrangements would be enough to make him come round to her point of view. There was still time. Just. But he looked, if anything, proud of Ella's determination and certainty in her plans. 'How will you support yourself?' she asked.

'We'd be paying towards her university fees and accommodation anyway,' Jon hurried to point out. 'So I don't really see why we should change that.'

'But...' Nothing came to her. She was defeated, her ammunition exhausted. 'Megan? Pete?' she appealed.

Pete's nose was hovering over his wine glass. 'Very drinkable Burgundy,' he pronounced.

Jon got up to fetch the bottle.

'Haven't you been listening?' Beth rounded on him, despite the warning in Jon's eyes.

'Losing your temper won't help.' Megan stepped in, having spent the past few minutes picking thoughtfully at her cuticle.

'Neither will ignoring the ramifications of them having this baby. If you hadn't—'

'Don't start,' Megan warned. 'I know what you're going to say, and I'm certainly not accepting any blame for this. I wouldn't do that any more than I'd blame you two. This is to do with Ella and Jake now. Not us.'

An awkward silence fell during which everyone looked anywhere but at each other. Beth kept her eyes fixed on the fireplace, shamed by Megan but unused to standing down in an argument. Then, on a nod from Jake, he and Ella stood up.

'Whether you like it or not, that's what we're doing. We're old enough to make these decisions ourselves. We're going back to

Mum and Dad's now. We'll see you later. Cheers for the beer, Jon.' He put his glass down just to the side of the drinks mat.

Pete was pushing himself to the edge of his seat, obviously keen to join the retreat. He was stopped in his tracks by a glare from Megan.

'But, Lulu…' Beth and Jon spoke together. The fact that she was leaving them to go with Jake was unbearable to both of them. Her loyalties had transferred so easily.

At the door, Ella turned. 'I'm sorry, Mum. I wanted you to be happy too. We're going to have the baby and we will make it work, with or without you.'

Then they were gone.

The two couples looked at each other.

'Well,' breathed Pete. 'Not what we were expecting.'

Beth turned on Megan. 'I feel as if we've lost her now. As if you haven't done enough.'

'What exactly are you accusing me of?' challenged Megan, doing up the one button on her jacket. 'Why are you still so angry with me when we should be pulling together?'

'She does have a point, Beth.' Jon was firm.

'For God's sake. As if you didn't know.' Beth barely suppressed her fury. 'I might have guessed the two of you'd gang up together.'

Megan stiffened.

Jon stared at Beth, astonished. 'What did you just say?'

'That's hardly fair.' Pete spoke at the same time as bending to tie one of his shoelaces, as if he was ducking for cover.

He was right. But Beth was damned if she would apologise. Jon got up to offer the olives, another drink, trying to bring the temperature down. Megan turned him away with a gesture that sent the olives flying over the ivory carpet. The colour had drained from her face and her expression was the fiercest Beth had ever seen it.

'I've done nothing.' Megan's voice was tight with rage, although she looked as if she might be about to cry. 'Nothing but be a mother to Ella when she's needed one. And at the time, when you were busy at work, it suited you.'

'We know what you think,' Beth fired back. 'But we've always been here for her. She knows that.'

'Ladies, please.' Pete put his arms out, palms down, patting the air as if levelling the atmosphere. 'This isn't helping.'

Megan leaned forward to help Jon, who was on his knees chasing the olives and putting them back into the bowl. When she sat up again, her expression had changed. 'Oh, God, let's not argue,' she implored. 'We're only going to make things worse. As far as I can see, they've made up their minds. There's nothing we can do about it except help them make it work. The more we try to dissuade them, the less they'll engage with us. You know that. And this is our grandchild we're talking about, after all.'

'As if I could forget.' Beth didn't want to feel this way about her first grandchild. She had always thought being a grandmother was something to look forward to, but in the future, in a conventional way. Not now. Not like this.

'Jake might not be the most obvious father material, I grant you …' Pete began, then stopped.

'Why couldn't you have supported me?' Beth's voice caught as she appealed to Megan. 'I've always relied on you. This is so wrong for Ella. I'm only thinking of her. Is it really what Jake wants?' As she buried her head in her hands, she felt Jon come round behind her chair. His hand rested on her shoulder, his thumb rubbing the back of her neck, before he squatted down to sop up the olive oil with kitchen roll.

'If Jake says he'll do something, he will. You know him. He won't let her down.'

Megan's voice came from a long way away, penetrating the dismal nappy-laden visions of the future that were whirring through Beth's mind. 'He's already done that.' She felt only despair. 'I can't understand why you can't see that. And you think he's too young too. I know you do. Why didn't you say something?'

'But, it's their lives,' Megan insisted, more gentle now. 'I'm not overjoyed about Jake's role in this. But if it is what he wants ... and I am surprised he does ... well, they have to be allowed to do things their way. You saw how they were together. We can't bend them to our will. We can only provide the arguments. And you've done that.'

'But a career in medicine will take her places, give her satisfaction, until the right time comes for babies ...' Beth stopped short. She would never convince them now.

'Not necessarily.' Jon's thumb stopped moving. 'You're thinking about your own life, not Ella's, and what happened to you. They're not the first to have a baby at that age. Megan's right. They'll cope, with our help.'

'That's not true. I am thinking about her.' Beth got to her feet. Jon had never disagreed with her publicly before. 'I'm going upstairs. I can't talk about this with you any more.'

As she shut the door, she heard Jon apologising to the others. 'It's difficult for her, but she'll come round.'

I won't, she thought. I don't see how I can when it goes against all our dreams.

This wasn't the first time she had felt like the outsider. All those years ago, when they'd first met, she'd had to work hard to infiltrate the tight little trio the others made. It had taken some time for Pete and Megan to accept her, but once they had, they had been indefatigably loyal friends.

All Megan had to do was support me, she told herself. I know she wanted to, but she's afraid of alienating Jake. He and Ella would come round, I'm sure they would. This can't be what she wants for him either. Pete won't care, but Megan ...

This time, though, there was no way back.

10

Megan was in the conservatory, laptop on the table. Even in winter, this was her favourite place to sit, staring over the top of the screen into her garden. It was the one room where no one would disturb her. The glass doors into the sitting room and kitchen were shut to keep the heat in the house and the cold out. She could hear the sound of the TV. If she turned around, she'd see Hannah sprawled over the sofa, surrounded by a plate of biscuits, yoghurt pots, coffee mugs and all the other detritus that she spread around her when she was 'cotching'.

Even though the heater was on full blast, without her Uggs, her long thick cardigan, thermals, fingerless mittens, and Diva curled on her lap, she reckoned she would be risking death from hypothermia. She pulled the scarf tighter around her head and neck, muffling herself as well as she could, then opened her inbox to reread Beth's email.

Megan missed Beth. She wanted to talk to her about the issues that were dividing them, of course, but there was everything else as well. She missed the gossip, the catching-up with what was happening at Beth's work, in her life. Beth's ability to see things in black and white meant she would understand how Megan might help Ben Fletton. Beth could assess a situation and offer sound objective advice better than anyone else she knew. Instead, an email had arrived the previous evening. Megan had read it several times, each time getting no closer to what was written between the lines.

Dear Megan

Nothing wrong with that exactly, except that Beth didn't usually bother with the niceties of addressing her, just got straight down to the message. Megan wasn't sure about this new formality.

I'm writing because I'm finding all this so difficult and it's impossible to talk to you. After all our years of friendship I thought I could expect you to support me. If Jake weren't the father, perhaps you'd see things from my point of view.

I've upset Ella, I know. She and I need to talk but she's not returning my calls. Please send her back home. We'd like her here so we can straighten things out as a family. Is that too much to ask?

I know our weekend at the Haven is coming up. I'm sure you'll agree that it's better we give it a miss this year.

Beth

A current of anger fizzed through Megan. If the two of them couldn't smooth this out, what was their friendship worth? Of course Beth was upset, but couldn't she see that her behaviour was only making things worse? For her to back out of their annual trip to the Haven was a real kick in the teeth. And why on earth did she assume that Megan was happy with the situation? This wouldn't be her first choice for Jake either. The future of Heavy Feather was far from certain, and he still didn't know what he wanted from life.

A part of Megan wanted to go upstairs, kick and scream and try to make the two of them see sense – it wasn't too late – but years of experience had taught her that that would be pointless. Confrontation only made things worse. She didn't have to look far to see proof of that. In fact, she had tried to point out all the potential pitfalls ahead of them. They'd listened, said they understood, but reiterated that they wanted the baby and they would make this work. So be it.

They hadn't left the house since they'd arrived back on Friday evening, two nights ago. They'd appeared for meals and for Megan's 'talk', but otherwise had spent most of the time in Jake's room. When Megan passed the door, she could hear them laughing and talking, just as they used to. Before, she hadn't given it a second thought. How could she have been so naïve? But Beth was right about one thing. Ella must go home.

Wearily Megan snapped shut the laptop and carried it with her into the kitchen, where she balanced it on the pile of unanswered post and unread weekend newspapers. She noticed the empty cake tins sitting on the side, their lids left upside down beside them. She would talk to Ella, then make some of the chocolate coconut macaroons Pete liked so much. Or should she be a better wife and encourage his diet? She rolled her eyes to the ceiling. Life was too short. He could look after his own body. He didn't need her for that.

In the hall, she stood with her hand on the banister and shouted up. 'Ella! Jake!'

'They're not still up there?' Pete appeared at her elbow, having finished sleeping off the lunchtime Merlot. 'Maybe you and I should ...' He jerked his head in the direction of their bedroom, leaving the suggestion unfinished. Her expression must have conveyed exactly what she thought of that idea. What *was* he thinking? She couldn't remember when they'd last had sex in the afternoon. He got the message and went to the kitchen, where she heard him rattling about making tea.

'Ella!' she yelled again.

A door opened and shut, then Ella turned the bend in the staircase above her. She was wearing an old navy blue jumper of Jake's that was ripped at the elbow, and a pair of his football socks over her leggings. Her hair was pulled into a high ponytail that left long wisps hanging round her face, emphasising its sharp contours. 'Sorry. Was the music too loud?'

'No, it's not that. Come into the kitchen for a second.'

Pete emerged with two mugs, grunted something unintelligible and went in the direction of the sitting room, Hannah and the TV. Ella made herself comfortable at the table, watching Megan get out the ingredients for the macaroons.

'It's been lovely having you—'

Ella interrupted before she could finish. 'It's been lovely being here. Thank you.'

Megan glanced over to catch Ella's smile. She was tucking some of her hair behind her right ear, attentive.

'But I think it's time you went home.' She immediately turned her attention to weighing out the flour, but she heard Ella's dismayed intake of breath. The latch of the door clicked as Jake joined them.

Clasping both elbows, Ella leaned across the table, her chin resting on her forearms. 'Can't I stay here? Please.' She drew out the plea as if she were a child begging for another story or to be allowed to stay up late. 'You've seen what they're like at home. I'd rather keep away till they come round.'

'Yeah, Mum. You won't notice we're here.'

Jake was standing close to Ella, his hand resting between her shoulder blades. Megan only glanced at them briefly as she spoke, turning to get the eggs from the fridge. Cooking and talking: great way of having a difficult conversation. Without eye contact, much more was said. She shooed Diva off the work surface. Affronted at this assault on her terrain, the cat stalked off towards the conservatory.

'But Ella has school tomorrow, exams coming up.' She carried on over Ella's protest. 'She needs a change of clothes. She has lots to talk over with her family. She has to go home.' She opened one of the drawers for a baking sheet, then remembered they'd had to use it as an emergency floor for the gerbil cage, and the other one was lost. The new roasting tin would have to do. She yanked it out, hearing something else clatter down behind the back of the drawer. 'You've both got to face up to what's happening. You can't hide yourselves away here for ever.'

'But, not today? Megan, you know you're my second mum ...' The compliment almost worked. 'If you can accept that we're having the baby and understand that Jake and I love each other and want to make it work, why can't she? We've talked everything through so carefully.' How self-possessed she sounded. It was easy sometimes to forget she was so young.

'It's the shock. That's all. She just needs time to readjust. Then everything will be different. You'll see.' But would the degree of intransigence that must have helped Beth to become such a successful lawyer get in the way?

'I know Dad's on my side,' Ella mused. 'But it's going to be *so* difficult living there. I'd much rather be here with you and Jake.'

'But Beth wants you at home.' Megan could imagine Beth's pain if Ella insisted otherwise.

'Only so she can give me another lecture.' Ella's eyes filled with tears, despite the effort she was making to hold herself together. 'I'm sorry you've fallen out, but she's so unreasonable. I'm not her and she can't live her life through me.' She looked at Jake for his agreement. He gave a nod of encouragement. 'She needs to look at it from my point of view too.'

'I don't think that's quite fair.'

'Mum, come on. It makes sense for Els to live here. Anyway, I've said she can.'

Startled by Jake's intervention, Megan looked up from the sugar she had begun to pour on to the weighing machine. He raised his hand to the curl of a ponytail on the crown of his head that was keeping his hair off his face. Even with that hairstyle, he was still a heartbreaker, with his long-lashed almond eyes and the 'interesting' scar above his lip from where he had been kicked in the face during a school football match.

'You can't send her home,' he insisted.

'I'm sorry, but I can.' But Megan was weakening. In Ella's shoes she would want to do the same. 'We-ell, perhaps if...' Then the thought of Beth reined her back. 'No,' she said firmly. 'You can't do that to your mum.'

'Great. That's decided, then. I knew you'd agree.' Jake only ever heard what he wanted to. He clasped Ella's hand. She looked at him with adoring gratitude.

'Jake! Hang on! I haven't agreed to anything.' But the battle, such as it was, was lost.

'I don't suppose you'd talk to Mum? Explain to her that I'll be here for a while?' Ella was twisting her stray hair around her fingers. She knew perfectly well what she was asking.

'No! Absolutely not. This is between you and her. Things are bad enough between the two of us without this. You really can't live here, Ella. I'm sorry.'

She should have insisted Ella go straight back on Friday, but emotions had been running so high. When they'd got home, Pete had shepherded her into the sitting room, where he'd put on some bluesy jazz, and they'd sat together, neither of them speaking, as she tried to absorb the implications of what had just happened and think ahead. Typically, he was unfazed. His laissez-faire approach to his children never changed. 'They'll find their own way,' he'd always said, absolving himself from any parental responsibility. For the first time, Megan wished she had been less forgiving of his attitude. He would be no help to her now. A yelp of laughter came from the sitting room.

'Don't you want me to?' How forlorn Ella sounded as the tears threatened again.

'You know it's not that. I'd love to have you here, but not when Beth and Jon want you at home. Imagine how much they must want to sort out what's going to happen, and how hurt they'll feel. You don't want that.'

'Well I'm hurt that she doesn't want our baby.' Ella's voice broke and she wiped away the tears with her hand.

Megan had to be firm. If she took even a step towards her, she would be in danger of relenting. 'Of course she does really. That's not what this is about. She's worried about you – as I would be about Hannah in the same situation. I know it's hard, but you must try to understand.'

'I have tried.' Tears were streaming down Ella's face now. 'But the way she sees it, the world's coming to an end. It's not as though I'm giving up the idea of doing medicine altogether. If all goes well, I'll just be deferring uni for a year, and then I'll be there with a baby. That's all.'

If only life were that simple.

'C'mon, babe. I'll come with you to talk to them. We'll explain together.' Jake passed her a bit of kitchen roll.

'Will you?' Ella blew her nose.

Megan saw the look that passed between them, and the strength that Ella seemed to gain from it. 'Jake, I think it might be better if you left this to Ella and her parents.'

'I thought you were behind us.' Jake looked outraged at the thought that she might not be.

'You're making this impossible! I'm not behind anyone.' She cracked an egg so hard on the rim of the bowl that the yolk slid in before she had time to stop it. As she tried to fish it out, it broke into the whites, making them unusable. She stopped what she was doing, slime dripping through her fingers, to make one last appeal. 'I just want everybody to be happy, and Ella moving in here will not help at this precise moment. Couldn't you both think about the rest of us for once? Please.' Despairing of ever being able to drum any sense or consideration into them, she sat down, elbows on the table, head in her hands, so they wouldn't see her tears of frustration.

Ella reached out and touched her arm. 'I'm sorry. I don't want to make it more difficult for you. But I can't go home. I can't.'

Megan knew that whatever she said would make no difference. Leaving her head in her hands, she shook it in resignation. She felt Ella remove her hand from her arm. She heard them leave the room and then the front door close.

An hour and a half later, she was watching *Bridesmaids* with Hannah and Pete, laughing enough to forget everything else for a short time. But as soon as she heard the front door again, her anxiety returned.

Please let it just be Jake, she said to herself. Please let Ella have seen sense and been persuaded to stay at home.

'Mum, can I have a word?' Her son put his head round the door.

'We'll pause it,' said Pete, stretching his legs out in front of him.

'Oh, God, it's Romeo and Juliet,' muttered Hannah. 'Mum, no. We can't stop watching now. There's such a good bit coming up.'

'Don't worry. I'll catch up with it later,' said Megan, lifting her head from Pete's shoulder. She patted his stomach, swung her legs off the sofa, yanked on her Uggs and straightened her apron.

A large black case stood in the hall. In the kitchen, she found Ella sitting at the table while Jake rummaged through the fridge. He pulled out a plate of cold sausages and held it out to Ella, who pulled a face. He helped himself and left the plate on the side.

'We told them Ella was going to stay here for a while,' he announced, looking pleased with the way things had gone. He bit into the sausage. Ella, however, was pale, obviously less certain of the success of their mission.

'Oh, Jake.' Why didn't the boy ever listen? 'Didn't you hear me when I said it was a bad idea?'

Ella's face fell. Poor child. This must be as difficult for her as it was for the rest of them. She needed at least one of the mothers batting for her. If Beth hadn't come round yet, then perhaps Megan should support her despite the inevitable hostilities that it would provoke. But what about the repercussions for the rest of them? Where would that leave Hannah and Amy, Jon and Peter? Long-standing friendships that were bound to be affected. She picked up the plate of sausages and returned it to the fridge.

'I didn't think you really meant it,' he said defiantly.

'I did mean it,' Megan corrected him. 'Ella, I don't want you to think I don't love you or don't like you being here. Of course it's not that. But I'm thinking about your mum and dad.' How often was she going to have to repeat that?

The phone interrupted them. 'That might be Dad,' Ella said in a small voice. 'He said he'd call.'

Not Beth, then. But Megan hadn't really expected to hear from her. Not after the last time.

She took the phone from the hall and sat on the stairs.

'Megan? It's Jon.'

'We thought it might be.' She straightened the rug in front of her with a foot.

'What are we going to do?' He sounded utterly beaten. 'Ella should be here with us.' He paused. 'We want her here. But she says you've asked her to stay with you.'

'That's not quite true,' Megan was immediately on the defensive. 'I got Beth's email and told Ella she had to go home. But she and Jake wanted her to stay here. They decided to go and see you to tell you face to face. I'm sorry. If it's any consolation, I think she should be at home with you too.'

His voice had triggered a memory of all those times years ago when he would come to her for advice. She had just started dating Pete, but her affinity with his flatmate was immediate and strong. She lost count of the hours they had spent discussing life, the women whose hearts Jon had broken or vice versa, the universe and everything else. Their closeness had been a crucial part of her twenties and early thirties. When he lost his heart to Beth and began spending all his time with her, Megan had quietly mourned the loss of their intimacy even as she and Beth became better and better friends.

She could see Jake and Ella whispering to each other in the kitchen, Jake's head thrown back as he laughed. They were completely caught up in their own bubble, careless of the trouble they were causing.

Jon's voice was in her ear again. 'Beth's beside herself. I don't know what to do, short of coming and dragging Ella home. Can't you persuade her?'

'I've tried,' Megan insisted. 'Really I have. But what can I do? I can't bar the door and I can't force her to do what she doesn't want. I know Beth's hurt – God knows I would be – but Ella's hurt too. She desperately wants Beth's approval.'

'I know.' He gave a long sigh. 'But you know what Beth's like. She wants the best for Ella, everything she didn't have herself. All that. She may not have been such a hands-on mother as you, but she does love our girls. Both of them,' he added, rather as an afterthought, as if he needed to explain.

'Of course.' Was he forgetting that she knew Beth better than anyone, possibly even better than he did? As Beth knew her. 'But Ella's very certain about what she wants. Like her mother, in many ways.' She heard Jon's rueful laugh at the other end of the phone. 'I think all we can do is let things shake down for a day or two and then regroup.'

'You'll make sure she's OK, won't you?'

'Oh, Jon. You know I will. But she's eighteen, not a little girl any more.' And you're going to have to get used to it, she thought sadly, as they ended their conversation.

How much easier everything had been when the kids were younger – and when we were younger too, she reflected, catching sight of herself in the window at the bend in the stairs. Not looking her best, feeling exhausted, and now no spa break to look forward to.

The anger she'd felt earlier returned. Beth should have phoned to discuss it instead of issuing orders via email as if Megan was one of her assistants. Megan had made the booking at the Haven this year. She'd certainly lose the hefty deposit if she cancelled now. Her reflection in the window confirmed what she already knew – a bit of a break was what was needed. But if Beth was going to continue hostilities, there wasn't much she could do.

As she gazed at herself, not really seeing, her thoughts took a new turn. Why not fight back instead of lying down and taking whatever Beth threw at her? The Haven would have been the perfect opportunity to thrash out their differences in neutral surroundings. They could have talked about their children and come to terms with what had happened. But Beth had denied them that chance.

Megan walked to the bottom of the stairs, unsure whether to return to the lovebirds in the kitchen or to the film in the sitting room, most of which she'd missed now. She heard Hannah laughing. Pete must have fallen asleep. She was hanging up the coats that had fallen off the end of the banister – again – when the idea came to her. Why not go to the Haven on her own? Just because Beth didn't want to go didn't mean she had to abandon the break too. Of course she didn't have to go on her own. She would ask Hannah to come with her. Her daughter would love all that spoiling, and with Megan as her wallet, she would almost certainly agree. To hell with Beth.

II

The hotel was in the rue de Seine, just off Saint-Germain. Outside their bedroom window Beth could hear the noise of a busy street market, and with it drifted up the rich smells of cheese and charcuterie, baking bread and roasting chickens. Over the shouts of the stallholders, she could hear a dog barking. A sharp female voice silenced it. Jon had left early for his meeting, leaving Beth with a morning to amuse herself.

Amuse. She almost laughed at the idea. She hadn't felt amused since Ella had told them she was pregnant, over two months ago now. Two months during which she had refused to come home and remained living with Megan and Pete. An uneasy entente had been reached, although they still trod on eggshells every time they saw her. She had been persuaded home for weekend meals, and Jon had taken her out for supper once or twice. She had been to school, registered at the hospital and was doing well, apart from a little morning sickness, but she still refused to move back under the same roof as her mother. As a result, Beth felt miserable, helpless and vengeful. Work distracted her, but not enough. By advising Ella to do what she believed was in her best interests, she had turned her daughter against her. But wasn't a parent meant to be an honest guide and adviser? Where had she gone wrong?

Her marriage had been affected too. Cracks were threatening what had been a reliably solid edifice. Of course Jon blamed her for what had happened. This trip to Paris was his way of trying to repair the damage. He hoped that being away for a few days might help her to see more clearly when she got home. She was only too aware how difficult this was for him. Of late, he and Pete had seen each other less frequently, divided between their friendship and their loyalty to their wives. Their regular dates in the pub had been put on hold. Similarly Jon was torn between his loyalty to her and his love for Ella, and she hated being responsible for that. But her instincts, so deeply ingrained in her, were impossible to ignore.

Perhaps he was right about Paris. The previous day, the city had begun to work its magic. They had strolled hand in hand through the Tuileries, wandered over to the Pompidou Centre to stand on the escalator, gazing out across the grey roofscape towards the Eiffel Tower, to their right the chalky domes of Sacré-Coeur rising from an island of trees. Over it all, puffs of cloud were blown about a spring blue sky.

In the evening they wandered out from their modest hotel and found a brasserie where they ate steak-frites and drank delicious red wine. After a stroll around the Île de la Cité, craning their necks at the illuminated façade of Notre Dame, they retired to bed, where they made long, lazy love as they had in the days before they had children. They'd reached across their differences and found each other again.

This morning, in his absence, she had planned to mooch around the shops and visit the Impressionists at the Musée d'Orsay. But she wasn't in the mood. She picked up the guidebook, leafing through it. The Picasso Museum. The Louvre. The Musée de Cluny. The cemetery of Père-Lachaise. She stopped there. She had never visited the cemetery, but what she had heard had made her curious.

Slinging her mac over her jeans and jumper, she left the hotel, taking the stairs rather than the steel cell of the elevator. Out on the street, she paused by a cheese stall, impressed by the number of different varieties, breathing in their smells. A queue snaked away from the bread stall, where two young men tried to keep up with demand. Voices – buying, selling, chatting – rose in the air. Next door, fat olives were being ladled from huge wooden barrels into plastic bags. Beyond that, stands of fresh fruit and vegetables were surrounded by customers shouting for attention. Beth squeezed through a gap to reach the pavement, where the crowd thinned out a little, and made her way to the Métro.

Half an hour later, she emerged into the bright sunshine at Père-Lachaise. Passing under the Métro sign, she approached a café facing the gate of the cemetery. She sat at one of the small round tables inside and ordered a *café noisette* and a croissant. Her only companions were a couple poring over their guidebook, and a young woman writing postcards. Beth sat quite content, watching the world go by. Outside, a very pregnant young woman stopped to chat with an older woman. They exchanged kisses and laughed as the woman put her hand on the girl's belly and exclaimed loudly. Beth looked away.

Since Ella had announced her pregnancy, there seemed to be a plague of young women who were either pregnant or pushing babies in elaborate buggies that took up most of the width of the pavement, got jammed in shop doorways and fitted awkwardly on buses. She studied them carefully, often trying to work out how old they were, whether any of them were as young as Ella. Occasionally they looked as though they might be. Those were the ones she fixed on, trying to see how miserable or content they were. A failure to smile, shadowy circles around their eyes, a child that refused to be pacified – all these were signs that confirmed the wisdom of her opinion. Nonetheless slowly she was coming to terms with the situation. Whether she liked it or not, she was learning to accept it.

She remembered her younger self. Of course she'd been nervous of having her abortion, scared that she might be irreparably physically damaged, that she might regret the loss of a baby for ever. But what else was she to do? And she hadn't regretted it. She had put it out of her mind completely and got on with her life. Even when she gave birth to the girls, she hadn't wondered what might have been. Until now. Ella's decision to keep her baby had prompted thoughts of Beth's own lost child and the other life she might have had. A girl or a boy? What would they have been like? What would she have made of her situation? Would she have stayed in Nottingham in disgrace? One thing was certain, she would never have met Jon, never had Ella or Amy. Fate's twists and turns had taken her in quite unexpected directions.

She paid for her coffee, then crossed the road to the cemetery. Despite the clear sky, there was a nip in the air that made her pull her mac around her. Walking up the slight hill, following the long tree-lined *allées*, her guidebook in hand, she found her way to Jim Morrison's grave. Modest, tucked away between other larger memorials, it was adorned with photos, candles, decaying flowers still in their cellophane, and even a couple of spliffs. His soulful eyes stared from a small, framed photograph. Gone for ever. How desperately sad. *Tempus fugit*, Beth reminded herself as she inspected a tombstone carved with a loving couple and their long-nosed dog. Life was short.

A toddler slipped the hand of its mother and ran ahead of its parents, who continued strolling together, the mother's left thumb hooked into the back pocket of her partner's jeans, and his right in hers. As Beth overtook them, she looked to see if the woman wore a wedding ring. She didn't. That was another habit that Beth had adopted. Not that the absence of a ring was significant. She knew that better than anyone. Having seen the emotional damage that divorce could inflict on children, she had long ago been convinced that what was important was the strength of the relationship, not the ring on the finger. Nonetheless, she was curious.

On her way to the back of the cemetery, hunting for Avenue Carette and Epstein's tomb for Oscar Wilde, her phone rang. She was taken aback to see Pete's name come up. He came straight to the point.

'Beth? Sorry to interrupt your trip. I couldn't get through to

Jon, but I thought you should know we've had some trouble here.'

She stopped still. 'What? Is it Ella?' She would never forgive herself if something had happened and she hadn't been there.

'No, no. Don't panic,' Pete chuckled. 'As far as I know she's absolutely fine. No, it's Amy this time.'

A lump in her throat prevented her taking the deep breath she needed. 'Oh, no,' she managed, sinking down on the edge of the path, remembering in time that sitting on a grave wouldn't do. 'What's happened? I thought she was with Natalie?'

She and Jon had listened to Amy's indignant protests about how she was old enough to be left on her own. Regardless, they had insisted that she spend the weekend at Natalie's, with her parents Hugh and Jenny. Beth had been determined that the one place she would not stay was at Pete and Megan's. Having one daughter resident under their roof was enough.

'She was, yes, but Hugh and Jenny were staying the night with friends in Oxford. I imagine Amy "forgot" to tell you that?' He gave a throaty cough. 'The three of them, Hannah, Nat and Amy, went on the lash and got absolutely trolleyed. Even by my standards.'

Beth supplied an appreciative half-laugh as she battled her anxiety and anger. 'Where did they go?' Why hadn't she checked the arrangements with Hugh and Jenny instead of trusting Amy? She should have known she'd get up to something.

'No idea. Some bar on Upper Street that accepted their fake IDs,' he carried on over Beth's barely suppressed sigh, 'then back to yours with a few friends. As far as I can tell, they were all completely pissed. God knows whether there were any drugs involved, but they swear not. At least one of them had enough sense to call an ambulance when Nat passed out. The police turned up and emptied the house. It's not trashed exactly, but as far as I can gather, you're not going to be altogether happy. Four of them were carted off to hospital. Nat was stomach-pumped and as far as I know she's still there. Hannah and Amy were brought back here by the police. They woke me up at five o'clock.'

'Where are they now?'

'Sleeping it off. If they surface today at all, I'd be amazed, given the state they were in. Amy was sick all over the bathroom ...'

Beth groaned.

'Don't worry. I cleaned it up. She'll be fine apart from a cracking hangover, but I just thought you ought to know where she was and what's happened.'

'I'm glad you called. Thanks so much. I'm just sorry you had to pick up the pieces.' But thank God he had. Safe in the knowledge that Amy was all right, however fragile, Beth began to imagine the state of the house.

'I didn't want to spoil your weekend ...'

'No, I'd much rather know. And thank you for taking her in.' She pulled her feet in to the edge of the cobbles and wrapped her spare arm around her legs, chin on her knee.

'Could hardly leave her on the street. And I'm sure Hugh and Jenny won't want her.' He chuckled at the idea. 'Now don't worry. Enjoy the rest of your weekend. I'll keep her with us till you get back. I don't suppose she'll be going anywhere when she eventually surfaces.'

'Can I ... er ... can I speak to Ella?'

A robin landed on a gravestone in front of her. It cocked its head and gave her a beady stare.

'Not here, I'm afraid. They've gone off somewhere.'

'Oh.' Beth was disappointed. 'Did she say where? Do you know when she'll be back?'

'Not sure. Tomorrow or the next day.' He sounded almost embarrassed, as if there was something he wasn't saying. 'A weekend thing. Try then.'

As they finished the conversation, Beth leaned her head against the cool stone of a sepulchre. Tomorrow? Where could Ella have gone? She was so used to having the children under her roof and knowing (or believing she knew) where they were all the time that when she didn't, she felt uneasy.

She might have known Amy would try something like this. Thank God she was all right. But suppose she hadn't been? Suppose she had been the one left lying in hospital – with alcohol poisoning … kidney failure … dead. Suppose she'd fallen drunk in front of a bus, or been taken advantage of in any number of ways. Perhaps she had been! And where had she ended up? At Pete and Megan's – exactly where Beth hadn't wanted her. She would not give up both her daughters to Megan. The pain she felt at the thought was almost physical in its intensity.

She stood up, returning to the cobbled streets of the dead, where the sun filtered through the branches of the chestnut trees flanking her route. As she walked, no longer noticing the names on the tombs, she began to formulate a plan.

By the time she met Jon for lunch, the plan had taken shape. They must cut their weekend short. She must get Amy back into the nest as soon as she could. She must talk to Ella and persuade her home. Megan's involvement with her family had gone too far. Beth must be the mother her daughters needed now.

'Absolutely not,' was Jon's immediate response as he cut into his *blanquette de veau*. 'We're not going home early. This weekend isn't just for my meeting; it's for us, and to give you a break. Amy will be perfectly safe with Pete and Megan. I know why you don't want her to be there, but you're overreacting. And we need this time together.'

He was right. They did. Last night had proved that. But …

'But we should be there to make sure she's all right.'

'She's with friends.' He ignored her choked protest. 'She was drunk, that's all.'

'But, the house …'

'Whatever done's done. It's not going to get worse because we're away. Anyway, we'll be back first thing on Monday. It's not as if we're talking weeks.'

'All the same . . .'

'I know exactly what this is all about.' He put down his knife and fork and concentrated on her.

'What? It's not about anything.' She faltered under his gaze. 'I just think we should be at home.' She loaded some salad and quiche onto her fork.

Sceptical, he raised his eyebrows. 'Not true. You don't like the fact that Amy's at Megan's. This is all about your feud with Megan. Darling, you can't expect the rest of us to fall into line behind you all the time. Pete's my oldest friend, I've known Megan for ever and Hannah's been Amy's best mate for years. We're not going to give them up just because you and she have fallen out.' He sounded weary. This wasn't the first time they'd had this disagreement. And it wouldn't be the first time they failed to reach a conclusion.

'I'm not expecting you to do anything,' she protested half-heartedly, although in fact of course that was exactly what she expected given the circumstances. Was it really so unreasonable of her to want some distance from the Westons, for a while at least?

'You know that's not true.' Despite disagreeing with her, he was still affectionate. 'You knew perfectly well that Pete and I had arranged to meet when you asked David and Nancy over for supper last week.'

'Well, yes. And I'm sorry. Sort of.' They smiled at each other. 'But how do you expect me to feel? Look what's happened. The few times I've seen Ella, she's been so distant. I'm trying my hardest to accept that she's having the baby, and I really do want to be the one sharing her pregnancy, not Megan, but … I don't know how to be. I don't know how to get over this. I don't even know where she is or what she's doing.'

'I'm sure she's fine. But you've no one to blame—'

'But myself. I get that.' Beth filled both their water glasses and banged the jug down on the table.

'Well, you did rather bulldoze your way through it all.'

'Bulldoze! That's not fair.'

'OK, not bulldoze, then. But you did make it very clear that you didn't think she should have the baby. Given that she's chosen to go ahead, you can't expect her not to be hurt by that. How would you have felt at her age?'

'It's not the same,' she said firmly. She remembered her own mother – diminutive, downtrodden, inadequate – and the way she had kept her at arm's length once she had left home, cutting her off almost completely once she was married and starting a family herself. She did feel guilty about that now. Why had she done it? Because her mother reminded her of everything she wanted to forget, everything she didn't want to be. But how must her mother have felt? At least she had Jennifer, Beth's older sister, who had stayed in Nottingham to bring up her family. History must not be allowed to repeat itself.

'Isn't the ball in your court? Aren't you the one who has to make the first move?' Jon interrupted her thoughts.

'But I can't pretend I'm one hundred per cent happy when I'm not.' She fought against the tears that stung at her eyes, blinking hard.

Jon reached across for her hand. She grasped his as if it were a lifeline. He gave her a despairing smile and a little shake of his head. 'Yes you can. Ella's taking control of her own life. The baby's going to arrive, and she'll need you then if not before. Don't you want to be involved with your own grandchild?'

A tear dripped from her nose on to her plate as she nodded. Of course she did.

They finished their meal in silence and were waiting for the coffees to be brought when Jon spoke again. 'How about a compromise?' The shadows under his eyes were darker than before, his face tired.

'What do you mean?'

'I'll see if we can change our ticket back to tomorrow, if it's not too ridiculously expensive. That way, we have another night

126

and part of Sunday – you've always said you wanted to go to the *marché aux puces*, so it seems a shame to miss it – but we'll be back in time for Amy to come home before school on Monday. How does that sound?'

She breathed a long sigh of relief. 'Fair.'

'In that case, we'd better get on. I'll ask the hotel to change our tickets, then I want to take you to the Musée Rodin. You've never been, have you?'

Beth shook her head. How she loved this man and his unexpected enthusiasms. He was still capable of surprising her. 'You know I haven't.'

'You'll like it.' He called for the bill and paid, then led the way into the street.

Walking a step behind him on the narrow pavement, Beth's mind remained on what was waiting for them at home. What she really wanted was the impossible – for everything to return to what they'd had before. She wanted Ella at home, not pregnant. She wanted Amy in any role other than that of the wayward teenager. She wanted her friendship with Megan back.

But none of that was going to happen. Things had changed irrevocably. By rights, they should be at the Haven this weekend, lazing about, being pampered, having a laugh together. Those days were over. At the same time as wanting her girls with her, she didn't see how things could ever be the same with Megan again.

12

Megan's eyes were closed in exquisite agony as the masseuse leaned down hard, pressing the point of her elbow deep into the knotted muscle of her shoulder. Her grunt of pain was lost in the whale music that whooped and mooed from the speakers. The lights were dimmed, the scent of aromatherapy oil filled the room, the towels were soft. Megan was almost relaxed.

In the next room, Ella was having a facial. Originally Hannah had agreed to come, but at the last minute she had ducked out – 'other plans' was her unsatisfactory, but typical, excuse. But there was no point in insisting. What could be worse than the luxury of the Haven in the company of someone who resented being there? Megan's quick phone call to check that they welcomed pregnant women met the reassurance of learning that they had specially tailored programmes for them. Ella was taken aback to be invited, but accepted – it was only a weekend after all. Megan took a small pleasure in knowing how much Beth would dislike Ella going with her. She was shocked to find herself delighting in such a petty triumph, but if Beth would not even meet her halfway … Wasn't all fair in love and war? Besides, which of them had declared war in the first place?

Having decided to go, she was determined to make the most of the weekend. But she found the place different without her old friend as company. She and Ella would never have the same sort of discussions together that only old friends had. Without those, there was nothing to make her forget the constant pangs of hunger that accompanied her whatever she was doing. She'd paid a fortune to be put through torture in the name of good health and to be given food that wouldn't keep a fly alive. Her stomach rumbled in agreement. It was two hours since her lunch of 'broth' augmented with a few lettuce leaves and a teeny mound of cottage cheese. Oh yes, and a glass of calorie-free water. Her abstinence was all the more painful for sitting by Ella, who was tucking into soup, grilled fish and vegetables. And pudding. However, she did feel a smug glow as she considered the pounds she must be shedding.

'Tea soon,' said the masseuse in sympathy, as she jabbed her elbow into Megan's other shoulder.

Tea. She anticipated the accompanying lemon and honey with a stab of pleasure.

As the attention moved from her shoulders, Megan let herself drift. Within what seemed like minutes, she heard the masseuse clear her throat. 'Just come round in your own time. Don't get up too quickly. There's some water on the side.'

More bloody water. At this rate, she would drown before the day was out.

Wrapping the obligatory white bathrobe around her and slipping her feet into white towelling mules, she left the comfort of the treatment room and made her way to the residents' lounge. Almost every chair was taken. The other women were of various ages, all of them robed into a comforting anonymity, their personal contours more or less disguised.

Megan spotted Ella on the other side of the room, dwarfed by the gigantic wing chair she had chosen, a file of revision notes on her knee. On her way over, she helped herself to a cup of tea, adding a particularly generous spoonful of honey and an extra slice of lemon. She glanced around her, but no one gave any sign of having noticed. All equally guilty, probably.

'How was it?'

Ella's hair was held off her face by a stretchy white band. Her face was luminous, having been comprehensively prodded and plumped and creamed. Megan had experienced the same treatment the previous afternoon as soon as they had arrived, and for a few brief moments had enjoyed the illusion of looking a few years younger. Ella looked up at the sound of Megan's voice.

'Heaven.' She stretched her arms above her head. 'Hannah must be crazy to turn this down.'

'Not too spartan for you, then?'

'We-ell … If someone were to pass me a massive slice of banoffee pie, I wouldn't say no.'

'Oooh, banoffee pie,' groaned the woman sprawled in a chair to her right. 'What I'd give for a piece of chocolate cheesecake.'

Megan laughed. 'Just a decent cup of builder's with milk would do me. And a biscuit or two.' She held the fine porcelain cup against the light and sighed. Every teatime she could remember at the Haven had been an invitation to food fantasy. Magazines opened to cookery pages were passed around. Conversations revolved around favourite meals or what would be on the menu the moment they got home. Few were the clients who managed to exist happily on the starvation rations, however attractively presented.

Ella's neighbour rose to her feet. 'Time for my colonic irrigation,' she announced.

Megan laughed at the look of horror on Ella's face. 'Nothing on earth would make me do that,' she whispered. 'Not even in the name of self-improvement. Massage and exercise are one thing, but that's an invasive treatment too far.' She took the seat the woman had vacated, feeling every massaged muscle cry with relief.

Ella leaned towards her. 'You don't think …' She stopped and beckoned Megan closer so no one else could hear.

Megan sat forward. 'What?'

'What if we escaped tonight and went to the pub? I mean, the food here's all right, I suppose, but you must be starving.'

'Ella! I'm shocked.' In Megan's mind's eye, a large gin and tonic materialised. 'No, I'm disappointed in you. How could you even suggest such a thing?' And a packet of crisps. Salt and vinegar ... She closed her eyes to banish the vision. No good. 'How could we get out?'

On the side table at the arm of her chair, a magazine lay open at a photograph of a glistening fish pie. She flicked the pages back to the fashion section, to a pair of jeans narrower than the drainpipes that ran down the outside of the formidable Victorian pile that was now the Haven. She would never be that thin again. What was the point in pretending?

'Just walk?' Ella sat up straight. 'It's not a prison. They can't stop us. I'm meant to be eating for two.' She rested her hand on her almost slightly rounded stomach. 'I've finished those chocolate chip cookies you smuggled in.'

Ella was right. The pregnancy menu was more than adequate, but unexciting. But what about Megan's own enforced diet and the half-stone she'd been vainly hoping to shift? For a moment, she wished the stash of ginger thins that she had polished off in the dead of the previous night were still in her drawer. But she hadn't wanted Ella to find out how weak-willed she really was. They'd had to be eaten.

'Oh, sod it. Let's do it.' The pub was bound to have some sort of salad on the menu that would assuage her guilt.

For the next half-hour they remained where they were, quite comfortable with each other. Having Ella around was like having a daughter without the bad bits. She didn't ask for money, borrow Megan's make-up or pinch her jewellery. She didn't come with the resistance that was hard-wired into Hannah; she was always easy to be with. And she was tidy. She even picked up the wet towels from the bathroom floor and put her clothes away. In the few weeks she had been staying with them, she had transformed Jake's pit into a room that was now navigable without having to stand on any of his belongings. Megan knew she should encourage her to go home, but the truth was she liked having her to stay and had got used to her being there. The pregnancy had been entirely straightforward so far, bar a little morning sickness, and she was no trouble. She went to school, carried on with her revision as if nothing had happened. Everything went more smoothly with her there. She made Jake happy. He appeared to have absolutely no regrets about the unexpected turn his life had taken.

Ella was lost in a daydream, staring through the window towards the extensive manicured grounds outside.

'What are you thinking?'

'About Mum.' She gave a heartfelt sigh. 'And about how we're going to be late for yoga if we don't go now.'

Megan groaned, bedded as she was into the comfort of her chair. 'We could always give it a miss.'

'No! We've paid for it. Look, almost everyone else has gone.'

Only one or two stragglers were left behind, dozing, sleeping off their latest treatments. In the corner, a waitress was clearing away the cups.

Reluctantly Megan got to her feet. 'OK, I give in. Come on then.'

The old basement kitchen of the house had been converted into a sprung-floor exercise space. The Haven didn't need a kitchen that size for the titbit diet they provided – however nutritious it was. Megan and Ella removed their robes and hung them in the locker room. In a rush of resolution-driven enthusiasm, Megan had invested in new exercise kit before coming. The leotard seemed to hold her in in the right places while not making exercise impossible. They followed the rest of the class into the studio, which had three mirrored walls and a ballet barre running their length. Exercise was one thing; seeing herself doing it was quite another – and from this angle, her kit was clearly not doing quite the job she'd imagined. She turned from her reflection only to catch it from another angle. Yet another reminder of why she should not go to the pub.

A lithe young woman welcomed them, and the keenies headed

straight to the front of the room, while Megan and Ella wedged themselves into position in the back row. They unrolled their mats and stood ready for instruction. Within minutes, Megan was feeling muscles she'd forgotten she had, despite the fact that it was only a beginners' class. Beside her, Ella was bending and stretching, holding positions without a grimace, casting sympathetic smiles in Megan's direction every now and then. The instructor kept an eye on Ella, advising her on simple positions if anything was going to be too much.

Having warmed up, they turned to the salute to the sun, from the mountain pose, stretching up into the extended mountain, then the swan dive down into a forward bend. Megan's hands came nowhere close to touching her toes, but no matter. This was not a competition, she reminded herself, nonetheless keeping a keen eye on the surrounding women. Eventually, they put the positions together into one flowing movement.

At that point, to her horror, the middle-aged curse of inappropriate flatulence threatened. She clenched her buttocks as hard as she could in an attempt to stave off embarrassment.

Into a lunge, then on into a down-facing dog. Balanced in an inverted V on her hands and feet, bottom in the air, pulling in her stomach for all she was worth, she was unable to stop the fart that exploded into the class, so loud it was impossible to pretend anyone but her was responsible. Mortified, she looked around, to find most of the rest of the class continuing womanfully as if nothing had happened. They swooped down through the plank into the cobra as one. If only they could see how ridiculous they looked. She tried to catch up and keep up, but her concentration was shattered. A blaze of heat rose from somewhere in her chest, tingling down her arms and up into her face, where it mingled with her acute embarrassment until beads of sweat were trickling down her hairline.

As they rose back into a second down-facing dog, this time in almost perfect control, she caught the eye of her neighbour, a rotund middle-aged woman with an unnaturally jet-black bob, who had been looking as if she was enjoying proceedings about as much as Megan. Their exchange of sympathetic self-conscious smiles was fatal. As Megan glanced away, she heard a muffled explosion, and looked back to see the woman's body shaking as she tried to organise her weight between her hands and her feet. Slowly her knees buckled and she sank down with a thud to lie helpless with laughter on the floor.

And again. Up. Inhale. Arms raised. Palms up. Exhale. Down. Inhale. Palms on the floor. Step back. Lunge. Inhaling as instructed, Megan lurched into the lunge, lost her balance and collapsed with the grace of a hippo beside her neighbour, who had yet to recover herself. Out of the corner of her eye she saw Ella roll on to her side with a snort. The three of them lay on their mats, unable to stop laughing.

'Ladies, ladies!' The instructor made her way to the back of the room. 'You're disturbing everyone else. Wind, of whatever kind, is a perfectly natural bodily function. Really nothing to laugh about.'

Shamed, the three of them reorganised themselves to repeat the asana faultlessly and noiselessly, but within seconds, they were reduced to gales of laughter again. The black looks from their surrounding classmates only made them worse. After a succession of pointed throat-clearings from the instructor, they were forced to leave the room. Yoga over.

In the changing room, they rewrapped themselves in their dressing gowns and rolled up their mats.

'I'm sorry,' apologised Megan, breathless. 'That was all my fault. And now I've made you miss the class.'

'Don't worry. I was hating every second anyway. All that pampering stuff, I love, but this … Just thought I should try and discover my core. Isn't that what's supposed to be important these days?' The rotund woman pulled a comb through her bob.

'Your core? I threw mine away years ago.'

The woman smiled and held out her hand. 'I'm Penny.' Megan took it and introduced herself and Ella.

On their way back to their rooms, Penny winkled out of the other two their escape plan for the evening, and invited herself along. 'A glass of Merlot and a plate of shepherd's pie … mmm.' She closed her eyes. 'I've been here almost a whole week, and I'm dreaming food now. I'm definitely in, if you're OK with that.'

Megan was OK with any kind of kindred spirit. Without Beth to keep her on the straight and narrow, reminding her why they were there, her spirit of rebellion was rampant.

As they walked down the long tree-lined drive towards the road that took them to the village, the three of them did their best to look nonchalant.

'Why do we feel so guilty? We're old enough not to have to conform to their rules if we don't want to,' Penny reminded them.

Megan had never felt the same rebellious urge on previous visits. She and Beth had always observed the rules and shed unwanted pounds together. The realisation that not being with Beth made the experience entirely different was bittersweet. She pulled out her phone and turned it on. 'It's weird not being connected to the outside world. Why do we pay through the nose to be deprived of everything we love? We must be mad.' She didn't need a reply. Like Penny, she enjoyed the spoiling part of the package; the rest she did out of duty, and hope that she might find the figure she lost a long time ago. But her real enjoyment had been in the undiluted time she spent with Beth, having a laugh, catching up.

As her phone came to life, a frenzy of missed calls arrived: all of them from Pete. He had been trying to contact her since that morning, when a particularly punishing aqua aerobics session had been followed by a catatonic steam room trance, lunch, then massage and yoga. Excusing herself to the others, she dropped behind them and called him.

'Meg! At last!' He sounded as if he'd been running, the one activity she knew was out of the question.

'I've been buffing the body beautiful. No time for worldly concerns. Is something wrong?'

Briefly he told her about what Hannah and Amy had been up to. 'But they're fine,' he concluded. 'I cleaned the worst of the bathroom last night, but I thought the least they could do was finish the job properly. They won't be wanting to do that again in a hurry!' His laughter reminded her why their marriage had lasted so long. These days, when love had turned into something more comfortable and passion had taken a back seat, his ability to see the funny side of things and make her laugh was, well, everything.

'What about Beth?' she whispered, hoping Ella wouldn't hear. But Ella was several yards ahead, deep in conversation with Penny.

'I called her this morning and told her. Thought she should know where Amy was. She didn't sound overjoyed, but what could she do?'

This was hardly going to improve things between them. But when Beth heard about Ella going to the Haven, as she surely would, and that she was missing a day of school, things would certainly not be pretty. Perhaps Megan should have thought about the potential repercussions, but her anger with Beth had made her instinctively hit back where it would hurt most. She wasn't proud of herself.

A car pulled up beside her; the driver's darkened window was being lowered.

'Got to go, darling. Thanks a million. Back on Monday. See you then.'

Out of the window poked the head of Anne Blackwell, the senior treatment manager. She was the fiercest of the staff. Her tight corkscrew curls wobbled with indignation as she spoke. 'Where are you going? You know we don't like you leaving the grounds during your stay here.'

'I know,' Megan replied, trying to think of a way to smooth the waters and failing. 'But just this once I can't exist with such a strict regime. And I've got a pregnant girl with me who needs to eat more.' The perfect excuse. Good.

'But she's had the benefit of our specially devised pregnancy menu,' protested Ms Blackwell. Through her red tortoiseshell glasses the woman's beady eyes darted from one to another of them, sizing up the situation.

'Perhaps. But she needs something more.' Treacle toffee pudding. Chocolate fudge cake. Crème caramel. Rhubarb crumble. The list was long.

Ms Blackwell raised both eyebrows, superior and slightly disparaging at the same time. 'Seems a shame to waste the opportunity, if only for a short time. You'd feel so much better when you go home.' Her eyes ran over Megan in a way that suggested she'd be mad to pass up such a chance.

'I'm sure you're right. My willpower just isn't there this time,' Megan said with some finality. 'Sorry,' she added, immediately cross with herself for apologising.

The wobbling curls retreated with a disbelieving shake, the window rose with a purr and the car moved off, crunching over the gravel. It didn't stop again. Megan caught up with the others and relayed what had been said. Penny's hearty dismissal of Ms Blackwell's homily fortified her desire to rebel. Hunger had them behaving like naughty children. There was no other excuse.

The pub was chilly, empty and unwelcoming, almost as if it was subsidised by the Haven to encourage any escapees to return immediately. They took a table by the unused inglenook fireplace, where a few church candles burned, and ordered food and drink. She asked for two large G&Ts for herself and Penny, an orange juice for Ella.

'I've been dreaming of this,' murmured Penny as a plate of lamb chops, potato dauphinoise and buttery carrots was put in front of her. The pub didn't run to shepherd's pie, although there

137

was a well-rounded if tannic Merlot behind the bar. She took a gulp before going on. 'My daughter gave me a fortnight here. A birthday present.' She scratched her head, dislodging the perfect symmetry of her hair. 'Funny, really. We don't speak for three years. Finally we make up and she's all over me, then she sends me away for a fortnight. She thinks it's going to do me good.' She prodded her ample spare tyre to show the challenge she was facing.

'Why didn't you speak?' Ella leaned back to let the waitress put her fish and chips in front of her.

'How long have you got?' Penny took a mouthful of her vegetables. 'Mmm. Food for the gods. Well, for those on the lower slopes perhaps. It's not *that* good.' She cut into one of her chops. 'But good enough for now.'

'Your daughter?' prompted Megan.

'Oh, yes, of course. Ginny. Long story, but she came into the butchery business with me.'

'You're a butcher?' Ella couldn't hide her surprise.

'Hard to believe, I know.' Pam spread out her neatly manicured fingers, which did indeed look unlikely instruments of slaughter. 'It all went well as long as we were stuffing sausages together and we knew who was boss. Me.' She shook with laughter as she dissected her chops. 'She wanted us to expand into breads and cheeses, with her heading up that side of the business. I thought she was trying to run before she could walk. She thought I was a dinosaur, past my sell-by date. Probably a bit of truth in both. We had a blazing row, said what we thought of each other – mistake! – and that was it. She went off and worked in a supermarket. Bloody ridiculous really.' She laughed again, looking at Megan and Ella, checking she still had their interest. 'All we managed was to upset everyone else in the family. Eventually, another butcher nearby started expanding their business in a very similar way to the one Ginny had suggested. This time I could see the potential benefits. I went to see her – we really did fall into each other's arms – and now we're working together again, and business looks as if it might boom. So happy ending, except this is her idea of a decent fifty-fifth birthday present.' She grinned. 'I won't be telling her about tonight.'

'Won't she sympathise?' asked Megan.

Penny shook her head. 'Oh, no! And I'm a bit scared of her when she disapproves. She can be very fierce.' This larger-than-life woman being in thrall to anyone was unimaginable.

As they carried on talking, Ella grew quieter, barely joining in. Later, when they were in bed, she whispered in the dark, 'Do you think Mum and me have fallen out for ever?'

'No,' Megan whispered back, not entirely surprised by the question after Penny's story. 'All it takes is for one of you to hold out the olive branch. That's a difficult thing to do, but it's all you need.'

There was a muffled hiccup, a sniff, and the sound of Ella turning over. Megan wondered what she could suggest, but within moments, despite feeling as though she had eaten an ox, or even a herd of them, she had fallen into a deep sleep.

13

To Jon's annoyance, the only train on which the hotel had been able to find seats left Paris mid afternoon. He had tried to persuade Beth to stay on, tempting her with thoughts of Montmartre, of a meal in a restaurant he had been recommended in the Marais. Despite wanting to please him, she had to get home. She wanted Amy there. She had to see what damage had been done to their nest. She wanted Ella home too. She would hold out a white flag to them both.

That morning, they had taken a pavement table outside Les Deux Magots, small white jugs of traditional hot chocolate in front of them as they soaked up the Parisian street life. They were still recovering from the night before, which they had spent in an underground jazz club Pete had recommended. They had sat in arched brick booths, drunk wine, swayed to the music, walked back to their hotel hand in hand along the Seine, kissed under a street light.

Now, as they sped through the French countryside on this grey April day, Beth retreated into her own world. She imagined how she would make things up to Ella, convince her that she had come round, that she would support her. But would she be able to pretend excitement when she still felt Ella might be making the mistake of her life? There were so many hurdles to be overcome.

As the taxi pulled up outside the house at last, they saw the hall light was on and the living room windows open. Jon looked up from counting out the right change. 'Isn't that Pete's car?' He nodded towards an old Triumph Spitfire in their space. Not the family Peugeot, but the classic indulgence that only he drove.

'What's he doing here?' Beth climbed out on to the pavement, yanking her case out with her.

'I think you're just about to find out.' He put his arm around her shoulders and kissed her. His kiss reminded her of the weekend they had just spent. She leaned into him and kissed him back, feeling his stubble graze her face before they separated and walked towards the house.

Halfway up the steps, they could hear music, heavy on the bass. 'That sounds like Amy's sort of thing.' Jon turned his key in the door and they went in.

The door to the sitting room was ajar. Music boomed into the hall. A pair of feet, crossed at the ankle, belonging to a seated man, were just visible. 'No. Not enough. I want it shining.'

They both recognised Pete's voice immediately.

'What on earth ...?' Jon pushed the door wide to find Pete lying back in a chair, with Amy and Hannah, surrounded by cloths, a bucket of water, wax polish and the vacuum cleaner, focused on the fireplace.

Hearing them, Amy spun round. 'Mum! Dad! You're early! Look, I'm really sorry. I can explain.' Dressed in an old tracksuit, red hair pinned to one side with a grip, she looked like a repentant twelve-year-old.

'Later,' said Pete firmly, before Jon or Beth had time to say anything. The shock of seeing Amy doing housework had robbed them of speech. 'Let's get this last bit done properly.' He turned and winked at the pair of them. 'Sorry it's not quite finished. Won't be long. I think there might be one or two breakages you might notice, though.' Amy's polishing intensified as he stood up and came to the door. 'Why don't we go into the kitchen? See if it gets your seal of approval while they're finishing off in here.'

Relieved that Amy looked none the worse for the weekend, Beth led the way. The kitchen was as they'd left it, apart from the empty wine and beer bottles that were regimented beside the recycling bin.

'No room,' Pete explained. 'I was going to take them back to ours, but you've seen them now.'

'How many people were here?' asked Beth, noticing a couple of spirits bottles among the ranks.

'That's that Château d'Yquem I was saving for a special occasion.' Jon picked up one of the bottles and turned it in his hand. 'What else have they drunk?' He busied himself checking the empties.

'About twenty, maybe. The girls are both so penitent at the moment, you'll probably be able to get the whole story. A couple of glasses seem to have been broken, and I think a vase in the bedroom.'

'The bedroom,' Beth repeated quietly. Not the pale green vase that Jon had bought as a memento of their Scandinavian honeymoon. Not that.

'I got them to change the sheets,' added Pete, as if that made everything all right. 'They're in the machine now.'

Beth sat down. 'They were in our bed …' Her voice faded away.

'I don't suppose there's a chance …' Pete hesitated.

'Of course,' said Jon, going to the near-empty wine rack for a bottle of red. 'Beth?'

She shook her head as he poured a glass for himself and Pete. 'Thanks so much for looking after her … and for this.' Her words seemed to come from somewhere else, but she made a vague gesture to indicate the tidying up and the cleaning.

'No problem. That's what friends are for, isn't it?' Pete winked. 'Lucky I was here. I'm off to France tomorrow – got to do a piece on the chateaux of the Loire. The punters love that sort of thing.' He took an appreciative sip of his wine.

Friends. Was that what he still was, after everything that had happened? Why hadn't he put his foot down earlier? He had just shown he was perfectly capable of it. Despite his being there for Amy, and so instrumental in the cleaning of the house, all Beth wanted was for him to leave and let them get on. 'I think I'll go upstairs and check,' she said, unable to sit there as if nothing had happened between the two families. She wanted to ask about Ella, but she didn't want to hear her news from him.

Upstairs, their room was as they had left it, bar the change of sheets and the absence of her favourite vase. She stared at the photo on the bookshelf. Her two girls grinned back at her from a Greek beach, Ella's face shaded by her straw hat, Amy wearing a reversed baseball cap. She remembered that holiday so well, when the only problems arose from indecision about which taverna or beach to visit. How simple life had seemed then.

She opened the top drawer of the chest and took out her jewellery box, deep-green leather with three drawers. As she sat with it on the bed, she fought an overwhelming urge just to sink back and go to sleep, shutting out all the problems. Instead she lifted the lid. Nothing seemed to be missing. There were the diamond and the sapphire half-eternity rings Jon had given her when each of the girls was born. He'd always promised he'd buy her a full one, one day. Beside them, his mother's diamond trefoil that Beth had been left in her will; the gold pea pod dented for ever after Amy tested her new front teeth on it was there on its delicate chain, as were the pearl drop earrings that Ella had borrowed when they went to Megan's niece's wedding the previous year.

When she returned to the kitchen, Jon and Pete were deep in conversation, discussing the football matches Jon hadn't once mentioned he was missing. She almost envied the camaraderie the two of them shared over the sport that bored her stiff. The music in the sitting room had been turned down. Amy must be feeling contrite. Beth made herself a cup of tea.

'Fancy a quick one down the Earl of Somerset?' Pete sounded tentative as he addressed Jon.

'I don't think so.' Jon looked to see Beth's reaction. She picked up the pile of new mail and started sorting it out. 'We've only just got back.'

Eventually, Pete left with an apologetic Hannah, but only after he had satisfied himself that the girls' work met with his approval. Even Beth was surprised by the high standards he applied. They were far less evident in his own home. This was just for her. She was touched. Amy had disappeared to her room, presumably dreading the inevitable showdown.

'You look exhausted.' Jon put his arms around her and she let herself relax, inhaling his familiar smell, her body fitting with his like two pieces of a puzzle.

'Not really.' She closed her eyes.

'Why don't I make supper?' he offered. 'You go and talk to Amy. Go easy on the riot act, though. Pete seems to have put them through their paces. They've been cleaning all day. That'll teach 'em.' He laughed.

'But it could have been so much more serious.' Visions of a hospital ward, Amy unconscious in bed, their house on fire, all their possessions trashed or stolen rushed into her mind.

'I know. And of course we should make her aware of that. But not tonight.' He stroked her hair from the side of her face and kissed her cheek, one of those gestures that had comforted her over and again through their years together.

She turned and kissed him in return. 'Did you want to go with Pete?'

'Not really. I'd rather be here with you right now, keep the weekend mood going a bit longer. But go and see Amy first.'

'I'll try not to say anything...'

'I know.' He gave a weary smile that only just reached his eyes. 'You might not be able to help yourself, but give it a go. For us. We're in enough trouble as it is.'

She stiffened. So he did still blame her for Ella's absence. But of course he did. Who else was there to blame?

He broke away from her, making it too late for her to object.

'Have we got any eggs? What else? I'll make omelettes.' He went to the fridge and took out some mushrooms. 'Good. Off you go.'

Being patronised never improved her mood. She left before she could say something she might regret. The tensions that Paris had enchanted away were already infiltrating their way back between them.

Upstairs, she tapped on Amy's door. She only just heard the small voice that muttered, 'Come in,' from the other side.

Pete's tidying schedule had had little impact on the chaos in here. Admittedly, it would have taken more than a couple of hours to make any significant impression. Some of the clothes had been shoved into Amy's laundry basket. Most of her shoes had been thrust higgledy-piggledy into the shoe rack that Beth had bought in a moment of foolish optimism. However, despite all efforts, the carpet was still barely visible. Amy sat marooned on her bed, wrapped in her duvet, her arm around one of the multitude of stuffed furry animals that competed for the bed space.

Beth picked her way across the room, collecting clothes and adding them to the pile of T-shirts on the chair. When she reached the bed, she sat beside her red-eyed daughter and just said, 'Oh, Amy.'

Immediately Amy threw herself at Beth's lap, where she lay sniffing as Beth stroked her hair. After a few minutes she scrabbled for a tissue in the sleeve of her top, which left far too little to the imagination, blew her nose and half sat up, snuggling into her mother. 'I'm really, really sorry,' she said. 'I really am.'

'What happened?' Now that she was alone with her daughter, Beth didn't want a row. She wanted to understand.

'Four of us went to the pub.' Amy was talking quickly, nervously, anticipating her mother's anger. 'I know I shouldn't have gone, but Nat's friend Sophie – well, her sister, Gemma, was going and she asked if we wanted to go too. Nat and Hannah said yes, so, like, I couldn't very well say no, especially as I was staying with Nat. Well, I couldn't, could I?'

Beth gave a despairing shake of the head. 'I suppose not.'

'Exactly,' said Amy, relieved at her support. 'So we went. I didn't buy any drinks or anything – Gemma's friends bought them for us. Then Nat suggested we came back here, or maybe Hannah did. I don't know.'

'Amy ...' She might as well at least tell the truth.

'Well, OK. I did. But I only meant the three of us. Nat told Sophie and then suddenly all the others were coming too.'

Beth could imagine. Empty house equals teen-magnet.

'I couldn't stop them. I knew you'd be furious, but they wouldn't listen. They found the drinks cupboard and the wine and helped themselves. I didn't know what to do. Really didn't. Then Nat passed out. We pinched her and shouted – one of the boys even slapped her – but she didn't come round. Gemma called the ambulance and then the police came and everything kicked off. I won't ever do it again. Cross my heart.' She criss-crossed her chest with her hand.

'You'd better not,' said Beth, hugging her. However rebellious a teen Amy was, things spinning out of her control had obviously taught her a lesson.

'I'll pay for the damage and the drink,' Amy offered, wriggling out of Beth's grip.

'But you've usually spent your allowance before you've got it. Anyway, that vase was a present from Dad.' Not everything was immediately replaceable. 'He gave it to me on our honeymoon.'

'No way.' Amy sounded horrified.

' 'Fraid so.'

'What shall I do, then?'

'You'll have to talk to Dad about paying him back in instalments, I guess.' She should be able to cover the amount eventually. 'And Pete's made you do such a good job, we won't have to get the cleaners in. That would have cost you the earth.'

'You think so?' Amy rallied a little and picked up her phone.

'How come Pete took charge?' The question had been nagging at her. 'Where was Megan in all this?'

'She was away. She went to that spa place you usually go to.'

So Megan had gone without her. Beth had assumed she would cancel the whole thing. 'On her own?' Despite her effort to be casual, her voice sounded oddly strangled. Even though she hadn't wanted to go, the idea of someone else going in her place upset her.

Now that the drama was over, Amy was busy texting. 'No. Hannah was going to go, but then she decided she'd rather be with me and Nat. So Ella went instead. They don't get back till tomorrow.' So insignificant was the detail to Amy that she didn't even look up.

Beth picked up the eyeless teddy at the end of the bed and stroked between its ears. What the hell did Megan think she was doing? Ella shouldn't be gallivanting about on spa weekends. She should be working when she could. Megan knew perfectly well how important these exams were. And they were only weeks away now. But that wasn't the only reason why Beth was upset. If anyone should have been there with Ella, it was her. Why had she not thought of suggesting that? Megan only suffered the deprivations of the Haven for Beth's sake, and would have been far happier on a city break somewhere.

'You OK, Mum?' Amy interrupted her train of thought.

'Just a bit surprised that Megan took Ella, that's all.' She failed to sound as nonchalant as she intended.

As Amy wriggled back under her arm, an avalanche of soft toys cascaded to the floor. Neither of them moved to stop it. 'Why? She is living there. And it would have been a waste not to take someone.'

'Yes. But someone her own age.' *Stop it.* Now you're sound-ing petty.

'Ella probably only went to be polite.' Amy kicked at a furry green tortoise with a red hat.

Even that small consolation didn't make Beth feel better. 'Amy?' she said tentatively, picking up the tortoise and placing it out of reach at the end of the bed.

'What?' Her phone bleeped and her attention turned back to reading a text.

'I'd prefer it if you didn't see quite so much of Hannah for a bit. Natalie too,' she added as an afterthought.

Amy's head whipped up. 'What? You're joking? You can't do that. Like, that's totally unfair.'

'No, I mean it.' She spoke calmly, convinced that this was the right course of action. The two families needed to distance themselves. 'I think you and Hannah … and Natalie … should cool things.'

'But that's silly. I'll see them at school.' The phone dropped on to the duvet.

'Well then, you can make do with that for a while.' Beth stared at Amy, daring her to contradict her.

'I know what you're doing.' Amy's face was white with outrage. 'What?'

Amy sat up straight, eyes blazing. 'This isn't about us, this is about you.' She overrode her mother's protests. 'Yes, it is. It's about you and Megan. You're punishing me to get back at her, not because me and Hannah have done anything wrong. We've apologised and cleaned and offered to pay. You just can't bear any of us having anything to do with Megan's family in case you lose us the way you're losing Ella. Well I don't blame Ella. You're a cow. And if I had the chance, I'd do exactly the same as her.' She threw herself back on to the bed and pulled her pillow over her head.

Appalled at what she had done, Beth reached out and put her hand on her arm. 'Amy, please.'

Amy pulled away from her as if she'd been scalded. 'Go away.'

Her yell was muffled by the pillow, but it was loud enough to be heard by Jon, who was standing in the doorway.

The despair on his face told Beth everything she needed to know.

14

In the taxi to the station, Megan stared down at her perfectly manicured hands. They hadn't looked this good since the last time she left the Haven. Somehow school got in the way of having perfect fingernails. The weekend had been a success. The last thing on earth she would have imagined herself doing was borrowing a girlfriend of Jake's to keep her company, let alone sharing a room with her. But, of course, Ella was more than a random girlfriend. They had known each other since she was born.

Over the last few weeks, those early days of motherhood that she'd shared with Beth had come to mind often. Jake had been a toddler when Beth was struggling with newborn Ella, as uncertain as many a first-time mother, looking to Megan to put her right. But, unlike Beth, Megan had preferred the school of muddling along, responding when her baby needed something. Extraordinarily, it seemed now, Jake had survived on his own terms. He came late to speaking, but was soon communicating in short sentences. He was a strong child and walked early, hauling himself up on whatever furniture was nearby. She never made him eat what he didn't like, with the result that he liked almost everything. He moved out of their bedroom when he asked to sleep in the cot in the room where his toys were. She hadn't insisted he move (or indeed do anything else) when the baby gurus decreed it, but let him dictate his own routine. She and Pete had been warned countless times that their sex life would suffer, but when they weren't catatonic with exhaustion, they found enough opportunities to suit them. Not always as conventional as before – on the kitchen table covered in flour (after they'd seen Jack Nicholson and Jessica Lange at it in *The Postman Always Rings Twice*), in front of the sitting room fire (after *Women in Love*) and even once or twice in the garage on the back seat of the car (they just fancied it) and in the bath (ditto) – but little Jake slept on undisturbed in their bed upstairs. She left potty training up to him too. Everyone got there in the end, she reasoned. Why make a thing of it?

Megan had found it hard to understand Beth's desperate desire for quick-fix solutions and watched, intrigued, as she struggled with a recommended routine, a little bit envious that Beth had a girl to dress up and mollycoddle. Did their individual approaches make a difference? Both babies had survived, one as apparently unharmed as the other by the variations in their early upbringing. Just as Amy and Hannah did a few years behind them.

Megan smiled to herself. Who would have thought that tiny scrap of a pink-swaddled baby that she remembered as if it was yesterday would turn into this self-possessed young woman sitting beside her so certain of what she wanted from life?

As if aware that she was in Megan's thoughts, Ella turned from her window. 'I'm glad we met Penny, aren't you? The others were all a bit up themselves.'

'If we'd stayed for longer, we'd probably have got to know them better,' Megan corrected her. She and Beth had never complained about the other residents. 'I doubt they're that bad. Your mum and I have met some perfectly nice women before.'

'Perhaps I was too young for them.' Ella gave a deliberately winsome smile. 'What about Brenda? You know, the one who wore her own leopard-skin slippers. And the facelift.'

Megan remembered the woman in the room next to theirs. A facelift? Really? She had assumed Brenda was just blessed with good genes and a total lack of interest in anyone else.

'Best bit?' she said, changing the subject.

'Oh, the pub, definitely. Then the facial. Oh, and the pedicure.'
She stuck out her legs as if she could see the varnish through her
shoes. 'Yours?'

'Just being away from home. Having nothing to do, no one
wanting anything of me, no arguments. Oh, and the pool.' That
long expanse of completely still blue water that she was one of
the few to use early morning or in the evening. While Ella lay in
their room revising, Megan's stately breaststroke had served her
well. Up and down, up and down. So well, that she had even
considered trying the local pool when she got home. But that had
only lasted as long as their stay. As soon as she left the building,
her good intentions dissolved just as they always did.

'And I liked talking after lights out.'

'Me too.' Every night they'd reminisced about their families.
Ella couldn't get enough of the events that had become shared
family folklore. On holiday, they'd all play long games of hide
and seek, when Ella would squeeze herself into the most difficult,
unlikely places. Once, Beth had been forced to call the police,
who found her daughter fast asleep in a hollow tree trunk down
the lane while her family were in hysterics imagining the worst.
They remembered Greece: the children's sailing lessons in a sea of
jellyfish; Scotland: Jon swimming out to rescue Hannah and Amy
from a rock as the tide came in to cut them off. They recalled
hours of swimming, beach rounders, cricket, Monopoly, jigsaws
and liar dice. They laughed about Pete, who never tried; Amy,
who was such a bad loser; Jake, who sometimes cheated; Beth,
who could never contain her desire to win, however young her
opponent; Jon, who angled his game so his daughters would have
a chance at victory. Amy had once tipped over the backgammon
board just as Jake was about to beat her. He didn't speak to her
for days.

When they'd laughed themselves silly remembering, they
moved on to the present. They could hardly ignore what was
happening between them now.

'I'm sure I've made the right decision,' Ella said unprompted on the last night. Megan had forced down yet another supper of nutritious broth following a day of rigorous virtual fasting, hot stone therapy and cupping (she still had the marks on her back). Lying stretched across one of the two double beds, eyes closed, a glass of diluted lemon juice at her side, she felt a new and improved woman.

'I'm sure you have too.' Excitement about the prospect of her first grandchild was quietly growing. Seeing Ella undress, Megan noticed that the baby had begun to show. How could she not respond to that? She was both touched and proud of the way Jake had stepped up to the plate, and impressed that the two of them had been so matter-of-fact in their planning. She would not have chosen this for either of them, but sometimes you just had to go with life's curveballs. Or you fought back, as Beth had, and risked disaster.

How could Megan forget Beth when her daughter was there with her, along with all the daily reminders of what they'd done together at the Haven? She smiled to herself. Beth would never have agreed to Ella's escape plan. But despite the G&T and the ham salad (her nod to the Haven's regime), she could not help feeling the usual glow of satisfaction when, at the final weigh-in, it was announced that she had lost four pounds.

'What shall we do about Mum?' asked Ella, breaking into her thoughts just as the taxi was pulling up outside Crewe station, in plenty of time for the London train.

'Wait till we're on the train.' Megan pulled her purse from her bag to pay. That 'we' disturbed her. She should really have asked another friend to come away with her rather than Ella. She tried to dismiss the voice that whispered, *How much do you really care?*

It was obvious that Ella had begun to miss her family. The longer she stayed with Megan and Pete, the more her talk was punctuated with funny stories of Amy's misdeeds – the smoking, the nose piercing, the faked letters to get off school swimming, the fake IDs – and Jon and Beth's reactions. Megan understood what was happening and resolved early on not to stand between Ella and her mother. Ella's anger with Beth was on the wane. As the baby became more of a reality, so her feelings were changing. She wanted to share her pregnancy with her mother.

As the train pulled out of the station, Ella could wait no longer. 'Well?' she asked. 'What *are* we going to do about Mum?'

Megan hesitated. 'What do you want to do?' A safe reply.

Ella sat with her bare feet on her seat, her arms around her legs and her chin resting on her bent knees. She wrinkled her nose, anxiety in her eyes. 'The thing is … Oh, I don't know. I love being with Jake, and with you of course, but I miss Mum and Dad. I even miss Amy – a bit. It's not that I want to go home exactly, except that I do.'

'Don't worry about us,' Megan hastened to reassure her. 'We'll understand if you go home.'

'Do you think Mum wants me?' Her brow furrowed.

'Of course she does. You staying with us has given you both time to think about what's happened and for her to accept that you're going to have the baby. Just wait till she holds it in her arms. You'll both forget all this.'

Ella still looked anxious. 'I hope so. What about Jake, though?'

'He'll be fine.' Megan wondered if he wouldn't even be a little bit relieved to have the pressure taken off. Everything had happened so suddenly, he too needed some space to adjust. 'It's not as if you won't see each other. A bit of distance will give you a chance to be sure of the next step.'

'He doesn't want us to live together, if that's what you mean.'

'Really?' This was the first time the subject had been mentioned in Megan's hearing.

'Mmm.' Ella chewed at her thumbnail. 'Don't worry. I don't think we should either. But I'm scared.' Her chin trembled and she put her forehead on her knee so her face was hidden. 'I know I said I was sure, but what if I've made the wrong choice after all?'

Megan didn't reply. She had learned her lesson. This was Beth's conversation to have, not hers. For all her bravado, Ella was deep down just a confused young woman needing someone to point the way. And much as Megan was prepared to do so, that person should be Ella's mother. Perhaps the pregnancy could be put on the right footing if she took a step back and tried to help the two of them mend fences. This baby should have the best start possible. Megan made up her mind.

'I'll talk to Beth,' she offered.

'Really?' Ella tipped her head and Megan could see the hope there. 'Will you?'

'I don't know if it'll help. We've barely spoken since we were all at your house.'

'But that's my fault, not yours. If she gives me a chance, I'll explain.'

Megan was touched by Ella's belief that the solution was that simple.

After supper, Ella and Jake had gone upstairs. Hannah was watching TV in the living room and Pete was somewhere on the Loire. Megan did her best not to resent his frequent travelling, but when a school day loomed large and she had to make a phone call she would rather not, it was bloody hard. The last time she got to go abroad without him was with a horde of rampaging schoolchildren and some other equally knackered teachers.

She took the phone into the conservatory. Pete had left a vase of red and yellow tulips on the table for her. He always left flowers when he went away. 'Just so you've got something to remember me by.' As if she could forget him.

She dialled Beth's mobile, unable to stop herself holding out one hand and admiring her nails again. The phone rang on. Relieved, but frustrated now she'd made up her mind to mend fences, she was about to hang up when Beth answered.

Megan's palms felt suddenly clammy. She wiped the free one

on her skirt, taking a couple of deep breaths as she flicked on the outside lights so that she could see the garden. The pansies in the tubs on the left of the terrace were closed up for the night, and a gentle wind riffled through the borders.

'Beth, it's Megan.'

The silence that followed was so long, Megan thought Beth must have put the phone down.

Then, 'Yes. What do you want?' There was none of the old warmth in her voice.

Don't react, Megan told herself. Don't react. Remember how you would feel if you were her …

'We should talk …' She stopped, annoyed with herself for starting with the obvious.

'What is there to say?' Worse than hostility was the chill in Beth's voice.

Megan held out the chunk of amber she wore around her neck, letting the light play on it. 'We should try to sort this whole thing out. Ella's unhappy.'

'Shouldn't I be talking to her, then?' Beth wasn't giving an inch.

'Beth, please …' She let go of the amber.

'What do you mean?'

'Be reasonable.' In the garden, everything was full of promise, coming into leaf. Clumps of daffodils trembled at the foot of the crab apple. Tulips stood proud in the pots she had arranged on the terrace.

Beth's intake of breath was audible. 'How can you expect me to be reasonable when you've done everything you can to take Ella from us?'

'Take her?' Megan had expected hurt, but not such a flagrant misinterpretation of the facts. 'That's simply not true. She chose to be here with Jake.'

There was a sound at the other end of the phone. A sob?

'You went to the Haven with her.' An accusation, not a statement of fact.

'But Hannah dropped out at the last minute,' Megan protested. 'I didn't want to waste the booking.' Even to her ears, that was a pretty lame excuse. She had known exactly how hurt Beth would be, but had chosen not to care. 'I'm really sorry. I didn't think. But can't we meet? Like it or not, we're going to be grandmothers in a few months.' Beth must be more used to the idea now. 'Can you believe it? I don't feel old enough.'

Silence.

Megan tried again. 'We always said we didn't want to be grandmothers until we were sixty. Hadn't we better face this together?'

Silence.

'I know you'd rather Jake wasn't the father. But we can't undo that.' There was an impatient sound at the other end of the line. 'All I can say is, he may be finding his way, but he's stood by Ella. They love each other.' Tracing the pattern of a peony on her skirt, Megan noticed that the age spots on the back of her hand had darkened, were more pronounced. She made a fist so that they almost disappeared.

'That's something.' Beth's voice gave a little.

'He's always stuck up for Amy, too. Last year in Rhodes, remember how he and his mate Baz protected your girls as if they were his sisters. If he says he'll stick by Ella, he will. You've no worries on that score.' That holiday had been one of their best yet, in a villa that Beth had found online. Every lazy day had been hot and happy. Jon and Pete would disappear to play golf (she hadn't realised Pete still had it in him) or spend hours swimming in the sea or chatting in the local taverna. She and Beth had lain by the pool, read and talked, sometimes making an expedition to one of the nearby towns or exploring the island. Their trip to the Valley of the Butterflies – a lush forested gorge that flickered with red, brown and white wings – was a high point. They had been enchanted as they crossed the bridges over a small river

157

running the length of the valley shaded by the trees, the sky a clear blue above them. They ate fresh calamari in the Fisherman's Shelter at the end of the beach, a glass of retsina each. The kids were happy left by the pool or on the beach by day, and spent nights in the tavernas and at a harmless nightclub in the local town. Neither of them had had any idea then of the twist of fate about to divide them.

'But they're so young.' Beth's voice was little more than a whisper.

'Which is why Ella especially needs all the support we can give her. Can't we find a way to mend our differences?'

A sigh.

Megan was holding out a white flag hoping Beth would take it. Outside, String had hopped over the wall and was prowling round the edge of the pond, ever optimistic, even though he had finished off the goldfish years ago. She knocked on the glass to discourage him. He looked up and sauntered towards the French doors.

'And her exams are coming up.'

Megan heard the note of accusation. 'She took her revision with her,' she said, sitting tight and trying again. 'I can't tell you how sorry I am about what's happened. I don't know what else to say, except that I miss you.' Saying the words brought home how true it was.

'Really?' asked Beth, sounding a little more robust. 'This is all so hard, though. Sometimes I even think I don't want us to have anything to do with your family any more.'

'But you can't mean that.'

'Can't I? You've undermined my relationship with Ella.'

'That's not true.' But, although she might not have meant to, there was more truth in that than Megan cared to admit.

'Why didn't you send her home when I asked you to?'

'I tried. Short of physically dragging her down the street,

I couldn't make her. She was devastated that you still wanted her to have an abortion. I felt desperately sorry for her.'

'We'd have made up.' Beth had recovered herself completely. 'If we'd had time together, we could have worked through all this. And then you take her to the Haven without saying anything.'

'For heaven's sake!' Megan lost patience. 'You were the one who said you didn't want to go. It was only four days. She enjoyed the pampering.' She shot another glance at her free hand.

'But she should be at home revising when she can. Her exams start at the end of May. What were you thinking?'

'I thought she needed a break. I told you, she took her work with her.' Megan's hand curled into a fist that she brought down on her knee.

Beth gave a short laugh, as if she didn't believe her.

'So what are we going to do?' Megan had one last try. 'The ball's in your court.'

Another silence, then: 'This is so difficult, especially after everything you said.'

Not that difficult, Megan wanted to scream. Instead, she said, 'You know I didn't mean it.'

Beth ignored her. 'I want Ella back home where she belongs. Can I talk to her?'

'Of course you can. She's upstairs. Let me give her a shout.' Megan stood at the bottom of the stairs and yelled Ella's name. 'It's your mum.'

Immediately Ella was running down the stairs, almost snatching the phone from Megan's hand. 'Mum! You OK?' She sat on the bottom step, hair falling over her face as she listened to Beth. Her toes curled and relaxed. Her left thumb rubbed between her ring and middle fingers, then stopped.

Megan moved away. As she watched Ella talk to Beth, her voice increasingly animated, she felt a lump forming in her throat. At least her call had achieved something.

15

A cloud had lifted from the family. Ella was coming home at the weekend. Jon could be heard humming in the garden. Beth's spirits had risen and her heart was back in her work. Ella's return was all it took. Even Amy's temper had improved, particularly when Beth didn't stop her after she announced that she was going to meet Hannah on Saturday lunchtime. Yes, *after* she'd done her revision.

Beth had talked to Ella for a long time that night she returned from the Haven, hearing the initial caution in her daughter's voice reflected in her own. Gradually the conversation had eased as they relaxed together for the first time since Ella had left home. Ella had even made her see the funny side to Amy's drunken night by telling her old scare stories of parties unwittingly announced to the world on Facebook. They had got off lightly by comparison, and Amy wouldn't rush to do it again. Eventually, they had agreed that Ella would live at home again but stay with Jake most weekends, depending on her exam schedule. When the exams were over, they might think again. But at least she would be with her family for now. She and the baby.

Beth pulled out of the parking space outside their house. Normally she would walk to the book group, but she had been kept later than usual at work. Anwar Malik was preparing to go to Pakistan to search for his daughter. The letters he had written to his ex-wife's family, to his, had drawn a blank. So far they had been unable to track down her whereabouts, and he was anxious that any necessary paperwork was in order. He was a desperate man. Beth reflected on the parallels that existed between his case and her own life. His plight seemed all the more poignant when she thought how broken she had felt when Ella left home to live only a few streets away. How much worse not to know if you would ever see your daughter again.

At least they would get a decent meal tonight. Claire, the host, was a professional private chef. Whenever it was her turn, she shamed the rest of the group by insisting that she would do all the cooking without any contributions from them. But what would adequately accompany Mrs Gaskell's *Wives and Daughters*? Stewed larks or boiled veal or something equally unpalatable?

Beth parked outside the modern block of flats near the canal. She was buzzed in through the front door and crossed the carpeted hallway to the lift, which whisked her directly into the flat as if she were royalty. The rich smell of a gamey casserole greeted her. Relief! By the lift door, a folded sheet was spread on the floor so all the guests could remove their shoes before stepping on to the pristine cream carpet. Through the door to her left she could see the dining table perfectly laid for eight: shining cutlery, sparkling glasses and candles already lit. Claire never did things by halves. Beth crossed the thick pile in her stockinged feet to where the hostess stood smiling at the doorway to the living room.

'Just in time for a Kir Royale – I've only got Cava, but you get the idea. Yes?'

'I'd love one.' Beth took the glass of rosy fizz from her. 'Cheers.'

From inside the room, the other members echoed her.

'From what I've been hearing,' Claire lowered her voice to a loud whisper, 'you probably need it.'

Beth raised an eyebrow as a question.

'You know,' Claire added conspiratorially. 'Ella. We've heard she's gone to live with Megan. That must be so difficult for you.'

'Except that it's not true,' Beth replied and went straight

through to join the gathering, leaving Claire gazing after her, puzzled.

Beth stood by the fireplace, not quite knowing what would come next. The others had heard their exchange and were watching her, expectant. Peggy was resplendent in beige and taupe, head nodding like a dog in the back window of a car, eager to get started; Fran was sporting one of her voluminous smock affairs with a Pomeranian puppy peeping out of her bag – 'Poppy, she's new. I couldn't leave her behind'; Susie, devoted mother of four, looked exhausted, and as if she'd been wearing the same clothes for weeks, which she probably had; Lucy, a high-rolling hedge-fund manager, had obviously come straight from work; Ruth, the frazzled mother of Bridezilla, was clearly relieved to have escaped the endless demands of her daughter; and finally Deirdre, a mildly spoken Pilates teacher, seemed to have applied her heavy make-up in the dark, or at least without the glasses that had slipped to the end of her nose. But there was no Megan.

'Why don't you sit down?' Lucy indicated the blue modernist sofa, which looked hideously uncomfortable. 'Are you OK?'

'Oh, absolutely,' confirmed Beth, feeling anything but. 'Everything's sorted out for the best now.'

'But it must have been a shock.' Ruth was needling for more information.

'Well, of course it was,' Beth conceded. 'But now we're thrilled.' Had she really said that? Reluctant to catch the eye of anyone in the group, she looked around the walls at the collection of bright watercolour landscapes reminiscent of English summer days. Yes, she had.

So the word was out. They had become the focus of the sort of gossip she scorned. Almost every day she was aware of how the distress of families could be intensified by misreporting in newspapers or magazines. Too many of her more celebrated or wealthy clients had suffered. A local book group discussing her affairs was nothing in comparison, but nonetheless, she didn't want to be its centre of attention.

'Megan's cried off,' said Peggy, puffing out her bosom like a pouter pigeon, realising that Beth wasn't going to satisfy their curiosity. 'So perhaps we should start.' Always eager to be out of the blocks, Peggy could be relied on to chivvy them into discussion. But not this time.

As Beth sat down, Lucy put her hand on her arm. 'I was so sorry to hear about Ella. It must be very hard.'

Beth swallowed. She propped up a geometric-patterned cushion behind her so it supported her back with the give of a brick, and cleared her throat. The others looked at her with greedy anticipation. 'I don't know what you've all heard, but perhaps I should clear this up straight away. Ella's pregnant. The father is Megan's son, Jake.'

There was a gratifying little gasp.

'Not really,' murmured Deirdre in disbelief.

Beth nodded in her direction. 'Ella spent some time with him while they got accustomed to the situation and what it means. Now she's back at home until she's completed her A levels, and then we'll take it from there.' She felt much better having said that, and she spoke so confidently that she felt quite calm. She was aware of six faces concentrating on her, waiting. Oh, yes. 'The baby's due at the end of September.' She took such a large swallow of her Kir that it went down the wrong way, making her cough explosively. Susie obliged by patting her on the back.

Beth had expected Megan to be there, assuming that was the reason she hadn't pressed for a date when they last spoke. That way, they would have their first meeting under the protection of the group, where nothing too damaging could be said. Nonetheless, she was relieved not to see her.

'It must have been awfully stressful.' Deirdre lengthened her ballerina-straight back, stretching out a perfectly toned arm towards Beth. 'I know someone who does the most fantastic cranial massage. That might help.'

'Thanks, Deirdre, but I'm fine. Really.' The idea of a stranger's hands anywhere near her brain – even outside her skull – did not appeal remotely.

'Megan hinted that things had been awkward between the two of you.' Ruth looked at the carpet as she spoke, clearly intending this as an opening to a more intimate conversation.

'Yes, Megan's been so upset.' Claire came into the room and plumped herself down beside Beth. The unforgiving modern sofa gave not even a little under her weight. 'Have you forgiven her?'

'Forgiven her for what?' Beth was startled by the question, but looked around her all innocence. 'There's nothing to forgive. Really,' she insisted. 'Shall we start?'

Put in their place, the others retrieved their copies of *Wives and Daughters* from their bags. Peggy always chose Victorian novels when it was her turn, something about revisiting her past and rediscovering the classics. This particular choice had an ironic resonance that could hardly go unmissed. Beth sat quite still as an unexpected moment of clarity struck her.

There *was* still something to forgive, wasn't there? But she couldn't find that forgiveness inside her, despite the newly sprouting seeds of gratitude towards Megan for looking after Ella. With her continuing resentment (of which she was not proud) and sense of betrayal came a constant and exhausting re-examination of her own inadequacies, exacerbated by what Megan had said. Her apologies, however genuinely felt, did not make anything go away.

Ella coming home had not marked the end of hostilities. How could it? Beth's emotions weren't chalked up on a blackboard that could be wiped clean, just like that. Like anyone else's, they were far more complicated and more deep-seated. However, she had to control them – for everyone else's sake as well as her own.

Then it came to her: subterfuge was the obvious answer. At

home, she said what she thought, always as open and honest with her family as possible. They knew exactly where they were with her. And that was what caused the rows. But it didn't have to be like that. From now on, things would be different.

Until now, she had divided herself into two: one personality for home, another for work. She tried never to show her clients what she really thought of them. If she felt anything hearing the tales of a wronged husband or wife, or she despised their desire for revenge, she never let on. They never knew whether she really thought they deserved the judgements handed down to them. Her celebrations with them were kept purely on a professional level. She was careful to remain as cool and as businesslike as possible, then let off steam when she got home.

So … if she pretended that she had got over what had happened, perhaps she would even come to believe it herself. If she didn't try, the relationships that were so important to Jon, Ella and Amy would break down completely and the family would suffer even more. It would be a struggle, but it wasn't too late.

'Beth?'

She had been aware that in the background Peggy had been holding forth about something to do with the marriage market in Victorian society, but she hadn't heard a word.

'Mmm? Sorry. I was miles away.'

'Are you all right to join in?' Susie spoke so kindly that Beth snapped to immediately.

'Yes, of course. I was thinking about something at work. Sorry.' Mention of work always got Susie's slightly resentful respect. She'd had a job once too – in advertising, as she was always keen to remind them – but had traded it all in for her family, thanks to her high-flying investment banker husband who was rarely there but who kept her in children and cash.

Just as they were getting to grips with their discussion about the novel, the doorbell rang.

Claire disappeared to answer it, and soon afterwards they heard the rattle of the lift doors, and a voice: Megan's. 'I know I said I wouldn't make it, but the parents had all left by six thirty. Jane and I hung around with a couple of the teachers, comparing notes for the school trip, and then I thought I might as well come along after all. I've read the novel and I really didn't want to miss your cooking. Is that OK?'

Any compliment on her food was a certain way to win Claire over. As a result, she almost succeeded in hiding how miffed she was that she would now have to lay another place and find an extra chair. From the sitting room, the others listened to the two of them reorganising the dining table.

Aware that, despite all denials, the group was keenly anticipating some kind of showdown, Beth steeled herself. As Megan came into the room at last, still wearing the fingerless mittens she always wore for cycling, Beth forced herself to smile. And Megan smiled right back.

Megan sat on an embroidered leather pouffe and leaned her back against the arm of the sofa. Within minutes, the discussion was back on track.

At eight thirty, Peggy called a halt and the group, only fortified so far by a few olives, trooped into the dining room. Beth sat beside Megan. Claire was as accomplished as a waitress as she was a chef, and the food was on the table immediately. As they ate, for once the book of the night was forgotten and the conversation turned to their lives.

Ruth began regaling them with Bridezilla's latest demand. Instead of the photographer Ruth and her husband had offered (a professional who was an old friend of the family and was offering mates' rates), she was insisting on a specialist wedding photographer who charged the earth. 'And who do you think is paying for all this?' Ruth asked plaintively. She didn't expect a reply.

'What about you two?' Claire asked Beth and Megan. 'Might there be a wedding in the family sometime soon?'

Heads turned.

Beth had to extricate a piece of shot from her mouthful of pheasant before she could reply. 'Oh, I don't think so,' she said airily, putting the pellet on the side of her plate. 'Jake and Ella have got a lot to think about first, haven't they, Meg?'

'They have,' Megan agreed quickly. 'It's early days.'

'Of course, they're both so young,' said Susie. 'But you'll be grandmothers together. I rather envy you that.' She clapped her hands.

'I'm not sure either of us is quite ready, are we?' asked Beth, wiping her mouth with the paper napkin from her knee.

'Oh, I don't know,' said Megan, as she began to collect up the plates. 'It might be fun. Babysitting but being able to hand it back at the end of the day. It's a cliché that rather appeals.'

Beth hid her uncertainty with a smile. 'I hadn't thought about it quite like that,' she said. 'Perhaps you're right. We'll make brilliant grandmothers. But I won't be taking up knitting just yet.' She pulled a face at the idea.

The others laughed, and Beth and Megan joined in.

Beth relaxed a little. This was working better than she had imagined. She could do this. And she would.

16

While Ella went to get a beaker of water from the cooler in the corner of the waiting area, Beth looked around her. On the small table beside her, a pile of well-read magazines offered celebrity gossip and TV schedules. The couple on her left held hands as they exchanged confidences under their breath, their eyes fixed on each other's. On her right, the wife sat silent, puffy-eyed, staring into the middle distance, while her sprucely suited husband fidgeted, checking his watch, tutting and returning to his paper. On the other side of the room, a slightly older woman sat alone, bestowing smiles on anyone who caught her eye, explaining that 'this is my fourth, so my husband hasn't bothered to come'. Her green cardigan was done up squint and one of her knee-length popsocks had rolled down to her ankle, revealing a shinful of varicose veins. She received the same embarrassed acknowledgement from everyone before she turned back to her magazine with a sigh. Every time a nurse walked past, all heads turned, hoping their name would be called.

Ella returned to her seat. 'Excited?' she whispered.

Beth nodded, although in fact she was feeling as jittery as if something dreadful was about to happen. But what was there to be afraid of? Having had two and a half months for Ella's pregnancy to sink in, she had learned to accept the fact. Nonetheless, the future was worrying, the unknown. She couldn't share her daughter's confidence that everything would work out all right. Experience had taught her that that was not always the case. Ella had made such a life-changing decision; what would happen to her and to the baby? To her longed-for career? Being here in the hospital, about to see the baby on a scan for the first time, was bringing a new reality to the situation. They weren't going to see a bundle of dividing cells, but a real baby: a person that was going to be born and be part of their lives for ever. Beth clasped her hands together, trying to steady herself.

A couple of weeks ago, Ella had got her to touch her belly for the first time to feel the baby kick. 'It's like butterflies fluttering through,' she said. But Beth hadn't felt a thing although she was reminded of her own pregnancies and her excitement when she first felt each of her babies move.

'I'm going to ask for a photo, so Jake can see.' Ella ran her hand over the bump that her floral top did little to conceal. 'If only he hadn't had that gig in Newcastle.'

But it was to Beth's benefit that he had. Without Jake's support, Ella had asked her to come with her to the hospital. Until now, she had kept both Megan and Beth out of the loop. Jake had gone with her to the twelve-week scan and the appointments where she wanted support. Being asked along to the twenty-week scan was the equivalent of being handed a mighty olive branch. They were both equally aware of the significance, although nothing was said. As was Jon. His pleasure that they were bonding over the baby at last had not gone unnoticed.

'Ella Standish.' A young woman in a white coat, clutching a thin file, emerged from the corridor. 'Come with me.'

'Come on.' Ella almost bounded from her seat, looking around for Beth, who followed half wishing she could run away yet drawn on despite herself. They were led into a small room where the lights were dimmed. Ella lay on the bed as she was asked, while Beth took the chair beside her, crossing and uncrossing her legs. The radiographer kept up a flow of innocuous chatter, pulling on her latex gloves and explaining what she was doing as she prepared Ella for the scan.

'Do you want to know the sex?'

Beth held her breath. The sex. This was a human being they were about to see. She realised that without her noticing, her shoulders had tensed up around her ears. She forced them to relax as Ella replied, 'No. I don't think so, thanks. I'd feel bad knowing ahead of Jake. You don't mind, do you, Mum?'

Jake. Hearing his name in connection with her daughter was still difficult. If it weren't for him … Beth stopped herself. What was the point? 'Of course not, Lulu. You must do whatever you want.' But she did want to know, she realised. She really did.

As Ella bared her stomach, pulling down her leggings and rolling up her top, a jolt of emotion shocked Beth with its force. Her daughter was really having a baby. Until now it had almost been a curiously abstract thing, but the reality of being about to see it made everything different. Ella, oblivious to Beth's distraction, was asking questions, gasping when the cool jelly was rubbed on to her belly. By her head was a small monitor, fizzing with snow. As the radiographer swept the paddle back and forth over Ella's bump, the snow cleared and what was quite unmistakably a baby appeared on the screen.

Ella gasped and reached out to grasp Beth's hand, her eyes never leaving the monitor.

'You can see baby quite clearly, can't you?' The radiographer fiddled with the dials in front of her.

Ella nodded. 'Yes, I can,' she said, breathless. 'Look, Mum.'

But Beth's gaze was already fixed to the screen. The process had cast her back through the years to her and Jon's first sight of Ella. So much had threatened to cloud their happiness then, but they were bound by nervous anticipation, neither of them knowing what the future would hold, certain of one thing only: that this baby was what they wanted more than anything else. And Ella had turned out to be everything they could have wished for. Beth was proud that they had a daughter who knew her own mind and had insisted on what she was certain would bring her most happiness. She was wrenched back to the present as her wedding ring was pressed painfully between her fingers in Ella's excited grip.

'We'll go to the right side first. There's the face.' The radiographer pointed at the grainy white image. 'The eye sockets. Mouth. You can see baby swallowing. There.'

Ella laughed, delighted. 'Wow! That's amazing.'

Beth took a deep breath, blinking hard to control the unexpected tears burning the back of her eyes.

'Here you can see the heart beating – and there, on the graph at the bottom of the screen. Nice and steady. One forty-five. That's pretty good.' A loud rhythmic thumping sounded in the room. Ella was riveted to the screen, then twisted back to Beth, her eyes shining. 'Can you see, Mum? Look!'

'Yes. Yes, I can.' Beth's voice caught in her throat.

'Look! There! Is that an arm in front of its face!' Ella pointed at a moving white line.

'Yes, and that's a leg – here. Baby's snuggled up to the placenta. That white structure's the umbilical cord.' The radiographer followed its line with her finger. Then the angle of the image changed and a tiny shape appeared in the dark gap between two indeterminate white masses.

'Is that a foot?' Ella spoke as if she couldn't believe what she was seeing.

'Yes, baby's moving around now, and here comes the other ...'

'Mum! Look!' Ella turned to make sure Beth was seeing everything she saw, that she was every bit as excited. 'Mum? Are you crying?'

Beth couldn't speak. She pulled a tissue from the box judiciously placed for patients and blew her nose. Ella laughed and reached out to be given one so she could blow hers too. For the next fifteen minutes they sat holding hands, Beth leaning on the pillow with her other elbow, exclaiming at what they were seeing as the radiologist explained the images and made her measurements.

'There. About ten inches long. Now I'm measuring the dia-meter of the head ... the circumference of the head ... a cross-section of the belly.'

'That's so cool.' Ella's eyes didn't leave the screen.

Beth was equally transfixed. This was her grandchild. The grandchild that, if she had had her way, would never have existed.

'I'm sorry,' she whispered, and kissed the side of Ella's head.

'What? Why? What are you talking about?' Ella looked round at her mother, puzzled. Then she understood. 'It's OK. It really is. We're here now, and it's gonna be great.'

The radiologist continued her work. 'The measurements are all good. You're twenty weeks, right?'

Ella nodded. 'You're going to give me some photos, aren't you?'

'Absolutely.' The radiographer ripped off some paper towel and began wiping the gel from Ella's stomach.

Eventually, she was dressed, upright, clutching the envelope containing her photos and ready to go. Even in the dimly lit room, her happiness was obvious, and in that moment, Beth knew that everything between them would be different from now on.

Megan was daydreaming on break duty. She glanced at her watch. Ella would have had her scan by now. A boy or a girl? she wondered. Not that it mattered, provided all was well and it was healthy. She missed Ella. She'd moved almost a month ago, but she still missed her company and the calm she brought to the house. The undercurrents of sibling rivalry between Jake and Hannah were back. Even at twenty-one, Jake resented any extra attention given to Hannah, even though she was hard at work for her GCSEs and needed all the parental support she could get. Only the other night he had objected that Megan always made Hannah's favourite meals, not his. How absurd. He wanted fish pie instead of chicken. A stupid argument broke out that would never have started if Ella had been there. Poor Jake was under pressure too.

Megan did up her jacket. She was ashamed of the one-upmanship she had felt while Ella was living with them. But Beth had obviously been equally uncomfortable at the last book group, despite her outward friendliness. Megan knew her well enough to see that. What did her apparent change of heart mean? That all was forgiven and forgotten? Pete had come home two nights ago from a drink with Jon saying they had been invited over for a family barbecue. Date to be fixed. Curiouser and curiouser.

A shout went up from the other side of the playground. She didn't need a crystal ball to know who would be responsible for any trouble. She walked over, careful not to run. Running would only instil panic. A fight had broken out. One of the teaching assistants was standing on the sidelines, ineffectually ordering the combatants to stop, unable to find a way into the brawl. A huddle of children were shouting encouragement. By the time Megan arrived, the initial fury had gone out of the squabble and the four pupils involved were rolling around exchanging perfunctory blows and hair-pullings. Except for one of them.

'Right, Ned.' She addressed the assistant. 'Take this lot to the other end of the playground. Go on, everyone, there's nothing for you here.'

The children dispersed quickly as Ned moved them away and began a game of rounders.

As Ben Fletton raised his fist, Megan caught it and pulled him from the top of the pile. He struggled against her at first, then, realising who had him by the arm, quietened down. Before he had time to register what she was doing, she turned him so he was facing away from the fight. 'Sit on the ground, Ben, and don't move.' Shocked by the speed with which he had been prised away, he did as he was told. Without him, the other three had broken apart. Ben's sidekick Steven was breathless, his T-shirt torn, one of his trainers kicked off in the fight. The other two were year fours: Jade, a fearless child who stood up for herself, and Will, one of her friends. Jade looked dishevelled but none the worse for wear. Will was trying not to cry as his hand came away from his nose smeared with blood. The knee of his tracksuit bottoms was torn.

'He wanted money from Will, miss.' Jade was first to defend herself. 'Fifty p. or else, he said.' She pushed back the curls from her flushed face.

Not again. 'I thought we'd spoken about this, Ben. It has to stop.'

Silence from the thunderous-looking nine-year-old.

'In which case, you had all better come with me to see the head. Will, I'll get Elaine to take you to the first-aid room to clean you up, then you can join us.' She beckoned to a year five teaching assistant.

As she led the children into the school, Megan felt utterly exhausted, as if her legs were moving through mud, a clamp around her brain. Usually she coped with the day-to-day rigours of her job. She enjoyed the children, relished the challenges involved in their education and was rewarded by the knowledge that she was making a difference to their lives. But Ben Fletton and his young cronies had her beat. There must be a way to deal with him, to help him, but she couldn't think what it was.

When the bell rang to mark the end of the day, she waited till the corridors had cleared of children before making her way to the hall, where they were having a meeting about the school fair. The steering group was composed of six parents, led by the indomitable Maureen Stocker. Generously proportioned, Maureen had the energy of a whirlwind and the tact of a heffalump. Every year, other pushy mothers attempted to stage a coup to oust her from her position as chief organiser, but she was a formidable fighter unwilling to share the role with anyone else, and she always came out on top, co-opting neutral parents to vote for her by fair means or foul. There were other mothers Megan might have preferred to work with – indeed had, during the much more pleasurable time when Beth had been chair of the parents' committee – but she could hardly object. Maureen's boundless energy, enthusiasm and inability to delegate were largely responsible for the ever-increasing success of the school fair.

By the time Megan reached the hall, the meeting was in full swing. Maureen was parcelling out the various stalls, taking suggestions and making plans. Seeing her in action made Megan long for Beth's firm, but less domineering, hand on the tiller. But those days had gone once Amy had left the school five years earlier. Five years that had gone like the wind.

'Megan, you'll be doing your usual baking, I hope.' Maureen turned the full force of her attention on her. 'And could you possibly make the guess-the-weight cake too?'

'I'd be happy to.' Her contribution assured, Megan let the flow of conversation wash over her, absorbing the key points, registering which of the committee was being instructed to do what, and making sure she looked as if she was engaged.

Having discussed every kind of stall under the sun, Maureen turned the discussion to the competitions.

'How about a beat-the-goalie?' suggested one of the two fathers who had dutifully turned up on the orders of his wife, who was currently beaming at him. The suggestion elicited murmurs of approval all round.

As Megan listened to them, she had a brainwave. Ben Fletton. He would be just the boy to put in goal. Football was his sport. Every morning before school began, he was to be found in the playground having a kickabout. Perhaps by being appreciated rather than punished, his attitude towards the school might begin to change. Thinking outside the box. This was the sort of strategising that Beth was always so good at. Perhaps Megan could do it too. It was a risk, but one she believed to be worth taking. All she had to do was convince the steering group. She braced herself. This should not be too hard if she presented the idea in the right way.

17

Was it going to rain? Beth glanced up at the gathering clouds. The forecasters had predicted a sunny May and June, but they were so rarely right. The weather in the previous few days had been anything but sunny. However, she was banking on the improvement so that they could eat outside. She looked around their garden, at the wide flagstoned path that joined the decking outside the house to that at the end, where the barbecue stood by the shed. On either side were raised beds constructed from railway sleepers planted largely with grasses and bamboos. Behind them the mingled purple, lavender and white clematises were coming into flower, while Jon's tireless efforts to achieve a moss-free, weed-free lawn looked as though they might be paying off at last.

'Dad wants to know where you've put the beer.' Amy skipped down the garden to join her.

To Beth's poorly disguised delight, the school had at long last taken a stand on hair colour. Under the new rules, the postbox red had been toned down to a dark conker colour – almost natural-looking if she squeezed her eyes half shut. Quite pretty. Today Amy looked pleasantly normal, barefoot in a too-short playsuit that came close to exposing more than was strictly necessary. But you couldn't have everything, and at least the Goth phase seemed to have passed on as quickly as it came. Jon had been right. That boy had never been seen again. Relief all round.

'By the washing machine, if not in the fridge.'

'It's a bit late to chill it now, isn't it? Anyway, the fridge is full. When's lunch?' Amy flicked her fringe back with a finger.

Beth looked at her watch. Nearly one o'clock. 'Soon. The others should be here at any second.'

Right on cue, they heard the doorbell, then Jock's frantic barking as he charged in its direction.

'Jock!' shouted Amy at the top of her voice, making absolutely no difference. 'I hope Hannah's remembered to bring the *Girls* box set.'

'You're not watching that all afternoon.' Beth hoped this barbecue wasn't a mistake. When she'd had the idea, she had been convinced of its brilliance, arranging it in the blazing heat of her conviction that she could repair the damage she had caused.

'God, Mum. Why not? You'll all be talking.' She drew the word out in the most disdainful way possible. 'And you and Megan will be making up while the lovebirds do their happy-families thing.' She stuck out her tongue to register her distaste, then ran back to the house before Beth had time to object.

Ever since her drunken weekend, Amy had been worryingly well behaved. More unnerving still, she had even been occasionally pleasant to Beth – even when nagged about her revision. Beth was grateful for small mercies. She stopped at the barbecue: none of that streamlined, easy-to-clean professional gas-fired type of thing for them. No, the dirtier, the more fiddly and more outdoorsy, the happier Jon was. He had never lost his attraction to boy-scout pursuits – one not shared by Beth. But at least they were reserved for outdoors. They hadn't used the barbecue since the previous year. Was this the best day to bring the thing out from hibernation? Perhaps not, but how better to demonstrate her new resolve than by asking the Westons over to make a new start? Nervous of the afternoon ahead, Beth gave the grid a brisk clean with the wire brush, delaying the moment when she would have to greet everyone.

Steps sounded on the path.

'Out of the way, fair maid. Your saviour has arrived.' An arm slid around her waist, then Pete pulled her towards him and kissed her on the cheek. 'This is what I've come for, isn't it? The barbecue, I mean. That and the beer, of course. And you.'

She forced herself to laugh and stepped to one side. 'In that order, I assume? Here you are, then.' She handed him the brush. 'Where are the others?'

Pete clasped his hands over the striped rugby shirt pulled tight across his paunch and displaying a not terribly seductive stretch of naked belly between it and his low slung belt. Beth looked quickly back to his face. He winked at her. 'Hannah and Amy took off upstairs like bats out of hell. Jon grabbed Jake to help him in the kitchen, and Ella wanted Megan to see something she's bought for the baby.'

Jealousy pricked at Beth. What was wrong with her? She and Ella were bonded again and she had nothing to fear, but ... she couldn't help herself.

'Yes,' she said, the memory of their successful shopping trip still sparking a warm glow. 'We bought a Moses basket. Hope we're not tempting fate.'

'Don't say that, old thing.' His eyes twinkled. 'I'm sure everything's going to be fine. I know it's not what you wanted for Ella and you're still hurting ...'

Beth was startled. Pete didn't do feelings. At least, certainly not outside his family. He had an enviable aptitude to let things blow past, never allowing himself to be affected by them – or so he made sure it appeared. That way lay an easy life. 'But I never said ...'

He started work with the brush. 'You didn't need to. I've known you almost since the day Jon picked you up in that supermarket, remember?'

She didn't have to force her smile at the memory of meeting Jon over the racks of Sainsbury's finest fruit and veg. She had been thirty and single, in charge of her life. Until that day, she had been very happy with her occasional liaisons, which gave her a reasonable social life, an even better sex life and no strings. Love at first sight was a notion she had always scorned. His opening line was to ask her if she knew where the Jerusalem artichokes were. Afterwards they both confessed they had fallen for one another immediately. Jon admitted that he had no idea what a Jerusalem artichoke was, but he saw the label on the shelf behind her and just read it off. The best excuse he could think of at the time. He then bumped into her twice (deliberately, she learned later) in two different aisles. Finally he wheedled her number from her at the checkout before laying siege to her until she succumbed. Two years later they had married. Pete was of course best man, Megan was a vastly pregnant witness and a random member of the registry office staff obliged as the other. They didn't involve their families. Not Beth's, because she didn't want them there. Not Jon's, because his mother had embarked on a Caribbean cruise for the over-sixties the week before.

'I can't help it,' she confessed now. 'I'm doing my best, but I can't help how I feel.' She stopped short at explaining how she was trying to deal with those feelings.

'I know, pet.' Pete stopped his work, satisfied that the grill was clean enough. 'You don't have to say anything. But the two of you had better get over this soon. We're all being affected. Now where's that beer?'

'Right here,' said Jon, coming out of the house. An excited Jock raced out behind him, jumping on to his hind legs then scooting towards Beth. 'I had a feeling you'd be after one straight away. Now let's get this show on the road or we won't be eating until midnight.'

'I bloody hope not.' Pete took the bottle held out to him. 'That's eleven hours. I need sustenance to keep this going you know.' He patted his belly, enjoying the others' laughter. 'Right, where's the charcoal? Let's do this.'

Beth left them to it and went back to the house, touched by

Pete's understanding. He could be a man of few words, but then you didn't need many if they were the right ones. Jon had been less sympathetic towards her recently. Perhaps his current anxieties were more to do with Ella's pregnancy now that her bump was visible. That must have brought home what was about to happen, made it real. For the first time Beth could remember, they had stopped confiding in each other. When she tried to express the confusion and panic that almost overwhelmed her whenever she thought about Ella's future, he brushed the subject aside. 'We've talked about this. It's happening. You're going to have to get used to it.' If she attempted to explain the distressing and continuing hostility she felt towards Megan, he didn't want to know. 'Get over it, Beth. How old are you, for God's sake?' In the end, she just stopped trying. Last thing at night they discussed nothing more than their days at work: her cases, so many illustrations of marriages in their last stages; his business successes and the new ventures he was considering. They never talked about what was dividing them. Or they didn't talk at all.

She found Jake in the kitchen, cutting up a string of sausages and pricking them. He looked up when he heard her come in, pushing his hair off his eyes with the back of his hand as he gave her that wide, even smile. He was a good-looking boy, no doubt about that – with those eyelashes, and a jawline to slice paper. But why would a boy like him want to be tied down by Ella, or anyone else for that matter, and a baby? How could their relationship possibly last?

'Jake, I'm so sorry. Amy or Ella were meant to do that.' She had asked them, then got sidetracked by a call from a colleague wanting out-of-hours advice on a custody case that would be in court first thing on Monday morning, when one of the most rebarbative judges on the circuit was sitting.

'Don't worry. Jon asked me to do it,' he said. 'It's quite relaxing.'

'I'll just get the chicken out of the fridge.' She opened the door. A bottle of Becks slipped out and smashed on the tiles. She just caught a second one in time. 'What idiot …' She stopped herself and, counting to ten, went to get a mop, refusing Jake's offer of help.

'Babe, what are you doing?' Ella arrived in the kitchen. 'You're meant to be a guest, not a galley slave.'

'And you were meant to do these, so I'm doing it for you.' He kissed her on the nose, then put his hand on the long stripy top covering her bump.

Beth stared at them for what felt like a second too long. Jon's words echoed in her head. This was happening. Get over it. She thought she had.

'I'll finish them.' Ella held out her hand for the kitchen scissors. 'You go and help Dad.'

Jake shook his head, although he got up to give her his seat. 'They don't need me. Look at them.'

Outside, Jon and Pete were talking, beers in hand, watching the flames. The two of them were entirely happy in each other's company, each able to anticipate the other's next move or phrase without needing a prompt. They had the sort of intuitive understanding that identical twins were meant to share. Although why Jon had decided to dress for the summer that morning was beyond Beth. Yes, it was almost June, but the sky was thick with gathering clouds.

'Ella, you can do the corn while I finish off the salad.' She pushed the tin foil and the bag of cobs along the worktop. 'Where's Megan?'

Ella laughed. 'I left her upstairs, going through the stuff we bought for the baby. She's offered to buy us a cot and buggy!'

So the competitive grandmothering had begun. Beth dug her fingernails into her palm. 'That's very generous of her,' she managed. Before she could retaliate by offering a car seat and a bouncy chair, she changed the subject. 'So what've you got planned for the summer, you two?'

'Festival season,' said Ella, beginning to peel the leaves off the cobs. 'How many are there, babe?'

'Five or six? Latitude, Bestival, Glasto ...' Jake paused as he dealt with the last sausage.

But these were names that Beth had heard of. Heavy Feather must be doing infinitely better than she'd imagined. 'That's amazing, Jake.' She began to slice an avocado. 'The band's doing so well.'

He looked up, that smile again. 'We're not playing at all of them ... well, at any of those ...'

'Mum! Switch on.' Ella chipped in, despairing. 'Heavy Feather isn't in that league yet. We're just gonna be hangin' out there, chillin'.'

'Oh.' Beth felt as small as it was possible to be made to feel by one's own child. Of course she should have known. But how? If they didn't tell her, how could she? And when had Ella begun speaking like that?

'Hang on, babe. We've got one gig in Victoria Park. Don't forget that.'

Ella stopped her work, put her arms around Jake and kissed him. 'I know, but Mum won't have heard of it.' She turned to Beth. 'Anyway, so once the exams are over, it's going to be one long party. Can't wait.' She reached up, pulled her hair on to the top of her head with both hands and twisted it, securing it with a wooden skewer.

'But ...' Beth was about to question the wisdom of this plan, given Ella's condition.

'But what?' Ella anticipated her. 'I'll be fine. Jake'll look after me.'

The two of them exchanged a conspiratorial smile that excluded Beth entirely. But she knew better than to pursue her argument. The important thing right now was for them all to enjoy the afternoon. She would talk to Ella later, when they were alone.

She must understand that being pregnant did make a difference, that your life wasn't your own any more.

Where was Amy? She and Hannah ought to be down here helping. Beth went into the hall and shouted up the stairs for her younger daughter. All she could hear was loud canned laughter coming from Amy's room. She tried again. This time the door opened, releasing a torrent of American voices.

'What?' The truculent Amy was back, influenced by Hannah's presence no doubt, showing off. She hung over the banisters. 'What do you want?'

'We need you down here.'

'No you don't. You've got loads of help without us.'

'Amy, please. I don't ask you often.'

'Mum. Chill out. Like we're in the middle of an episode now. We'll come down when it's finished. OK?' The door shut, muting the babble of voices.

No, it wasn't OK. But she didn't want to have a full-scale row in front of the Westons. Not that they hadn't witnessed such rows before. But not this afternoon, when she was doing all she could to convince everyone that bridges were finally being repaired, that they were getting back to some sort of normal. Annoyed, she returned to the kitchen.

'I don't know why you let her speak to you like that,' said Ella, who was concentrating on wrapping the last of the cobs. 'Anything else?'

'Nor do I.' Being criticised by Ella for the way she did or didn't deal with Amy only made Beth feel more inadequate. 'You could start taking things outside for Dad and Pete.'

'Can I help?'

The voice from the door made Beth turn. 'Megan! Hi.' She forced her facial muscles into a smile. Megan flung her arms wide, more expansive than usual. Beth went over to kiss her on both cheeks as if bygones were bygones. She hoped Megan didn't notice the small part of her that held back as she went through the motions. *Try harder*, whispered that little voice inside her. 'Love the dress,' she said. 'That lilac's great on you.'

'Thanks. Love the cardigan.' Her smile was returned.

'Really?' Beth considered the sage-green cashmere that Megan must have seen thousands of times before. Was the unnecessary compliment a sign that Megan was feeling just as awkward and wanted things better between them? Was that a good or a bad thing? Should she be regretting the impulse that had driven her to suggest this get-together?

Jake and Ella exchanged another look, this time one of relief muddied with frustration with their mothers. Beth understood every familiar nuance.

'Well?' said Megan. 'Can I? Help, I mean.'

'You could help me, if you like.' Ella thrust a dish of marinading chicken towards her. 'These need to go outside in a min. Haven't you got a drink?'

'I think I'll wait. What are you two up to?'

'I'm just hearing about their plans for the summer,' Beth said, wondering if Megan was aware that her son was about to drag a heavily pregnant Ella around the country.

'I know. All those festivals. Makes me wish I was young again.'

'Not me,' said Beth firmly, wishing Megan had at least echoed her caution. 'All that mud, and I never want to sleep in another tent again as long as I live.'

'God, do you remember that awful time in Anglesey?' Megan put the dishes down on the side. 'Jake, you must have been twelve then, and Ella, what? About nine?'

'How could we forget? Dad persuaded us that camping was the ideal children's holiday. In the south of France, maybe. But Wales ...'

'It rained so hard we were virtually washed off the campsite.' Jake started laughing.

Beth pulled a face at the memory. Jon had insisted on digging out his old canvas tents instead of investing in something more

185

hi-tech. 'Remember how the sides of the tent snapped in the wind all night, letting water through wherever anyone touched them. And you all insisted on staying up, scared stupid by Jon and Pete's old ghost stories. Then my airbed leaked, so by morning I could feel every stone. Never again.'

'Mum, it was brilliant,' corrected Ella. 'We had a wicked time. Remember cooking breakfast on the fire in the morning. Those massive sausages.'

'It was awful,' Megan corrected her. 'We couldn't find enough dry wood. We had to buy one of those foil barbecue things from the campsite shop and cook three sausages at a time. It took for ever.' She laughed. 'Why on earth didn't we take a Primus stove like everyone else?'

'Because Jon and Pete were convinced their boy-scout training would see us through. That's why we had those dreadful old-fashioned tents. Thank God for the White Swan.' Beth pictured the grey stone building half a mile down the road from the campsite. Spartan inside, but warm and with a sympathetic landlady who took pity on them.

'Remember the steam rising from the kids when they sat by the fire?' Megan shook her head as if unable to credit her memory. 'We put up with one more night in the rain and that was enough.'

'You insisted we stayed in that hotel with the pink bathroom down the corridor,' said Ella. 'Didn't we all squish into two tiny rooms? I remember there were little china ornaments on every ledge. I loved those.'

'Really?' Beth had no memory of them at all. Nor of the bathroom. 'I only remember how cramped we were, with every square inch of floor space covered with mattresses and our clothes hanging over the two small radiators and the end of the bed.'

'And the owner kept telling us to keep quiet or be careful.' Ella reminded her.

'God, yes. And we couldn't go anywhere because all our clothes were soaked and it kept on raining.' Beth grinned despite herself, her point proven. 'We never camped again.'

'Only because you and I put our feet down.' Megan helped herself to a crisp.

'Yes, well it won't be like that this summer. It's not going to rain.' Ella was certain.

Ah, the optimism of youth. Beth could barely remember it.

'What's going on in here?' Pete was at the door, his face shiny with sweat, a smudge of charcoal on his cheek. 'There's no time for slacking. We're almost ready to start cooking.'

One by one they trailed down the garden with everything the cooks needed, balancing it all on the side of the nearest flower bed. As the first piece of chicken went on and the marinade hit the coals, smoke billowed over the garden fence. Their next-door neighbour rushed out to take down her washing. Beth tensed. She would have to apologise. Perhaps she could give her the chocolates she had noticed that someone had left in the hall.

Jake took over drinks duties, and kept everyone's glass full or a bottle of beer in easy reach. He left the barbecuing to Pete and Jon – knowledge born out of long experience. The two men were in their element, with Jon in charge and Pete an obliging sous-chef.

'We need some music,' announced Amy, finally appearing with Hannah. She plugged in the iPod dock and threaded the cable through the window so The Beatles' 'Back in the USSR' belted down the garden at full volume.

'Turn it down, Amy!' Jon had to shout to make himself heard.

'It's The Beatles. You like them,' she yelled back, unable to believe he was objecting to the choice.

'Not this loud.' He marched up the garden and ripped the iPod from its moorings. There was a sudden silence. 'And what about the neighbours?' He handed it to Amy. 'I must have told you a thousand times.'

'Maybe they're out,' she suggested uncertainly.

'They're not. OK?' He turned on the heel of his Birkenstock and returned to his position at the barbecue. More smoke rose as the sausages started splitting and fat fell on to the coals below. The others stared at him, surprised by his outburst.

'He's never happy.' Amy put the iPod on the table. 'Well, now we're here, what do you want us to do?'

'Nice timing,' observed Ella. 'We've nearly done it all.'

'You mean we could have stayed upstairs and watched the next episode? I said there were enough people here.' Amy was outraged. She tucked her arm through Hannah's. 'Let's go.' With her very short pleated skirt, her long white socks and her hair (a rather lank blonde since the pink had been dyed out) in two bunches set high on her head, Hannah looked like jailbait. Why didn't Megan or Pete say something? Beth wondered.

'Hang on.' She stopped them mid getaway. 'You two can lay the table. Everything's in the kitchen. I left it there because I was waiting to see whether we should eat indoors or out.' She looked up at the sky, where the clouds were massing, obliterating the little piece of blue there had been.

'In.'

'Out.'

Her daughters spoke simultaneously. Everyone laughed.

'Let's give Meg the casting vote.' Ella opened her arms towards Megan, inviting her opinion.

Megan made a great song and dance of sucking her finger and holding it into the wind, scratching her head and screwing up her eyes as she deliberated. The children exchanged those despairing looks.

'Come on, darling,' interrupted Pete. 'We can't wait all day.' The smell of barbecuing meat drifted across the garden.

'Oh, honestly!' she objected with a smile. 'OK. I say outside.'

Glancing upwards to question the wisdom of this decision, Beth nonetheless led their two youngest indoors to press the knives and forks into Amy's hands and the napkins and bread into Hannah's. 'Thanks, girls.'

They did the job if not exactly with grace, not entirely without it either. They still needed those Brownie points. Megan helped with the plates and glasses, asking Beth about the garden and admiring the new bed that she'd planted the previous year, wondering if she'd like some cuttings. Nothing controversial, nothing personal. Beth smiled as she put the dressing on the salad, answering her questions quite equably. Perhaps they would get through this.

18

'Who's taken the plate?' Pete turned from the barbecue, brandishing a sausage in the tongs. 'Jock!' he roared, grabbing everyone's attention, including the dog's.

Jock lay on the grass behind the raised bed on which the plate had been perched. Around him were the remains of the sausages. He was inching forward on his stomach, making quick work of what was left. He froze at the shout, then his nose shot out to snaffle another. Pete advanced on him with a yell. The dog looked up at the sausage in the tongs, ever hopeful.

'Oh, don't be angry with him,' pleaded Amy, running forward to protect Jock by flinging her arms around him. His tail wagged as he gave her face an appreciative lick. 'Pooh, you stink of sausage.' She laughed as she pushed his head away.

'No wonder you're fat.' Pete addressed the dog as he crossed the grass and picked up the couple of sausages that were left.

'No he's not,' protested Amy, scratching Jock's chin.

'Ahem! Pot, kettle,' observed Megan. The others smiled.

Pete's jokes about his own weight were one thing. Those from anyone else hit a sensitive spot, judging by the dark look he gave his wife as he returned to the task in hand. 'You can have these later, Jock. Maybe. As for the last three ...' he waved in the direction of the barbecue, 'they've now got a rarity value beyond compare. Who wants one?' Recovering his *amour propre*, he pulled in his stomach as far as he could. 'Me, fat? Huh!'

'Sorry,' called Megan. 'But you did ask for it.'

'Don't say any more.' Pete returned to his post. 'I *have* lost a couple of pounds. Doctor's orders.'

'Drop it, Mum,' advised Jake, giving that look again to Ella, who returned it with a sympathetic smile. Parents!

Beth's hackles rose. She picked up her glass. Time to help Jon get the food on plates and to the table.

Megan inclined her head towards Jake and zipped her lips with a hand. She walked beside Beth down the path and picked up one of the serving dishes.

'Let me,' Beth said, reaching out to take it. This was her job.

'No, really,' Megan insisted, stepping in front of her. 'You sit down. I'm happy here.' She began to help Pete transfer the meat on to the serving dishes.

Beth was stopped in her tracks. Unless she made a ridiculous and unnecessary scene, she had no choice but to return to the table. As she did so, she wrestled with herself. She must stop letting everything get to her. They were here to have a good time. Old friends, together. She sat down. A single raindrop landed on a festive paper napkin. She looked up as another fell on her cheek.

'Careful, you two,' she called to Amy and Hannah who were playing ball with Jock. She could foresee broken windows, spilled food, barbecued ball.

Amy ignored her and threw the ball again. Hannah hesitated, looked at Beth, then threw it back. Jock barked sharply as he rushed back and forth between the two girls, twirling in circles, jumping up at the ball, nipping at their hands.

Jon was giving a running commentary on the art of barbecuing to anyone who would listen. They had all heard it many times before, but no one appeared to mind – apart from Beth whose irritation levels were rising. He was quite happy turning the chicken, examining the corn and halloumi. 'Nearly there.'

'Beer, Dad?' Jake offered, picking up a Becks from the table. Ella disentangled herself from him as he rose to his feet. Beth wished she would be a little less demonstrative in front of them. She wasn't used to seeing her daughter so loved up. But better say nothing. She bottled herself up again.

'Don't worry. You stay there. I'll come and get it,' Pete replied, leaving his post to Megan.

Hannah threw the ball and Jock dashed after it, darting between Pete's legs, unbalancing him. As Beth watched, time slowed. Pete lifted his left foot. For a moment, he was absolutely still, poised on one leg, then he crashed to the ground.

Jon was first beside him. 'Are you all right?'

Pete turned himself round and sat up. 'Oof. Winded.' The knees of his corduroys and his palms were stained with grass. He winced as he rubbed his hands together, running one over his left arm. 'Bit of a sore wrist, nothing major.' He let Jon help him to his feet, and gave an embarrassed laugh as he brushed back what was left of his hair. 'Bloody dog. He's a menace.'

'I'm sorry. We should have left him inside where he can't do any harm.' Jon grabbed Jock by the collar.

'You can't have forgotten how he ate that birthday cake Beth made you?' Pete said.

'I'd forgotten. He wouldn't do that now.' That was a much younger, more athletic Jock who'd leaped on to a chair to snaffle the cake that had been left on the kitchen table while Beth organised someone to turn off the lights.

'If you say so.' Pete looked doubtful.

'Amy!' Beth beckoned her over. 'Would you take Jock? Come and sit down, Pete. We can do the rest.'

With Pete back on his feet, everyone returned to what they doing. Jake gave his father his beer, patting him on the shoulder. 'All right, Dad?' Then he sat back on the garden bench beside Ella, his hand on her thigh, squeezing up together to make room for Pete.

Pete nodded his thanks and sat down with a grunt.

'Where are the tongs?' shouted Jon. 'Someone's moved them.'

Jake picked them up from the grass and took them over, averting what looked about to be a major panic. Jon could get surprisingly touchy if the barbecuing, at which he deemed himself so expert, looked in danger of going wrong.

'These are all that were spared.' Megan brought over the plate of three sausages to put on the table. 'Are you really OK? That was quite a fall.'

Pete's usual flushed complexion was rinsed of colour but he managed a smile. 'Bit of a boneshaker, but give me a few minutes. Not as young as I was, that's all.'

Amy and Hannah had hotfooted it inside with Jock, before any blame could be laid on them. At that moment, the rain began to fall in earnest, slowly at first, but gathering momentum.

'Wrong call,' said Beth a little too loudly, feeling the responsibility for Pete's fall. Her daughter, her dog. 'We should have stayed inside.'

Megan glanced round. 'Something wrong?'

Beth shook her head. 'Nothing at all,' she said through gritted teeth, before going inside for an umbrella, leaving Megan to orchestrate the move indoors. In the hall, she stopped for a second. *What's wrong with you? Breathe deeply. Calm down.* All she wanted was to relax with her family, but even the smallest things were niggling at her: Jon's lecture; her children's behaviour; Megan's over-assiduous efforts to help; the dog. Normally she wouldn't have thought twice, just gone with the flow. But, today, everything was different. *Try harder*, said her inner voice. *Try harder.*

Outside, only Jon was left, hunched over the barbecue turning the sweetcorn packets, the last of the chicken and the halloumi. He straightened up to take a swig of his beer and look at the sky. Above them the clouds were thunderous. The others had taken everything indoors. Megan stood by the French windows, staring out. She signalled something. Beth ignored her, opened the umbrella, the largest she had been able to find, and went out to shelter her husband and the barbecue as best she could.

'They look ready,' she suggested as the rain fell more heavily, splashing off the umbrella and pinging on the lid of the barbecue. 'In fact they look a bit overdone.'

'No they don't.' He turned them again.

She was surprised by his sharpness. 'What's wrong?'

'With me?' He didn't look at her. 'Nothing at all. I could ask you the same thing.'

'What do you mean?' But she knew the answer.

'You're like a cat on hot bricks.' He wiped a hand on the leg of his shorts, smearing them with charcoal. 'Relax, for God's sake. You're making everyone jumpy.'

'I *am* relaxed,' she objected, clenching her fists, feeling the nails dig into her palms. 'You've been out here all the time. You don't know. You're just worked up because it's raining. You always do this if things don't go to plan.'

He gave her a disbelieving glance. 'That's rich coming from you.' He picked up the tongs. 'Everything's difficult enough without you making it worse. And what happened to the kebabs? I thought we were—'

'I thought we had enough without,' Beth interrupted him.

'Pity now that Jock's wolfed the sausages.'

In the old days they would have laughed, but now rage fizzed up inside her. She kept a cork on it as she passed him the serving plate, catching him hard on the side of his wrist.

'Careful!' He rubbed his arm before snatching the plate from her hand.

As he bent to load it up, the set of his shoulders betrayed his exasperation. And she was trying so hard. If only he realised how hard.

'Sorry,' she apologised. 'Accident.'

He clanked the lid of the barbecue back into place and they hurried through the rain towards the house, not speaking.

In the dining room, Ella had dug out a gingham tablecloth and matching napkins. Amy and Hannah had spread the cutlery and plates around. Jake was fetching the drinks from the kitchen, making sure everyone had what they wanted, while Pete sat at the head of the table, holding out his glass for something to wash down the paracetamol someone had given him. 'Drink and drugs should do it,' he pronounced and swigged them back.

'I hope there's enough,' said Megan, cutting the sausages in half before offering them around.

Was that a criticism? Beth stiffened, but said nothing and let Jake pour her a large glass of red wine. The kids were chatting about *Girls*, oblivious to the undertow of tension in the room.

Ella was next to her, sawing through a charred piece of chicken. Beth glanced at Jon to see if he had noticed, but he was concentrating on the sweetcorn, wrapping them back up in their foil. 'They're not done,' he pronounced. 'I'll have to stick them in the oven.'

'Dad?' Ella passed her plate to Megan, who shook her head as she poked at the chicken with a fork.

'Something wrong?' He banged down the tray of sweetcorn on the side table. Megan and Beth looked up at once.

'The chicken's burnt on the outside and raw in the middle.' Ella held up a bit on her fork to show him. 'We can't eat this.'

'Nonsense.' He walked around the table and took the fork from her hand. 'It can't be. I've done this hundreds of times.'

'Not for at least a year, though.' Beth realised too late that her contribution was less than helpful.

'Let's send out for pizzas,' suggested Amy.

'Yay,' muttered Hannah.

Jon glared at her. 'We'll do nothing of the sort.' He sat down and started to dissect his own chicken. He grunted. 'How can that have happened?'

'Ella's right,' said Megan, putting down her knife and fork. 'Mine's the same.'

'I'll put them back on the barbecue,' he said, standing up.

'That won't help,' offered Pete. 'If the inside's cooked, the outside will be charcoal.'

'It is now,' said Amy.

Beth went into the hall for paper and pencil. 'I think you'd better give me your orders.' What a pain.

The wait for the pizza delivery seemed interminable. Beth piled the unsalvageable chicken on to a plate and put it in the kitchen as the others picked over the food that was left. When she returned, she tried to smooth things over with small talk fuelled with more wine. 'What are you up to, Hannah?' she asked, taking a swig, waiting for the alcohol to level her out, smooth her nerves. 'Lots of revision, I bet. Salad while we wait?'

She heard Amy's embarrassed 'Mum' under her breath, saw Ella's glance at Jake.

But Hannah didn't seem to mind being asked. She smiled brightly as she helped herself. 'I've done loads—'

'Really?' interrupted Megan incredulously. 'Have you?'

'Er, yes, I have actually.' At least Hannah kept her scorn in reserve for her own parents. 'Anyway, you were the one who said I should revise in small chunks and give myself rewards when I hit my targets.'

'Not that small,' said Megan, removing a piece of onion from her salad.

'What sort of rewards?' asked Beth. In the past, she and Megan had often traded tips for conning their children into getting them to do what they wanted.

'Well, on Saturday we're going to the Jo Cooper gig … in … Hackney …' Her sentence tailed off as she became aware that Amy's eyes were popping as if willing her to look in her direction. Several desperate shakes of the head told her to stop talking before it was too late. Jo Cooper made regular headlines with his heavy drinking, his serious drug habit and his high-profile girlfriends, and was often front-page news as he entered and exited court, up on one charge or another. He was the current bad boy of rock. Even Beth had heard of him.

'Really?' asked Beth, pretending she hadn't noticed a thing, but storing up the information for use later. 'What about you, Jake? Got any more gigs lined up?' She raised her glass again. Jon had chosen the wine well.

'Gigs!' Ella raised her eyebrows at her mother's use of the word.

But Jake studied his plate. 'One or two since Germany. We're writing some new songs, though. But I've just started work in a photographic studio.' Ella clasped his hand and squeezed it in support.

'He's pretty good with a camera,' Pete cut in. 'Got a good eye.'

'I'm not taking the photos, Dad. Just assisting. You know,' he replied to Beth's interested expression. 'I help set up the shots, using the light meter to get the light right, all that sort of stuff.'

'That might make a good alternative career,' she said brightly, tactlessly. She took another drink.

An uneasy hush fell. At last, Ella spoke. 'Jake's a musician, Mum. That's what he does.'

'Of course. I didn't mean ...'

'It doesn't matter,' said Jake. 'I'm not an idiot. I know people think we might not make it.'

'Yes you will.' Ella supported him, echoed by Amy and Hannah.

'Have you even heard his music?' asked Amy, not waiting for Beth's answer, confident what it would be. 'It rocks. It really does.'

'Actually I have,' said Beth, aware that she was about to dig herself in deeper. 'And I, er ...' She willed someone to help get her out.

'Well it's not really aimed at us, is it?' said Megan, giving her the first pull upwards.

'Exactly. I'd be worried if you liked it.' Jake gave her another.

Ella grinned at him while Amy and Hannah nodded their agreement.

The doorbell rang.

'The pizza,' said Jon, tearing himself from the half-hearted conversation about Cambodia he was having with Pete at the end of the table. His interest was tempered by the fact that he clearly still blamed himself for having messed up lunch.

As he took delivery and returned with a pile of boxes that he proceeded to decant on to plates, the talk of Pete's recent trip expanded to include the others. He was telling them about his two guides, who had both been sent to children's camps while their families were divided and destroyed under the Pol Pot regime. 'One of them never saw his father and oldest brother and sister again. He was only six when he was sent to the camp and forced to work in the fields. Can you imagine what that must have been like for a small child? You lot have had it so bloody easy.' Apart from visits to the Killing Fields, Angkor Wat and the surrounding temples, his other stories mostly involved falling in and out of the Foreign Correspondents' Clubs in Phnom Penh and Siem Reap and who he met there. 'So bloody hot, we had to take full advantage of Happy Hour.'

'Cheer up, Jono,' he added. 'This isn't like you. It's Saturday, the Gunners are going to win. We've got food and drink. All's well with the world. This pizza looks good.' He poured drinks for those who wanted them, ignoring Jon's black look.

'Anyone for ice cream and meringues?' asked Beth at last. She had bought raspberry meringues on impulse when she passed one of the new bakeries that had opened on Upper Street.

Megan's hand flew to her mouth. 'Oh, but I made a pudding. It's only a chocolate hazelnut cheesecake. I left it in the car. Shall I get it?'

Beth looked at her. *Only.* 'We don't really need—' she began.

'Why not?' Jon spoke over her, lifting his glass. 'We've had the pizza, we might as well have a bit of everything.'

'But I didn't expect…'

His look silenced her. She poured herself another glass, aware that he was watching. She should take it easy. But by now, she wasn't drinking to enjoy. She was drinking to get through. And so, by the look of it, was he.

While Megan went to get the cheesecake, Jon turned the conversation to summer holidays. 'Yesterday, one of the guys involved in Scents and Sensibility offered me their family villa in the north of Majorca, near Deia. You kids up for that?'

'When is it, Dad?'

Beth could tell immediately that Amy had something else planned.

'End July/August. Someone else has let them down. Of course, Mum and I could always go by ourselves. You don't have to commit now.'

Beth took another sip. Why hadn't he mentioned this earlier? The least he could have done was discuss it with her first. They'd rather put holiday plans on hold with so much going on. She prayed that neither Pete nor Megan would think they were invited. She couldn't cope with that. Not yet.

Jake and Ella exchanged a look that prefaced them extracting themselves from the arrangement.

'The thing is, Dad, I, well, I don't know how to put this. But the thing is, we're going to be at Green Man and Shambala then – Jake's blagged the tickets.'

'Have you really?' asked Amy. 'Lucky. I wanna go.'

'Ah,' said Jon, momentarily taken aback by his daughters' lack of enthusiasm. 'I see. Oh, well.'

'But Lulu,' Beth chose her words carefully, knowing how they might be taken the wrong way. 'Wouldn't you prefer to be in a villa? You'd be so much more comfortable. I'm sure Jake could miss the festivals this year.'

By the look on their faces, anyone would think she had suggested he commit hara-kiri.

199

Ella kissed his cheek. 'No, I wouldn't. I'd rather be with Jake.'

'But he can come too.' Now he's one of the family. But she couldn't bring herself to say it.

'But, we've got the tickets.' Ella's pout had been her weapon of choice throughout her childhood, and she brought it out now.

'You know what, Jake,' Beth persevered. 'I'm really not sure Ella should be going to all these festivals. You'll need to rest, darling.'

'Mum, per-lease. I asked the doctor at my last check-up and she said it would be fine. I mean, Majorca would be great, but just not this time. Perhaps next year – with Bessie.' She put her hand on her stomach.

'Bessie?' said Pete, emerging from his memories of the Far East. 'Not really?'

'Dad!' laughed Jake. 'Of course not. We don't even know whether it's a boy or a girl. We're saving that surprise.'

'I still don't think it's a good idea.' Beth tried again, despite the looks she was getting. Outraged from the kids. Puzzled from Pete. The most pointed was from Jon, the imperceptible shake of his head suggesting they would be better discussing this later. His lack of support disappointed and infuriated her. But what did she expect any more? She topped up her glass.

'I think we're old enough to make up our own minds,' said Ella. 'Don't you, Meg?'

Megan was backing in through the door with both hands full. Jon jumped up to help her.

'About what?' she said, putting two plates in the centre of the table as Amy, at a gesture from Beth, started to help clear away the first course. 'I made these macaroons too. I thought we might like them.'

Cheesecake *and* macaroons. If that wasn't overcompensation, Beth didn't know what was.

'About going to all the festivals,' Ella insisted. 'Mum doesn't think I should.'

'You'll have a great time,' said Megan, as she concentrated on cutting the cheesecake into even slices. 'Might as well make the most of your last couple of months of freedom.'

Ella left the table to get the meringues with *See!* written all over her face. Beth felt frozen with fury. By contradicting her, Megan had undermined her again and succeeded in scuppering what might have been their last family holiday together.

Reaching out for the pile of pudding plates, Megan registered Beth's expression. 'I didn't mean to ...'

'It's fine,' said Beth tightly. 'I'm just worried because she'll be so pregnant by then.'

'Oh. I'm sure it'll be OK,' said Megan, sounding uncertain as she tried to restore the mood. 'If the doctor thinks it's all right. But, of course, it's not up to me.' She passed a plate to Jon, then Pete. 'Are you sure your wrist's all right?'

'Bit swollen. Nothing to worry about.' He brushed aside her concern as he helped himself to a pistachio-green macaroon with his other hand, already forgetting the doctor's advice about his weight. 'She's probably right, Beth. But, if you're worried, talk to the doctor together. Anyway, when the time comes, you may feel differently.'

Jon looked grateful for Pete's intervention. 'Quite. Let's just see how things pan out.'

Feeling thoroughly ganged up against, frightened of what she might say if she spoke again, Beth excused herself to make coffee. Alone in the kitchen, she went to the French window and placed her forehead on the cool glass, watching the rain trickle down the other side. The afternoon would soon be over. She had failed to make things better. The atmosphere in the dining room was unbearable. These sorts of nit-picking disagreements would become a regular thing between the families, now inextricably tied together. Two warring grandmothers making life impossible for everyone.

'What *is* the matter with you?' Jon came in and began

rummaging in the drawer for more pudding spoons and forks. The hostility rose from him in waves.

'You asked me before, and I told you. Nothing. I'm just not keen on the idea of Ella cavorting all over the country in the back of Jake's van when she's heavily pregnant.' Why couldn't he understand that? Why wasn't he supporting her?

'You're ruining the afternoon. Can't you at least try to be pleasant?' He slammed shut the drawer.

'I'm doing my best.' Beth crossed the room to fill the kettle, but turned the water full on so it splashed out over the worktop.

The two of them faced each other. She had never seen him look so strained. His weekend pepper-and-salt stubble stood out against the pallor of his skin; his clear blue eyes had assumed a hardness she didn't recognise. What was familiar was a certain sadness that she saw in her own eyes when she looked in the mirror. What had happened to them? She moved towards him, but he held up a hand, preventing her from getting too close. 'Well it's a bloody poor best. They're our oldest, closest friends and you're being unbelievably rude to them.'

'It's not my fault you didn't cook the meat properly. Don't take it out on me.' Beth turned from him to get out the blue and white coffee mugs.

'I'm not talking about the food. I'm talking about you. Get off your bloody high horse and get over yourself. You're the one who's the problem here – not Ella, not Jake and certainly not Megan.'

'How can you say that? Have you any idea …' Her hand was shaking too much for her to spoon the coffee into the cafetière.

'I think I've got a pretty good one, actually.' He was at the door, about to leave the room, when he had second thoughts and turned to her. 'Why do you have to be so controlling?' His brow furrowed in puzzlement. 'Why can't you just let go? This is so selfish.'

Controlling! Jon never spoke to her like this. *Selfish!* She was thinking only of Ella. Ella and her future. Something he didn't seem to consider.

'What do you mean, controlling?' she hissed, aware of the others in the next room. 'I'm doing everything I can to make things better.'

'No you're not. You're making things impossible. If it was just about Megan, I could put up with it. But it's Ella, too.' He put the spoons and forks down on the side with a clatter, shaking his head. 'I feel as if I don't know you any more. No wonder she turned to Megan when she was in trouble. I don't blame her.' He paused, leaving Beth reeling. But he hadn't finished. 'It's not your life, Beth. It's hers. Ella's. Our daughter.' He was talking to her as if she was a recalcitrant two-year-old, spelling out his meaning. He wasn't even going to try to understand ...

Her pent-up resentment and frustration raced to the surface and an overwhelming urge to hit him, to hurt him, to make him react possessed her. Unaware of anything except her blind rage, she barely heard her own words. 'Except for the one thing you seem to have forgotten.' Borne on a red tide of anger, she didn't hear the footsteps coming towards the kitchen door. She barely registered the look on Jon's face, the little colour draining from it. His eyes were wide, his mouth opening as if to say something. But she had heard enough. She was oblivious to everything except the fury that had taken her over. 'Just one small thing.' She emphasised every word.

They stood rooted to the spot. He shook his head as if unable to believe what was happening. His eyes warned her not to go on, his hands lifted in appeal.

But she was carried forward, unable to stop herself. 'She's not your daughter, is she?'

'Beth, please.' He reached out towards her.

'She's never been your daughter and she never will be. But she is mine. So whether I "control" her or not is, in fact, absolutely none of your bloody business.'

As soon as the words had flown from her mouth, Beth's mind cleared. She stared at Jon aghast as he steadied himself against the table. These were the words she had vowed never, ever to say, whatever happened, however hard she was pushed. But too late. There they were – in the open: words that could never be taken back.

They stood motionless as the significance of what had just happened sank in. And at the door, beyond Jon's appalled and shen face, stood Megan and Ella, who had both clearly overheard every word.

19

'What can Beth have meant?' Pete was sprawled in the comfy chair by the fireplace, strong mug of tea and a raspberry macaroon at his side. Megan had made a makeshift sling for his arm out of one of her old Indian scarves.

'No idea.' Megan held her own mug in both hands, its warmth comforting when she felt such turmoil inside. Outside, the rain was still sheeting down. 'She's never said anything to me to suggest that Jon wasn't Ella's father. Nor has he.'

'It can't be true, can it?'

'Why would she say something like that if it weren't? It must be.'

'I thought you knew her better than anyone.' Pete leaned forward to take his mug from the tray that was balanced somewhat precariously on a pile of old magazines on the ottoman. Sorting them out was a long-deferred rainy-day activity. Megan rescued the tray and put it on the floor before switching her gaze to him.

'I thought I did too. But, she's never even hinted … It's weird. If it's true, then she's not the person I thought she was at all. And to come out with it like that. In front of Ella, too.'

'That poor girl,' mused Pete. 'Do you think she'll move back here?'

'No.' Megan could imagine the fallout. 'Don't let's get involved. I've learned my lesson.' She stretched out her legs and sighed. 'Anyway, we should think of Jake. I think he needs some space of his own. He'll be able to support Ella and the baby better if he's got a bit of distance. They're what matters now.'

'Won't Beth need you?'

Megan gave a resigned smile. 'You really don't get it, do you? I was trying so hard this afternoon, but everything I did got under her skin. I know she was trying too, but between us we've made things infinitely worse. It was OK for me to be close to Amy and Ella when it suited her, but not any more.' She sipped her tea as she considered the situation. 'I still can't get my head around the idea that our friendship's over.'

'I don't believe that. We've all got along for so long, that's not going to stop now.'

She heard the anxiety in his voice. Not having Jon around would be like losing a limb for him. She thought for a moment. 'But it's never going to be the same again. How can it be?'

'But, why hasn't Jon ever said anything? To you, if not to me?' Pete rubbed the bridge of his nose, clearly perplexed.

'Because men don't?' Megan suggested, then ignored his 'pah' of objection.

'She never said anything at all to suggest …?' Pete's journalistic instincts were kicking in, his nose already truffling out a story.

'Never. Don't you remember when they told us she was pregnant?'

Pete nodded, grimacing as he moved his injured arm to be more comfortable.

Nearly nineteen years ago, Jake had been a testing two-and-a-half-year-old, going through a bad sleeping phase, unable to settle when he went up. Normally Megan didn't bother about him, knowing he'd drop off in the end, but with Jon and Beth coming round, she wanted him out of the way. The doorbell rang just after she'd come down from putting him back to bed for the umpteenth time. She had been nowhere near ready, not even changed, not a dash of make-up, the first course only half made. But none of that mattered when she saw their beaming faces as she opened the door. Jon was holding out a bottle of champagne, his face split by a ridiculous grin. She guessed immediately.

'You're not?' she had shrieked as they all hugged. Pete and Jake came bundling down the stairs to see what the fuss was about.

Beth nodded, her eyes shining with happiness. 'We are.'

Jon's arm was around her shoulders. 'Yup,' he said. 'We're finally having a baby.'

It wasn't a secret between them that they'd been trying for a couple of years. Jon had confessed to Pete, and then to Megan, his anxiety that he was firing blanks. Beth was convinced that she must be infertile after a teenage abortion. She would never go into any more detail than that. They had resisted IVF, leaving it as the very last resort. Or so they had claimed. Megan didn't know what to believe any more. In the meantime, Beth tried everything from ovulation kits to going teetotal to acupuncture and every kind of alternative therapy, crank or otherwise, to help her relax. One of those must have worked. Or time. Or so Megan had always assumed.

That evening had gone down in their shared history as one of the happiest, even including the celebrations of the births of Hannah and Amy, who had been born two days apart two years after the arrival of the very precious Ella. But second babies never merited quite the fuss of a first, and certainly not when the first had been as special and long-awaited as this one. That night, Beth had been radiant, Jon over the moon, Megan and Pete thrilled to see their best friends made so happy.

Had there been any signs that that Jon wasn't Ella's father? Not that Megan could remember. Pete used to joke about Jon's enthusiasm for those NCT antenatal classes that he himself had found numerous excuses to skip. He had almost missed Jake's birth altogether thanks to a delayed plane, whereas Jon and Beth had shared every moment of Ella's. When he eventually tore himself away from the hospital, Jon had come straight over to share the experience with Pete and Megan. Who else? She smiled, remembering how he wouldn't shut up. Going on and on as if they were the first couple ever to go through the miracle of birth.

Since then, he had been … well, Ella's dad. No more, no less. No child could have wished for better. As Beth's career stepped up a gear and she became a partner in the firm, Jon had deliberately trimmed his professional sails so that he could be at home when needed, waiting until the girls were more independent before he expanded his portfolio. Of course, they'd needed a succession of various kinds of childcare, coming to rely on Megan as a backstop during the holidays, but Jon was a devoted father to both his daughters. He had never shown any kind of favouritism. Nothing. A perfect dad.

Megan looked across at Pete: not such a bad one himself. He was trying to wiggle the fingers on his left hand, his face screwed up against the pain.

'Are you really OK?' she asked, leaning over. 'Why don't you let me take a look?'

Gingerly Pete withdrew his arm from the sling. 'Actually, it's bloody sore.' He rolled up his sleeve to reveal a livid and swollen wrist. 'It didn't hurt much at first, and then, well, it didn't seem so important in the light of everything else.'

That was true. In the stunned silence that had followed Beth's announcement, Megan realised that the best thing she could do to help was to get her family out of there and leave the Standishes alone to deal with this bombshell. She had heard Ella's shocked little cry and had felt her shrink back as Jon took a step towards her, his hand outstretched, but she hadn't stopped to see what happened next. This was a family drama that didn't need her as a bystander.

She had returned to the dining room immediately. 'Come on, Jake, Hannah, Pete. We need to leave. Now.'

Startled, they all stared at her as the sound of Ella's sobbing carried through the house.

'What's happened?' asked Jake urgently. 'Is Ella OK?' He tried to push past his mother, but she just grasped him firmly by the shoulders.

'She's fine. But something's been said that Beth and Jon need to sort out with her now, without us being here. Family business. We should leave them to it.' She waited for a beat as no one moved. 'Really.' She picked up her bag and pulled out the car keys.

'She might need me.' Jake stayed where he was.

'This once, they're better on their own,' Megan reassured him. 'Trust me. Come on. You can phone her later, when the dust has settled.'

'But you can't just go like that.' Amy stood up from the table. 'We've got more *Girls* to watch, haven't we?' she asked Hannah, who nodded half-heartedly, realising her mother was serious. 'What's going on, anyway?'

Pete was on his feet, his good hand on Hannah's shoulder. 'Come on, pet. Do as Mum says. Sorry, Amy.'

From the kitchen, they heard Jon roar, 'We promised, we absolutely promised that we would never, ever mention him again. Never. What were you thinking?'

Beth's answer was inaudible.

For once, Jake and Hannah didn't argue, but allowed themselves to be ushered out without any goodbyes. Jake hung back, anxious, then, seeing Ella wasn't looking for him, hastened out of the house. Amy followed them down the hall, past the kitchen. The closed door didn't block the sound of urgent voices and the occasional sob. As the Westons left, Amy stood on the doorstep looking bewildered. 'What shall I do?' she wailed.

'Go inside, Amy darling,' Megan advised as she got behind the wheel of the car. 'They'll explain. This is family.' She slammed shut her door and they drove off, leaving Amy on the doorstep, looking lost.

No, there hadn't been any time to think about Pete's wrist. Since they'd been home, apart from his agreeing to her suggestion of a sling, they had been far too busy speculating.

'Come on. Finish your tea, then I'll take you to A&E. You

should definitely have that X-rayed. That bloody dog. They never trained it properly. They should have locked it in the house.'

'There's no point taking all this out on the dog. It wasn't Jock's fault.' He was right, of course, but loading her guilt on to something else helped.

As she put her empty mug on the tray, the doorbell rang. They looked at each other. Pete raised an eyebrow.

'Not Ella, I hope. I've had enough for one day.' He took a macaroon.

They heard one of the kids racing downstairs to the door. Unable to resist, Megan went to look. Hannah and Amy were hugging each other on the doorstep. As they separated, Megan could see that although Amy looked shaken, she was toughing it out. She went into the hall and hugged her. 'Are you OK?' Stupid question.

'Mmm. Like ... well ...' She looked confused. 'Dad explained that he's not Ella's real dad.'

Hannah gasped, her eyes like saucers. 'No way?!'

'Mum and Ella are shut in the kitchen, so Dad suggested I came over here for a bit and they're going to talk to me later. Is that cool?'

'Of course,' said Megan. She could hardly turn her away. 'Come in.' She stood back to let the two girls pass her.

Amy hung her black bomber jacket on the bottom curve of the banister. 'It's hard to get your head round. I mean, like, Dad's been our dad ever since day one.'

'And that's what you've got to remember,' said Megan. 'That's not going to change.'

She heard Pete clearing his throat behind her, reminding her not to get too involved. But she had to comfort Amy, who, despite the brave face, was clinging for dear life on to Hannah's hand.

'Yeah,' said Amy. 'But, the thing is ... if Dad's not Ella's dad, then maybe he's not mine either. I mean, he swears he is, but how do I know he's telling the truth now?' She tossed her head so her fringe fell back out of her eyes.

'I don't think they'd lie about that, not after what's just happened,' suggested Megan. 'Besides, you look just like him. Your hair, your nose, the shape of your eyes.'

'Everybody says that, so it must be true. But then I was thinking … if he isn't, then someone else must be.' She perked up a little. 'I mean, I could be the daughter of a prince, a famous film star, a millionaire – anyone.'

'Well you could be, but I don't think it's terribly likely.' Megan couldn't help laughing.

'It might be Paul McCartney,' said Hannah, warming to the theme. 'Didn't your mum meet him once? Or George Clooney! Did she ever meet him?'

Megan gave her a look.

'Or even Prince Charles,' suggested Amy, topping them all.

'Imagine! That's so gross.' Hannah made a disgusted face at the thought of her friend's mother shagging the heir to the throne, and the two girls burst out laughing while Megan tried to keep a straight face.

'How's Ella? Is she OK? Shall I go round?' interrupted Jake, who had come halfway down the stairs, and was leaning over the bend in the banister.

'Really upset,' said Amy. 'They wanted me out of the way, so I don't suppose they'll welcome you.' She pulled the box set of *Girls* out of her bag and handed it to Hannah. 'You left this behind.'

'Poor Ella,' said Megan. 'What a bombshell. This'll be so hard for her.'

'But she should take the positives from it.' Amy looked at Megan in all seriousness, pulling down her dress so it covered the tops of her thighs. 'I mean, like, Dad's OK, but her real one might be better.'

'I don't suppose it's very easy for her to see it like that at the moment.' Megan tried to make Amy understand the gravity of the situation. 'Try and imagine. One of the things she's always believed about her life has been removed. Who her dad is is a part of who *she* is. Do you see?'

Amy looked thoughtful. But her solipsistic view of the world would not allow her to involve herself so deeply in someone else's life, or not for too long.

Pete coughed again. 'Shouldn't we be going?' he called. In other words, you're getting in way too deep. Back off. Leave the girls to it.

'Yes, we should.' Megan was grateful for his interruption. 'I'm just taking Dad to A&E. I think he might have broken his wrist.'

'Really?' Amy stared at the Indian scarf as Pete emerged into the hall. 'What? From tripping over Jock?'

'God, Dad. You poor thing. Does it hurt?' Hannah hesitated. 'You actually *are* my dad, aren't you?' She nudged Amy, who giggled.

Pete grimaced. 'Certainly am. Think I'd have stuck around this long if I wasn't? Help me do up my cardigan, there's a good daughter.'

'Dad! That's so rude.' But she helped him all the same.

Half an hour later, Pete had been admitted to a reasonably quiet A&E and they were waiting for him to be seen. Megan couldn't help noticing that half the people waiting didn't look as if they were in need of emergency treatment. The worried well of north London. One woman was bent double over a sick bowl, her anxious husband stroking her back and looking around for a nurse. A drunk with blood trickling down the side of his face wove through the rows of seats, telling anyone who would listen how a friend had bottled him in a pub. 'A friend, I'm tellin' ya,' he kept repeating. 'Well he's no friend of mine no more.'

'I don't blame him,' muttered Pete, his patience waning. 'I'd have done the same thing given half a chance.'

Megan tried to take his mind off their surroundings and the sticky discomfort of the black plastic seats. 'Do you think Jon will call?' She looked away from the over-bright notices giving helpline numbers for the suicidal or the alcoholic, or advice on hygiene.

'I should bloody hope so after all this.'

There was a clunk as a boy with his arm in a makeshift sling got a can of drink from the vending machine.

'I can't imagine what he must be going through.' Jon's stricken expression was still clear in Megan's mind. 'He's been such a great dad to Ella.' She couldn't help voicing the question they had both been avoiding. 'But if he's not her father, then who is?'

Pete gave a slight shrug. 'God knows. I don't remember Beth being with anyone when they met, do you?'

'She wasn't, as far as I know. She always gave the impression there had been a string of admirers who came and went, but nobody special. She always put her work first.'

'You don't need long-term to get pregnant. Jake and Ella could tell you that.'

'I know, but we were caught up in their whirlwind as much as they were. Remember?' But, since then, she and Beth had had years during which they'd discussed every aspect of their lives. Or so Megan had thought. What else was there to do while they sat at the side of a playground, watched swimming galas and sports days, did the washing-up in one of the various cottages they'd shared on holiday? How had they missed this? They'd had plenty of opportunity. Now she thought about it, though, Beth had always been quite circumspect about her love life before Jon.

Before they could discuss it any further, Pete's name was called. Megan stood to support him, linking her arm through his uninjured one so she could shepherd him down the corridor behind the nurse.

*

Two hours later, they were on their way home with Pete's wrist manipulated, set and temporarily bandaged. An appointment for the fracture clinic had been made for two days later, when it would be checked and plastered. She could tell he was feeling better: the colour was returning to his face and he had started worrying about the trip he was taking on the Scottish Far North Line later in the week, complaining about the nuisance of having a wrist in plaster.

'It won't stop you raising the odd dram or two, I'm sure,' she countered.

Despite the lateness of the hour, lights were blazing from every window of the house when they pulled up outside.

'Well, at least the burglars know someone's in,' grumbled Pete as he clambered out of the car. 'How many times do I have to remind them who pays the bills?'

As soon as they were through the front door, Jake and Hannah came to see how he was.

'Where's Amy?' asked Megan.

'Jon came to collect her,' said Jake. 'He said he was hoping to see you.'

'How was he?' Megan wished she had been there. If nothing else, she could have listened to him as she had in the past.

'Fine. Looked a bit rough, I guess.'

'What else did he say?' Why were the men in her family so reticent when it came to the important details?

'Nothing much. Just came in and said Beth wanted Amy to come home.'

'Have you heard from Ella?'

Pete coughed a warning, but she couldn't turn off her concern just like that.

Jake followed them into the sitting room, where Pete was struggling with the top of a whisky bottle. 'Do you think you should, Dad?'

'For Christ's sake,' Pete roared, frustrated at not being able to open it one-handed. 'Isn't a man with a broken wrist who's been hanging around the hospital all night entitled to a soothing glass of something when he gets home?'

'All right, all right. Chill out.' Jake took the bottle, poured him a couple of fingers and passed it to him.

'Thank you.' Pete collapsed back in the armchair, exhausted.

'Well?' pressed Megan, refusing a drink with a shake of her head. As she sat down, she realised how tired she was. Diva sprang into her lap, purring like a traction engine as she circled before settling herself.

'What do you think? She's devastated. But she's strong, too.' Jake pulled at the fingers of his left hand so that they clicked one after the other. Megan flinched, but didn't comment. 'She wants to meet him.'

'Not the father?' She was shocked. Poor Jon.

'Not *the* father, *her* father,' Jake corrected her. 'She has a right, don't you think?'

'Did you suggest she should?' She had a horrible feeling that, yet again, a Weston was too embroiled in Standish family matters for their own good.

He looked sheepish, crossing his arms across the logo of his T-shirt. 'Well, we talked. I don't see how you could disagree.'

'Did you think about the ramifications that might have?' Megan said softly. 'Did you think about how insisting on seeing him might affect Beth and Jon, their family?' How could he be so thoughtless with his advice?

'Yeah, well. They should have thought about that themselves.' His look said the subject was closed.

Megan was too tired to argue. Too tired even to ask if he knew who the father was. More than anything, she wanted to phone Beth to offer her a shoulder to lean on. But she wasn't going to risk being rebuffed again.

20

Beth would have given anything in the world to take back what she had said. Instead, her words ricocheted around the room, bouncing between her and Jon, and Ella: the one person in the world who should never have heard them.

Nineteen years ago, she and Jon had agreed that no one need ever know the truth of Ella's conception but them. All they had wanted was a family – at almost any cost. For two years they had dealt with a switchback of soaring hope when they thought Beth might be pregnant and disappointment when she was not, the highs and lows intensifying with time. She blamed herself: the abortion. When they were at last presented with this unexpected chance at happiness, unconventional as it was, they had surprised even themselves by grabbing it. They buried the secret of Ella's natural father between them, believing that what Ella didn't know wouldn't hurt her, that they could keep it secret for ever. The trust they had shared, strong and unbroken, was a measure of their good marriage. Then, in one stupid, unguarded, angry moment, fuelled by drink, Beth had lobbed this ticking bomb into their midst.

'Beth!' Jon's expression belonged to a man losing his grip on a cliff face with thousands of feet of empty space beneath him. He turned towards Ella, his hand out, but she backed away from him.

Beth couldn't move. She couldn't speak. Her arms were dead weights at her sides, her feet too heavy to lift. There was a rushing in her ears, a sense of being swept away beneath the surface of something with no way back. She had to reach out, save herself. At the same time, she knew exactly what she had just done. The box was open now. Nothing she could do would stop its contents getting out. Her control over them was lost and only she was to blame for the hurt that would be inflicted on those she loved.

'What the fuck do you mean?' Ella stepped into the room as Megan melted away behind her. 'That he's not my dad? What are you talking about?'

Beth focused on her daughter standing in front of her, arms crossed, face flushed with indignation and disbelief, eyes teary as she looked first at her mother, then her father, then back again.

'Well?'

Looking at Ella, Beth could see her own panic reflected in her face. She had just ripped away one of the foundation stones of her daughter's life without having anything with which to replace it.

On the other side of the room, Jon was coming back to life. Beth longed to go over there and hold him, to undo the pain she had just caused. But a stranger had replaced the man she had loved for more than twenty years, his face dark and unforgiving. Any such move would be unwelcome.

'What the hell have you done?' His voice broke through her thoughts. 'We promised, we absolutely promised that we would never, ever mention him again. Never.'

She could think of nothing that would excuse her.

A huge hiccuping sob burst from Ella. At last, Beth reacted. She reached out to her daughter, taking her in her arms, feeling her body shaking. Behind Ella's back, Jon slammed the door, shutting them in together.

The noise made both women jump. Ella prised herself out of Beth's hug and pulled out a kitchen chair.

'Mum! I asked you what you meant.' She sat down and waited, wiping her eyes.

Jon took another chair. He looked as if his legs would barely support him. He ran his fingers through his hair before putting his head in his hands and letting out a long, despairing sigh.

'Mum!' Ella insisted, her face as unhappy as his.

Eventually, Jon looked up at Beth. His eyes were red-rimmed, glassy. 'I think you'd better tell her everything, don't you?' He turned to Ella. 'But, Lulu, when you've heard what your mother has to say, I want you to remember this. Look at me.' He waited as she turned to face him. 'Right from the very beginning, I've loved you as if you were mine, and as far as I'm concerned you are. Nothing will ever change that.'

'Mum.' This time the urgency had been overtaken by bewilderment. Ella's hand lay on her stomach, moving in small circles, comforting her baby, comforting herself.

Beth's eyes closed as she took a long deep breath. Crossing the kitchen felt like wading through mud, every step an effort.

Jon kicked out a chair for her on the opposite side of the table. She took it. The wine she had drunk earlier had left a sour taste in her mouth. She ran her tongue around her teeth and swallowed, wishing she had a glass of water.

'It's a long story.' She held out her hand to Ella, but her daughter ignored the gesture and kept on stroking her stomach. Round and round.

'We've got plenty of time,' said Ella. 'All night if need be.'

'Your exams.' The irrelevant thought popped into Beth's head from nowhere.

'Nothing tomorrow. And even if I had, this is way more important. Don't you think?' The sarcastic edge to the question cut through Beth.

At this reminder of life outside the kitchen, Jon's head snapped up. 'I think I should see what Amy's doing. I heard the others leave. Perhaps she should be part of this.'

'No,' said Beth immediately. 'I can't tell them together.'

'Why not?' he asked, his eyes hard. 'Amy will have to know sometime.'

'Jon. Please do this one thing for me.' The way he could hardly bear to look at her was tearing her apart. 'Please.'

He waited.

'I need to talk to Ella alone first. That's only fair. If you could just explain to Amy what's going on, then, if she wants me to, I'll tell her the whole story too.' As she spoke, her reason began to return. Perhaps she could make this all right. If she explained clearly, Ella would understand. But Jon? Would he ever forgive her?

He left the room and they heard his heavy tread on the stairs. Beth got up, poured herself a glass of water and put the kettle on to make tea. Ella's eyes didn't leave her as she moved around the room, but neither of them spoke. At last, Beth put the mugs on the table and sat down. Ella leaned on her elbows, rested her chin on her hands and just stared at her as if she was seeing her for the first time, waiting for her to speak.

'This goes back a long way,' Beth began, ignoring the impatient curl to Ella's lip. 'To before you were born, to before I even met Dad. Even if we had agreed to tell you, I'm not sure I could have done, because you might not have understood. Perhaps you won't understand now.'

'Try me,' said Ella, her voice expressionless.

Shivery with nerves, Beth clasped her mug of tea. 'Before I met Dad, I hadn't had any really serious boyfriends. I dated, of course, but I was so wrapped up in my work that I guess I put men second and they could tell, so they didn't hang around. Or I didn't meet the right one. You see, I was so desperate to make a new start in life for myself. I wanted more than anything to get away from home. When my mum married Barry, Dad was long dead. She'd done her best bringing me and Aunt Jen up alone, but money was tight, and she struggled.'

Ella's face said she'd heard this all before. But she hadn't lived in that tiny house that reeked of cigarette smoke and chip fat. She didn't know what it was like to bathe in a tub in the kitchen in lukewarm soapy water that the rest of the family had already used, or to go to an outside toilet where spiders waited to ambush you in the dark. She had no idea what it was like not to have any privacy, to share a bedroom with your sister, to find your only escape route through books that the others sneered at, singling you out as 'odd' at school. Beth wasn't going to try to explain now. Too much else was at stake.

She held her hands up. 'OK, I'll keep it brief, but some of that is relevant and I want you to understand. When Barry turned up in our lives, for Mum it was like the second coming. She worshipped the ground he walked on. And to begin with, Jen and I thought life was going to get better at last.'

Beth paused as she remembered that first Christmas with Barry. They'd had a proper tall Christmas tree, presents for each of them. They were both given quilted nylon dressing gowns: hers pink, Jen's pale green. Beth got a pile of second-hand novels and Jen a set of Rowney watercolours and a sketchpad. They all sat down to the table to have a real Christmas dinner, with a turkey instead of the more usual scrawny chicken and baked potatoes. Cooking was not one of her mother's strong suits. The whole occasion reminded her of something out of Dickens' *Christmas Carol*. Usually they ate with their plates on their laps in front of the Queen's speech, her mother tippling from a bottle of sherry. For the first time since Beth could remember, at least since her dad had died, her mother's smile stayed in place all day. She giggled like a schoolgirl when Barry paid her a compliment, or gave her the gold necklace that must have fallen off the back of a lorry, or carved the turkey, or suggested he stay the night.

'But, in fact, life got worse. They were so wrapped up in each other that there wasn't room for us as well. Barry could do no wrong in her eyes. But when she wasn't watching, he'd tell us we were in the way, that we ought to leave school and start earning. I vowed to get out of there as soon as I could. But it was school that gave me my exit route. Jen left when she was sixteen and got a job at Boots, but I stayed on for my A levels – Barry hated that – and was encouraged by a couple of my teachers to apply for a place at university.'

Remembering was like watching a film about someone else. Although she was describing her own life, at the same time it had nothing to do with her.

'But, what about me?' Ella insisted.

'I'm coming to that.' Beth swallowed, still nervous. 'You know, I was the first in our family to get their A levels, never mind go to university. But I was so determined to get out of there that nothing – absolutely nothing – was going to stop me.'

Ella inclined her head, her face drained, her mouth drawn into a tight straight line, impatient for Beth to get to the point. She turned her mug, making a series of wet circles on the tabletop.

'I studied law, but of course you know that too. After three years at uni I did my professional exams at Guildford, and then I came to London.' The excitement she had felt getting on the train. The terror when she got off at St Pancras and had to find her way to the room she had rented in Peckham, wherever that was. 'I did my articles in London with Taylor Parsons, and that …' she took a mouthful of tea, as she summoned up her courage, 'was where I met Gerry. Your father.'

She had Ella's full attention now. Her mug was still and she was watching Beth like a hawk watches its prey. But all Beth saw was Gerry. She had tried to forget him, but that was impossible when confronted by his likeness every day for the last eighteen years. Not even Jon had been aware of that.

'He was one of the senior lawyers in charge of the articled clerks, but he took me under his wing from my first day. I had been given a pile of matrimonial files and told by the other lawyer looking after us to get on with it, but I hadn't the first idea what I was meant to be doing. Gerry took pity on me and bothered to take time to explain.'

'Or fancied you,' muttered Ella, trailing her finger through the liquid on the table.

'Maybe.' Beth was not going to be deflected now. 'But I learned fast. Lots of the work was dogsbody stuff, but if you got on with it and worked hard on the cases you were given, they entrusted you with more responsibility.'

She remembered long hours of working late into the night reading files, and days punctuated by the most menial of tasks: the photocopier that jammed if you didn't put the paper in exactly right; the impatient queue behind her; the mugs that were always waiting to be washed up; the papers to be filed, the files to be returned to the archive.

'And Gerry?' Ella hesitated over his name.

'Gerry was great. He looked out for me. We'd go for the odd drink after work, or have a sandwich at lunchtime if he was around. He'd give me advice, explain what I didn't understand, discuss the cases he was working on with me so I got to learn the ins and outs of the system.'

But she couldn't bring herself to explain how, from the very first, she'd been drawn to him. He was in his forties, older than her by about twenty years, tall, distinguished, sandy blonde hair, an infectious grin, a dimple on his chin – just like Ella's. He was unlike any of the older men she'd met before. He was interested in what she thought, he shared his enthusiasm for their chosen branch of the law and he made her laugh. She'd known from the beginning that he was spoken for, that every day he commuted to and from his wife and four children, who lived in a big house somewhere on the fringes of London. But she was lonely, living in a poky room in a flat shared with strangers, and responded eagerly to his friendship.

'And of course, I got to know him. He wasn't the love of my life. Your dad's that ...'

'Spare me, please,' muttered Ella. Her finger stopped moving. Beth took care with what she was saying, wanting Ella to understand. 'One day, he gave me a recording of *Carmina Burana*. I'd never heard of it.'

He must have bought it on his way back from court. They had gone for a drink that evening, he suave in his suit, she neat in her new dark dress with its white Peter Pan collar. The wine bar was advertising Beaujolais Nouveau and he had ordered a bottle. He mentioned having been to a concert and had thought she might be interested. She took the gift, understanding as she did that her acceptance was loaded with another significance too. But her cultural education was part of her seduction. Gerry opened her mind, recommending all sorts of books, music, films she didn't know. She lapped them up, hungry to expand her knowledge and develop a critical awareness.

'He taught me how to appreciate so much in life. And yes,' she said to Ella's mistrustful gaze, 'eventually we began an affair, but not for a long time. Nobody knew about it. If they ever suspected, nothing was said. He was married—'

Ella gave a small gasp.

'Yes,' Beth affirmed again. 'And he had children.'

Ella's eyes were wide, her face rapt.

'He was never going to leave them,' Beth went on. She couldn't let herself stop now. 'I knew that. To his credit, he never pretended. And to mine, I never asked him to.'

The boundaries of their relationship had been set out right from their first discreet hotel assignment in Soho. Everything was forgotten as Gerry slowly undressed her, admiring her, touching her, kissing her. He taught her more about the pleasure her body could give and receive than she had ever imagined possible. This was a long way from the clumsy fumblings that had got her pregnant when she was sixteen. Their liaisons had been brief by necessity. At lunchtimes they had to return to work; in the evening, the 10.15 train provided a strict deadline. The subterfuge gave an added frisson to the whole affair. As the years passed, they occasionally got to spend an intensely pleasurable night together, but that was never a prelude to anything more permanent.

'But, how do Dad and me fit into all this? I still don't understand.' Ella's hand was back on her stomach.

'I'm coming to that.' Beth smiled at her, a smile full of regret. Not for her past, but for the fact that she had put them in this position: the storyteller and the listener anxious for the conclusion. But was there ever such a thing as a perfect ending? Not every thread could be knotted off neatly. Life wasn't like that. 'Our affair lasted for about ten years. Yes, a long time. I had other boyfriends too. That was allowed,' she excused herself in the face of Ella's silent disapproval. 'Gerry accepted that our relationship couldn't be exclusively on his terms. I was a young woman, for God's sake.'

She stopped, calming herself down. And I didn't want to be alone, she remembered. I enjoyed the company of men and I enjoyed sex. Gerry had taught me how. But that was not something she needed to go into.

'None of that matters. The arrangement worked for us, and I'll always be thankful for everything he taught me. My life would have been quite different without him.'

'And Dad?' prompted Ella.

'We met in Sainsbury's – a bolt from the blue.' She couldn't help a swift smile at the memory. 'But you know that. I knew immediately that what I felt for him was different to anything I'd felt before and that I had to put a stop to my relationship with Gerry. By then, he had moved to another firm and we were seeing each other much less often. He was pleased for me. We agreed to be friends, to keep in touch, but that was all.' She paused and went to pour them both another cup of tea. 'We'd been too big a part of each other's lives to be able to let go completely.'

She sat down again, staring into the garden, lost in the past, before she went on. 'Dad and I were so happy together, right from the word go. But I was in my early thirties and my biological clock, which hadn't given a single tick till then, suddenly went bananas. I desperately wanted to have a baby. Dad felt the same. More than anything, we wanted to have a family together. Our careers were on track ...'

Ella tutted, understanding an implication about hers where, for once, none had been intended.

'We were ready, and we thought it would be so easy. Megan and Pete had Jake. Other friends were starting their families. But not us. I lost count of the number of times I thought I might be pregnant, then nothing. I can't tell you how disheartening that sense of failure was for us.' Remembering how she and Jon had tried so hard to support each other, tears pricked her eyes. 'Then I met Gerry again. By then, he and his family had moved to York, but he was in London for two nights. He called me. We met and I told him everything.'

Four short sentences that did nothing to convey the overwhelming sense of desperation she was feeling when she went to meet him, or what happened. His hotel in Covent Garden was opulent, panelled and discreetly lit. She walked in, apprehensive, knowing she should not have come. But, seeing him sitting at the bar, nursing a whisky, had been like coming home. His smile told her that nothing had changed. He would listen. He would know what to do. Over a pre-dinner drink, she began to talk. She told him about her abortion and consequent fear of infertility. He wasn't shocked or embarrassed, but just took the story in his stride and encouraged her to keep talking as they moved to their table for dinner. He answered her questions about his work, about his own family, his marriage. She confided in him her hopes and fears for her relationship with Jon: her hopes for its future, her fears that the absence of children might destroy them. He comforted and reassured her. When she started crying, he suggested they had a nightcap in his room. She always believed that what happened next had not been planned by either of them, although somewhere in her subconscious she must have known what might happen when she accepted his invitation. Their old patterns of behaviour had reasserted themselves. Cocooned in the warmth and comfort of the hotel room, the outside world had disappeared and for a brief time they were able to leave their problems outside, focusing on nothing more than each other. Beth barely noticed the move from the comfortable chairs to the emperor-sized bed.

Afterwards, on her way home in a taxi, she had felt a terrible gutting shame. Filled with self-loathing, she had tried to justify her behaviour to herself. But there was no justification. Jon would be destroyed if he ever found out what she had done. She consoled herself with the firm knowledge that she would never make the mistake of seeing Gerry again, and that Jon would never know. She would return to their marriage, and they would keep trying for their baby. Nothing would change.

She looked across the table at her daughter. 'But, nine weeks later, I discovered I was pregnant.'

21

'But how do you know Dad's not my father?' asked Ella, clearly desperately hoping that Jon might still be in the frame. 'How can you be so sure?'

They had come too far for Beth to allow her to think that was a possibility. She owed her the whole truth.

'Because I told him, Lulu. I had to.'

She played with the links of her bracelet as she relived her confession: the one time their marriage had been under serious threat. That night, late in June, Jon had come in from work excited about their holiday plans. They had agreed after much soul-searching that if they couldn't have a baby, they would throw themselves into a life without children. Their first step was to be three weeks trekking in Nepal. He'd heard they could extend their Langtang trek through the Gosainkunda lakes to Helambu, so they would take a different route back to Kathmandu. He looked at her face as she sat slumped in the sitting room. 'What's the matter? I thought you'd be keen on the idea. Don't you want to go any more? I thought we'd agreed?'

'We had, but something's happened.' Her heart felt as if it was battering against her ribs.

He sat opposite her, searching her expression for clues, finding nothing. 'Well?'

'I'm pregnant.'

She would never forget the stunned joy that obliterated his concern at a stroke. For a moment he sat quite still, as if unable to believe what she had just said. Then with one stride he crossed the distance between them and swept her up into a bear hug. 'But that's fantastic news. Are you sure? Oh, my God!' He did a little jig on the spot, then pushed her away so he could look at her. 'You *are* sure?'

She nodded miserably, unable to share his excitement.

'Well then, what's wrong? This is everything we wanted. If it's Nepal, don't worry about that. Nepal will still be there another time.'

That was when she told him about Gerry. Neither would she ever forget how his face changed. Momentary disbelief gave way to hurt that in turn gave way to a terrible anger. But that wasn't part of Ella's story. Beth took a deep breath, hardly daring to look at her daughter, unable to bear her fascinated distaste. 'We agreed that when you were born, we would have a paternity test done.'

'Why? If he was going to pretend I was his, what did it matter?' Pain registered in her eyes.

Glossing over the hellish weeks that followed, during which she believed that Jon would never forgive her, Beth went on, 'It didn't. He just needed to know. I can't explain more than that. But, believe me, he has never mentioned it again. The result made absolutely no difference to his love for you.'

For nine months she had carried Ella, uncertain who her father was. But deep down she had always known. The dates, combined with her and Jon's history of failure in conceiving, were too much to ignore. The knowledge had inevitably diluted her excitement. She had watched Jon constantly, alert to his slightest change in mood, trying to detect what he was thinking, terrified that he would leave her, unable to bear her betrayal and its consequences.

'Why didn't you have an abortion?' Ella's voice was hard with dislike. 'You know, like you tried to make me.'

'Because we wanted you more than anything. You have no idea how wanted and loved you have been.' How would she ever make her understand? How could she, after everything that had happened after Ella announced her own pregnancy.

'More than I love this one?' Ella looked down at her bump.

Beth smiled at her. 'Just the very same, I hope.' She couldn't stop herself from adding, 'But we were older than you, married, with settled careers; our time was running out.'

But the smile was not returned. 'Yes, you said.' The resistant Ella was back. 'And what about Gerry? Where's he?'

This was the question Beth had been dreading. 'I don't know.' She pulled at her wedding ring, twisting it back and forth on her finger.

'You don't know!' Ella's eyes sparked with rage and disbelief. 'How can you not know where he is? Has he ever seen me? What did he say when he did?'

Beth shook her head, unable to speak. She had promised Jon she would never contact Gerry again, and she had been true to that promise.

'What? Never? Wasn't he even curious, this Gerry? My father.' She said the last three words with venom.

The front door slammed.

'He doesn't know.' Beth's whisper was so quiet, she wondered if Ella had even heard. She looked up, her vision blurred with tears.

'You didn't tell him?' Ella's astonishment robbed her of anything more to say.

Beth shook her head. 'No,' she murmured. 'No, I didn't tell him.'

They were staring at each other in silence when Jon came back into the room. 'Amy's gone to Hannah's. I didn't think it was fair for her to be here right now.'

Beth felt stronger with Jon beside her. This part of the story belonged to him too: to the three of them. 'I've never seen him again. I wrote to him saying that I had made a mistake and that I loved Dad and our marriage came first.' She stretched out her hand for Jon, but he stepped out of her reach.

'A mistake?' Ella's outrage was mixed with sadness. 'Is that how you think of me, then?'

'No, of course not.' Jon stood behind her, his hands on her shoulders, supporting her. 'What Mum meant was that she shouldn't have threatened our marriage. In fact her mistake in seeing Gerry gave us exactly what we had been longing for. You.'

'Why did you even tell Dad?' Ella asked, shaking off his grip. 'If you weren't going to have one of the abortions you're so keen on, why didn't you just let him believe I was his?'

Beth shrank in the face of her ferocity, but kept her nerve. 'I had to tell him because I loved him. I couldn't lie to him, not about something so important. If I had, it would have driven us apart in the end.'

The three of them were silent, each lost in their own thoughts, Beth revisiting that ghastly time.

Of course she had considered an abortion. It would have been so easy. Just like the time before. No one would have been any the wiser. But, this time, she wanted a baby. And Jon wanted a baby too. Wasn't even Gerry's baby better than no baby at all? They had both reached a point where they believed they would never conceive one together. This was an unlooked-for chance. Jon had listened as she explained her relationship with Gerry and what had happened. He heard her out and then left the house. He didn't return until the next day, by which time she was beside herself worrying that something might have happened to him. He'd been walking, he told her. He had no real idea where he had been. His furious disbelief at her betrayal had kept him going until dawn broke.

They'd had to decide what to do so quickly. Was it wrong to suggest he bring up another man's child as his own? They only had a few weeks to make the decision and, if they went ahead, agree how to present the pregnancy to the world.

The first weekend after she confessed, Jon had stormed off to his mother in Kent. As well as being a very merry widow who enjoyed her wide circle of friends and local charity work, Elaine remained firmly at the centre of her family, completely involved in her three sons' lives. She loved Beth as she loved her other two daughters-in-law, welcoming them all equally into her nest, making sure none of them felt an outsider. Beth adored her. Elaine was everything her own mother was not.

To this day, Beth had no idea whether Jon had told Elaine the truth about the pregnancy. If he had, it was never discussed or alluded to. Elaine's subsequent treatment of Beth was as warm as it had ever been, and her joy over Ella's birth was unconfined. All Beth knew was that when he returned from that weekend, Jon was a changed man. Instead of the angry, jealous, humiliated husband who had left her in London, he had come back stronger, focused, with his mind made up.

For her, that weekend alone had been hellish as she oscillated between excitement and guilt, happiness and despair. Jon would never ask her to have an abortion, but if the baby was going to present the threat to their marriage that she feared, should she go through with one on her own? If she did, would the knowledge of what she'd done divide them even further? But if she didn't ... what then?

The change in him was visible as he walked into their living room to find her on the sofa, stuffing her tissues under a cushion. But her red eyes and blotchy face were giveaways. He hadn't spoken at first, just sat down beside her and let her cry, until eventually he had broken down too and they sobbed together. He told her how betrayed and angry he felt, how he feared that he might never be able to love the baby as if it was his. They sat up talking all night. At last, he had laid down his conditions and they had made their pact. Gerry would never be mentioned again, or contacted. Ella would be Jon's child, and no one would ever know different.

How confident they had been that that was how it would always be.

'And yet you could lie to me?' Ella's voice was hard, the words tumbling like pebbles into the gap between them.

'But it wasn't a lie,' protested Jon. 'Not in that sense. We never mentioned it again. We didn't need to because we agreed that although I wasn't your father biologically, I would be in every other possible way. And I have been.'

He sat at the other end of the table, desperate for her to believe him. Beth shivered again. All this was her fault. How would she be able to make amends?

'Isn't your biological father the one that matters?' Ella's tone didn't change.

'No!' Jon and Beth spoke at once.

'The father who's there for you every day of your life is the one that matters.' This had always been their fervent belief, the one that had supported them since Jon decided to stay with her.

'But you never gave Gerry a chance. Maybe he would have been.'

'Trust me, he wouldn't.' Beth remembered being shown photos of Gerry on holiday, surrounded by three ash-blonde daughters, his one precious son and his smiling wife. 'He had his own family and he was always quite clear that he was never going to rock that boat. Never. That was the deal. It was better for him not to know. And better for us.'

Ella's brow wrinkled as she considered this. 'And Amy? What about her?'

Amy. Difficult Amy. Of the two of them, she was the one who was most like a cuckoo in the nest. And yet … Beth turned to Jon, letting him speak, remembering their unadulterated joy when she discovered she was pregnant for a second time.

'I am her dad,' he said, quietly.

Ella gave a small 'oh' as Beth took up the story again.

'We didn't think we would have another child. I hadn't been able to get pregnant before you, and nothing happened after. Then, two years later, completely unexpectedly, after a blissful holiday in France with Megan and Pete and Jake – you know those photos – I was pregnant again. And this time there was no doubt who the father was.'

A tear rolled down Ella's cheek.

The photos were mementos of such a happy time. They had stayed in a gîte in the Dordogne: a small French farmhouse with three attic bedrooms that Pete had come across when researching one of his summer travel pieces. A perfect fortnight. She and Jon were as happy as they had ever been, their joy only enhanced by the existence of Ella. The sun had shone on them for the full two weeks, while they spent long lazy days by the pool, reading and playing with Jake and Ella, or leisurely explored the neighbourhood beyond the tiny hamlet. At night, the four of them would sit outside on the terrace, drinking local wine, eating the food that they'd bought at the market, playing backgammon and cards while the children slept upstairs. Not long after they got home, Megan and Beth both announced they were pregnant.

'Well, lucky Amy.' There was no mistaking the bitterness in Ella's voice.

'Don't be like that, Lulu. Please.' Jon reached out and took her arm, stroking her hand. For a second, it looked as if she would snatch it away, but then she decided against.

Beth couldn't bear to look at them: two of the people she loved most in the world, utterly devastated thanks to her thoughtlessness, her lack of control.

Eventually, Ella stood and went to Jon, putting her arms around him. She kissed the top of his head, then pulled up a chair so she could sit beside him. His relief was like watching a light being switched on.

'It's just such a shock. I don't know what to say.'

'I know.' Beth felt so ashamed.

Ella steepled her fingers, then clasped them together. 'I'm just trying to take it all in. Trying to work out what it means. And of course I'm jealous of Amy.' Her voice quavered. 'I want you to be my dad too. Really want you to be.'

'But I am,' Jon insisted again, twisting to look at her.

'I know. I heard you. Really.' She reassured him with a squeeze of her hand. 'I think I'll just go upstairs for a bit. Maybe talk to Jake.'

'Of course,' Jon agreed.

Beth stared down at the table, feeling numb. She longed for Ella to come to her, to put her arms around her and kiss the top of her head. Instead, her daughter walked to the door, turning towards them as she opened it. How young and vulnerable she looked again.

'I suppose I should thank you for telling me at last.' And then she was gone.

Beth breathed out. She felt too shaky to stand. 'I'm so, so sorry. Nothing I say can tell you how terrible I feel. I don't know what happened.'

Jon picked up the empty mugs and put them by the stacked lunch plates on the side. 'Why, Beth? Why? We promised. Doesn't that mean anything to you any more?'

'There's no excuse. None. Will you ever be able to forgive me?'

'I don't know,' he said, finally. 'I don't know what to think. If this means Ella won't have anything to do with me, then no, I don't think I will. I'm going to get Amy. I can't talk to you now.'

She watched him leave the room. Then she was alone with her thoughts. Moving like an automaton, she started filling the dishwasher with everything that had been piled up from lunch. As she completed the familiar routine, she went over what had just happened.

The pregnancy had been a gift. Jon had believed her when she swore she would never see Gerry again. If she did, he would leave her – child or no child – and there would be no going back. Keeping her promise was not hard. Jon was everything she had ever wanted. The moment Ella was born, she had him in the palm of her tiny hand. When they found out she was definitely Gerry's, he said nothing. Beth saw his face close up as his hope was extinguished, but he was already besotted. They never spoke of Gerry again. Jon had been true to his word and had brought Ella up as his. She could ask no more of him.

And Ella. What about her? She was a bright young woman with her head screwed on tight. She had made up her own mind about having Jake's baby, despite the pressure that Beth had heaped on her. She had survived their estrangement, and was almost through her exams – although how she'd done it, Beth found it hard to imagine. She had her mother's determination to get what she wanted from life. Beth had to respect that. Ella would make her own mind up about this, too. Perhaps when she'd had time to think about what both of them had said, she would understand why they had done what they had.

Where was Gerry now? Beth wondered. She had never felt guilty about not telling him about Ella. She knew he would not have wanted things complicated any more than was necessary. Their arrangement had suited both of them, but it had been strictly private. Nothing must ever intrude on his happy home life – that was the deal. He would be retired now. She imagined him portly and balding with his grey-haired and elegant wife, surrounded by blonde children and their partners and children. They would be prosperous; he would be a non-exec director of various boards, play golf perhaps. Life would have turned out exactly as he would have wanted it. That was the privilege of the alpha male.

And what of her? What now? She recalled her mother, her stepfather, everything she had escaped. How hard she had tried to give her children what they deserved, not only materially but emotionally, too. She had worked hard, both because the need for escape through achievement was hard-wired into her, and because she wanted her family to have what she had gone without. Where her own childhood achievements had been greeted by a mystified silence, she made sure when her turn came that she lavished praise when it was due and celebrated every success. She couldn't blame her mother for being beaten down by life, for having her dreams and aspirations knocked out of her. But she could blame her for the lack of love she'd shown to her two daughters.

She rarely saw her family. They inhabited such different worlds, there was barely a bridge between them. Her mother still lived in the same house with Barry, living off his undoubtedly ill-gotten gains, both nervous of the fact that her daughter had something to do with the law. And Beth didn't want to know what went on – another reason to keep her distance. Jen was married with four children of her own and a life that was poles apart from her sister's. Her husband, Derek, was in insurance and spent his weekend washing the car, mowing the grass, doing odd jobs around the house, watching football, having a beer with the lads. Jen looked after the kids and the tatty but tidy home, while he went out to do the hunting and gathering. Neither her mother nor Jen could help Beth now. They simply wouldn't understand.

She finished washing up the larger plates, pulled a tea towel out of a drawer and started to dry them.

But who *would* understand? Who could she talk to? For the first time in over twenty years, Beth had an overwhelming urge for a cigarette. She took a peppermint from the tube she kept in the tea and coffee cupboard. There was no one she could turn to. Jon had his own demons; he didn't need to be burdened with hers too. And Megan … Well, Megan had always been there for her, but not now. Why did she have to be standing at the door with Ella when Beth had snapped? Now the secret was out, and not just with Ella. How would they get through this? *Would* they get through this?

She gave a low groan. She didn't want to talk to anyone else about Gerry, or to have to start justifying her past behaviour. Even if she had wanted to unburden herself, who else was there? She was used to keeping her private life just that. There was no one in the office she would share confidences with – ironic in the light of what had happened with Gerry so long ago. She allowed herself a small smile. She had few close friends. Acquaintances, yes, but close friends, no. Jon had been enough for her, and their friendship with Pete and Megan had reached all the places that her relationship with him and the girls didn't. She hadn't needed more.

She had no idea how much time had passed. She was aware of Jon and Amy returning, heard the murmur of their voices in the hall. But neither of them came in.

Should she go up to Ella? Make sure she was all right? No. Ella was better left alone. She would come down when she was ready to talk. Beth would wait.

Sitting at the kitchen table, she leafed through one of the Sunday colour supplements, taking in nothing as the words and pictures blurred under her eyes. She got up and opened the kitchen door. She recognised an angry Shostakovich cello concerto coming from Jon's room. Upstairs, a door opened and closed.

She returned to her magazine, feeling as if her life had left her. Was this what her mother had felt like when her father died? Despairing and alone? But they were hardly in the same boat. Beth at least looked forward to her job in the morning, whereas her mother had only had her daily drudge on the cigarette production line to face.

Were those footsteps on the stairs? She waited, hoping they were Ella's, hoping she was going to be forgiven. The handle clicked, and the door opened. Ella had changed into her pyjamas and monkey slippers. Her dressing gown hung open. She had swept her hair up into a topknot, which meant that her pinched face and red eyes were plain to see.

'Lulu?' Beth asked, tentative.

'Could we have some hot chocolate in the sitting room?' There was a new strength in Ella's voice. She squatted down to pet Jock, who put his front paws on her knee as she tickled him under his beard. She dodged the lick directed at her cheek.

'Of course. You go through and I'll bring it in.'

Within a few minutes, Beth was carrying in a tray with two mugs of hot chocolate and a plate of shortbread. She remembered how hungry she had been all the time when she was pregnant. They sat together on the sofa, waiting for the drinks to cool down. Ella took a biscuit. Beth watched her turn it in her fingers.

'I've been thinking.' Ella took a bite, then put the biscuit on the edge of the plate. She pulled her dressing gown around her and did up the belt above her bump.

'Yes?' Beth tried not to anticipate what was coming next.

'I want to meet him. Gerry, I mean.' Her eyes fixed on Beth's, not allowing her to look away.

Beth took a deep breath. 'That's really not possible.' This was a can of worms that should not be opened.

'Why not?' Ella's gaze remained on her.

'One, Dad would be terribly upset.' Beth felt flustered under her daughter's scrutiny. 'And two, I've no idea where he is.'

'I've already asked Dad, and he says he doesn't mind.'

'You have?' Of course Jon would mind desperately. He must.

'Yes. I knew you'd say I shouldn't so I thought I'd go ahead before you had a chance.' She patted the sofa and Jock jumped up beside her and settled with his head on her lap.

Beth could picture Jon in his comfy chair, resigned, sad, as Ella made her request. He would do anything to make his girls happy. Always had. He always put his own needs second.

'Jake and I were talking…'

Was Jake already taking over from them as the moral keystone of Ella's life, now she was having his baby? That would take some getting used to.

'… and I need to meet him. I'm not going to do anything stupid. I've thought about all you said and need to think some more. Obviously Dad is my dad. He's the only and the best dad I've ever known. But we're having this baby and I need to know his or her grandfather. And he should know he has a grandchild.'

He probably already had several grandchildren, and Beth was

238

as sure as she could be that he wouldn't want anything to do with this one. It was a complication that the old Gerry would never have countenanced.

'I really think it's better to let things lie,' she said cautiously. 'You don't know what you'd be stirring up. Think of his family.'

'They don't need to know.' Ella was adamant. 'We could meet in a hotel, anywhere. I don't want anything from him. I've survived without him so far. But I do need to see him. Just once.'

'Lulu, you've no idea what that'll do. You don't know him.' But her fear was selfish. Inside her welled a deep terror that any meeting between Gerry and Ella might mark the end of their happy family. Right now, there was still a chance she could salvage things. But she might be wrong about how Gerry would react. The man she knew nineteen years ago might have changed. Then what?

'That's the point, isn't it?' Ella raised her eyebrows as she cocked her head on one side. 'Mum, you can't refuse me this. I'm eighteen, I'm having a baby. I'm making my own life at last. Get real.'

'No, Ella. I'm sorry, but it's out of the question.' She would not let their lives spiral any further out of control.

'It can't be out of the question. You can't tell me about him and then deny me the chance to meet him.'

'I said no.'

'For once, you're not in control of this. He's not your father, he's mine. And I want to meet him.'

'Ella, please. I'm asking you not to do this.' It would take their family one step nearer the precipice.

Ella looked at her with disdain. 'If you won't find him for me, then I'll find him for myself.'

'You won't be able to, and anyway, think of Dad. Please.' Her last attempt at persuasion fell on deaf ears. She hadn't bargained for Ella's tenacity.

'I can, and I will. How hard can it be? You told me he worked at Taylor Parsons. I'll find him on the Internet. There must a register of family lawyers or something. You said he'd moved to York. I'll start there. I've got enough to go on.' She stood up, conversation over, and clicked her fingers. Jock jumped to the floor.

Once Ella started searching, it wouldn't take long. Beth thought quickly. 'All right,' she said. 'I'll do it.' If she took the responsibility, she might at least be able to limit the ensuing damage. Perhaps Gerry would refuse to see her.

When Ella went to bed, Beth stayed downstairs, besieged by thoughts and memories that she once believed had been locked away for good. The past was another country that she had no desire to revisit, however briefly, especially not when it might threaten the happy home and the family she and Jon had worked so hard to build.

When she eventually arrived in the bedroom, Jon was curled on his side in bed, his light off. She could tell by his breathing that he was still awake. She undressed and slid between the chilly sheets to lie beside him. He didn't move. He didn't speak. Beth lay on her back, feeling the warmth from his body but not daring to roll over and touch him, frightened that he would reject her. She couldn't blame him. She stared through the dark towards the ceiling, hearing his shallow breaths, the sharp cry of a fox in the street, feeling nothing but dread. What had she done?

22

Megan looked around her. The cars delivering for the fair had almost all left the playground. Only one remained: Janis Brewer, unloading the piles of new and second-hand children's books she had managed to scrounge for her stall. Down by the play area, smoke was beginning to rise where four fathers had been roped in to manage a massive barbecue for the mountains of home-made hamburgers and hotdogs. Beside them, their wives were setting up a drinks stall: Pimm's (an advance on the usual beer and warm white wine, reflecting the changing demographic in the catchment area) and masses of soft drinks. Down one side wall were ranged the rest of the stalls: clothes, books, used toys, bric-a-brac and home produce. Along the other were the activities: skittles, welly-wanging, face-painting, lucky dip, treasure hunt, tombola and throwing the sponge (Megan had been coerced into taking the 3.30 slot). Over everything fizzed a general air of expectancy as months of planning and preparation came to fruition.

Outside the school gate, the queue was growing. Megan raised her programme to fan herself against the heat, moving to one side as a line of mini-majorettes were led out of the school hall to the lower playground, where they were going to kick off proceedings with a rousing display. They looked adorable in their shiny red and white costumes. Behind them fluttered a flock of proud mothers, still reaching out to tweak a costume, hold a hand, give encouragement. Megan smiled as they went past.

'Good luck, girls. You look fabulous and I know you're all going to be great.'

There was a lot of excited preening as the dance teacher raised her crossed fingers in response.

'Megan! Have you seen Julie Archer? I want to be sure she's got the raffle tickets and one of the money aprons.' Maureen, bursting with her master-of-ceremonies role.

'Last seen over by the bouncy castle.' Megan watched the chief organiser's ample backside swaying off in that direction.

She looked at her watch. Two o'clock. Time. She raised her arm to catch the head's eye. Jane looked up from where she was helping straighten out the clothes stall, folding, arranging and hanging – a fairly pointless exercise, since the whole stall would be reduced to a mountain of indistinguishable garments within moments of the gate opening – and nodded.

'Let battle commence,' she yelled.

The other stallholders looked up and visibly braced themselves, particularly those doughty ladies on the cake stand. Megan could see her own cupcakes stacked on one side beside Maureen's fairy cakes, knowing that underneath the table her six loaves, three cakes and trays of biscuits were waiting to be produced when the first rush had died down. She had been baking every evening that week. She had also made the fruit cake for guess-the-weight. Never let it be said that she didn't do her bit.

She crossed to the gate and inserted the key in the padlock, just as the sound of music rose from the lower playground and the first waft of frying onions and hamburger drifted to where she stood. As the gate opened, she stood back to let an unstoppable tide of people flood the playground. The advance guard – most of them women – made a beeline straight for the cakes or the clothes, determined to bag the best. Behind them came a stream of families with assorted buggies and older children, there for the fun and to support the school.

After fifteen minutes, the atmosphere had relaxed, the cakes had been decimated, the best items of clothing had gone. This was the time Megan liked most, when the playground was full, but not frantic, and people had begun to enjoy themselves. She stopped at the sweet stall and treated herself to a small bag – in a good cause, after all.

'Can you help Susie on the craft stall, miss? Keith's had to go home to let his daughter in. He says he'll be back in half an hour.'

Unable to answer thanks to the wodge of treacle toffee that was gluing together her upper and lower teeth, Megan nodded and mmmm'd her agreement. This was where she was in her element. She loved getting down and dirty with the kids. Give her paper, a tube of glue, a few crayons and some glitter and sticky shapes and she was happy. Better than that, she could make the kids happy too. Witness her success in the summer holidays at ArtOfficial with Ella.

She looked up, half expecting to see Beth, Ella and Amy crossing the tarmac. They had come to the summer fair out of loyalty every year since the girls had been pupils here. But, of course, they weren't to be seen. What was she thinking? They wouldn't want to support her now. As she helped glue some finger puppets together, she thought of the baby, her grandchild. The word produced a glow of excitement. Would he or she be a pupil here too? How wonderful would it be having her own grandchild in the school. She imagined walking a little girl into the reception class with Ella, helping her settle in, keeping an eye on her in the playground, just as she had with Hannah. But perhaps Ella would have a boy . . .

'Miss! What are you doing?' The little girl beside her tapped her on the hand.

She let go of her daydream and focused on her task, to see that she was sticking together puppets that had yet to be coloured in. 'Well spotted, Sophie. Let's see if we can unstick them now, then you can colour them.'

'Looks like you need a hand with that.' The voice was familiar,

243

with its inflection at the end of the sentence. But it couldn't be. She looked up. It was. Ella was standing beside her, more pregnant than when Megan had last seen her, her skin radiant. She had never looked more pretty.

'You're here! How are you?' They had brushed past each other once or twice as Ella made her way to Jake's room, but had barely spoken properly.

'Fine, thanks … I don't know how, but, well …' She shrugged her shoulders. 'You know.'

Megan wasn't sure she did. She took Ella's hand. 'I didn't think you'd come.'

'Of course we came. Amy's over at the bottle stall with Hannah.' Ella took a chair and sat down. 'Look at this queue, already. Now, what about this mask?' She turned to the small boy next in line and showed him a monster mask. 'Do you like this?' He beamed and nodded. 'You'd better start colouring, then. This green pencil?' She handed it over on another nod, took the coins gripped in his hand, and watched him start some frantic, but concentrated, zigzag colouring. 'Who's next?'

A pair of giggling year threes presented themselves. 'We want to make the purses, please.'

'Come on, then. Find yourselves a space.' She picked up the pile of purses ready made in bright fabrics, so that they could choose one each, and then began to help them pick out fabric shapes, sequins and beads to stick on, at the same time as making sure the boy had a red crayon for his monster eyes. Looking up at Megan, she smiled. 'Go on, go and do whatever else you have to. I'm fine here.' 'Are you OK with that?' Megan asked Susie, whose own children had disappeared in the crowd.

'Of course. If Ella's as good as she was last year, well …' She left the sentence unfinished and waved Megan away. 'On you go. Now, who's next?'

No longer needed, Megan left them, passing the face-painting stall, where four artists kept up with the heavy demand, churning

244

out satisfied tigers, Spider-Men, butterflies, kittens and flower fairies. The fact that Ella and Amy were here had lifted her spirits. She hadn't realised how gloomy she had felt recently, until the gloom had lifted. Perhaps, even if her and Beth's friendship had broken down, she did not have to lose the girls as well.

'Megan, there you are.' Maureen waddled up to her. 'I can't find Ben Fletton. He's supposed to be the beat-the-goalie at three o'clock. Have you seen him? I've got to check everyone's got enough change.'

'Oh, no.' Megan looked around the playground, but saw no sign of Ben. 'I thought I'd persuaded him he'd enjoy it. I'll find him for you.' She had fought to get her idea through, against the objections of the parents who knew the boy. In the end, though, her persistence had won the day. She refused to believe that he couldn't be helped.

A quick search of the playground was fruitless. Drawn by some inner instinct, Megan went towards the staff bicycle sheds behind the school building. Sure enough, there was Ben, with Billy and Sid, two of his cronies. Sid was on his knees, fiddling with something. Ben was leaning over him, issuing whispered instructions. As she got closer, she realised what was going on.

'Sid! Leave my bike alone! Right now!'

Three shocked faces lifted to look at her. Ben immediately tried to hide what was in his left hand. A cigarette. The smoke and the smell gave him away. In his panic, Sid dropped a pack of tiny nails, one of which he'd been driving into the tyre of her bike, hammering it with the pump, which was now pitted with minuscule dents. The nails scattered across the concrete between the boys and Megan. Billy stared at her, alarm in his eyes, knowing the trouble he'd be in if his parents found out where he was.

'Ben. Give me that, please.' She held out her hand for the cigarette.

He cupped it in his hand and took a swift, defiant drag before handing it to her, filter first, blowing a stream of smoke after it.

She waved a hand to disperse the smoke, then stubbed out the cigarette on a wall. Sid was on the ground, scrabbling for the nails.

Megan took a deep breath, willing herself to keep control. 'I'm not going to say anything now. I don't want to spoil the fair for everyone else. But we will talk about this on Monday. Right now, I want you to go to your beat-the-goalie slot, Ben, and do your bit for the school, for once. Do you think you can do that?'

Ben nodded, surly. 'S'pose.'

'Well, go on then. You don't need these two in goal with you.'

She waited while he slunk off towards Maureen, who had followed Megan without her noticing and was hovering at the side of the building. Maureen nodded at Megan, who then turned her attention to the other boys. Without Ben's presence, they had lost their swagger. 'What am I going to do with you two? You know you shouldn't be doing this.'

'Ben gave me the nails, miss.' Sid passed her the packet. 'He told me what to do.'

'Telling on your friend isn't cool either,' she warned, examining her tyre for damage. Judging by the three or four bent nails on the ground, Sid hadn't had much joy getting through the rubber. 'So … if the tyre's damaged, I'm afraid I'll have to ask you to pay for a new one. Or your parents, depending on how expensive it is.'

Billy visibly paled. 'My dad'll go mental, miss. Please don't tell him.'

'You should have thought of that before you started. Now get back to the fair, and don't let me catch you round here again. I'll see you in my office on Monday before school.'

There. They had the whole weekend in which to worry about it. That was the best punishment she could think of right at that moment. She bounced the bike up and down on its front wheel, but the tyre seemed undamaged. So Billy's father was unlikely ever to find out. But Billy didn't need to know that just yet.

In the lower playground, the dog show had taken over from the majorettes. Whose bright idea was this? Surely guaranteed to provoke tears or chaos, or both. Megan stopped to watch the dogs, big and small, being paraded by their proud owners, glad that she wasn't a judge. That honour had fallen to Jane, who was choosing the dog most like its owner. At the moment she was bent over Susannah from year four and her fluffy bichon frise, sporting matching pink bows in their hair.

Was that Beth? As she climbed the steps into the big playground, Megan thought she recognised the back of her head, her hair tied back like Ella's, her green linen jacket. But by the time she had negotiated her way round a couple of year fives admiring their overenthusiastic Labrador and a feisty Border terrier, and exchanged a few words with their parents, Beth – if it was her – had gone. In previous years they would have met up at the school gate at the very end of the fair and gone home together for a post-mortem cup of tea or something stronger. Megan longed to be able to offload about Ben and her bicycle, her attempts to tame him, not to mention the trials of dealing with Maureen. But not this time.

'Mum! Look what I've bought!' Hannah appeared by her side clutching a tiny black and white kitten to her chest. 'Isn't he cute?'

'But we've got two cats already,' Megan protested, unable to resist reaching out to stroke between its ears with a finger. 'String'll have him for breakfast.'

'No he won't! Anyway, I could keep him in my bedroom.'

Megan moved to one side to let a gaggle of boys pass, their hands full with hamburgers. 'I don't think so.'

'Mum, go on. Please.'

At that moment, Amy appeared behind her. 'I knew you'd love him.'

'Let me take him home, and we'll see.' Hannah let the kitten inch its way up to her shoulder, where it snuggled into her neck.

'If I'm right, then you'll have to find him another home.'

'Maybe we could have him?' Amy suggested. 'Jock wouldn't care.'

'Your mum might,' Megan said, reaching out for another stroke. The kitten squeaked in appreciation.

Amy shrugged, as if to say she didn't care. 'Can I hold it?'

Hannah passed the kitten to her as if it was a piece of porcelain. 'What shall we call him?'

'Let's go home and decide. We'll get a box to carry him from Maureen. Laters.' With that, the two of them headed towards the gate with their prize.

Megan knew exactly who would end up looking after the little creature, just as she had looked after every one of the menagerie that had come through their door, from the rabbit ultimately decapitated by a fox through a range of gerbils, hamsters and goldfish to Athena, the white rat. She had been a sucker when it came to all of them, easily talked round by the kids. Just as she would be this time. Picturing the additional pawprints on the kitchen worktop, the hairs on the chairs, she could just imagine what Beth would say when presented with a kitten. But that was no longer her business. Besides, after Diva and String had established the pecking order, the kitten would no doubt adapt to its place in the family.

At the beat-the-goalie stand, quite a queue had lined up to get the ball past Ben. As she watched from the sidelines, Megan could see he was in his element. A quite different boy emerged as he weaved and dived and reached, letting almost nothing past. Between shots, he wore a broad grin on his face. 'Line up, line up,' he shouted, quite the market trader. 'You won't get one past me. Betcha can't score!' The challenge was too much for most of the boys to resist; some of the fathers too. But he was tough to beat. So, she had been right after all. He had stepped up to the plate. Perhaps there was hope for him.

The afternoon was turning out better than she had envisaged.

She glanced at her watch. Five minutes until her turn on throwing the sponge. She walked across to take over from Jim Morrow, the much-loved overweight ex-hippy who taught one of the year six classes. She noted with some relief that his head, sticking through the cut-out over the body of a much skinnier pantomime dame and her black cat, was almost dry.

One of the helpers passed her a plastic poncho. 'Should keep the worst off your dress.'

Jim extricated his head from the hole, brushing a few drops of water off his ponytailed hair. 'Thank God that's over and that they're such bloody awful shots. Are you next?'

' 'Fraid so.' Megan adjusted her poncho. The plastic stuck to her bare arms.

'Good luck! I've never felt quite so vulnerable.' He laughed. 'All those kids determined to get their own back for tellings-off and bad marks. The girls are worse than the boys! Makes me think I won't tell anyone off next year at all!'

'Thanks for the warning. Now I'm really looking forward to it! At least Ben's busy in goal, or I'd be really worried.' Megan glanced at the children milling around on the other side of the board, all of them looking relatively unthreatening. She was fairly sure Billy and Sid wouldn't dare. 'Here goes.'

As she got into position and stuck her head through the hole, one or two of the children pointed and clapped. With only her face exposed, Megan immediately understood what Jim had meant. There was no hiding place now. She could see him in the distance, heading towards the hamburger stand, his hand on the shoulder of one of his twin daughters.

'Ready, Megan?' asked the woman running the stall, having taken the first customer's money and given them a sponge.

Megan eyed the grinning year six with pretend trepidation. 'As I'll ever be.'

The girl laughed and danced her feet back from the dripping sponge. Perhaps it would be easier not to look at the throwers, not to see their determination as they screwed up their faces in concentration and took aim. Megan shut her eyes. There was a thud as a sponge hit the board at about the level of her stomach. Then another to the left of her head. She could hear the kids laughing, egging one another on. The spray from a hit just below her chin rose over her face. She shook the worst of it off, and opened her eyes. This was not quite as bad as she'd feared. In a lull between customers, she looked around. So it *was* Beth's green jacket she had seen earlier. There she was talking to Jane at the treasure hunt, the two of them laughing together.

Thwack! Another sponge landed just shy of Megan's face. And thrown by one of the fathers! He gave a shrug of apology and handed the next sponge to his son. Jane was pointing towards her, laughing. Beth turned to look. The smile was wiped off Megan's face by a sponge on the chin. She closed her eyes and took a deep breath. She must have been here for five minutes already. Surely. Only another fifteen to go. Sponges rained down around her. Cold water ran down from the shots above her head on to her hair and down the back of her neck. So much for the bloody poncho. She shut her eyes and shook her head. When she opened them, she saw Beth standing opposite her, with Jane at her side.

'Can't resist,' shouted Jane, who threw a sponge wildly wide of the mark.

She must have done that on purpose, Megan thought. No one was that hopeless.

'Go on, Beth. Your turn,' Jane encouraged, indicating the bucket.

An odd look had crossed Beth's face that Megan had trouble interpreting, but she knew one thing: it wasn't friendly, more the dawning recognition of an unexpected opportunity. She wouldn't, would she? Megan shut her eyes, trying to put herself in Beth's position. When she looked again, she saw Beth holding a large sponge, dripping wet from the bucket. Her eyes followed, alarmed, as the sponge was lifted, pulled back behind Beth's shoulder, elbow bent (unlike the gentle underarm technique that Jane had employed). There was a determined glint in Beth's eyes as they narrowed in concentration. Her mouth tightened; she raised her hand and moved it a fraction to the right, then her arm flashed forward, releasing the sponge.

Megan saw only a blur of colour as it sped towards her. But when it hit, she felt it quite clearly. Splat! Right in the centre of her face, momentarily blinding her and leaving her gasping, her mouth filled with water. The sponge dropped to the ground.

'Bullseye!' The cry went up from the surrounding children and parents, followed by a cheer. Could she hear Beth's voice among them?

Pulling her gracious loser's face from somewhere very deep inside her, Megan shook the water out of her eyes, wishing she could reach around the board to remove the strands of hair from them. She forced her facial muscles into an almost generous smile that would tell everyone, but especially Beth, that she had not been hurt physically or emotionally, that she was not smarting inside. How could Beth have done that in front of so many people? But as she refocused furiously on the laughing crowd, the first thing she noticed was that Beth was no longer standing there. There was a flash of green jacket over by the cake stall and then Megan lost track of her as another sponge thwacked on to the board. What a coward. Brave enough to hit the mark, but not to face the consequences.

One thing was crystal clear to her. Despite her efforts, Beth had not got over their differences. The moment had presented herself and she had taken full advantage of it, leaving Megan bitter, angry and soaking wet.

23

Beth put her laptop back into her bag. The train to York was far busier than she had expected. Although she had a table seat, the conversation around her was distracting. She had hoped to bury herself in her work throughout the journey, so she wouldn't have to think about what was waiting at the other end of it. However, what with the young man beside her absorbed in a noisy bleeping game on his phone, and the woman across the table insisting on reading snatches of her book out loud to her friend, there was no hope.

She leaned back and stared out of the window, watching the countryside flash past. Had she done the right thing by writing to Gerry? She had, as Ella predicted, found his contact details without much difficulty. The Internet and a bright assistant saw to that. She had shied away from phoning him. Somehow that was too intimate after such a long time, and given what she had to say. It had taken a whole evening to compose the letter that she finally sent. Not too familiar, not too distant, suggesting that she had a good reason to ask him to meet her again, but not specifying what it was. He had replied immediately. Yes, he was well. She wouldn't be surprised to hear that he was retired. But he was kept busy on various boards and with his charity work. The golf course, too. Yes, he could be in York on both the days she was suggesting. Could he take her out to lunch to discuss whatever it was? He was intrigued.

As well he might be. But what about her family? She dreaded

the effect this rendezvous might have on them. Despite her protests, she had refused to let Ella come with her.

'I must do this bit on my own. I owe it to Gerry to break the news to him alone, just as I did to you. Once he's absorbed the fact that he has another daughter, he'll decide how to play it. Remember, this will be as much a shock for him as it has been for you.'

'Yes. But I should have an equal say as to whether or not we should meet. Remember to tell him that,' pointed out Ella. 'He can come here, or I don't mind going to York.'

Beth had wearily agreed. All her best intentions for her family had backfired catastrophically and now she was experiencing the fallout. But of one thing she was certain: whatever happened, Ella would never abandon Jon. As far as she was concerned, he was her dad. She had reassured him of that over and again.

But even if he believed her, would he be able to trust Beth again? They had been such a tight team for so long, bound by their mutual love and respect for each other but also by the secret they had shared. But what had once bonded them was what was now driving them apart. If only she could wind back the clock.

And Megan. Beth was mortified by her behaviour at the school fair. She had been enjoying catching up with Jane, who had suggested they go over to the stall and have a throw. It was meant to be a laugh. But when she was confronted by Megan, completely at her mercy, some avenging demon had taken over. When the sponge hit her with such a smack, Beth had felt genuine shame. That was what had made her flee without even apologising or staying to check that she hadn't hurt her. And in front of all those people.

She had tried to persuade Ella against contacting Gerry, but Ella was absolutely set on her right to meet her biological father. 'Suppose something goes wrong with the baby at birth? We might need to know his blood group or something,' she had insisted. Meanwhile, Jon, who claimed to accept Ella's need to see Gerry, distanced himself from Beth as much as possible, going out, or shutting himself in his room under the pretext of work. His silences affected the whole family. Amy had escaped the house as often as she could, often returning with the smell of cigarette smoke on her clothes or drink on her breath. When questioned about her remaining exams, she followed her father's example, shutting herself in her room with her school books, laptop and phone. All of them were operating separately from one another, each caught up in their own world, unable to communicate or make things better.

Beth prayed that her visit to York might be the first step to rebuilding what they once had, although it was hard to see how. As the train sped northwards, her thoughts went round in decreasing circles.

The announcement that they were approaching York station took her by surprise. She had been so lost in her thoughts that the journey had passed in a flash. She checked her watch as the people around her began to pack their things away, get their luggage down. The train was exactly on time. All of a sudden, nerves paralysed her. She sat motionless as they pulled in beside the crowded platform. She watched the passengers waiting to board. If she just stayed there without moving, the train would take her on to Edinburgh or even Aberdeen, putting plenty of distance between herself and her problems. She was half tempted to sit where she was, although there was really no escape. She would only have to come back and face them another time. The carriage was emptying. It was now or not at all.

Her family. Just the words gave her the impetus to make the titanic effort required. She got to her feet and edged her way down the aisle and off the train, pushing through the passengers who were already boarding. She had refused Gerry's offer to meet her. A public reunion would be too difficult. Instead, he had given her the name of a hotel and restaurant somewhere just outside the city.

She found the cab rank, gave the driver at the front of the line her destination, and climbed in. In the back, she tucked herself into the corner to minimise the slippage factor and pulled out her make-up bag. There was no point in turning up looking like the living dead. She added a bit of colour to her cheeks, a slick of lipstick. She readjusted her hair, which she had partially pulled back and clasped at the back of her head. Her favourite summer dress, a deep turquoise, fitted, with three-quarter sleeves, was appropriately businesslike but comfortable. She put her mirror away. She was as ready as she would ever be.

With everything back in her bag, she stared blindly out of the cab window, waiting, apprehensive as they approached her destination, pulling up outside a large William and Mary country house built of warm red brick. She gazed up at the three floors of windows, which seemed to stare back, unwelcoming, making her even more nervous of what she would find behind them. She paid before climbing out of the cab and walking through the gate and up to the porch. Trust Gerry to choose somewhere as comfortable but imposing as this. She asked at reception and was pointed in the direction of the dining room. She glanced at her watch again. Five minutes late. Just right. She had rarely felt this apprehensive, not even when appearing in court in front of the most intimidating of judges. She crossed the chequered marble floor towards the wood-panelled room.

'I'm meeting a Mr Worthington,' she told the maître d', who hovered by a small desk by the door. He inclined his head, said something to a nearby waiter, who led her into the restaurant. Large windows overlooked a terrace where people were eating under cream parasols. Beyond them stretched acres of well-tended gardens, leading to a ha-ha, then parkland.

A few people sat indoors, out of the heat. An elderly man was alone at a corner table, absorbed in the menu. He looked up when he became aware of the waiter's approach. He started as he caught sight of Beth, then pushed his chair back to stand up. His dark suit was expensive, well cut.

'Beth.' She would have recognised the voice anywhere, with its very slight northern inflection. It took her swooping back to the last time they had met. But how he had changed. Once, their age difference had seemed insignificant, but now the twenty years between them showed. As he greeted her, she took in the grey hair, the slightly rounded shoulders, the deep wrinkles – ones that hadn't been there before – the thin lips, the liver spots on his veined hands. He wore glasses now, and beside his chair was propped a wooden walking stick. But the shape of his face was the same, the cleft in his chin still there and his eyes were as blue and alive as ever. He might be an old man now, but he was unmistakably Ella's father.

'You haven't changed,' he said. 'I'd know you anywhere.'

She let the waiter pull out her chair, allowing her time to compose herself as she sat down.

'A glass of champagne? To celebrate our meeting again.'

Was champagne appropriate, given her reason for being there? But she squeezed out a 'Why not? That would be lovely.' After all, she didn't have to drink it.

He gave the order to the waiter before turning the full glare of his attention on her.

'So.' He steepled his fingers, reminding her of the way Ella made the same gesture, and stared at her over them, bouncing them against his chin. 'Why now? After so long.'

Of course he had suspected something. She was grateful that they weren't going to go through the motions of small talk. He had always preferred to get straight to the point. The meal would have seemed interminable if he'd insisted on them waiting until it was over before letting her explain. Even after all this time, he knew her. As she did him. Already she was calmer. Now that she was with him, telling him of Ella's existence didn't seem the hardest thing in the world after all. He would know what to do.

Just as he always had. Even so, she hesitated. 'I'm not sure where to start,' she began.

He smiled. 'Then let's order first and get that out of the way.'

She saw him notice her hand tremble as she held the menu, but he looked away. 'The fish is always very good,' he said, as if he did this every day.

The flutes of champagne arrived, their order was taken, they were left alone. He picked up his glass. 'To us,' he said. 'How good it is to see you.'

'To us,' she echoed. After all, that was what this meeting was about. Them. And Ella. She took a small sip, the bubbles pricking on her tongue.

'Come on, Beth. You haven't come here for nothing.' He set his elbows on the table and leaned forward, his gaze fixing her. 'You're bottling something up. I could see it the moment I set eyes on you. Let's have it.'

Could he have guessed? What other reason could she possibly have for coming to see him? Perhaps he thought her marriage had ended and she had come to ... to what? *For heaven's sake, woman. Just tell him. Get it over with.* So she did.

He didn't interrupt, just waited for her to finish. His expression betrayed nothing.

'A daughter.' He sounded not so much surprised as bemused. 'Did you think I wouldn't want to know?'

'It wasn't that.' How would she ever begin to explain what had gone through her mind so long ago? 'We weren't going to see each other again. We both knew that. You had your family. I was in love with Jon, and we wanted a baby more than anything. You knew that. I told you that evening.'

'You did.' He leaned back in his seat as the waiter put Beth's chilled gazpacho in front of her, then gave Gerry his ham hock ballotine.

'Honestly?' She dropped some croutons into her soup and stirred them around. 'I didn't think you'd want to know. You always made it so clear that nothing must interfere with your home life.'

He looked as if he was about to interrupt.

'And that was fine by me,' she added hastily, not wanting to be stopped now. 'When I realised I was pregnant, I saw no point in telling you. I knew you wouldn't want me to have your baby. But I had to tell Jon. Perhaps it's difficult to understand, but I couldn't get rid of it when we wanted our own so much. Yes, I'd had an abortion before, but this was different. It was as if we were being presented with a chance. Jon was devastated, of course. He couldn't believe that I would sleep with anyone else. I had to convince him that it had meant nothing.'

Gerry looked faintly amused.

'It was a terrible time. It took a lot of talking, a lot of thinking, before he began to believe me. He always said that he wouldn't have let me have my abortion if he had been around to look after me. And we wanted a family so badly. Eventually he agreed that, if we kept the baby, I would promise not to have anything to do with you again.'

'And since then you've been happy?'

What did he want to hear? She couldn't tell. She moved her spoon around in the soup again, but didn't have any appetite. As he studied her closely, looking for an answer, she was remembering her childhood, the struggle she'd had to establish herself in her chosen career, her unsettled love life until she met Jon. All of a sudden, she knew the answer. She had known it all along.

'Yes,' she said firmly. 'He's the best thing that's happened to me.' Gerry had meant something else to her. He had supported her, educated her, helped her achieve what she wanted in life. Perhaps she had believed she loved him, but in fact she hadn't known what love was. That was the one thing he hadn't taught her. Long afterwards, when she thought about their relationship, she supposed one of the reasons it worked was because in some ways he represented a kind of father figure to her. The father she had never had. She didn't need Freud to help her work that out.

'Then why make a special journey to tell me this now?' He took a mouthful of ballotine, shaking his head as if he didn't understand. 'You could have kept me in the dark for ever.'

'Because Ella's pregnant.' How could she begin to explain the sequence of events that had led her to blurt out the truth? 'And I told her about you.'

He raised an eyebrow. 'Why then?'

'Long story. Drink was taken, and I was pushed too far. All my fault. And now she wants to meet you. So I've come to ask if you will.' There.

'Oh.' None of the expected fireworks, no protest, nothing. He rubbed his chin, thoughtful. 'How do you feel about that? And Jon. What does he think?'

'He's desperately unhappy about it, of course, but doesn't feel he's in a position to prevent her.' She straightened her napkin to cover her skirt, unable to meet his gaze.

'So while I was a secret, everything rolled along smoothly, but now I'm out of the closet, everything's changed.'

'Exactly.' Beth's throat was choking up, her eyes stung. She dug her nails into the palm of her hand. She must not cry. 'I don't know what to do.' Here she was again, asking him to sort out her life. Hadn't she learned anything at all in the years since she had last seen him? 'Do you want to meet her?' Please say no. Please. But she knew he wouldn't refuse her.

'Dear Beth.' He put down his knife and fork and pushed his plate further from him. 'I've got three daughters of my own to worry about, plus a rather spiky daughter-in-law. I'm stunned to hear of Ella's existence and I'm curious about her. Of course I am. But I don't need another responsibility at this time in my life. Especially after Melanie's death.'

'Your wife's dead?' Now it was Beth's turn to be shocked.

Somehow she had never imagined the happy family life that had cocooned him so completely ever coming to an end.

'Two years ago. Pancreatic cancer. It was brutally quick.' He wiped his mouth, remembering. 'The children were torn to shreds. She was an incredible wife and mother. We all miss her dreadfully and I don't think this would help them.'

His family had always come first. But what about hers?

'What shall I tell Ella?' She imagined returning to her daughter with the news that he wanted nothing to do with her; the upset that would follow. He had to help her cushion the blow. He owed her that at least.

Their conversation paused as their plates were removed, the waiter enquiring if there was anything wrong with her soup. She reassured him, saying she wasn't hungry.

Gerry gazed at her across the table. 'What do you want to tell her?'

'That I made it all up, that Jon's her real father.' She gave a bitter laugh. 'But it's gone too far for that. I can't tell any more lies. I could have pretended to meet you, pretended you'd refused to see her … but I couldn't do that either.'

'What's she like?' At last. So he was interested in her after all. 'Does she look like you?'

'No. Like you.' She dug about in her bag for her phone and brought up her most recent photo of Ella, smiling with Jock on her lap in the garden.

'Much prettier,' he mused, staring at it.

She gave a short laugh. 'And just as determined to have her own way.'

'Excuse me, but I think that may be a characteristic she's inherited from you.' His eyes twinkled at her over the top of his spectacles.

They both started to laugh.

'Perhaps. But she knows what she wants. At first, I didn't want her to have this baby … I'm still not entirely sure it's the best thing. But it's too late for doubts.'

Gerry looked surprised. 'Even after you'd decided against an abortion to have her?'

'But that was different. Surely you can see that. She's so young, and hardly in a stable relationship.' She sat back in her chair, picturing Jake, his flop of hair, his shy smile. 'Jake's a sweet boy, but he's hardly husband material. He's only twenty-one, for God's sake. He's as unprepared for what's about to hit them as she is. I'd hoped for so much more for Ella than this. She was all lined up to go to Cambridge to study medicine. She says she'll defer her entry, but I wonder if she'll go at all.' She took a sip of her champagne and sighed. 'All I wanted was for her to be successful and happy.'

'But who's to quantify those things?' he asked thoughtfully. 'My daughters have all ended up with lives I would never have predicted for them. Phoebe's an actress, Ellen's an economist and Tess is a stay-at-home mum. I'd say each of them was equally successful in their own way – well, Phoebe has yet to make it to the West End, but she's happy with the small successes she's had. And we're happy for her. Oscar was the exception: he followed me into the law.'

'You surprise me. In fact, you sound a bit like Jon.' Beth spoke quietly. This was an altogether different side to the man she had known so long ago. When his daughters and son were young, she would have predicted that he'd have wanted the same career success for them as she did for Ella.

'Then he must be a much better man than I.' He smiled. 'I came late to Melanie's point of view. She was always much more relaxed than me about what they all did with their lives.'

So she had been right. 'Did you ever tell her about us?'

He smiled, a distant look in his eyes. 'No. If she guessed, she never said anything. Our marriage worked as it was.'

'Was there anyone else apart from me?' She couldn't help herself, not out of jealousy, but curiosity now.

'No.' He threw his hands in the air, laughing at the idea. 'I was never a womaniser. It was only ever you. But we had fun, didn't we, and no harm done.'

'But harm has been done – not to your family, but to mine.'

'Only afterwards – and that could have been avoided.' As he absolved himself from all responsibility, a shutter seemed to slide down over his eyes. So he blamed her. And in all truth he was right to. But she knew that she and Jon had made the right decision.

'I accept that,' she retorted, her tone brisk. 'But I wouldn't be without Ella, not for anything. And neither would Jon.'

'Then why do you need me?'

'We don't. But Ella does. Imagine what she's feeling.' She waited while her tomato and courgette tart was put in front of her. 'You're a missing piece of her identity.'

He shook his head.

But she was not going to give up. She had come all this way for Ella and she was determined to do her best by her, however much it went against what she herself wanted. She tried again. 'This is the first time I've ever asked anything of you. I know how much you've given me in so many ways, more probably than you ever realised, but I'm asking you to see her. Please.'

It was one of the most difficult requests she'd ever made. Difficult because, deep down, she didn't want him to agree. However, seeing him might put some of Ella's demons to rest. If she knew of his existence but never met him, she might always be wondering, imagining what her father, her baby's grandfather, was like. Having opened the box, Beth owed it to her to try to shut it as tight as she could.

Gerry deliberated as he helped himself to vegetables. How was he going to reply? Beth knew not to push him. When she refused wine, he ordered himself a glass of Montrachet, but still he gave no indication of what he was thinking. Her request hung over them as they ate. They had come a long way from those dinners and lunches filled with wine and laughter as they discussed their cases, compared what they were reading or listening to, analysed what they had seen at the cinema, caught up with who they had seen, what they had said.

Despite being on tenterhooks, Beth filled the gap by telling him about Ella, about her childhood, her likes and dislikes, her academic prowess, the differences between her and Amy. As she spoke about her family, she prayed he would make the right decision, whatever that was. When he didn't respond beyond the odd nod or smile of acknowledgement, a short question, she started telling him about how her career had progressed, her partnership in the firm, and the recent case of child abduction she had been handling. He listened, commented, laughed on cue, but still he didn't answer her.

Eventually, he finished his chicken and leaned back, unbalancing his stick, which landed on the floor with a crack. He bent to pick it up, then hooked it over the back of his chair before turning round to regard her gravely.

Did he realise he was about to throw her family a lifeline? Or not. She could hear her pulse pumping as she waited for his verdict.

He cleared his throat, put a hand to his collar, hooked a finger inside then removed it. 'All right,' he said.

She waited for him to go on, putting her knife and fork on the plate beside her unfinished meal. She couldn't eat any more.

'I'll come to London and I'll meet you both. Or I'll meet you both with Jon, if that would help. I won't see her alone.'

'You will?' Dread inched through her.

'Yes.' He smiled, letting the young Gerry she remembered emerge. 'I'm not doing this for you, mind. I'm doing it for her. If she is as keen as you say about meeting me, she won't let go until she does. But I will make it absolutely plain to her that

263

there won't be another time. And my children must never hear of it – ever. Understood?'

He raised his glass, and she chinked her water glass against it to seal the agreement.

'Yes. And Ella will understand too.'

She had no doubt that Ella would stick to her word for Jon's sake, but what would she make of this man who was old enough to be her grandfather? And Jon. Would he want to be there too? Perhaps meeting Gerry would prove to Jon that he was not the threat he might imagine. But her success in her mission was bittersweet. Would this be enough to bring Ella back to her? To reassure Jon that he was loved by them both?

24

Something bad was about to happen. What exactly, Megan had no idea, but she could feel it coming. Since getting up, she had felt unaccountably on edge, but had no idea why.

The noise in the assembly hall was deafening as the teachers led in their classes, one after the other. The children sat on the floor, each class in an approximation of a straight line, while the teachers and teaching assistants took seats at either end so they could supervise them. The older children were at the back, fidgeting, giggling and whispering, despite the rule of silence and their teachers' warning looks. Last to come in were the reception class, the sweetest of the lot, holding hands, looking around them and sitting obediently at the front.

Once they had all settled, Megan ran her eyes over the pupils before addressing them. 'Good morning, everyone.'

'Good morning, Mrs Weston,' they chorused back.

She watched Ben pick his nose and flick his find over the heads of the kids in front of him. He judged it perfectly, just as his teacher was distracted confiscating what looked like a penknife from one of the boys nearer her. His goalie stint at the fair had briefly paid off. He had not been in any kind of trouble since. Megan was already trying to think up ways she could reinforce her experiment in the next school year. A couple of birds flew past the window against a clear blue sky. Thank God it was nearly the end of term.

Broad shafts of sunshine beamed through the open skylights as she introduced the theme of the morning – Ramadan – and invited one of the year five classes up to the stage to explain the festival and its traditions to the rest of the school. Despite their evident enthusiasm, Megan's attention wandered as she scanned the audience for troublemakers. She caught one of Ben's classmates whispering to him and pointing to one of the girls in the year below.

At last, the interminable presentation drew to a close. She must gently remind Eleanor, the class teacher, of the age range of the audience next time. The decibel level rose as the children left the hall for their classrooms. Megan returned to her office. She wasn't teaching until the afternoon, but had plenty of admin to get through.

She had only been in her office for half an hour when there was a knock at the open door. She glanced up to see Marilyn Booth, one of the year five teachers, looking unusually harassed.

'I've brought Ben and Jaden to see you, Megan, as the head's still out at her meeting.' She stepped inside and pulled the door to, lowering her voice as she did so. 'I can't have them in my class any longer. They're too disruptive. I've done my best and I know it's almost the end of the school year, but they're spoiling everything for the others. This morning they were spitting at the backs of the kids in front of them before sticking chewing gum in Bethany's and Daisy's hair. We're going to have to cut it out, so they're both hysterical. I just can't cope with this any more. I'm sorry.'

'All right.' Megan maintained her composure. She was a past mistress at never showing how ruffled she was inside. That had been a large part of her job. 'I'll take it from here. Where are they now?'

'Sitting outside.'

On cue, there was a bang as something hit the partition wall of her office, and a loud groan followed by snorts of laughter. The two women rushed to see what had happened. Ben was standing holding a chair, while Jaden was lying on the ground, one hand on the back of his head, blood oozing through his hair on to his fingers.

'He took the chair away as I was sitting down, miss.' Jaden's eyes widened as he took his hand from his head and saw the blood.

'Put the chair down, Ben.' Megan had rarely felt so angry with a young child. 'Sit on it and don't move. I mean it.'

Cowed by the sight of blood and her obvious anger, Ben did as he was told, watching as they examined Jaden's scalp.

'I think it probably needs stitches,' concluded Megan. That was too much for Jaden; his bravado cracked and he began to whimper. 'Could you call his parents, Marilyn? If they can't come, one of us will have to take him. Come down to the first-aid room, Jaden. Ben, you stay right here till I get back.'

Once Jaden was settled in the first-aid room, a piece of lint bandaged tight to his head, Megan left him with a teaching assistant and returned to her office. Ben was still slumped on the chair outside. As soon as he saw her coming down the corridor, he sat up, his expression changing from a sullen blank to confrontational. Megan summoned her last vestiges of patience, She was not going to be beaten by this child, however much he got to her.

She held open her office door. 'Ben. Come in.'

Hands in pockets, eyes to the floor, he followed her, shutting the door behind him.

'Sit down.'

He did as he was told. She took the seat across the low table from him, waiting. After a few minutes, he looked up, his eyes beady, challenging. 'It wasn't my fault, miss.'

She raised her eyebrows at him. 'I think we both know that's not true, don't we?'

He looked down and scratched at the knee of his jeans. 'If he'd sat down when I said, it wouldn't have happened.'

'But Ben, you shouldn't have moved the chair at all.' Be calm. Be reasonable. 'Jaden's badly hurt.'

Silence.

'When he's back at school, I want you to apologise to both him and his parents. Do you understand?'

He shrugged.

'I said, do you understand, Ben?'

'Yeah, suppose.'

She only just heard him, but that was better than nothing. Perhaps she was getting through to him at last. Hallelujah!

'Now, this isn't the first time you've been to see me this term, is it?' That might have been a nod of the head, she wasn't sure, but, encouraged, she went on. 'And your mum's been in as well. I've given you numerous chances to convince me that you've understood that your behaviour needs to change, including being the goalie at the fair, when you did a great job.'

The boy glanced at her briefly, glowing at the praise. But only for a moment.

'I'm trying to help you, Ben, but you still persist in being one of the worst-behaved boys in the school. Why do you think that is?'

Ben shook his head and swung his leg so that he kicked the table. The vase of flowers jumped. 'Don't know.'

'You should be setting an example, not terrorising the little ones.' Appeal to his better nature. He must have one.

He mumbled something.

'What? I didn't quite hear you?'

He looked up again. Megan didn't like the sullen expression she saw darkening his face. 'Who says I've got to do what you say?' he asked. The deadness behind his eyes was frightening.

Megan was aware that she was entering unknown territory. This child had no fear of authority, no concept of consequences. He refused to observe any of the boundaries reasonably set by the school; only saw them as obstacles in his way. He wasn't going to respond to her entreaties. She had been wrong to think she could help him.

'I do.' She made herself as authoritative as she could, but for the first time, she was experiencing fear. Fear for him, and fear for herself. She wiped her palms on her skirt, counting silently to five, slowing her breathing.

This time, he smothered a laugh. He was sneering at her. No other child in the school did that. Even the worst of them retained a modicum of respect for her authority. But she would not let him get away with it. If he wouldn't respond to reason, then she would have to resort to old-fashioned punishment. There was one sanction that she didn't want to evoke, but what choice had she?

She stood up and walked to the long windows of her office, overlooking the playground and the park beyond. Deep breath. Control, she reminded herself. Don't let him get to you. She adjusted the neck of her blouse in her reflection, examined her nails, noticed one broken, then turned. He hadn't moved; his leg still swung back and forth against the table.

'Please don't do that, Ben.'

He looked up at the sound of her voice, hearing its change of tone. He knew she meant business this time. He kicked the table again. Harder.

Megan took the vase and moved it off the table, then sat behind her desk, feeling more in control now that she was on its other side and looking down at him. There was no need to be kind any longer. 'I'm afraid, Ben, that if you can't see that you've done wrong and won't apologise, there's only one thing we can do.' She paused.

His leg was still. A dog barked in the park. The reception class was led chattering into the playground below.

'You won't go on the class trip to Chessington.' There. The trip to Chessington World of Adventure was a treat given to years five and six at the end of the summer term. To say it was one of the highlights of the school year was an understatement. 'Instead, you'll come into school and do your usual classes – alone. And I'm removing you from the football team until next term, when … *if* your behaviour's improved, and *if* you're chosen again … I'll reinstate you.' That would mean he would miss the last two matches in the local schools trophy and the kudos that went with being in the team.

Ben's face was white. For a second, she thought he might leap up and attack her. But he didn't. 'You can't do that,' he objected.

'I just have. I'm sorry, Ben, but you leave me no alternative. If you think better of things, then come and see me.' She stood to signal that the meeting was over.

'Bitch!' The word was muttered, but loud enough for Megan to hear quite clearly.

'Forget that, Ben.' She gripped the edge of her desk with both hands, her knuckles white. 'No football team next term either. And I will be speaking to your parents again. This can't carry on. OK, you can go.'

She watched as he left her office, her pulse rapid, aware that she had just made matters much worse. His punishment would only encourage his rebellion. But what else could she do in the circumstances? Once again he'd pressed all the buttons that made her react. To retract the punishment would only be seen as weakness on her part and leave her open to more abuse. She would talk to Jane and Marilyn about him as soon as they were free.

That day, any such discussion proved impossible. Jane was in a meeting and didn't get back until after lunch, by which time Marilyn was in class and leaving at the bell to get home to her sick mother. She was delighted to hear that Ben had been excluded from the class outing, but agreed that they needed to discuss what more could be done to tame him, and that banning him from football would only cause more trouble – with him and his friends.

After her two classes that afternoon, Megan had stopped by

the head's office, but Jane had been on the phone. She put her hand over the mouthpiece. 'Sorry, Meg, but I'm horribly tied up. Can it wait till tomorrow? Or perhaps I could call you this evening?' Without waiting for an answer, she turned back to her call, waving Megan away.

Was Ben Fletton the worst thing that could happen to her that day? Megan hoped so, but that weird sense of premonition was still there. On her way home, she was almost knocked off her bike as she circled the small roundabout at the end of the road. She had been distracted, thinking how much better she could have handled things, and hadn't seen the car coming from her right. The little red Fiat cut through the centre of the reserve and swerved straight in front of her, then sped off without stopping, leaving her so shaken that she had to get off and push her bike the rest of the way home.

No one was in. Exams were over at last, so Hannah must be out with friends. As soon as the term was done, a bunch of them were going down to Newquay so they were busy planning. God help Newquay. Jake must be at the studio or on a shoot somewhere. At least he was throwing himself into his work now, seeing it more and more as a job than a hobby, taking his responsibilities seriously. And Pete was travelling – no surprise there – in Ireland for four days this time, writing up the Ring of Kerry.

She sighed. He hadn't always been a travel journalist. Their life had been more settled when he had been on-staff, editing the travel pages, sending other people out to write, going away less frequently himself. But since the pages had been cut back and he'd been put on a freelance contract, he'd had to do more of the work himself. It was less lucrative this way, but he was good at it, his contacts were second to none, and it gave him a sense of purpose. He was a reliable travel hound who could turn the work around fast. Good for him, but less so for her, stuck at home alone with her problems. Going away meant he often chose not to involve himself with them.

The sun was still shining, so she opened the doors of the conservatory into the garden. Fizz, the kitten that had never left after the school fair, skittered out behind her, quite at home now. Diva arched her back as he darted by, but did no more than that. She and String tolerated the incomer, making clear who was boss with the odd hiss or swipe of a claw. Fizz had quickly got the idea.

The garden was looking its best. There was even a pale yellow lily flowering on the pond for the first time. She wandered around, measuring progress, deadheading, pulling out one or two weeds that had appeared since the weekend. She was particularly proud of the herbaceous border, which she had transformed through trial and error over the years until it was as close to a country garden as she could get. Purple verbena, neon-blue delphiniums, assorted lupins and hollyhocks vied for space, providing a backdrop for her favourite love-in-the-mist and scented tobacco plants, and the wild geraniums and rock roses that scrambled over the edge of the lawn. Facing it was the bed that she had devoted to shade-loving shrubs, ferns, foxgloves and hellebores.

She turned on the sprinkler. As the drops of water danced in the sunlight, tapping lightly on the leaves, she pulled her lounger under the pergola. Beyond the clematis and climbing roses the sky was cloudless, interrupted only by the white vapour trails of planes criss-crossing the city. As a child, she would spend hours wondering about their destinations, looking them up in her atlas, wondering if she'd ever visit. But now? She closed her eyes, inhaling the delicate scent of the sweet peas trained up the bamboo wigwams beside her. Whatever Pete was doing, wherever he was, as far as she was concerned there had never been anywhere better than home.

Her peace was interrupted by the sound of her mobile. For a second she was tempted to let it ring, but remembering that it could be any one of her family, she dragged herself up and went inside.

'Megan? It's Jane. I'm sorry I couldn't speak to you earlier.'

Megan opened the fridge, took out a jug of iced tea and poured herself a glass. While they got the niceties out of the way, she sat at the conservatory table, her attention only half on Jane's anxiety about the quality of the maths teaching in the school in the light of a new government directive. She had a feeling that this was only the preamble to something else that the head was delaying addressing. Then she heard her say, 'Megan I'm afraid something's happened.'

Here it was, whatever she had been dreading all day, rolling towards her, gathering momentum. She stared outside, fixing on a butterfly fluttering around the sweet peas. 'What?'

'This isn't easy.'

'Jane, come on. How long have we worked together? You know me. Just say it.'

'There's been a complaint.'

Was that all? Teachers were complained about all the time; usually it was a misunderstanding and they managed to solve the problem quite easily. 'About who?'

'I'm afraid it's about you.' Jane paused.

'About me?' Megan sat straight, on her guard. 'What about me?' One thing of which she was confident was that her conduct at school was beyond reproach.

'I'm afraid you've been accused of hitting one of the children.' A pause.

'What?! Oh, don't be ridiculous.' Megan put down her glass. This must be a wind-up. 'You know perfectly well I'd never do that. Never.'

'Of course I do.' Jane was mollifying. 'But you know as well as I do that we have to take every complaint seriously.'

'You don't mean ...' This was what Megan had been waiting for. The moment came closer.

'I'm going to have to suspend you pending an inquiry.'

'Jane, that's ridiculous.' Megan was quite calm. 'Who's made the complaint?' She had a feeling she knew.

'I had Josie Fletton on the phone after school. She must have phoned as soon as Ben got home. Apparently there's a bruise on his arm where you hit him. She's photographed it.'

'I've never laid a finger on any child, ever. However much I might sometimes have felt like it.' Her attempt at levity fell flat.

'This is a very serious allegation, Megan. I wouldn't joke about it.'

Jane had never spoken to her like this before. At once, Megan realised how damaging this could be to her and her career.

'I would have come round to see you, to warn you, but I've got to go out this evening. I thought it was important you know, though. She's accusing you of conducting a campaign against him that culminated in your slapping him this afternoon.'

'But I didn't,' Megan protested. 'If there's been any campaign at all, it's been his. He's constantly harassing the younger children and winding up the teachers. Ask Marilyn.'

'I will, and I believe you, but she says she has a witness. Micky Lonsdale.'

Megan was flabbergasted. 'But Micky must have been in class then.'

'Apparently not.'

'Have you checked with Marilyn?' She felt the first flutterings of panic.

'I haven't been able to. But of course, I will first thing to-morrow.'

'Jane? You do believe me?'

'Of course I do. But I have to go through the procedures, you know that.'

'I do,' agreed Megan, reassured, but at the same time anxious.

'Try not to worry. I'll see you in the morning.'

At least she was to be allowed into the school the next day.

Megan walked out to the lounger, her mind racing. As she sat down heavily, there was a loud crack as one of the legs broke. She landed on the ground with a shout, her arms and legs in the air like a swatted fly, iced tea all over her. She didn't move for a second, feeling the liquid soaking into her blouse. Bloody Pete! He'd promised to mend the thing before he left. Why couldn't he ever do his share of chores when he said he would?

She manoeuvred herself out of the wreckage, lifting her right arm. A bruise was already forming down the length of her triceps. Wearily she headed for the house once again, this time to change. All she had wanted was a quiet, relaxed hour in the garden as the sun went down.

She changed into a loose linen dress, returned to the fridge and poured herself another glass of tea. Outside, she shoved the lounger into Pete's potting shed. He'd get the point. Instead of risking a repeat performance, she sat on the wooden seat. She couldn't relax now. Her arm throbbed as her thoughts returned to Jane's phone call, running over everything that had happened between her and Ben that afternoon. There was nothing she had done that could be interpreted either as holding him or slapping him. A memory of him shutting the door came to her. Why hadn't she opened it? They had it drummed into them that office doors had to be open if you were alone with a child. Why? She was just finding out. This had to be a conspiracy cooked up between the boys to see her in trouble. Well done, lads. It's working.

There was nothing she could do until she got to school and checked out Micky's story. Ben would be enjoying this. He was smart enough to have woven a convincing set of lies and was unlikely to back down. No, he would take pleasure in provoking trouble for her, if he could. How Megan missed Beth right then. She would think of all the possible outcomes and work out the best way of dealing with them. When it came to incisiveness and objectivity, there was no one like Beth – except when it came to dealing with her own life.

Megan closed her eyes, letting the last of the sun warm her face, but her thoughts wouldn't slow down. Not only school, but all the other potential trouble spots whirled through her head – Beth, Ella and Jake, Hannah and Newquay, Pete and her. She turned her focus on Ella and Jake. Would they stay together? Should she encourage Jake to make something more permanent of their relationship? What would happen when the baby was born? Would Ella give up her starry future? She was worrying over the answer to each question when her phone rang again.

Praying that this was Jane to say that Josie Fletton had retracted her accusation, she answered without checking the number.

'Jane?'

'Meg?' Not Jane, but Jon – one of the people she would least have expected.

'Yes.' She was wary, wondering what on earth might have happened. Were things about to get worse?

'I wondered if we could talk.' He sounded equally cautious.

'What is it?'

'It's Beth. I don't know what to do. I need some advice. You know her so well, and you know me. I thought you'd be able to help.' Cautious, but at the end of his tether.

'I'll try.' She hesitated. 'But I'm not sure how well I really do know her any more. Go on.' If there was anything she could do for him, she would. For old times' sake.

'Not over the phone. Can I come round, tomorrow evening maybe, or the one after? We've got a houseful and I can't just disappear.'

'Whichever you like's fine with me. Pete's away as usual and I'm not doing anything much.' Except planning a funeral for my career.

'Are you OK?' Sometimes more sensitive to her moods than her own dear husband, he had always had a knack of knowing when she was down.

'Oh, just something at work. You don't want to know.'

'Tell me tomorrow when I see you.'

She looked at the phone after he'd hung up. Perhaps she would. In the absence of Beth, and with Pete away, she could use a friend.

25

Megan hurried down the corridor to her office, her determination that Ben Fletton was not going to outwit her driving her forward. She had been over and over what had happened the previous day and was certain that nothing she had done could possibly be interpreted as any kind of physical abuse. The Flettons had no case. The bruise, if there was one, must have been inflicted by someone else. She wouldn't put it past Ben to have given it to himself.

She had been behind her desk for only seconds when the head put her head round the door. 'Shall we?'

When Megan saw Jane's awkwardness, she realised this was not going to be as straightforward as she'd hoped. Jane brought in two coffees and they sat together where Megan and Ben had sat the day before.

'This whole thing is ridiculous,' Megan began. 'Ask Marilyn. Ben's been a nightmare all year. He deliberately stirs up trouble, and ends up here because the teachers can't cope. Yesterday Jaden had to go to hospital thanks to him. Read the first-aid log. Afterwards he was so uncooperative and rude that I took him off the Chessington trip and the football team. That's all that happened.'

'I believe you, if that's any consolation.' Jane clasped her hands on her lap. 'But ...' She let the word hang there, closing her eyes, taking a deep breath. 'We have to follow the protocol. I spoke briefly to a friend on the council last night and he confirmed that I've no choice but to suspend you pending a hearing. I'm so sorry.'

'But how long will that take?'

'As quickly as we can arrange it. Of course, the fact that the holidays are about to start may draw things out a bit, but I'll try not to let them. And I'll have a word with the chair of governors ...'

Their meeting was brief. All that remained was for Megan to pick up what she needed and go home, until she was summoned. As she left the school, she passed various mothers in the corridor dropping off their children. She greeted a couple, but instead of the usual smiles, they muttered replies and turned away. She knew what this meant. Word was out already. Some of them had got wind of the charge against her and were gunning for her. She'd seen this happen before to a teacher when she was training. In the knot of women at the school gate, she spotted Josie Fletton's blonde updo. As she approached, they stopped their chatter, a couple of them staring at her, hostile, before they turned back to the others. She was sure she heard the words 'bruise' and 'bitch' as she passed. So this was how a witch hunt began.

For the rest of the morning, she tried to get hold of Pete. She didn't want to talk to anyone but him, not just yet. Either there was no signal or his phone was off. By lunchtime, she was steaming. Why was it that whenever he went on one of his trips he felt he had to immerse himself in the experience without any forays into the humdrum life of home? He always complained about how his travelling companions phoned and emailed their families all the time. He himself would only deal with work-related contact during the day, limiting himself to evening calls home (often when she was in bed and he was the last person she wanted to hear from), assuming she would cope without him if there was an emergency. And if something happened to her? She could have killed him.

Gardening provided a predictable palliative. As she snipped and pulled, repotted and planned, she came to a resolve. This situation was nothing but a hiccup in her long career: the most serious, but a hiccup nonetheless. She would not let it get to her. Worrying about a process she couldn't affect was pointless.

She wished she could talk to Beth. But those days had gone. Perhaps she should just pick up the phone and try. But the afternoons of the barbecue and then the school fair had demonstrated the distance between them. Beth obviously felt it as much as she did. Megan didn't relish the idea of further humiliation by asking for help and being turned away. But surely they needed to come to a truce before their grandchild was born?

She occupied herself through the rest of the day, then made an early supper. With no one else to cater for, she treated herself to cheesy scrambled eggs and the remains of the apple pie and cream. Since there was nobody there to see, the calories didn't count. And a glass of wine. She picked up a book. *The Poisonwood Bible*. Oh, the tyranny of the book group. She wasn't in the mood, so she put the damn thing down and switched on a cookery show, muting the sound, just to keep her company. Perhaps she could stop going to the group at last; Beth clearly wouldn't want her there now. She could make new friends at that knitting shop on the high street, or by taking up yoga or Pilates. Perhaps she should join a choir, except she couldn't sing, or take up bridge, or aqua aerobics for the over fifties. The possibilities were limitless, but the idea of them depressed and exhausted her. Perhaps her dwindling energies would be better directed into one final attempt at building a bridge between her and Beth.

The doorbell interrupted her deliberations. She wasn't expecting anyone except the kids, and she didn't even know whether she was really expecting them. Jake hadn't made an appearance for a couple of days, staying over with friends, she assumed. And Hannah? She seemed to be celebrating the end of exams endlessly. Megan sighed. Only the results would tell them whether she had done enough work when it had mattered.

She did up the button that had come adrift on her shirt – could she really have put on weight since last summer? Obviously, yes – and squinted through the spyhole to see Jon standing there. In all the years she'd known him, she had never seen him look so rough. He was dressed casually but carefully. His face was drawn, he hadn't shaved and his eyes were shadowed.

'Sorry. I couldn't wait until tomorrow.' He leaned against the jamb as she opened the door.

'It's fine. I'm not doing anything and everyone else is out.' Concerned at his pallor, she took him into the garden. 'I'll get us a drink. Wine OK?'

He nodded. 'Thanks.'

As she pulled out the glasses and found a packet of peanuts, she wondered what on earth had brought him here. They hadn't spoken since the day of the barbecue. She imagined that things had not been easy for him since then. She hadn't wanted to make the situation worse or embarrass him by phoning. If he needed her, he would call. She couldn't help wondering, yet again, who Ella's biological father could be. She also reminded herself not to get involved. Tread carefully.

She took everything out to where Jon sat on the garden bench, his head tipped back, eyes closed. 'Nuts?' she asked.

'Not far off!' He straightened up and looked at the small bowl she was offering. 'Oh.' He helped himself and picked up his glass.

'That bad?' She sat beside him.

'Worse, probably,' he replied. 'You were there. You've seen Amy. You know.'

'So it is true?' She hardly dared ask.

'Of course. Beth would never come out with something like that if it weren't. Hasn't Ella been here to share it all with you?' Was that a trace of bitterness that she heard? No, she thought not. Jon wasn't like that.

'I've seen her a couple of times, of course, but she didn't really want to talk to me. She's learned her lesson and she's got Jake now.' Her restraint gave way and she couldn't hold the question back any longer. 'But if you're not her dad, who is? Pete and I can't remember Beth ever talking about anyone else.'

'She never told anyone about him, that's why. And she wouldn't have talked to you; after all, you were – you are,' he corrected himself quickly, 'my closest friends. Weren't those the days? Life was a hell of a lot simpler then.'

'Hardly!' Megan protested. Had he forgotten all those dramas they went through together? 'Don't you remember when Katie dumped you? You were distraught. Pete and I were practically on suicide watch for months …'

'Lord, yes. I'd almost forgotten.' He gave a hollow laugh. 'It seemed like the end of the world back then. If only I'd known …'

'Quite,' said Megan. 'I wonder what happened to Katie.'

Only months after Megan had met Pete, the three of them had gone island-hopping in Greece together. Katie had been sitting on the passenger deck of the ferry from Piraeus to Paros, strumming a guitar and singing. She was bronzed, beatific, with a low, husky singing voice that reminded them of Marianne Faithfull. They were all entranced.

Megan remembered the floaty long skirts, long straight hair tied with a band around her forehead, flawless skin, arched eyebrows and the earthy aura of patchouli oil that followed Katie around. A hippy through and through, she drifted around Jon's life for almost a year. He was totally besotted. Then one weekend she disappeared with a fellow musician, giving no warning, leaving a note explaining she had gone to an ashram somewhere in India 'to find myself'.

'God knows. I never heard from her again. Just that note. She left all her things, remember?'

'How could I not?' Megan was the one who'd eventually bagged them up and donated them to the Oxfam shop.

After Katie's disappearance, Jon was wary of women. Each relationship he embarked upon was short-lived, as he refused time and again to commit, scared of the same thing happening again.

He would spend hours confiding in Megan. So many hours of coffee and talking, they must have kept the entire Brazilian coffee industry afloat. The more time they spent together, the more Megan had wondered whether she had chosen the right flatmate. Pete was great fun, but she and Jon had a connection of another kind. But before anything could develop between them, he met Beth, and the merry-go-round took another turn.

'I don't remember life being simple then at all.' She poured them both another glass, offered the peanuts. 'But tell me what Beth meant.' She flapped away a wasp.

'That's why I wanted to see you.' He took her hand. She was slightly surprised, but made no move to take it back. 'I've got to talk to someone.'

As Jon told the story of Gerry and how he fitted into their lives, Megan watched his face. At the start, he was impassive, almost as if he was tired of the whole business, but as he began to talk about Ella and the effect the discovery had had on her, his expression changed. He didn't need to say how regretful he was that she had found out like this; Megan could read the sorrow in his eyes. Nor did he need to say what he felt about Gerry or how puzzled and angered he was by Beth's behaviour. That was all written there too. Eventually, when he had brought Megan up to date, he paused, then said, 'Beth's been to see him, to talk to him about meeting Ella.' Looking wretched, he took a sip of wine.

Megan felt so sorry for him. 'You must hate the idea of that.'

'You've no idea how much.' He screwed his face up, clenching his fist. For a second, she thought he might break down.

'But, can't you stop them meeting?' she asked, trying to think of a solution.

'It's what Ella wants.' He spoke as if he had lost all hope.

And, as always, Ella gets what Ella wants. But Megan kept that thought to herself.

'I don't even think Beth wants it to happen,' he went on.

'But I don't really know what she wants any more. We're barely speaking. She knows how angry I am. And she's eaten up by guilt. Doesn't know how to make amends. Trouble is, even though I know she's been on a knife edge since Ella got pregnant and went to you, and then Jake … I can't forgive her for letting it all out like that. However pressurised she felt. Not after all these years and everything we promised each other.'

'I don't blame you.' Megan refilled their glasses.

He stretched out his legs. 'But suppose when she meets this Gerry, Ella decides she wants to know him better. I don't think I could bear it. I want to be adult and reasonable about the whole thing, but it's tearing me apart. I'm jealous of the bloody man. So jealous. I want to be Ella's father in every way – and I never will be.' He punched the arm of the bench.

Megan admired his honesty. 'She won't want to,' she tried to reassure him. But on what grounds could she say that? 'You have such a good relationship with Ella, she's not going to abandon you like that. How could she?'

'But she might. He might charm her. After all, he charmed Beth.' His frown deepened.

'Jon!' She couldn't let him torture himself like this. 'For heaven's sake. That was years ago and completely different.'

'She always promised she would never see him again. I believed her, but suppose she has? Suppose now she's seen him, it all kicks off again.'

The way he was looking at her said he wanted her to contradict him. 'Didn't you say he was older than her? He's probably on his last legs, a Zimmer at least.'

He managed a wry laugh. 'Bed-bound and incontinent. One can but hope!'

'Don't!' She shivered. Without the sun, the evening was unexpectedly chilly. 'Infirmity and death. Dementia.'

'Somehow I think that's sadly not the case. He's coming down to see us at the weekend. For tea.'

'You're kidding?' Megan imagined the four of them sitting with fingers crooked, porcelain cups, a cake stand of fancies on a white damask cloth. No, that would never work.

'I wish I was. Ella's so excited, I can't rock the boat. She's been through too much recently. But Beth knows perfectly well how I feel about the whole thing.'

'Haven't you talked about it?'

'I told you. We're hardly speaking. I can't. I don't trust myself.'

Megan didn't know how to react. Instead, she went for the safe option. 'I think we need another bottle, don't you? Let's go inside while I think.'

In the sitting room, the table lamps gave a soft light against the growing dusk outside. While Jon went to the upstairs bath-room, Megan kicked Hannah and Jake's debris of magazines and DVDs under a side table, where they would be less visible. She put the wine and the glasses on the table in front of the sofa, then sat down and waited. Opposite her, above the fireplace, the portrait of a handsome young woman looked back at her – an old favourite in their collection that she hadn't looked at properly for ages. Painted in the forties by an unknown artist, but Megan didn't care about his identity. She could interpret what he must have felt for his sitter. And she for him.

'I do love her,' she said to Jon as he returned, indicating the picture with a nod of her head. 'Look at her eyes, the way she's looking at the painter.' She sighed.

'You're such a romantic.' Jon sat beside her, pouring them both another glass.

'Rubbish!' Megan was beginning to feel pleasantly mellow, but she didn't stop him. If he had come for her company, she was happy to oblige. Besides, what had she got to get up for in the morning? Why hadn't Pete called so that she could tell him what had happened at school? At that thought, she picked up her glass. 'To us,' she said. 'Pete's away again. And you and Beth aren't speaking. What a success we've made of our lives.'

As they drank, she was aware that he was watching her, a strange look on his face. What was he thinking? She glanced down at her lap, self-conscious, then crossed her legs and studied her foot.

'You've always been there for us,' he said. Ush? Was he slurring his words?

'Did you have a drink before you got here?' She hadn't meant to sound so schoolmarmish. She sipped at hers.

'Just one,' he admitted with the grin of a schoolboy who'd been caught out. 'Well, perhaps two. Anyway, where were we?'

'You and Beth not talking. Ouch!' She put her glass down and rubbed the corner of her eye.

'Oh, yes.' His expression changed. 'And bloody Gerry, who's coming whether I like it or not. It's all arranged. Nothing I can do.'

'Oh, Jon, there must be something. Talk to Beth.' She rubbed again. Must be an eyelash.

'I told you, it's no good.' He leaned towards her. 'Got something in your eye?'

'Probably an eyelash.' She felt it stinging. 'I'll go and slosh some water on it. Won't be a minute.' She started to stand up.

'Hang on. Let me see. Maybe I can get it out with a tissue. Here.' He pulled a neatly folded one from his jeans pocket and leaned towards her. His face was so close to hers that their noses were almost touching. His finger was gentle on her face as he pulled her lower lid down. 'I see it. Hang on.'

She could smell the wine on his breath, his limey cedar scent. She realised she was holding her breath and let it go with a sigh as he dabbed the tissue against her inner eyelid.

'Got it!' Triumphant. 'Better?'

She nodded, unable to look away. She knew what was about to happen. Could anything be more corny? She stifled a giggle, but she did nothing to stop him. The two of them were in a bubble all of their own, careless of the outside world. His lips were soft, the kiss feather-light. That was enough. Beth. Ella. Pete. They whirled through her head, making her draw away. But, before she could think again, he pulled her back towards him. His tongue was in her mouth, his lips on hers. He held her face between his hands. She hadn't been kissed like this for years. This couldn't be happening. It was thirty years too late. Then her thoughts stopped as her body responded to him and she abandoned herself to the moment. She felt the cushion behind her slip to the ground, heard the phone crash to the floor.

'We shouldn't ...' she managed.

'We should.' She was taken aback by the urgency in his voice.

Her left arm was hurting where it was pinned behind her. She hoped the veneers on her front teeth would survive as they clashed with his. They hadn't been tested quite this vigorously before. His reading glasses fell from his shirt pocket. The sofa creaked. His knee jabbed into her thigh as the TV remote drilled into her left buttock. She reared up and they both tipped to the floor, almost heedless of the side table that went with them.

His hand was on her right breast, and he was saying something she couldn't make out, his voice lost between her chin and her collarbone. She spared a second's thought for which bra she had on – the black, she hoped. Decent. And then she was lost again. So this was what it was like with someone who wasn't Pete. It had been so long – just the stuff of fantasies for years. The kisses went on and on, sensuous, probing, arousing. She hoped he wouldn't put his hand on her waist, suddenly self-conscious of her newly acquired extra pounds. But another kiss took her far away from such considerations.

He was having some trouble with the buckle on his belt, so she helped him with it, not considering the consequences. She felt his hand on her hip as he levered himself on top of her. Her skirt was rucked up beneath her. Her sciatic nerve gave a warning dart down her left leg. She tried to move into a more comfortable position, but the weight of him prevented her. Then he kissed her again and she sank back under a wave of delirium.

At that moment, the front door slammed. 'Mu-um? Where are you?'

Megan rose to the surface as surely as if she'd been shot from an underwater cannon.

Footsteps on the stairs. Thank God. Normally Hannah would have gone straight into the kitchen. 'Get off,' she whispered, coming to her senses in a second. What on earth had they been thinking? 'Quick.'

She struggled to her feet, sorting out her skirt, doing up her blouse (quickly covering not the black but the old beige bra), taming her hair with her fingers in the mirror before slipping on her sandals. Behind her, Jon was tucking in his shirt, adjusting his trousers and straightening the troublesome buckle. He righted the table as Megan tossed the cushions back on the sofa and they heard Hannah coming downstairs.

'Mum?'

'In here.' Megan rubbed her cheeks, hoping that the telltale flush was dying down.

Hannah put her head round the door. 'I thought you must be in bed. Oh! Hi, Jon.'

'Hi.' He looked up from the travel brochure he'd found on the floor, adjusted his specs on his nose.

'I'm off out again. Just going round Nat's. Is that OK?'

'Of course. When will you be back?' Megan's voice sounded oddly pitched, but Hannah didn't seem to notice.

'If you give me the money, I'll get a cab back by midnight.'

Megan couldn't be bothered to argue. She just wanted Hannah out of there. 'Take it out of my purse.'

Hannah disappeared and they heard the front door slam. They looked at each other. Megan felt herself blushing.

'Christ! What happened?' Never had a man sobered up so fast. His eyes were wide with alarm. 'I didn't mean ...'

What didn't he mean? 'Coffee?' she suggested.

He nodded, looking appalled at the prospect of having been so nearly caught out by one of their children. 'Do you think she realised?'

'Realised? I don't think you need worry. As far as she's concerned, we're dinosaurs, way too old to even be thinking about sex. No, she won't have realised.' But thank God she had come home when she had. Any later and it would have been a whole lot worse – in all sorts of ways. Dinosaurs or not, desire had definitely got the better of them. 'Drink equals geriatric aphrodisiac. We probably couldn't have got any further anyway,' she joked. Perhaps they could just pretend it hadn't happened.

He looked at her, grateful, but both of them knew the truth.

26

'This is a terrible idea.' Jon's voice floated out from behind the wardrobe door. He emerged with a shirt and a jacket.

'I know you don't want to meet him.' Beth sat in front of her mirror and slipped in a knotted gold earring. 'I do understand.' She concentrated on brushing her hair, unable to look at him, unable to bear seeing how much he was hurting.

'Well why the hell suggest it, then?' Leaving his clothes on the bed, Jon disappeared into the bathroom.

Beth heard the sound of running water, and had to raise her voice to make herself heard. 'Because we thought it was a good idea, that it would help Ella.'

Jon put his head out of the door, toothbrush in hand. 'Who's this "we"? I thought you and I made the decisions when it came to what's best for this family.' He disappeared again. This was the same hostility he'd shown towards her when she had told him she was pregnant with Gerry's child, and it frightened her. She couldn't blame him, but she was scared of what he might do, of what was going to happen to them.

'Of course we do.' She raised her voice to be heard over the sound of his sluicing and spitting. 'But Gerry suggested we all meet together. And I think it's a good idea.' She picked up her favourite gold and enamel bracelet, a present from Jon on her fiftieth birthday, and slipped it on her wrist.

'And the fact that I don't doesn't matter?' He returned to the room, a white towel wrapped around his lower half.

'Of course it matters.' What was wrong with him? Why

couldn't he see how she had been thinking of all of them? She wasn't absolutely sure any more how this meeting would help, but if Ella saw the three of them being civilised about the situation, perhaps it would do some good. 'I just thought Ella came first.'

'Pity you didn't think that when you blurted it all out!' He disappeared again.

That hurt.

As she heard him getting into the shower, she wrestled with her conscience. Whether or not meeting was the right thing to do, it was too late to change their minds now. They were due at the hotel in less than an hour. She wondered how Gerry must be feeling. Nervous? Excited? Calm?

She pulled on her coral dress and took her sandals from the rack. That morning, when she had tried for the umpteenth time to tell Jon about her trip to York and what exactly had been said, he'd refused to listen to more than a few words. Instead, he'd chosen to spend lunchtime mowing the lawn. Eventually, he had stamped inside, cutting her dead, leaving it till the last possible moment to get ready. She understood his fear that Ella and Gerry would get on well, and that Ella would somehow stop loving him. But love wasn't a tap that could be switched on and off. When he met Gerry and saw him with Ella, he would realise that that would never happen.

Jon emerged from the bathroom, a cloud of steam in his wake. With her back to him she watched his reflection in the mirror as he dressed. The gym and those regular tennis games had paid off. He was close to being as lean and muscled today as he had ever been. His arms were tanned as far as the short sleeves of his tennis shirt, his legs as far as his shorts.

'Ready?' she said, watching as he put on his blue linen shirt. 'Don't be scared.'

'Scared? I'm not scared of him.' He gave a short laugh at the idea. 'I just don't want to meet him. Is that so hard to understand?

I've never wanted him in our lives. You promised he wouldn't be. And you've broken that promise.'

She reached for his hand. 'I know.' She felt those wretched tears threatening again as he turned his back on her.

'When are we leaving?' He pulled up his trousers, zipped his fly.

As if he didn't know. 'Any minute. I'll just go and check that Ella's OK.'

'Of course she will be. This performance was her idea in the first place.' He rubbed his hair with a towel, then peered at himself in the wardrobe mirror as he combed it through before roughing it with his fingers. 'Why the Regency?'

'Because I thought we'd be better on neutral ground. And the Regency's quiet.' She hadn't wanted Gerry to see where she worked, and it was unthinkable that he should come to their home. Everything was arranged now. She knew what Gerry was going to say. This meeting was something they just had to get through. In a couple of hours, it would be over and their lives would be their own again.

She went out on to the landing. 'Ella?' She waited for a reply.

'Just coming. Nothing fits, though.'

Though she was hardly huge, Ella's pregnancy was definitely showing now. To Beth's surprise, among the sea of troubles, the thought of the baby gave her a kind of joy. Although she still had her private reservations, she was coming round to the baby a little bit more every day. Ella was blooming, obviously happy and confident with her decision. Jake was revealing himself to be a steady, more thoughtful partner than Beth had ever imagined.

Jon followed Beth downstairs, where they stood in the hall waiting. He slipped on a dark jacket, then took it off and hung it up again. Beth jumped as his arm brushed her shoulder.

'Sorry,' he said. 'I know I'm not helping, but this is so bloody difficult. I've never wanted to meet this man, and I certainly don't want to now. I'm only going along with this for Lulu and in the hope that it will help us to have some sort of civilised future together.'

Grateful that he had said something at last, Beth turned. 'I know.' She squeezed his arm. 'I can't tell you how much I wish I'd never put us in this position, but I can't keep on saying sorry. He'll soon be gone.'

He moved away from her touch. 'I can't help it. I don't want him in our lives.'

'He's not going to be. I've told you.' She raised her hand to her necklace.

'How do you know?' he pressed her. 'How do you know that once he's met Ella he won't want to see her again? And then again? How do you know she won't want to see him?'

'Because I know him,' she insisted. 'He's an honourable man.'

'So you say,' he scoffed. 'But he wasn't so honourable twenty years ago, was he? You were a married woman.'

'Don't. Please. That sort of remark's beneath you.' But she hadn't a leg to stand on.

Before they could continue, they heard Ella's door shut and looked up together. Outside, a car horn beeped.

Ella raced down the stairs. She was wearing a floaty floral dress, leggings, her hair in a topknot, a minimum of make-up. 'That'll be the taxi!' She bent to get her pumps from the shoe rack and put them on. 'Ready?'

'Yes,' said Beth, bursting with pride. 'Yes, of course.'

Jon didn't speak, just opened the front door.

The minicab was stuffy and stank of stale smoke and lemon air-freshener. Ella screwed up her nose and opened the window wide as Beth gave directions. The driver took them to the end of the road and turned left. Beth felt Jon tense beside her. 'Odd route,' he muttered, then carried on to criticise every aspect of the journey under his breath. 'Why are we going this way?' 'Shouldn't we turn right here?' 'Much quicker to go down there.'

If the driver understood, he didn't rise to the bait. Beth bit her lip, knowing that anything she said would be fallen on and ripped apart. Ella stared into the wind, a hand over her mouth, clearly willing the journey to be over.

At last, they pulled up outside the hotel. They were shown into the lounge, where Beth had booked the table in the far corner, tucked away from the rest. The place was busier than she had expected, with several tables occupied by middle-aged ladies dropping from their shopping and reviving themselves with cups of tea, glasses of pink champagne, plates of cakes and sandwiches. The thick carpet, heavy curtains and dim lighting gave an air of comfortable opulence, a cool retreat from the muggy summer day outside.

Jon didn't look to left or right as they crossed the room and was visibly relieved to see they had arrived before Gerry. He chose the chair that faced the door. Beth and Ella sat either side of him. After ten minutes, when there was still no sign of Gerry and their tea had been served (Jon insisted on just a pot of tea and scones, no cakes – 'We're not celebrating anything'), Beth pushed back her chair, unable to stand the tension another moment.

'Why don't I go to the lobby and make sure there isn't a message for us?'

Jon looked as he was about to say something, but then thought better of it, leaving her to do just that.

As she stepped out of the room into the marble-floored foyer, she breathed a sigh of relief at getting away. Perhaps Gerry wasn't going to show. All she wanted was a message saying so, and then they could go home and start again.

'Beth?'

He had come after all. True to his word, as always.

'I'm sorry I'm late. Getting a taxi from the station was murder.' He looked the part of a gentleman caller in his cream trousers and dark linen jacket, navy blue and white polka-dot cravat tucked into the neck of his shirt despite the heat, a straw panama in one hand, walking stick in the other.

She noticed a tic at the corner of his right eye. So, he was not as unperturbed as he'd first seemed. She kissed him lightly on the cheek, then, anxious that the gesture might be inappropriate, stepped back.

'You look lovely,' he said, appraising her. 'That coral colour suits you.'

'I was wondering whether to give up on you,' she said, now not wanting to allow anything at all personal between them. She was going to deal with this as if she was at a meeting at work, shutting off the emotional side of herself. If she could do that, she would cope, and that would help Jon and Ella get through this too.

'I hope we're doing the right thing,' he said as he followed her into the lounge, as if they were co-conspirators.

'I don't see we have a choice,' she said, turning her head towards him abruptly, surprised but relieved by how detached she still felt from him.

'I could have refused.'

'I knew you wouldn't.'

He gave a small smile.

She led the way through the tables to where Jon and Ella sat. They stopped talking and got to their feet. Ella's face was flushed, her eyes shining with excitement. Jon could not have looked less happy if he had tried. Around them sounded the clink of cutlery and china, the discreet murmur of voices.

Beth stood beside his chair, her hand on its back. 'Jon, this is Gerry. Gerry, this is my husband, Jon.'

Jon's eyes narrowed just a fraction as he took in his wife's former lover, appraising him. Gerry held out his hand, withdrawing it quickly when he realised Jon was not about to reciprocate. Beth moved on swiftly, pretending she hadn't noticed.

'And this is our daughter, Ella.' She had planned that 'our' carefully. She wanted to make it quite clear to them all that Gerry was not part of her life or her family. But, as she said it, she realised nonetheless how easily the word could be misinterpreted. By the thunderous look on Jon's face, he had clearly taken it the wrong way. Gerry seemed oblivious. He was smiling at Ella, who was staring back as if she had seen a ghost. She lifted her hand and put her finger on her dimple.

'I've got your chin,' she said.

Jon sat down loudly. 'And his eyes. Blue.'

And his hair colour, and his height, and the shape of his face, thought Beth, but she said nothing. She had always been aware of how much Ella resembled Gerry, but seeing them together was shocking. There was no mistaking their relationship. Jon must be finding that impossible.

'Tea?' she said, too brightly, hoping that they could at least be civilised.

'Would you excuse me for a minute.' Jon stood as suddenly as he had just sat down. 'I won't be long.' He headed out of the room, Beth's eyes on him, anxious.

Gerry took the chair next to Ella. 'Well!'

For once Ella seemed to have lost the power of speech. She was just staring at him, eyes wide.

'When's your baby due?' He grasped for conversation.

'September,' she managed.

'She's deferred her university entrance for a year,' said Beth, although she'd already explained when they met before.

'I'm going to do medicine,' added Ella.

'So … a doctor,' said Gerry, unnecessarily.

This was awful. Beth glanced at her watch. Four o'clock. How soon would he leave or could she bring this politely to an end? Not until he'd said what he'd come to say. She willed him to get it over with.

Jon was making his way back to the table; it looked to Beth as if he might have been crying. He sat down, clearly not about to contribute to the conversation.

'How many children have you got?' asked Ella, although Beth was sure she had told her.

'Three daughters and a son.' Gerry went on to describe them one by one, as he had done to Beth a week earlier, obviously relieved to have something he could talk about. 'And I gather from Beth that you have a sister?' He reached out to help himself to a scone.

'Yes. And she is mine. In case you were wondering.' Jon's cup rattled against its saucer as he put it down.

'Dad!' Ella's face registered her shock that Jon could be so rude. The three of them stared at him as he ran a finger inside his collar, his face flushing.

'I wasn't, actually,' said Gerry. 'I realise this must be extremely difficult for you, but please remember that it is for me too. I had no idea Ella even existed until last week, whereas you've at least had years to get used to the knowledge that I'm her father.' He seemed quite unruffled as he pulled at the cuff of his shirt, though he left the scone untouched on his plate.

'I'm not interested in how hard it is for you. And it's not up to you to judge how I must be feeling. You have no bloody idea.' Jon got to his feet again.

'Jon!' Beth put out a restraining hand.

'Dad, don't!' Ella looked panic-stricken.

'I can't sit here and drink tea as if nothing was happening. We've met. That's enough. I'll leave you three to sort out whatever it is you're sorting out and see you both at home later.'

'Dad, please.' Ella grabbed his wrist. 'I'd like you to stay.'

'Lulu, I can't.' He put his hand on hers. 'I'm sorry. You know I'd do anything for you, but this is asking too much.' He planted a kiss on her forehead and left the table without even looking at Beth.

How could she ever have imagined that this would go well? She couldn't have been in her right mind. 'Excuse me for just a minute.' She followed Jon out, desperate to call after him but not wanting to cause a scene. She had no idea how he would react. By the time she reached the door of the hotel, he was halfway into a black cab, staring ahead, his face set.

'Jon, stop!' she called. Heads turned, then looked away. The uniformed porter held the door of the cab open as she rushed towards it. Jon leaned forward, towards her.

'Please,' she pleaded. 'For Ella.'

'Beth, I can't. This isn't Happy Families. Do this if you must, but it's too much to expect of me. I thought I could do it for Lulu, but turns out I can't.' He slammed the door, taking the porter by surprise.

Beth watched the taxi turn into the traffic, the back of Jon's bowed head. What had she done?

She returned to Ella and Gerry. Ella was clearly upset by Jon's abrupt departure, but Gerry was doing his best to keep a conversation going. He turned to Beth when she arrived at the table, offering them both a refill. The scones and jam lay between them, ignored.

'I'm sorry to have caused that. You seemed so certain he'd be OK.'

'I thought he would be.' She took her seat as he poured. 'He told Ella he was all right with us contacting you.'

Ella's eyes were on Beth, anxious, imploring.

Gerry uncrossed his legs and looked at his watch. 'I've got a taxi coming in half an hour.'

Ella gasped. 'So soon? But we haven't …'

'I never meant to stay for long,' he explained. 'I only came because Beth asked me to. I was curious, I admit. And although I'm very proud that I had a hand in your being on the planet, given what's happened here I don't think it's a good idea for us to meet again, do you?'

Speechless, Ella shook her head, her hand stroking her bump.

Beth reached for her cup, nervous, although she knew what Gerry was about to say.

'Look.' He held his hands out towards Ella. 'Please don't misunderstand me, but I already have four children, and three grandchildren. This may sound harsh, but I don't need another one any more than you need another father. I think they'd be horrified to find out about your existence, a little like the way Jon evidently feels about me.'

'But there are things I want to ask you.' Ella found her voice at last.

'Are there? Is there anything you really need to know? You've managed without me till now and I think that's how we should continue.' His hand rose to his cravat and straightened the knot.

'Why did you come, then?' It was anger that sounded in her voice, not hurt. She stared at him so furiously, he couldn't look away.

'I said. Because your mother asked me. Because you wanted me to. And I felt it was better to say this face to face.' His hand dropped to his lap.

Ella shook her head. Strands of hair untangled themselves from the topknot to hang over her cheeks.

'Anything you want to know, just write to my lawyer and ask. I'll make sure he replies.' He gave a sharp nod, as if he was instructing some underling.

'So that's it?' Beth heard Ella's disappointment and disbelief. 'You agreed to come all the way here just to tell me that?' Her chin wobbled a fraction.

He nodded gravely. 'I think it's for the best, don't you? We shouldn't know each other any better.'

'Perhaps.' She stood up, her eyes brimming with tears. 'I'll be back in a minute.'

Beth watched her retreat, helpless. Nothing she could do or say would make this better.

Gerry stretched out his legs. 'Phew!'

'Did you plan that little speech before you came?' Beth was stunned by his self-assurance. Although he was right in principle.

Ella would never have let the matter go until she had tracked him down. He had to put a stop to her involvement with him, however brutal. Not just for his own sake, but for theirs too.

He splayed his fingers on the edge of the table and studied his neat, square-cut nails thoughtfully. 'No, I hadn't intended to be so blunt. But once I saw you all together, and how hurt and angry Jon is, it made sense. We've satisfied Ella's curiosity and she'll get over what I've done. The baby will help, I'm sure. We're not going to get to know each other. I'm sure she's a great girl, and that I'd like her, but it would be a mistake.'

A waitress came over and bent to speak to him. 'Your taxi's here, sir.'

'Thank you. And could you bring us the bill?' he said, taking his panama and stick from the back of his chair. 'I didn't come down just to see you. I met an old friend for lunch and I'm going to stay with my eldest daughter tonight. It's all worked out very nicely.'

He'd just fitted them in as if they were a dentist's appointment, no more, no less. When the waitress reappeared, hesitating over whom to present with the bill, Beth put her out of her misery by taking it and reaching for her purse.

'Let me,' said Gerry, putting out his hand. 'I insist.'

He expected everything to be on his terms. But not any more. Beth put the cash into the folder. He raised his eyebrows, looked amused, but let her pay. She enjoyed the triumph, however small.

All that remained was to say their goodbyes, confident that they would never meet again. They waited for Ella, who, when she returned from the Ladies', was polite and brisk, not letting herself give away her real feelings. She and Beth watched him leave the room, his limp more obvious than Beth had noticed before. Once they knew he was safely in his taxi, it was their turn to leave.

27

Jon had phoned Megan from the Green Man, sounding distraught, asking if she would meet him. Casting aside her lingering resolve, she threw on her most flattering summer dress, dashed on tinted moisturiser, mascara and lip gloss, and set off. The pub was midway between them, convenient but hardly salubrious. She found him sitting in the garden at the back, a scrubby bit of wasteland where the grass had been worn away to dust, decorated with fag ends and a couple of empty crisp packets. Couldn't he have chosen to meet somewhere a bit more pleasant? There were five or six combined bench-tables, each with a large rusty ashtray under a faded parasol fluttering in the breeze. Two were occupied by canoodling couples, who must have been there since lunchtime, judging by the empty plates and glasses piled up around them. Jon sat alone at the corner table, beside a Christmas tree still dressed in its festive outdoor lights, forlorn in the summer heat. His back was to her, an untouched pint in front of him.

Megan edged around the side of the table and climbed in opposite him. Staring into the distance, a million miles away, he jumped to attention as she sat down. 'Megan! Thanks for coming. Drink? Let me get you something.'

She half stood. 'Don't worry, I'll get my own.'

'No, let me.'

They both laughed.

'A lime and soda, then, if you insist.'

He disappeared inside. Nice blue shirt. Chosen for Gerry's

visit, presumably. She could only assume that was why she had been summoned – to be a sounding board. Although a part of her hoped it might be something more. *Stop it! Now! You're just a bored housewife whose job's on the line and who needs a sympathetic shoulder. He belongs to someone else,* she reprimanded herself sharply. *Even if she's no longer a friend, he's off limits.*

While she waited for Jon to come back, she amused herself by listening to the conversation of the young couple on the next table, who were busy debating where they should spend their honeymoon.

'If we haven't got the money, let's stay in the UK,' he proposed. 'We're hardly going to be outside much.'

She giggled. 'But I want sun, Jamie. Spain or Greece or somewhere.' She snuggled up to her burly boyfriend and they kissed.

Love was in the air for some. Recalling the excitement of that youthful passion, dimmed in the face of jobs and mortgages and children and age, Megan wished she were young again. If anyone had ever expressed the same wish to her, her response would have been a brisk, 'You're as old as you feel.' But it wasn't true. You could feel as young as you pleased, but you couldn't ditch all that life experience that made you cautious, anxious, or even reckless when faced with opportunity. She would never know where that couple would end up honeymooning, because they were whispering now, aware of her interest, and Jon was back with her drink and a whisky chaser to accompany his pint.

'Bit early for that, isn't it?' she asked, anxious. She didn't want to be responsible for carting him home completely pissed.

'Don't worry. It's just the one.' He sat opposite her, rolling up his sleeves. The sun caught the dark hairs on his arms.

'Well?' she said, inviting the explanation for her summons. 'How did it go?'

'Dreadful.' He took a nip of his whisky, waiting as it burned his throat. He shook his head in disbelief. 'I behaved appallingly. They'll never forgive me.'

Megan could feel the sun on her cheek. She angled herself so that it warmed her back instead. If she kept quiet, he would fill the silence with whatever it was he wanted to tell her.

'He was so fucking … egregious.' He picked the word carefully, then shook his head. 'Him and Beth! I just don't see it.'

'It was a long time ago,' Megan offered. 'He must have changed.'

'Even so. He's in his seventies, debonair, wealthy I'd guess, in good nick, the sort that knows how to handle every situation.' He struck the table with his fist.

'That doesn't sound so bad.'

If he heard her, he didn't take any notice. 'But you know what really got me? Ella looks just like him. She's got his eyes, the same shape face, even his bloody dimple on her chin. Remember how we used to tell her the story of how a fairy had touched her there, to mark her out as special? I couldn't believe it. Actually, I couldn't bear it. Of course, Beth must have seen the resemblance every day for the last eighteen years and never said a thing. How could she, after I made her promise we'd never mention him? But that's what upsets me. She must have thought about him constantly. How could she help it? And Ella will never look like my daughter. Never. She'll always look like his.'

Megan listened as he described the tea party, the pain that he felt on meeting the man who was the one thing he could never be. Ella's natural father. His suffering was plain. He looked thoroughly wretched. How could she not feel anything but sympathy? How could Beth have put him through this? What had she been thinking? She reached across the table to place her hand on top of his, trying to convey that she understood, that she was there for him.

He flipped his hand over to clasp hers, but he didn't look up. Megan was aware that the honeymooners were leaving the table beside them. Once again, she and Jon seemed to be entering that bubble. Did he feel that too?

'You're a good friend to us,' he said. 'Always have been. I'm sorry to offload on you. If Pete were here, he'd tell me to man up. And perhaps he'd be right.'

But he's not, thought Megan. And if he were, what happened last night would never have happened.

'I should have hung on and supported Lulu, whatever I was feeling.' His grip on her hand tightened. 'All these years I've been able to distance myself from the truth by telling myself that he was no different from a sperm donor, an anonymous somebody who helped us out. Mum managed to persuade me to see it like that.' He gave a rueful laugh. 'I've even been grateful to him, for God's sake! But meeting him … that was never part of the deal.'

'Come home with me.' Had she really said that?

Jon looked up, startled. 'What?'

Blood rushed to her face. 'I just thought it would be nicer than sitting here,' she justified. 'Hannah and Jake are both out. So we'd be on our own.'

'Is that really a good idea after last night?' He at least smiled at the memory. 'We should probably both forget that, for all our sakes. Don't you think? Put it down to drink.' But he hadn't let go of her hand. 'I really don't need any more on my plate right now.'

'You're probably right,' she agreed hurriedly. Was that the faintest twinkle in his eye?

'Nice idea, though,' he added as an afterthought.

'You're just being kind,' she said, surprising herself again.

'No,' he said, looking at her at last. 'It is a nice idea. But not one we should do anything about. I don't know what's going to happen to me and Beth, but it wouldn't help. Besides, what about Pete?'

Flustered, she took her hand away, and this time there was no mistaking the relief in his face. 'I don't know why I said it. Silly of me.' She sipped her lime, buying time as she gathered herself together, appalled by how forward she had been. And what about

Beth? The kids? Wishing she could wind the clock back to before she had embarrassed them both, she returned the conversation to his family. 'So what do you think's going to happen with Ella and Beth now?'

'If only I knew.' He grasped his head with both hands, rubbing them back and forth as if that would clear his thoughts.

'Jon, listen to me.' Their eyes met. *Stop it.* 'Go home to Beth and the girls. Make up for running out on them. Show Ella how well you can handle this, whatever you're really feeling. You can do it. You must. Whatever happens, you won't lose her, I'm sure.'

'What about Beth? What if she and Gerry ...' He couldn't finish the thought.

'Talk to her.' This was why he had called her. So that she would tell him what he wanted to hear, reinforcing what he thought he should do. She was mortified. What on earth had she been thinking? That they would embark on some sort of superannuated affair? She was married to his best friend, for God's sake. The absent Pete. When Jon had turned up last night, they were both at a low ebb and needed company. No more than that. They were drunk, disinhibited, and had leaped at the opportunity for a bit of physical comfort. Old friends. That was all it was. But, however successfully she could rationalise the moment away, she couldn't pretend she didn't feel just the smallest fragment of regret.

'You're right, as usual.' He finished his whisky. 'Got a peppermint?'

She smiled and shook her head.

'I'll get some on the way home, then. Don't want to go in stinking of drink. God knows what'll be waiting.'

'No,' she agreed sadly. 'That wouldn't help at all.'

'What a creep! And he's my father!' Ella tossed the ball as hard as she could, and Jock skedaddled after it. 'I can't believe it!'

After a tearful half-hour at home, she and Beth had decided to clear their heads by taking Jock to the park. Oblivious to what was going on, he was having a high old time, racing after the ball, picking it up, dropping it and haring off after another dog or a squirrel. Beth felt utterly wrung out, regretting now that she had given in to Ella's demands in the first place, that she had expected too much of Jon. She should have managed things far better. She picked up the skanky old tennis ball that Jock had dropped at her feet. 'Yeuch. This isn't ours.' She chucked it towards an empty bit of grass, with Jock in hot pursuit.

'If I hadn't got pregnant, none of this would have happened. You wouldn't have fought with Megan, you wouldn't have shouted at Dad, I wouldn't have found out about Gerry and insisted on meeting him. This is all my fault.'

'No, it's nobody's fault.' Beth only wanted to console her. 'Life sometimes just runs away with itself, especially when it comes to families. People equal baggage and secrets, secrets that are often kept in the interests of others. But they always get found out in the end. As we've discovered. There's no point going over old ground. What's done is done. We can't undo it. We can only try to put things right and move on.'

'Mum, you're so wise.' Ella tucked her arm through Beth's.

'Well, don't sound so surprised.' But Beth was smiling even as she pretended to be hurt.

'You know what I mean. But you and him!' Ella screwed up her nose as she fell back into step. 'It's so weird. Although I know he's my father, I didn't feel any connection with him at all. None. I thought I would. Or that I *might*, at least. And now I feel … not cheated exactly, but a bit, I don't know, flat, I suppose.'

Beth patted her hand. 'But you've got a perfectly good dad. You don't need another.'

'That's not fair. I never said I wanted another one. I love Dad. Full stop. But I just had to see for myself. Perhaps it wasn't the best idea, as it turns out, but it was my first reaction. All that blood group stuff was just a stupid excuse.'

'Well, when Dad gets back, make sure you tell him that.' Beth stopped to let a toddler steer her doll's buggy past them, veering one way then another. As she stood still, she wondered where Jon had gone.

'I will.' Ella paused, unhooked herself from Beth, picked up the ball and threw it again. She turned to look at Beth, scrutinising her. 'What did you see in him? I mean *really* see in him?'

'I told you.' Beth felt uncomfortable revisiting the subject. She wanted to bury it where it belonged.

'Tell me again.' Ella stopped by an empty bench under a plane tree and sat down, patting the space on the seat beside her. Beth obliged, leaning back, stretching her legs out and crossing them at the ankle, reminded of all the times Ella had demanded a bedtime story. She would tap the edge of her bed as she urged one of them to sit down with a book. How fast the years had flown.

Beth took a deep breath. Just as when Ella was tiny, she couldn't refuse her. 'He was kind to me when I needed someone to be. He was funny, urbane – qualities I'd never really known before. At least not close to. Think of Barry, my stepdad. They couldn't be more different.' The girls had only met him once – a terrible visit encouraged by Jon. Barry's sighs, finger-drumming and clock-watching had made it plain they couldn't leave soon enough. 'Mum wouldn't have known what to make of Gerry. In a way, I wished she had met him back then; her reaction would have been priceless.'

'But you must have had boyfriends?' Ella narrowed her eyes, as if she was imagining Beth when she was young.

'Of course, but I was so driven, so determined, that I didn't allow enough time to make the relationships work. I'd left everything I knew behind in Nottingham and I had to make a go of it. Failure wasn't an option. I was far too proud.' Ella slid along the seat and slipped her arm through Beth's. 'But I've told you all this. Perhaps the fact that he was older than me made a difference. A bit of a father figure, maybe, though I hate to say it.'

'Weird.' Ella bent to clip on Jock's lead and tie it round the leg of the bench. He lay in the shade, tongue out, panting, his eyebrows twitching.

'And believe it or not, he was pretty sexy in those days.' Beth tipped her head back to look through the leaves, annoyed with herself for adding that. She didn't need to justify herself, or excuse him. She could still remember that first time he'd come to her rescue, knowledgeable and patient, as she floundered through the unfamiliar mound of paperwork. There'd been an unmistakable flicker of electricity that she had ignored for as long as she could, not wanting to be deflected from her work.

'Did you love him?' Ella's voice returned her to the present.

'No.' She watched a green parakeet land on a branch above her head, swiftly joined by another, their presence announced by loud screeches. 'Perhaps I imagined I did for a bit, but our relationship wasn't about that – more about a really close friendship, the sort you can only have with someone you see every day and have so much in common with, and occasional, but great, sex.'

Ella made a face. 'Oh, please. Too much information.'

'Well, you did ask.' But it was true that the two of them had never really talked about sex that openly, beyond the cautionary contraceptive chat. She found herself back-pedalling. 'The whole thing happened so long ago that it's hard to explain even with hindsight. Basically, it ran on his terms.'

'He hasn't changed, then. That's awful.'

'But that's what I keep telling you,' Beth insisted. 'It wasn't. That's what I wanted or needed then. The arrangement suited us both and it helped me get on. Admitting that now sounds terrible. But we didn't harm anyone. Then I met Dad and every-thing changed. If I saw Gerry at all, it was as friends, except for that one night you know about. And I can't regret it, because you were the result. And you came at just the right time – my career was established, Dad and I were married …'

'Not like me.' Ella looked down at her bump.

'No, not like you at all.' Beth patted Ella's leg.

'But you're glad I'm having my baby now, right?'

Glad? No, that wasn't what she felt. The excitement she had experienced at the scan was still there, but overlaid with a definite sense of resignation. Who was to know what might have happened in an alternative universe? Not having a baby might have led to another situation with which Beth would be equally unhappy. Anyway, what about the thrill she'd felt those times when Ella guided her hand to her belly and she felt the baby kick? That was what was important now.

'I'm looking forward to this as much as you,' she said. But that wasn't exactly true. However much she might love this child – and she would – she was dreading the disruption that would come with it, although she was at least now confident they would somehow cope. Of course, she would far rather Ella was qualified, happily married, and not having her baby under their roof. Was that so hard to understand? So selfish? Just as she had begun to look forward to a new stage in her life with Jon, one that gave them some of the old freedoms back. Would that happen now?

'Good.'

Beth looked away across the park, to the young families and groups of students enjoying themselves. She heard her thoughts echoing Jon's. *This is her life. Let her make her own mistakes.* He was right. She saw that now. She should take a step back, stop trying to control her daughters. She had taken charge of her own life at their age, made those important decisions on her own – and so should they. All she had to do was be sure to be around to pick up the pieces if the worst happened. And perhaps it wouldn't. On the other hand, if Ella were older, it might be different, but was she really equipped to make these choices alone? Was stepping back the right thing to do when Beth's experience told her that her daughter was making a mistake?

'Can't you and Megan be friends again?'

Beth turned towards Ella, who was staring at her, blue eyes

intent. She pictured Megan in her garden, enjoying the sunshine. That was where she'd be now. Glass of rosé. Relaxed.

'I don't know,' she replied, quite honestly. 'We seem to have reached an impasse. I can't see how we can go back to square one now. Too much water under the bridge. Too much said.'

'I wish you would, for mine and Jake's sake, if nothing else. You not speaking makes everything so difficult. I feel disloyal wherever I am.'

Beth smiled. So Ella still had that mile-wide solipsistic streak that came with every teenager. 'To be honest, there are other more important things I've got to see to first.'

'Dad?'

'Exactly. And Amy. I've rather neglected her, what with one thing and another.'

'She'll be OK. She's tough as old boots. And she's happy now Jake's got her tickets for Latitude.' Ella bent to untie Jock, who leapt to his feet, tail wagging. 'Get down, you idiot.'

'I hope so.' The summer holidays were on them, exams over at last. 'Are you sure you're going to be OK at all these festivals you and Jake have got planned?'

'Mu-um! Don't! I'll see what it's like next weekend and then decide. I really want to go and have fun. It's been a tough few months.'

For once, Beth decided not to say any more.

As they walked home, Jock pulling in front, Beth thought about the summer ahead of them. Not long until she and Jon were due to go to their borrowed villa in Majorca. Right now, she couldn't imagine them on holiday together at all. But Paris had helped them once; perhaps Majorca would too. A compromise had been reached with Amy after Jake had come up with those Latitude tickets. She would come with them to Majorca after all, bringing Natalie with her. Hannah had Newquay and a fortnight's internship at a women's magazine, so there was no question of her coming. Ella and Jake would go to their festivals, and if Ella changed her mind about joining them, she could. Beth hoped she would. They would leave all this disruption behind and regroup as a family. And when it was over, there would be the baby ...

28

Was there any point in getting up this morning at all? Megan pondered. She did need to relieve the increasingly painful pressure on her bladder, and she supposed she should go to the meeting at school. Jane had called the day before, hinting that she had news but she couldn't explain just yet. The bedroom window, which Megan always kept open whatever the time of year to cool her hot flushes, rattled in a gust of wind. But, under the duvet, she was warm, alone, cut off from the world at large and keen to remain that way. She wanted her job back. She wanted her life back as she knew it.

After half an hour of dozing, coming to and hearing snatches of the news on the radio, then drifting off again, she gave herself a stern talking-to. *Come on, woman. Go into battle for yourself. You didn't hit the boy, and Jane believes that.* She got up, had a brisk shower and dressed to impress: smart trousers, T-shirt and jacket; make-up. Nothing much she could do about her hair except brush it into a half-baked short-lived submission. She would not show those mothers that they were getting to her. Instead of cycling, she took the bus, determined to arrive looking in charge.

By the time she arrived at St Columbus, the majority of parents had dropped off their children and left. There was a small gaggle around the gate who nodded embarrassed hellos, but nothing worse than that. Head held high, she ran up the steps and buzzed to be let into reception.

Jane came to fetch her as soon as she was announced. The door clicked shut behind them as they entered the corridor of offices and classrooms. Jane didn't beat about the bush. 'Josie Fletton's bringing in Ben. And Micky and his dad are already here.'

'Oh, God.' Megan's spirits sank. 'Do we have to do this? I thought it was going to be more formal, council-led, school governors. All that.'

'So did I.' Jane stopped just before they got to her office. 'But there's been a change of heart. Micky and Ben have had a big falling-out. They were caught fighting outside the school two days ago. Since then, Micky's changed his story.' She gave a reassuring smile.

'No!' All at once, the sky outside seemed bluer, the sun brighter. 'Why didn't you say anything yesterday?'

'I couldn't. Not until I'd seen his father and talked to him. If you could just wait here, I'll bring them in.' She showed Megan into her office and went to get the others.

Megan stood at the window behind the desk. The threat of her enforced absence becoming permanent had reinforced what she already knew: that St Columbus was in her blood. She had been part of the school too long to give up on it, or for it to give up on her. When she'd thought she was going to lose it all ... She stared across the empty playground to the park beyond. With the trees in leaf, she could only make out the edge of the football pitches and tennis courts. She needed to be here.

Someone cleared their throat. She spun around. Jane had returned, accompanied by Josie and Ben Fletton. Josie resembled a flustered chicken, except she was dressed in a pink tracksuit, with large fiddly earrings that jingled when she moved her head. Ben looked sulky and unrepentant. Behind them came a timid Micky Lonsdale and his dad, a well-built cabbie who didn't look as if he would take any nonsense. Micky was sporting a nasty black eye, and a bandage on his left wrist, presumably trophies from his recent argument with Ben.

'Right,' said Jane. 'I think you all know each other, so why don't we sit down.'

Megan took a seat by Jane, while the others shuffled into place around the table. Sitting on chairs low enough for primary children slightly distracted from the gravitas of the meeting. Megan waited as Jane began the proceedings.

'Now. Just so we're all quite clear. Ben has accused Mrs Weston of hitting him. That's an extremely serious allegation to make about any teacher. Mrs Weston has been suspended since his accusation, pending a disciplinary hearing. However, Micky...' she paused and looked in his direction, 'has changed his statement in which he said he saw the incident.'

The boy faltered under the glare both Flettons gave him.

'Go on, son,' encouraged Micky's father, putting a beefy hand on his son's shoulder. 'Tell her what you told me.'

Megan longed to be able to help the child, who looked frankly terrified. But, with his father giving him support, he finally spoke. 'I didn't see nothing although I was in the corridor.'

He gazed up at his dad, who nodded encouragement. 'And? Why did you say you did?'

Micky looked at his knees, determined not to catch anyone's eye. 'Because Ben said he'd stop the others speaking to me if I didn't.'

'And why are you telling us now, Micky?' Jane's voice was gentle, coaxing.

'' 'Cos Billy told me he was going to do that anyway. Then Ben took my money for the after-school club, and we had a fight.' Micky's voice was so small and scared that nobody moved so that they could hear him clearly.

'Poor little sod came home in tears,' added his father. 'He didn't want to tell us, but we've talked about bullying ever since his brother suffered a few years ago. Secondary school that was. He knows you have to stand up to them.' He glanced at Ben, who swung his leg and kicked the table.

His mother slapped his thigh immediately. 'Ben! Stop that.'

'So what do you have to say, Ben?' Jane's voice didn't change, but Ben didn't reply, just ran his fingers over his buzz cut.

'Ben. The teacher's talkin' to you.' His mother jabbed his arm.

'Yeah, well.' He dug his hands into his pockets.

'So are you agreeing that you told Micky to lie for you?' Jane pressed him gently.

Ben just stared at her, feral, challenging, like a fox stopped in the street at night.

'Well then.' Jane refused to be disconcerted. 'If you won't defend yourself, I can only assume it's true. Which brings us to the bruise on your arm. Are you still claiming that Mrs Weston is responsible for that?'

Ben fixed his eyes on a spot on the floor, refusing to look at any of them.

'No? Josie, have you got anything to say about that? Or Micky, perhaps?' Jane was like a dog with a bone, refusing to give up until she got what she wanted.

Megan's gaze flicked between Ben and Micky, waiting for one of them to speak. Josie fidgeted on her seat, touching her updo, studying her nails. Micky's dad nudged him. 'Just say what he told you, son. You might as well. You're halfway there now. It's the right thing to do.'

Micky looked up, clearly still scared, but gaining strength from his father. 'He said his dad did it.'

Josie was immediately on the edge of her seat. 'He said that? Ben! If you are lying to me, I'll ...' She raised her hand, bright with varnished nail extensions, then lowered it again.

No wonder Ben was such a problem child. Not even his mother had faith in him. His parents ran the pub a couple of streets away from the school: a renowned rough house that frequently had squad cars pulling up outside. They let their children run wild. Megan had seen Ben hanging out with the Meadows Estate gang. At the age of ten, for God's sake. With those sorts of examples to follow, it was no surprise that he behaved the way he did. Finally, Megan realised that there was nothing she could do to help the boy. The forces operating on Ben outside the school were too great for her to contend with. She was a fool for ever having believed she could.

'Losing our tempers won't help,' interjected Jane. 'The reason I've got you all here is because I would like to sort this out before I'm forced to take things to another stage. Mrs Weston denies she laid a finger on Ben. Micky has admitted he lied. So, Ben, I'm giving you this chance to put matters right. If we find out later on that you've been lying, the consequences will be much worse.'

'Are you threatening my boy?' Josie's feathers ruffled even more, but at least she was speaking up for him at last.

'Of course not,' Jane protested. 'I'm just trying to explain that it would be best if he were to tell the truth. Otherwise we may have to take this to another level. Mr Lonsdale, perhaps you would like to take Micky and wait outside while I speak to Ben?'

Micky was visibly relieved as they left the room, his dad's meaty hand on his shoulder. When the door had shut behind them, Jane turned again to Ben, who seemed to have shrunk in his seat. His bravado had deserted him, and Megan almost felt sorry for him. If her career weren't in the balance, she would have.

'So, Ben,' urged Jane. 'What did happen? Did Mrs Weston hurt you in any way? That's all I want to know. You're not going to get into trouble for telling the truth.'

There was an outraged explosion from Josie, but a glance from Jane stopped her saying anything more. All eyes were on Ben, who squirmed in his seat. His eyes moved from one of them to the next. Megan couldn't help but give him a small smile of encouragement. To her surprise, a tear rolled down his cheek. He wiped it away fast, but in that moment, she knew she was safe.

'No,' he said, his chin on his chest.

'I'm sorry, Ben. Can you explain what you mean?' Was Jane pushing him too hard?

'She didn't hit me. My dad done that. He hurt my arm.' The

316

words came out in a rush. He cowered as his mother raised her hand again.

'Josie, please,' Jane remonstrated. 'That won't help.'

Josie lowered her arm, looking thunderous.

'I just want to be absolutely clear, Ben. You're saying that Mrs Weston did not hit you after all?'

'Yes.' He sniffed. 'I just wanted to pay her back for not letting me go to Chessington.'

'You stupid little sod.' Josie poured all her scorn into her words, then half laughed and shook her head.

'Thank you,' said Jane. 'Is there anything you want to say to Mrs Weston before you go?' She turned to Megan, trying to hide the triumph and delight on her face.

He shook his head, fixing his gaze on the floor. 'Sorry.' He cleared his throat, then repeated it so Megan could hear quite clearly.

'Thank you,' she replied. 'Thank you for telling the truth.' There was nothing more to say. Their history was over.

A short time later, the Flettons and the Lonsdales had left the school, a further meeting between Jane and the Flettons to be arranged. When Jane returned from seeing them off the premises, Megan flung her arms around her. 'Thank you so much.'

'Don't thank me. Once I got the call from Mr Lonsdale, I had a feeling everything would work out. Of course I knew you weren't guilty. We've worked together for far too long for me not to know that you're a fine teacher who would never lay a finger on any of the children. But I had to play by the rules.'

'So what happens now?'

'Term's as good as over, so why don't you take the rest of the day off, then come back tomorrow?'

'That's kind of you,' Megan replied, about to burst with joy. 'But I think I'll just go straight to my office and carry on as if this hasn't happened. I've got plenty to do.'

As she walked along the corridor, she couldn't stop herself

humming. Just as everything had seemed to be tumbling around her ears, justice had prevailed after all. Perhaps, if she waited long enough, her other troubles would be resolved too. At this very moment, she believed anything might happen.

Beth turned the envelope over. It had lain in her bag for the last two days, shoved in there the moment she'd read the note inside. A sheet of watermarked cream wove paper. No address. No phone number. Just a scrawled date in the neat italic writing that she hadn't seen for so long. Then the message:

Dearest Beth (*Dearest?* How could he?)

After so long, this has been a terrible shock. I may have seemed harsh when we met, although I warned you what I would say. I hope you'll forgive me. Jon's distress at my visit was all too evident and confirmed to me that it's far better for me to retire from your lives before any more damage is done. Coming down to see you was a mistake. Ella seems a girl you should both be proud of, but she really is nothing to do with me and, heartless as it may seem, I am pleased to leave it that way for everyone's sake. However, I'm enclosing a small gift that I hope may help her and the baby.

And so, farewell. We had fun, didn't we?

Gerry

In her other hand, trembling slightly, was a cheque for ten thousand pounds. He had to have the last word.

How bloody dare he? Did he think she and Jon weren't able to provide everything that Ella needed? They certainly didn't need or want his charity. Or was this guilt money? Did he think he could absolve himself from any responsibility by buying Ella's silence? But if that was what he wanted, why hadn't he sent the cheque directly to her?

She hadn't mentioned the letter to Jon or Ella, unsure about the best way of dealing with the problem. She had even considered tearing the cheque up and saying nothing. But that would be foolish. There had already been too many lies and secrets.

She had come home early today after meeting Anwar Malik again. He had returned from Pakistan with only a couple of flimsy leads as to his daughter's whereabouts, but really none the wiser about where she had gone. She hated being so powerless to help him as he sat in her office, despairing and desperate to be reunited with little Aiysha. But until she was found, there was little more Beth could do. At least, despite the difficulties that came with them, she had her daughters at home with her.

She heard the front door and braced herself. 'In here,' she called.

Ella put her head round the door, a spotted scarf hiding most of her hair, knotted above her forehead. Beth was reminded of the scarf her mother wore to do the housework. 'Where's Dad?'

'In his room. Do you think you could ask him to come in here? I've got something I need to talk to you both about. I've been waiting for you.'

'God, Mum. Not another secret? Please.' Before Beth could say anything, Ella laughed and backed out of the room.

Beth laid the cheque on the coffee table, in plain sight, and waited, her gaze drifting to the large photos of her two girls. She hoped she was doing the right thing.

Ella returned, pushing Jon into the room, both her hands on his hips. He laughed as they dodged the chair by the door. Beth was struck by how much more relaxed he looked with every day that passed. Slowly but surely his fears about losing Ella's affection were abating, although his anger with Beth was taking longer to recede, every now and then slipping out through a gesture, a word. Finding their way back into their marriage was going to take some time. Or had she hurt him too deeply for recovery to be possible?

'You wanted us?' His expression was wary; alarm bells were obviously ringing.

'Yes. There's something I've got to share with you both. It arrived a couple of days ago and I haven't known what to do with it. So …' She pointed at the coffee table.

Jon came over and picked up the cheque, puzzled. 'What's this?' He pulled his reading specs out of his pocket, then stood with his back to the fireplace, leaning against the mantelpiece, as he took it in. She could see the back of his head in the mirror, the spot where his hair was thinning. He flicked the cheque with a finger as he looked up. 'Who the hell does he think he is, buying his way into Ella's favour? Why didn't you just throw this away, or send it back?'

Beth had dreaded his anger but was equally determined not to retaliate in kind. 'I thought about it, but then I thought I should show it to both of you and we should decide together.' She leaned forward and passed the note to Ella, who was curled up, feet underneath her, on the sofa. She read it quickly, then handed it back. To Beth's relief, Jon made no move to read it. He had turned away from them, his reflection revealing his clenched jaw, the closed look in his eyes.

'I don't want his money.' Ella crossed and uncrossed her arms in front of her. 'What's it for, anyway? Is he buying me off?' Her face showed her outrage.

'I don't think it's that.' Beth kept calm. Despite having his back to them, Jon was watching them like a cat. 'I think he means it as a goodwill gesture. A goodbye, if you like.'

'Exactly. Paying me off.' Ella ran her finger along her lucky charm bracelet, stopping at the tiny silver microphone Jake had given her.

'No. Babies are expensive. You told him your plans for uni. Perhaps he thinks this will be a small help.' Had she gone too far?

'Have you spoken to him?' Jon's face was flushed as he turned, his eyes narrowed.

'Absolutely not. I don't want to see him again.' She accompanied each word with a gentle punch to a cushion. 'How many times do I have to say that to convince you? All I want is for us to be happy again. Us and Amy. Where is she, by the way?'

'Out buying wellies for Latitude.' Ella laughed, breaking the tension. 'Best be prepared!'

'Look.' Beth prepared to lay her cards on the table. 'I want you two to decide what to do with this. If you choose to tear it up, so be it.' Her hand found its way to her necklace; her finger hooked around it, moving back and forth.

Jon was staring at the note but he didn't pick it up. 'That's a lot of money to throw away, Lulu.'

'Yes, but it's from him. I really don't want it.' Ella unfolded her legs and went to join him at the fireplace: father and daughter in cahoots. They were about the same height. Ella blonde, Jon dark, her face oval, his long and thin, her with a dimple, him without. 'Are you OK with that, Dad?' She took the cheque from his hand.

Jon scratched his head, thoughtful. 'I'll be honest. I didn't like him. I don't want anything to do with him, but ... Lulu, you'll need all the help you can get. Financial, too.'

She pulled a face.

'I understand that you don't want this money,' he went on. 'I wish he hadn't sent it too. But he has, and I wonder whether we shouldn't put it into a rainy-day account for Bessie. That way you don't have to use it unless you're really on your uppers and for some reason we can't help. Or Bessie can have it one day. You never have to spend it at all, but it's there.'

'You want me to accept it?' Ella's surprise was palpable.

'What I really want is for all this to go away,' he said. 'But what if you need this money one day? What then?'

As she listened to them debate the options, Beth welled up with pride. Jon was doing his best to be reasonable when he must be dying to tear the cheque into tiny pieces. His thoughts were for Ella and her future, not himself. Ella understood her father, too. She didn't want to hurt him by accepting the money. She was making it crystal clear to Jon that she had no future with Gerry, whereas she did with him.

And what of Beth's future with Jon? In a couple of weeks they would be in Majorca. They could use that time to try to mend fences, make things better between them. They had overcome Gerry once before, but could they do it again? She wanted their marriage back, to know that Jon trusted her again. That was all that mattered to her now. That and her daughters' happiness.

'Take it, Lulu,' Jon was saying. 'Put it in a high-interest account or buy some premium bonds or something. I'd like you to. Honestly.'

'Really?' She hesitated, then accepted the cheque he was holding out to her and tucked it into her pocket. 'Well, I won't spend it.'

'Not even on a new pair of dungarees?'

They all looked down at the ripped knees of the ones she was wearing and laughed.

'Not even.' She put her arms around Jon's neck and kissed his cheek. 'Thanks, Dad. You're the best.'

After she had left the room, Jon sat down beside Beth. 'God, I hate her taking his money.'

'Then why tell her to accept it?' Beth asked.

'Because I thought the decision should be hers, not mine. And I meant what I said. I quite like the idea of her taking the money off him and then never spending it. It's a silly sort of revenge, a kind of last laugh, except he won't know.' He gave a little smile, but then doubt crossed his face 'You haven't spoken to him about this?'

Beth reached out and took his hand and kissed it. 'I promise.'

He didn't pull away.

29

The leaves on the trees had begun to change colour. Summer was almost over. Megan was considering how horribly quickly the holidays had passed when she heard Jake's intake of breath as the cyclist disappeared from her offside wing mirror. She tightened her grip on the wheel. The mistake had been giving him driving lessons for his eighteenth birthday. Since he'd passed his test first time, he'd been an insufferable back-seat driver – even when in the front seat – who knew every inch of the road and every quirk of the car better than her. Whenever he asked her for a lift, she vowed never again. Luckily for him, she had conveniently forgotten that resolution and had agreed to take him to pick up the band's van from the garage.

'Would you like to drive?' she asked through gritted teeth.

'No. But you did nearly hit him.' He took his hand from the dashboard, where he'd used it to brace himself.

'Jake! I was nowhere near him. If you're going to criticise, then let's change places.' She swerved into a parking space that opened up at the side of the road, enjoying the fact that he gripped the side of his seat. She undid her seat belt and started to open the door.

'Mum, stop it! I won't do it again, OK?'

She slammed shut the door and refastened her belt. 'You'd better not.' She turned the key in the ignition and they continued their journey.

She was enjoying having her boy around again. Except for this morning, when he was definitely the worse for wear. (His drinking habits had been handed down from his father.) She had a strong suspicion that he hadn't gone near the shower, and by the look of it, he hadn't changed his clothes from the previous night either. That was assuming he'd taken them off at all. He'd been away a lot over the summer: at work, staying with friends, at music festivals, the last one of which had been at the weekend. He'd arrived home wrecked, with a bag of dirty washing that had been dumped in the kitchen. She was damned if she was going to open it, so there it still sat, just inches from the washing machine.

She herself was just back from a last-minute trip to Croatia with Pete. The two of them holidaying together hadn't been the wildest of successes. She'd begun to realise that to function their best as a couple these days, they needed other people around them, even if it was only their children. Better still would be Jon and Beth, like the old days, but they hadn't seen them all summer. She had missed Hannah, who had greeted with scorn the suggestion that she might go with them. Jake had also been busy doing his own thing, without Ella as it turned out. After Latitude, Ella had apparently come to her senses. Sleeping in a tent when heavily pregnant had not been the fun she had been determined it would be. She had given her remaining festival tickets to friends and had gone with her family to Majorca after all, explaining to Jake that the four of them needed time together in the light of everything that had happened. Megan had missed seeing her too, but cheered herself with the thought that no doubt she'd be around this evening now that she and Jake were both back home.

She signalled right and pulled into the middle of the road. 'Is Ella coming over tonight? I haven't seen her for ages.'

Jake grunted an affirmative.

'Did she have a good time in Majorca?'

'Yeah.'

'Jake!' She spoke sharply enough to rouse him from his torpor.

'You could at least try to give me an answer. I'm only asking about Ella.'

'Yeah, right. Sorry.' That was it.

If she hadn't been driving, she would have throttled the boy. What on earth was the matter with him? Even with a hangover, he wasn't usually this uncommunicative. He might make more of an effort, especially given that they hadn't seen much of each other over the summer.

After a minute or two, Jake spoke. 'I can't go through with this.'

'What?' Megan's mind had moved on to Beth, wondering what she must be feeling now that the due date was only a couple of weeks away, wondering about her and Jon, wishing they could talk.

'The baby. The fatherhood gig. I don't know if I can do it.'

Her instinct for self-preservation kicked in just in time to prevent her from driving straight into the car in front. She braked hard. 'Of course you can.' She was brisk, as the consequences of any wavering crossed her mind. 'It's too late now.'

'I don't know, Mum.' He heaved a deep sigh. 'I really don't.'

Megan had no alternative but to focus on the road ahead. At the next set of traffic lights, she shot him a sidelong glance. Why hadn't she noticed how pale he was, how thin his legs looked in those skintight black jeans? He cut a forlorn figure hunched over in the passenger seat, picking at one of his thumbnails. He didn't return her gaze.

'What do you mean? I thought you and Ella were blissfully happy.'

'We were. We *are*. No, we're not. I don't mean that. Fuck! I don't know.' He banged the car door with his fist, and stared out of the window.

As the traffic started moving, Megan turned her attention back to the road. 'Being nervous is OK, you know. It's understandable,' she said.

'It's not nerves, Mum.' He banged the door again. 'I love Ella and all that, but it's got too much.'

She gripped the steering wheel tighter. This was exactly what she had been afraid of from the very beginning. She had been so proud when he'd thwarted her expectations and seemed to take on the responsibility Ella had presented him with. This was what Beth had foreseen too.

'I want to be in the band without having to be on a guilt trip every time we go away.' He swept his hair off his face. 'I want to enjoy my life.'

'But Ella wouldn't—'

'I know she wouldn't mind,' he snapped, as if his mother was a halfwit. 'At least that's what she says. But *I'd* mind. Don't you see? It's too much pressure.' He stared out at the parade of shops they were passing.

She came to a halt as a lorry manoeuvred into a narrow opening, blocking the road. 'Jake, Ella's having your baby. You're both very young. It's not surprising you're having cold feet.'

'But don't you see, it's not just the baby. It's both our families too. Everything was so chilled out before. Fun. The summer and the festivals were fun. Now it's a fucking nightmare.'

'Jake!'

'But it is.'

He swung round from the window, his hand sawing up and down his seat belt. 'You know what I mean. First it's the baby. Then it's you and Beth. Then it's Ella's exams. Then Jon turns out not to be her dad after all. On and on. And none of it's gone away. We talk about it … well, she does, all the time. I listen and I do try to help, but will it ever stop?'

How best to help her son? It was so easy to give advice to other people's children, but so much harder with your own. She searched for the words which would help, which would make emotional sense.

'It will,' she tried. 'Once the baby's born, everything will calm

326

down, you'll see. It's just the anticipation that's making everyone more jumpy than usual. Just give it time.' But how long would it take?

He grunted again. There was something he wasn't saying.

'But it's not really about any of those things, is it?' She turned into the gateway of the garage where they were picking up the van, and pulled into a parking space. Neither of them made a move to get out. She switched off the engine and freed herself from her seat belt so that she could turn and concentrate on him. 'Have you met someone else?'

He shook his head and gave a hollow laugh. 'Of course not.'

'Then what? If you don't tell me, I can't help you work it out.'

'I'm twenty-two,' he said angrily. 'I don't need your help.'

Megan was shocked by the fury in his voice. He might be twenty-two, but he clearly did need her help. 'Then why tell me any of this at all?'

'I don't know.' He reached down to grab his bag from the floor of the car.

'Jake,' she said urgently. 'We must try to sort out whatever's bothering you. Ella's about to have your baby.'

'You think I'm not aware of that?'

She made every effort to stay calm. 'Of course.' Perhaps better not to say more but wait to let him speak.

'Look.' He glanced at her, making sure he had her attention, then looked down at his lap, where he was pushing repeatedly at the cuticle of his thumb. 'I love her but I don't want to be tied down. I'm young, I'm having fun. I don't want that to stop. That may sound selfish ...' This time, when he looked up, his expression was more challenging, as if daring her to gainsay him. He flicked back his hair, confident again.

'It does.' She ran her hands around the steering wheel, then gripped it tight. His summer spent largely apart from Ella must have been a huge reminder of everything he would be missing, and driven home how much his life was about to change. But

327

if he were to back off now, what would that do to Ella? To the already fractured Standish–Weston relationship? 'Oh, Jake. If only we'd discussed this before.'

'Saying that isn't helpful at all.' He opened the passenger door and got out before turning and bending down to face her. 'Thanks for the lift. I shouldn't have said anything. She's coming over tonight and we'll talk. We'll work it out. You'll see her then.' He straightened up and slammed the door. There was a moment of silence and Megan let out her breath slowly. Then he was leaning down again, looking stormy.

She wound down the window so she could hear whatever it was he had to say. 'Jay ...?' her voice held the wooing, tender note she had used towards him when he was tiny.

He was having none of it.

'And I've been fired by the studio,' he shot at her. 'So I'm not going to be a photographer either. Get used to it.'

Stunned, Megan watched him walk towards the office, tall, lanky, bag slung across his body, bending his head as he went through the door. He didn't turn and wave. She sat there for a second, feeling sick. He couldn't seriously be thinking about breaking up with Ella only a fortnight before their baby was due. Who would do that? How could any child of hers be so super-humanly selfish? It was too easy to imagine the upset it would cause. Some of Beth's worst imaginings would be proved right. Megan didn't want that. And losing his job, too ... It wasn't as if Heavy Feather was having the success he and his bandmates dreamed about. That was still a long way off. She leaned forward and banged her forehead gently on the steering wheel, three times. There was a knock at the window.

'You all right, miss? Can I help?' A young boiler-suited mechanic was looking at her with concern.

'Never better, thanks.' She forced a smile, turned the key in the ignition, reversed out and turned into the road. There was no point waiting for Jake. In any event, she had no wish to arrive home exactly when he did, if indeed that was where he was even headed once he picked up the van. She needed to think. Since she had last spoken to Beth, the Standish family had drawn in their horns and kept themselves to themselves. Not that she had been expecting to see them, given recent events, but this was the first summer for almost as long as she could remember that they hadn't gone somewhere together, even if only for a long weekend. Pete was always so good at finding the right city break or that idyllic, well-appointed cottage with a view. He hadn't met up with Jon for ages. Was that down to Beth? Or Pete being away so often? Or could Jon be feeling guilty about their drunken fumble? He wouldn't have said anything to Beth, would he? Surely their connection went way too far back for that.

She was sure that Hannah had been secretly upset at being passed over for the Majorca holiday in favour of Natalie. She had put on a good front, protesting that her work experience was far more important than a holiday anyway, but Megan could read her daughter like a book. Better, in fact. After all, work experience could be changed, or abandoned. Not that she would encourage that, of course. Had Amy transferred her number-one-best-friendship to Nat? Girls were fickle, but Amy and Hannah were like sisters. Beth had always been expert in the art of subtle suggestion – could she have had a hand in the decision?

When Beth had invited them to that disastrous barbecue, Megan had thought her friend was holding up a white flag. She'd accepted the invitation because she wanted them to move on too. But, come the day, Beth had so obviously not wanted – or been unable – to extend her hand in friendship at all. The whole occasion was one of the most fraught they had ever spent together, even without Beth's outburst. After that, the family must have needed time on their own to recover. But this battle between them had gone on too long. Would the birth of Ella's baby make a difference? Not if your feckless, head-in-the-clouds son detaches himself from proceedings before they begin, she told herself, fighting the temptation to descend into gloom.

Hours after arriving home, Megan heard the van pull up outside, footsteps, the door, voices murmuring in the hall, then silence. A kiss? Perhaps everything was going to be all right. After all, a job wasn't everything. The door to the living room opened, so she put down the Sudoku that she had been half-heartedly puzzling over. Diva and String leaped to the floor as she moved, disturbing them in the process. Ella stood half in the room and half out, as Fizz took the opportunity to dart past her and into the kitchen. She was tanned, and her bump was more pronounced than ever under her tight blue and white stripy top and maroon leggings. Behind her, in the shadow, loomed Jake.

'Hi, Megan.' She came in and kissed Megan on the cheek. She smelled of summer flowers.

'Ella, how are you?'

'Great.' She looked down, laughing, hand on her stomach. 'As you can see.'

'But you haven't put on any weight at all apart from the baby,' Meg marvelled, remembering the stones of lard that accompanied her own pregnancies, hidden under voluminous smocks. Things had changed.

'I know. But it was so hot in Majorca, I was never very hungry.' She tucked a strand of hair back into the pile swept up on her head.

'Was it fabulous?'

They both sounded so formal, as if something had changed between them.

'Great. At least I had a bed – much more comfortable than a field somewhere. And much quieter.' She turned to Jake. 'You should have come.' She didn't seem to mind that he only replied with a shake of his head. Remembering their earlier conversation, Megan's anxiety returned. If they split up, how would that affect the baby? Would their family even be part of its life? She could barely concentrate as Ella regaled her with stories about the villa, its infinity pool, its shady kitchen 'that you'd have adored', the ping-pong table, and the local disco where Amy and Natalie spent every night, lying comatose on the beach or at the poolside by day.

Megan felt a lurch of resentment. What about Hannah? She should have been there. If it weren't for Beth's absurd overreaction, her daughter could have had a wonderful holiday too. She corrected herself swiftly: it wasn't up to her to organise Hannah's summer. 'Dare I ask about your A levels?' she said, deliberately changing the subject before she blurted out something she might regret. 'You've got the results by now?'

'Didn't Jake say?' Ella looked at him with despair. 'A stars for biology and physics and As for chemistry and philosophy.' She grinned, pleased with herself. 'I never dreamed I'd get there – given everything else that was going on.' She looked down at her bump and gave a little shrug. 'I'm really pleased. So ... once the baby's born and I've got us sorted ...' she ran a hand over her stomach, 'next stop, medicine.'

'You're still set on it, then?' Ella's determination and drive were either impressive or alarming. Megan was unsure quite which.

'More than ever. I've just got to be organised.' She turned again to look at Jake, who was picking at something on his T-shirt. Organisation was certainly not one of his strong suits. The older these two grew, the less alike they seemed to be, in so many ways. Was that a good thing? Jake looked up and, with a jerk of his head, indicated that they should go upstairs. He looked so uncertain that Megan wished she could scoop him up and change his life for him. She let out a long breath. He had got himself into this situation ...

She picked up the Sudoku again, then, realising that she had misplaced a number early on, making the thing unsolvable, scrawled zigzags over the squares, tearing the paper, before tossing it on the floor. If Jake had meant all he said that morning, he

331

must be breaking the news to Ella now. Surfing through the TV channels, she was unable to find anything she wanted to settle on. Her mind was all over the place, anxious about what was going on upstairs, but, even more than that, about what was going to happen to this baby. Were these two going to be able to provide it with everything it would need? Here she was, aching to be a part of its life while aware that Ella's first port of call would be her mum from now on. But she and Beth should be providing a united and welcoming backstop, not what they were offering now.

Biscuits! She would soothe her troubled soul by making some. Or bread. That was the answer.

She went through the conservatory into the kitchen, Fizz pouncing at her feet then skittering away, spooked by nothing. Diva sat on the worktop out of the kitten's way, licking the inside of the frying pan. Megan shooed her off and put the pan in the sink. Hannah was going to be late. Pete was meeting some ex-colleagues in the pub and had called to say he'd been held up. Megan knew what that meant. He'd roll in after eleven. She put some leftover fish pie on a plate for them to microwave when they got home. Sitting at the kitchen table, she leafed through her folder of recipes torn from old magazines, scribbled down after a dinner out, culled from friends. But nothing inspired her. She wasn't in the right mood, not while Jake might be explaining his confused feelings to Ella. How would she take it? Megan rolled her shoulders, trying to ease the tension from them as she waited for the storm upstairs to break.

Back in the sitting room, she returned to her chair, eased off her shoes and leaned back against the cushion, lurching forward to try and catch the tiny carpet moth that caught her eye. Missed. She watched it flitter past the fireplace, envying its freedom (short-lived, if she had her way). She tried the TV, finally settling on a repeat she hadn't seen of a build-your-own-dream-home series. Property porn: the exact antithesis of the mess of her own home, though how irritating were the smug smiles of the overenthusiastic would-be home-makers. Her eyes glazed over as their underground house ran into one problem after another.

She wondered what was happening upstairs. She went into the hall. Silence. She tiptoed up a few stairs. Nothing, just the sound of distant music. She returned to the sitting room. Was this not being allowed to know what was going on another milestone in parenthood that she had to accept?

If Pete were here, he'd switch off the TV in frustration, but she was lulled into a mindless trance. When the show ended, bed beckoned. She would have a long, hot soak before enjoying the luxury of having their huge double bed to herself, a mug of hot chocolate on the side table with a couple (at least) of biscuits, and a good book. She had read somewhere that drinking two hot chocolates a day warded off dementia and had adopted the habit without difficulty, discounting her already tightening waistbands.

With only the mirror light on, she lit three lavender-scented candles, ran the bath as hot as she could take it and dripped in some 'Deep Relax' bath oil. She chose not to weigh herself (something she meant to do once a week, but rarely did now she was warding off mental disintegration with hot chocolate), took one of the newest towels out of the cupboard (still softish, not like the ones she had hung outside so often they were like scratchy cardboard), switched on the radio so it would be obvious to the others that she was in there and tuned in to Classic FM. Downstairs, the door slammed. After a few minutes, he heard Hannah's footsteps on the stairs and her shout of 'Goodnight.'

' 'Night,' she replied, before dropping her clothes on the floor, one by one. She took the tube of hydraquench face mask, squeezed out a blob and applied it liberally. In the bath, she shut her eyes and let herself float, drifting with the music, enjoying the scent of the candles.

By the time she got into bed, she had managed to ease any

tension so successfully, she was asleep before she finished her chocolate and the book slipped from her hand.

She woke with a start. Had someone called her name? Pete was beached beside her, snuffling gently in his sleep. God only knew what time he had got in. The smell of lavender she'd gone to sleep with had been overlaid with the smell of stale beer. The blue digital clock face told her it was four in the morning.

'Mum!' There it was again. Urgent, but not loud. She was dragged from semi-consciousness by the sound of footsteps in the corridor.

'Jake? What is it?' Her head was off the pillow as he opened the door. Pete murmured something, pulled the duvet up and snored louder.

'It's Ella. She thinks something might have happened to the baby!' She could barely see him in the dark, but he sounded panic-stricken.

'What do you mean?' Megan sat up, quite calm, as her synapses started to fire.

'She says it hasn't moved for hours.'

Megan relaxed. 'I'm sure it's nothing. I'll come and talk to her.' She got up, grabbed her dressing gown and followed him out of the room. Pete raised his head from the pillow and let it fall back, dead to the world. 'It's probably just gone quiet. That can happen when it's ready to be born.'

'Born?!' Jake's face was a picture. 'You don't mean …'

'I'm sure it's not that,' wailed Ella, emerging from Jake's room in one of his old T-shirts and trackie bottoms, her arms around her belly, fear written all over her face. 'I've been lying in bed for hours, waiting for something … anything …' She sniffed, and her eyes filled with tears. 'This never happens. Not ever. I can't remember when it last moved it's been so long.'

'You don't think you might have dozed off and missed something?' suggested Megan. 'Just the smallest sign.'

'No. I've been watching the clock. I'm sure something's wrong.' She was increasingly frantic.

'I'm sure it's nothing to worry about.' Megan put her arm around her shoulders and took her back into Jake's room, where she sat her on the edge of the bed. 'Now wait here while I call the hospital for you. They'll know what to do.'

'Tell them it's been hours.' Ella grabbed her hand.

'Don't worry, I will. Jake, why don't you make us some tea?' Giving him something to do seemed wise. Anything to stop that horrified, glassy stare. Megan extricated herself from Ella's grip and went to find the phone.

Minutes later, having made the call, she returned to find the pair of them on the bed, sipping tea. She was relieved to see that Jake had come to his senses and was calming Ella, stroking her brow, reassuring her. As soon as Megan walked in, Ella sat bolt upright. 'What did they say?'

'That there's probably nothing to worry about but that we should go in, just to make sure.'

Ella's eyes were wide with panic.

'I'm sure it'll be fine. Let me just get dressed and I'll drive you. When you're ready, Jake, could you call Beth and Jon and tell them what's happening?'

'Oh, no, they're not there,' gasped Ella. 'Mum's at a conference. You'll have to call her mobile. Mine's in my bag. Her number's on that.' She edged herself towards the edge of the bed.

'And Jon?' Megan asked.

'He's gone to Gloucester, and Amy's at Nat's.' She stood up. 'Where have I put it?'

'Stay there. I'll get it.' Jake yanked his jeans over his boxers, hopping across the room to fetch Ella's shoulder bag. She began to make the call, but Jake took the phone from her. 'I'll do that. You concentrate on getting what you need to take with you.'

'Give me a minute.' Megan returned to her bedroom and groped about in the half-dark for her clothes, grabbing the first things that came to hand – gardening jeans, T-shirt, old grey fleece – and slinging them on. Pete didn't stir, just kept snoring. Ella was standing shivering on the landing, waiting for Jake to be put through to Beth. Hannah's door was firmly closed. She'd always been able to sleep through anything. There was no point in waking her now. Megan found the old picnic rug in the chest and wrapped it around Ella's shoulders. 'Let me just get the keys.'

'Yes, now,' she heard Jake say. 'Yes, we're going to the hospital. Mum's taking us.' She could imagine the unbridled joy that Beth would feel when she heard that. 'Yes, of course you can.' He passed the phone to Ella.

'Mum?' Her voice shook. 'I didn't want to worry you … No. Are you coming? I wish you were here … No, we'll be fine.'

Jake kissed the side of her temple. She turned to him with a smile.

'Is she coming?' asked Megan.

'She's in Birmingham so she won't be here for a while. She's leaving as soon as she can,' Ella explained. 'She's going to get hold of Dad and tell him.'

Outside, the night was chilly. Clouds chased across the moon. Megan opened the passenger door. If she were the one present at the birth of their grandchild, Beth would never forgive her.

Ella climbed in, gathering the rug around her. 'Come on, Jake.'

He was hanging back, looking anxious, as though hoping he wouldn't be needed. He reluctantly followed instructions and climbed into the back. He touched Ella's shoulder. 'It'll be OK, Els.'

She reached up and held his hand. 'But you don't know, do you? I should have told you sooner. Suppose—'

'Shhh,' he comforted her. 'We'll be there soon, and then we'll know. There's no point in getting upset yet.'

Megan was impressed by his recovery. She was dying to ask if everything was all right between them again, but this was hardly the moment. Ella had stayed the night. Perhaps Jake had bottled it at the last minute. Perhaps he had changed his mind. The questions whirled pointlessly through her head as she manoeuvred the car out of its space. She heard Jake's impatient 'tsk' as she bumped into the cars both in front and behind, setting off one of their alarms. She didn't stop to wait for whichever neighbour it belonged to to come out, but headed off, forcing herself to concentrate on nothing but getting them to the hospital without hesitation, deviation or accident.

30

In Birmingham, Beth was wide awake, reeling from the news that Ella was on her way to the hospital with Megan. Once again, she was on the outside and not by her daughter's side, where she should be. But this was unreasonable. *Be grateful that Megan's there, looking after things. It's hardly her fault that you're up here on business.* Then she heard Megan's voice: '... all very well when *you* needed me to be a mother to them ... But when *they* need me to be one, you don't like it.' No, she didn't. Megan was right.

Suppose something happened to Ella? She'd heard the panic in Jake and Ella's voices. She should have asked to speak to Megan, who would be calm in the face of emergency. How serious might the baby not moving for a few hours be? She reached for her laptop on the bedside table, then shut the lid. Googling would only make her more anxious. Surely being admitted to hospital was a belt-and-braces measure. If they were seriously worried, wouldn't they have said so?

Leaving Birmingham now meant that she would be unable to deliver her paper to her fellow lawyers in the morning, but that couldn't be helped. She had promised Ella she would be at the birth if asked. She had to get there, whatever the outcome. That was where she wanted to be; where she belonged.

The pair of them had come a long way together over the last months, and the bond had been sealed by those two weeks in Majorca. While Amy and Nat had slept through the mornings, Beth and Ella had lain by the pool together. Often Jon joined them – more and more often as the days went by – abandoning the shade and his latest military history tome. They had talked and talked, pulling apart their reactions to the pregnancy until they understood them better. They'd discussed Megan: how close she and Beth had been and how much Ella wanted peace to be restored between them.

'It's so important,' she had pleaded. 'None of us can settle.'

Beth had remained non-committal. They'd talked about the baby, Ella's plans and how Beth and Jon would fit in. They'd talked about Gerry– how could they not? – assuring one another that he was out of the picture for good. After so much analysis and confession, Beth had, at last, accepted that she had to let her daughters go. If she did, they would use their wings and fly, coming home because they wanted to be there. Ella had made it clear that, if her mother insisted on trying to control them, she wouldn't stay around any longer than necessary. Beth couldn't lead her life for her. Just as nobody had led hers. 'Mutual respect and space to breathe, Mum. That's what we both need.'

On this subject, she felt anything but rational and quite re-moved from the cool professional she had always striven to be. What she wanted was to be with her daughter. She *needed* to be with her daughter.

Ella had also said that she wanted Beth with her when she went into labour. Her, not Megan. Letting her down was not an option. Beth pulled up her knees and, in the pallid orange glare of the street lights that leaked through the gap at the top of the curtains, called Jon. She waited, listening to the ringtone, but there was no reply. She smacked the bed in frustration. Dialling reception instead, she eventually got a sleep-deprived concierge, who gamely tried to assist. The first train would get her into central London, just minutes from the hospital, at seven fifteen. A taxi, or a rental car, by the time they found one, would hardly be quicker.

There was no point trying to sleep. Once dressed, she packed her overnight bag, flinging her sponge bag on top of her clothes. Sitting at the desk, she tried Jon again. When he still didn't pick up, she fired off a couple of explanatory texts, confident he would phone as soon as he saw them. She emailed her colleague from the university to explain what had happened, attaching her paper so that he could read it for her. She experienced a moment of guilt; she had never done such a thing before. Then she sat on the bed and waited.

Time turned slowly. At five o'clock the phone rang, making her jump. She grabbed it, feeling sudden fear. If anything had happened to Ella or the baby ...

She registered Megan's number. Oh, God, no.

'Megan?' Her voice was little more than a whisper.

'Yes.' Megan's was controlled, matter-of-fact. 'I thought I should phone you as soon as we had some news. First of all ... Ella's fine.'

Thank God. Beth let out the breath she had inadvertently been holding. 'And the baby?' She dreaded the answer.

'Fine.' Megan almost laughed.

Beth collapsed back on the pillow. 'Really?'

'Yes, really. Just a scare. They've run a CTG and whatever else they do.'

'So where are you now?' Beth propped herself up on an elbow.

'Still at the hospital. Ella's waters broke about twenty minutes ago but there was some meconium there so they've decided to keep her in so they can monitor things as she goes into labour.'

'I wish I was there.'

'You mustn't worry, she's in the best possible hands. She's quite calm and Jake's with her. He's being brilliant.' Beth could hear that Megan's pride was mixed with surprise. 'And you'll be here soon. You know what labour's like. We'll probably be waiting for hours.'

This was the reliable, no-nonsense Megan Beth had almost forgotten. But all the same, she was there and Beth was not.

'I'll be with you as soon as I can. The train should get in just after seven.' She was so choked with relief, she couldn't say much more. As she hung up, she wondered how Ella was really coping. Excited or scared? Or both? She should have asked. The thought of her daughter in pain or terrified was the stuff of nightmares. She reassured herself that, if anything were wrong, Megan wouldn't have spared her. It sounded as if there was more than a good chance that she would reach the hospital in time. She shut her eyes, and gave herself up briefly to the bed's firm embrace. Until now, she had experienced such mixed feelings about this moment, frightened of everything that it would bring. But her fear was at last being chased away by excitement, anxiety, longing to be there.

Ella had been two weeks overdue when the doctors decided to induce. Even then, she had been reluctant to show herself, and Beth was in labour for a good eighteen hours. She remembered the day quite clearly: the sleepless night on the ward; the early start; the wait to go into labour; Jon's nervous arrival; the delivery room; the cheerful West Indian midwife. It went down as one of the best days of her life, up there with meeting then marrying Jon, and the birth of Amy to complete their family. Being presented with Ella, a bloody scrap of a thing, while Jon cut the umbilical cord with tears streaming down his cheeks, was a moment that would stay with her for ever. They had been so happy then, just the three of them in their bubble, not knowing what the future would bring. She checked her watch. Surely the taxi must be due soon.

By the time the concierge called up to say it had arrived, she was ready, sitting on the edge of the chair, coat on, case and bag beside her. On the train, she found an empty table seat and spread open the newspaper she'd bought, but was unable to concentrate on a thing. Sensible thought was impossible. At that moment, nothing mattered more than being with Ella.

*

Six o'clock. Megan let her hand drop to her lap. Her eyeballs felt as if they'd been coated with molten lava. She moved about in an attempt to get comfortable on the plastic-covered chair that she should have wiped before sitting down. Her elbow slipped off the thin wooden arm as she shifted her hips to the left and slumped awkwardly to one side. She righted herself, trying not to wake Ella, who was managing to doze between contractions and the occasional visit from the midwife.

Soothing cream walls with a round ticking clock facing the end of the bed, around which was the paraphernalia associated with birth. Nothing much had changed since Megan had had Hannah. No real human comfort, just machinery in case something went wrong. Or, to make sure nothing does, she corrected herself. Sixteen years ago, almost to the day, she had waddled up the hospital steps in her maternity dress commando-style, having been unable to bend over to put on her underwear before she left the house. She had insisted that she didn't need a wheelchair, being determined to stay on her feet until the last possible moment. That was what expectant mothers were told back then. Keep moving for as long as you can. Pete had arrived from work half an hour later – surprising that he had arrived at all, given his well-vocalised dislike of the gore that had accompanied Jake's birth. 'All right for you,' he always joked, slightly to her annoyance. 'You were at the other end of the proceedings. I got an unadulterated view.' But arrive he had. Having made sure she was comfortable in the delivery room, he went off to the canteen for a coffee and a sandwich, as confident as she that they would be there for hours, in a repeat of Jake's birth. By the time he got back, Hannah had arrived and was at Megan's breast. He had missed the whole caboodle.

Jake had gone outside for yet another cigarette. The only thing Megan loathed more than him smoking was the smell he brought back in with him. His clothes spoke of the smokers clustered in the covered area outside, even at this hour, drawing on their little white sticks as if they were their last. And they probably would be for some, she reflected, remembering the sleepless, gaunt wheelchair-bound patients she had seen out there.

Ella groaned and shifted slightly. They were still waiting for her to go into full-blown labour. The flurry of their arrival and her waters breaking had calmed down thanks to the regular checks. The last midwife had examined her, pronounced herself happy and left them to it. No sign of Beth or Jon yet. Megan glanced at the clock. Time hung heavy. She almost wished she didn't have to see them. Beth would not want her here. Would Jon? But this was her grandchild too, she reminded herself. She had every right to be here if Ella wanted her to be. And although they might be less close than they had been, Ella had said nothing to suggest that she was unhappy with Megan's presence. Megan was unsurprised but sad that Ella's loyalty had shifted back to her mother. That was how it should be, of course, but she had so enjoyed their special closeness while it lasted.

She picked up the well-read copy of a women's magazine she'd found outside. Without her glasses, which she'd left behind in the hurry of leaving, she could only read the headlines. She sat staring at the pictures of Z-list celebrities that she didn't recognise. How could she be so out of touch? She started as the magazine slapped against the floor. She must have dozed off again. As she bent to retrieve it, the door swung open. She braced herself. Beth?

'Everything all right in here?' A different midwife came in and familiarised herself with Ella's notes as Megan relaxed. 'I'm just going to check you over.'

Ella stirred, grimacing as she tried to sit up and a contraction set in. 'How long will it be?' she gasped. 'It is going to be OK, isn't it?'

'Take it easy, dear. It's going to be fine.' The midwife unhooked the thermometer and clipped it to the end of Ella's finger. 'How often are they coming?' She looked at Megan.

'About every ten minutes, maybe less.' Megan looked at Ella

for confirmation, feeling guilty that she hadn't been keeping a proper tally. Ella nodded.

'Why don't you get yourself a cup of tea while I do this?' The midwife took away the thermometer and started to unravel the baby heart monitor. 'Baby seems in no hurry and I'll be done by the time you get back.'

'I don't mind,' said Ella. 'Really. Do go.'

The idea of a cup of strong builder's had a sudden ambrosial appeal. Megan hoisted herself out of the chair, her arm parting company from the chair with a ripping sound where her bare skin had stuck to it. 'You sure?' she said, rubbing the spot.

Ella nodded as the midwife pulled back the sheet covering her and opened her hospital gown.

The labour ward was hushed, punctuated by the odd squeak of a shoe on lino, the sound of a door opening or closing, lowered voices in the corridor or occasional screams from one of the delivery rooms. Down the corridor was the relatives' room, with a vending machine in one corner. The room was empty. Megan rooted around in her bag among the crumpled receipts, chewing gum tablets that had escaped their box, keys and other flotsam. She dug out her purse and slapped a couple of pound coins into the machine, but nothing happened. Then she noticed the inadequate biro'd sign: SORRY, NO TEA OR COFFEE. Her mouth felt as fetid as the bottom of a small rodent's cage. She had to make do with a can of cola that clunked into the tray. Rather than return to Ella immediately, she decided to let her have some privacy for a minute. She sat down with a long sigh, and ripped the ring pull.

What would happen to their two families now? Was it too late for Beth and her to bridge the distance between them? Megan would always be watching her step with Ella and the baby, worried about how Beth would react. She couldn't live like that. Their friendship had once been like a hand-knitted jumper, well worn and comfortable. Now it was holed; it could be patched and darned, but however skilled the workmanship, it would never be quite the same again.

This baby needed the support and love of a family, but unless Jake was just suffering from last-minute nerves, what had divided their families seemed to be dividing him and Ella too. Megan closed her eyes, mulling things over, looking for answers. And Jon. What about him?

'Can I have one, Mum?' Jake came through the door.

She jumped, jolted out of her daydreaming. 'Sure.' She dug into her bag, but he stopped her with a hand on her shoulder and bought one for himself before coming to join her.

'You look exhausted,' he said, stretching himself over a chair, arms and legs extended.

'Thanks. That's made me feel a lot better.' Her smile felt as though it might crack her face open. 'You don't look so great yourself.'

'I've no idea what's happening, is why.' He shook his head as if trying to clear it.

'Did you tell Ella how you were feeling?'

'I tried. But you know what happened?' He lifted his can and tipped his head back to drink.

'How could I?'

'She said that she'd been thinking too, and perhaps I was right. Looking after the baby and studying is going to take up all her time, so perhaps we'd be better off just friends. Go back to being the way we were, and then see what happens.' He looked cast down by the idea, turning the can in his hands, staring at it as if it was going to provide the answer.

Megan was confused. 'But isn't that what you wanted?'

He looked up, his eyes glassy. 'I thought so, but now she's agreed with me and made it so easy, I'm not sure that it is any more. I'm not sure it's really what she wants either, but she's saying it for me. God, Mum, it's so hard. We were going to talk about it this morning and sort out what was best, and then

345

this …' He gestured in the direction of Ella's room. 'Now all I want is to be there for her.'

She allowed herself a wry laugh. 'That's love for you,' she said, then leaned forward to pat his thigh. 'Perhaps just go along with it for now. It's hard to believe, but it will all become clearer. This isn't the time to try to sort things out. Why don't you go back in there and I'll come along in a minute. Beth should be here soon too.'

He pulled a face. 'You're not going to make things difficult, the two of you?'

'Of course not! We do know how to behave.'

The raised eyebrow and downturned mouth suggested doubt as he unfolded himself from the chair. 'I'll see you in a minute, then.'

They both looked at the door, hearing footsteps coming in their direction, but they passed and carried on down the corridor. Megan threw her can at the bin and missed. Jake binned it for her, then gave her a hug, kissing her temple. She leaned into him for a second, enjoying their closeness. Her eyes were shut as, just for that moment, she forgot everything else.

After he'd gone, she let herself doze in the chair. She was woken by the door opening.

'Beth!' Megan sat up straight, rubbing her neck where it had stiffened up, What was the time? Would Beth turn her presence at the hospital into some kind of confrontation? Over-compensating for her dread, Megan said too cheerfully, 'Everything's fine. Ella's down the corridor, with Jake.'

'The nurse said you were here. I wanted to thank you.' Beth looked tired too, but ready for a day at the office. Megan regarded her own tatty flats, which she'd slipped on in a hurry, then Beth's nude courts, her work suit. She was probably only going to stay briefly. Her office would be calling. Megan buried that thought as Beth gave her a lukewarm smile.

346

The lukewarmth of it hurt. After all they had meant to each other.

'No need.' She straightened up in the chair. 'I've always said your girls are like family.'

The two women looked at each other, wary, like two warriors sizing each other up. They made no move to embrace or kiss, as they once would have done.

'Why don't you go home and get some rest? We'll call you when something happens.'

Megan bristled. She wasn't going to let Beth tell her what to do. 'I'd rather stay. Assuming you don't mind.'

'What? Both of us be at the birth?' Beth looked surprised, as if this was the last thing she'd expected.

'Why not? It won't be the first time it's happened.'

'Because it's not what Ella planned,' whipped back the reply.

'But she didn't plan any of what's happened tonight. You know how babies and plans don't work!'

'I don't know ...' Beth paused.

Megan didn't wait for her to finish. 'Why don't we go and see what's happening?' she suggested, leading the way.

The ward was beginning to come to life now that the day staff had checked in. A murmur of voices came from the nurse's station, the rattle of a trolley. As they walked down the corridor together, Megan registered that not only was she exhausted, she was ravenous too. She should have found a canteen and got something to eat. No doubt there would be time for that. She opened the door to Ella's room.

Ella and Jake were alone, talking. He took her hand just as she gasped in pain, rubbing between her shoulders with his other. Whatever they had been taught in their antenatal classes had obviously sunk in. As Ella gave him a quick look of gratitude, he took a flannel from the basin and wiped her brow. When the pain subsided, Ella flopped back against her pillows.

'Mum! You made it!' She started to get off the bed.

347

Beth turned to Megan. 'We'll be fine now,' she said.

'But can't I ...' Megan stopped as she caught Ella's eye. If Ella wasn't going to ask her to stay, she shouldn't make a scene. Ella glanced up at Jake, who shrugged his shoulders.

'I'll call you as soon as there's some news.' Beth began to settle herself on one side of the bed.

Ella cleared her throat. 'Actually, Mum, I think Jake and I would like to do this on our own after all.' Her voice was quiet but firm.

Beth stared at her, confused. 'But I thought you wanted ...' she began, then stopped.

'I know. But we didn't plan on everyone being here at once, did we?' She looked at Jake for support, taking his hand.

'What Els is saying is that we can't have one or other of you in here – that wouldn't be fair. Having both of you, when you're barely speaking to each other, isn't going to work. We've decided that we'd like you both to be at the hospital, of course, but just not in here with us until after the baby's born.'

Despite her disappointment, Megan felt so proud of Jake at that moment. However nervous he might be, he was prepared to face down the mothers together, for Ella's sake. A consummate diplomat. But Beth looked shattered. She was trying to hide it, but Megan understood. She knew ... she just knew what Beth was feeling.

'Sorry, Mum.' Ella and Jake spoke together, then glanced at each other and laughed.

Beth recovered herself, bent over Ella and kissed her forehead. 'We'll be down the corridor.' She came over to Megan, shepherding her out. 'This is hardly the time to argue.'

31

Out in the corridor, Megan slumped against the wall. 'Well, that's us told!'

Beth's face was ashen, and her eyes shone with tears. She took a tissue from her bag and blew her nose.

Megan felt for her. 'Come on. Let's go and find a coffee.'

Beth sniffed. 'I think I'd rather stay up here, just in case I'm needed. I don't understand what just happened in there.'

'Yes you do,' objected Megan. 'You and Jon wouldn't have wanted anyone else there when Ella was born, would you? Imagine having us in there together after everything that's gone on? Can you blame them?'

Beth shook her head. 'But you weren't meant to be there ...' She stepped back to the other side of the corridor to let a woman in a wheelchair be pushed past.

The two of them faced each other, backs pressed against the walls.

'Don't start,' Megan warned. 'Not now, and certainly not here. Nobody could have predicted what's happened.' As Beth began to say something, she cut in: 'Isn't it about time we buried the hatchet? For their sakes if not for ours. Life's going to be impossible otherwise.'

'After everything you said?' Beth tucked her tissue into her bag. 'I don't know if I can.'

'Said in anger,' admitted Megan. 'Besides, I seem to remember you gave as good as you got.'

Beth's mouth lifted at the corners at the memory.

'We can't talk in the corridor. If you won't come down to the canteen, I'll bring you up a coffee.'

Beth nodded. 'Thanks. Give me a minute or two on my own first.' She walked towards the relatives' room, her head bowed as if she carried the cares of the world. Megan waited. If she was disappointed at being excluded from the birth, Beth must be a hundred times more so. But the kids were right. If they were going to make a go of things, this was their moment. Their happiness was what mattered. And perhaps she and Beth … but the thought didn't go any further as she saw Jon coming towards her from the opposite direction, his face racked with anxiety.

'Everything's OK,' she said as he reached her.

He tipped his face to the ceiling, as if praying for something. 'Beth's got to get here on time,' he murmured. 'Got to. I know if she's here when the baby's born, everything will be all right.'

'She's here.' Exhausted, Megan felt as if her legs were dissolving, unable to hold her any longer. Her heart was thumping. He must be aware of it, surely. She made a superhuman effort to stay on her feet.

'Thank God.' As if knowing exactly what she needed, Jon led her over to a couple of chairs by the nurses' station and they sat down together. 'Where are they?'

She leaned forward as the nervous energy that had been keeping her going drained away, leaving her as weak as a kitten. 'Down the corridor, third door on the left. Beth's in the relatives' room.'

He looked surprised.

'They wanted us out of there,' she explained.

He gave a weary grin. 'Quite right. A head-to-head between the two of you is not what's needed … I'll just see Beth and check everything's okay, then I'll make myself scarce. We don't all need to be here.' He clasped both her hands. 'Thank you for looking after Ella.'

She looked down to her lap, where her hands were locked in his. *For God's sake, woman, pull yourself together.*

He let go of her.

'The coffee machine in the waiting room is broken.' She made a vague gesture towards the door. 'So I'm going to the canteen.'

'Perhaps I'll see you down there.' He grinned at her. 'I need something after that drive.'

'I'd like that,' she murmured.

He cleared his throat, looked uncomfortable then righted himself. 'Yes, well. I'd better see what's happening first.'

She watched him walk down the corridor, neat in his jeans with a deep green sweater around his shoulders. If Hannah hadn't interrupted them, that evening might have had a very different ending. But he probably hadn't even given her a thought since they last met. How hard it was to have a long-buried fantasy brought to life then have it gently but definitively dismantled.

As she waited for the lift, she switched on her mobile. She'd have to ring Jane to explain why she wouldn't be at school today. She had two missed calls from Pete. Once she was outside, she called him back.

'Where the hell are you?' he roared. 'Woke up and you were gone. Hannah's gone to school. House is empty. You know how to worry a man.' Then he laughed, as if nothing could have worried him less. As far as she knew, he had never questioned their relationship, and as a result, she trusted him implicitly too. Her disloyalty in thinking of Jon as anything other than as a friend was shocking.

As she began to explain, Megan couldn't help a smile. She gazed at the lift doors. For heaven's sake, what was there to smile about? Yet, as they talked, her smile broadened into a grin. Face it. Pete had always been the one with whom she was going to walk into the sunset, like two Start-rite pensioners. Never Jon. He had been in love with Beth since the day they met. Agreeing to bring up Ella as his own had proved that.

'I never heard a thing,' she heard Pete say as she described their rushed exit from the house.

'Hardly surprising when you were snoring like an elephant.'

'Don't hit a man when he's down, darling. I'm suffering for it now.' He groaned. 'Feeling a bit mothy around the edges today, so I'll wait here for any news. I've got a couple of deadlines to get to grips with. Jake bearing up?'

'He's splendid,' she said. 'Coping well.' There was no point even beginning to explain the question mark hanging over Jake and Ella's relationship. He would only say that they would sort themselves out in time. And, of course, he was right. One way or another, they would.

She hung up, pausing for a moment to breathe in some fresh air and let the late summer sun warm her face. She listened to the hum of traffic, shouts from people in the street. Outside the hospital, the world went on as usual. Being inside was like being on another planet where everything ran to another set of timetables and rules. She went back in, followed the signs to the canteen, ordered an Americano, an almond croissant and a Danish. She needed an energy boost if she was going to be able to function. Now Jon was with Beth, she'd wait a while to take up the coffee.

Around her, several weary-looking young doctors were hunched over their breakfasts before they went on or off duty. One or two early outpatients were killing time before their appointments. How long would this labour last? She wouldn't leave until the baby was born. Jake needed her support, however little Beth might want her here.

Time drifted by as Megan stared into space, considering the future, wondering where they would all be in years to come. Eventually, she heard someone pulling out a chair, felt a touch on her shoulder. Surprised, she glanced up to find Jon looking down at her. She blinked, eyes aching with tiredness. After the night they'd had, she must look awful. 'Is everything all right?'

'I'm definitely surplus to requirements.' He smiled. 'I've just come down to grab a decent coffee before I leave. I didn't expect you still to be here. We thought you must have gone home after all.'

'I'm meant to take Beth a coffee. But, in any case, I can't leave until it's all over.' She felt self-conscious in the clothes she had thrown on without thinking.

'Of course.' He rubbed his cheek, thoughtful.

'Actually, to be honest,' she brushed crumbs into her hand and dropped them on to her plate, 'I think Beth wanted me out of the way.'

'I'm sure that's not …'

'We both know it is,' she said firmly. 'But I'm not going to be told what to do. This is my grandchild too.'

'Same old Megan,' he grinned. 'Always your own woman. Don't look so surprised. It's been true ever since I first knew you. How could we forget it's your grandchild too after all we've been through?' He gave her a meaningful look. 'Beth's just nervous for Ella. You know what she's like.'

'Only too well!' She knocked back the dregs of her cold Americano. 'But of course I understand that. Really.'

Jon tapped his spoon against his saucer. 'Megan …'

Despite everything, her heart leapt a little.

She made herself look at him. 'Yes?' She knew what he was about to say but didn't try to stop him.

'Can't you sort things out between you?' he asked. 'Please. Life would be so much better for the rest of us. And what better moment than now?'

Upstairs, her grandchild was making its way into the world. That must mean something. She allowed her gaze to rest on his face for one … two … seconds. Then she looked away. Jon was not hers.

'I don't know,' she said. 'We'll have to see.'

*

In the relatives' room, Beth had company. An older woman had come in shortly after Jon had left. After nodding at Beth, she settled herself in a chair and got out her knitting, a small stripy something. Her veined hands bent and stretched with the movement of the needles, her cloud of grey hair bent over her work. Another expectant grandmother, Beth assumed. Judging from her composure, this was not her first. She looked up and exchanged a smile with Beth, then returned to her knitting. Beth felt so strung out, she could barely sit still. If only she had something with which to occupy herself, to distract her from what was going on down the corridor. She was glad Jon had left; she couldn't cope with his nerves as well. As for Megan ... It suddenly hit her: she wanted Megan there.

Eventually, the click of the needles stopped as the woman untangled the different-coloured balls of wool in her bag. 'Your first one?'

'Yes,' Beth replied. At first she spoke tentatively. 'Well, my daughter's. Her boyfriend's mother and I don't get on too well, so they don't want us in there for the birth.'

'Quite right,' said her companion. 'I don't hold with everybody crowding in while it's going on anyway. You're better off waiting till after. Where's the other grandmother? Is she here too?'

'She brought them in.'

'They must be close then.' She paused her knitting. 'What made the two of you fall out?'

'She was my closest friend until Ella discovered she was pregnant.' Once Beth had started unbuttoning herself to this stranger, the relief of saying something meant the words kept on coming, encouraged by the considered attention she was being given. The knitting stayed on the other woman's lap. Her head cocked to one side as she heard Beth out, her earrings glinting in the light. Beth found herself explaining how the war – because that was what it felt like to her now – between her and Megan had begun, and what had happened between them since.

As she described the hostages taken – for what else was it when Ella went to live with the Westons? – the collateral damage inflicted on all their families, the attempted peace offerings that had been consistently thwarted, her companion became more and more absorbed, nodding, asking the odd question for clarification.

Eventually, Beth drew to a close. 'There. So that's it. A bloody mess we've made of things between us.'

'Children can cause terrible problems. Mine were no angels either.' The woman picked up her knitting again and began the next row.

Mesmerised as she watched her companion weave one colour then another into the pattern, Beth found the rhythmical movements quite soothing. She looked at her watch. What was happening down the corridor?

'Babies don't always solve the problem, but they often make us realise our priorities, and then things change.' The woman picked out a small ball of lavender blue and began to work it into the knitting. 'Perhaps this one will enable you all to have a new start.'

Beth waited for her to say more, then realised there was nothing more to say. This woman didn't know them, had no real idea of the tangle resulting from their conflicting personalities and desires. Only they could adjust their priorities and start again. 'Is that what happened to you?' she asked.

'More or less,' the woman answered. 'More or less.' She obviously didn't feel the need to unburden herself in the same way as Beth.

'Your daughter?' Beth was intrigued and prepared to hear the story. But at that moment, the door opened to admit Megan with a coffee. So she had stayed after all. Of course. Beth was glad. She hadn't registered before, but Megan was looking extraordinary. Her hair was all over the place, and she appeared to be in her gardening clothes.

Picking up on Beth's look, Megan excused herself. 'I know, I

355

know. I got dressed in a hurry, in the dark.' She passed the coffee to Beth. 'Sorry I've been so long. I went into a bit of a daze, and then Jon came down. I left him finishing his coffee.'

'Don't worry. We've been talking.' Beth inclined her head to indicate the other woman, who gave no sign that she knew who Megan was. 'I lost track of time too.'

The three of them sat waiting as the minutes ticked by. After polite conversation ran out they sat silent, Beth and Megan flicking through magazines, staring into space, trying to control their anxieties. The only other sound was the regular click of the other woman's knitting needles. After what seemed an eternity, a smiling midwife put her head round the door. All three women started, their eyes on her, eager for news.

'Mrs Standish?'

Beth jumped to her feet, expectant, anxious. 'Has something happened?'

'Jake and Ella asked me to tell you that you're a grandmother.'

Beth heard Megan clap her hands and gasp. She felt an over-whelming burst of joy as her face split into a wide smile. If it weren't for Megan grabbing her arm to support her, her legs might have given way.

'A gorgeous little girl,' the midwife went on. 'Born ten minutes ago.'

'Can we see them?' They spoke at the same time.

'Just give us a few minutes to clear up. We'll let you know as soon as they're ready.' The door shut behind her.

All at once, Beth and Megan were in each other's arms, hugging as if nothing had ever divided them. Just as suddenly, they separated, their arms dropping to their sides, a sudden wariness taking Beth by surprise. But they had hugged. That in itself was a start.

'I must phone Jon.' She picked up her bag and felt for her phone at the same time as experiencing an urgent need to sit down. 'Perhaps I'll catch him before he's gone too far.'

He picked up immediately and she told him the news. Hearing his excitement made her wish he was with her. She wanted to share this moment with him. 'I'll turn around and be back there in five,' he said and hung up.

For the next few minutes, Beth barely took in what was being said to her. She was dimly aware of Megan calling Pete to break the news, of Jon arriving. Of congratulations, kisses. But the fact that Ella had had her baby safely was what really mattered. All she wanted to do was see them both; hold them tight. At the same time, she felt the tension she'd been carrying with her for months give a little as a feeling of lightness, of joy, began to take its place.

The midwife couldn't return soon enough. But, at last, she did. Beth and Jon made for the door together, but Beth hesitated.

'Are you coming, Megan?' she asked.

Megan got out of her seat, then stopped. There was a tiny pause, once again punctuated by the click of the knitting needles.

'No, you go,' she said. 'You go first. I'll come in a few minutes.'

Their companion nodded her approval.

Beth retraced her steps and kissed Megan on both cheeks. 'Thank you.'

Megan glanced at her watch.

'That was very generous,' said the woman. Her needles kept on moving. 'A small thing but a big one at the same time.'

'No, not really,' admitted Megan. 'Ella's her daughter and they've been through a lot to get here. She should be there first. Ten minutes won't make a difference to me. But it might to them.'

Having said that, she proceeded to count every one of those minutes as they ticked past. She didn't want to talk, just to imagine what seeing the baby for the first time would feel like. At last, the time came. As she stood to go, slinging her bag over her shoulder, her companion looked up at her. 'Enjoy her,' she said. 'The first one's very special.'

As Megan walked to the birthing suite, she felt as if she might pop with excitement.

The first people she saw when she entered the room were Beth and Jon. They were bent over a swaddled bundle in Beth's arms. Ella and Jake looked up, both pale but radiating pride and happiness. Jake stood, withdrawing his arm from Ella's back but letting his hand rest on her shoulder. 'Mum!'

Megan walked towards them, feeling tears hot on her cheeks but laughing at the same time.

'Come and meet Daisy,' he said, a broad smile spreading across his face. 'And we're all sorted now, aren't we, Els?'

She nodded, beaming back at him. 'We're going to be fine.'

He enveloped Megan in an enormous bear hug. 'I'm so proud of you both,' she whispered, her voice catching with emotion. Somewhere behind her, she heard Beth say something to Jon, and then his reply: 'Wait. It's her turn now.' She turned to them, and to the baby.

'Daisy,' said Beth, 'meet your other grandmother.' Her eyes were red but she was smiling broadly as she stepped forward to pass the bundle to Megan. 'We're grandmothers! Look! Isn't she gorgeous?'

Megan cradled the baby and felt her weight settle into her arms. She stared down into the tiny pink face, eyes shut, a perfect nose, rosebud lips just parted, blonde hair like peach down. 'Hello, Daisy,' she whispered.

'It all went according to plan,' Jake said, coming over to stroke his daughter's forehead with a finger. 'Ella was amazing. She remembered all her breathing and, in the end, the birth was quite quick.'

He sounded like an old hand.

'Thanks to you remembering it too and reminding me.' Ella laughed. 'I couldn't have done it without him.'

And you? Megan wanted to ask Jake. Are you OK? But, instead, she stared in awe at her granddaughter. 'Seven pounds eight ounces,' Jake went on. 'The tiniest fingers and toes. Not much hair, but she's so beautiful and she's even got Ella's dimple.'

'Are you sure?' asked Jon quickly. 'I didn't notice.' He moved close to Megan and leaned over Daisy.

'Oh, yes,' confirmed Beth. 'Didn't you see? Just like ...' She stopped and touched Jon's shoulder.

Jon shook his head and his expression changed. For a moment, Megan thought she saw sadness there, but then it had gone and his eyes lit up again. 'Just like Ella,' he said.

'I hope you two grandmothers are going to behave now she's born?' Jake addressed them both.

There was a silence. An awkward one that was filled with regret.

Beth looked at Megan in a way she hadn't looked at her for months. The now familiar hostility had vanished. Perhaps ... perhaps they could be friends again, but in a different way. They would be bonded by the practicalities and pleasures of grand-motherhood from now on.

'Are you?' he insisted.

My God, thought Megan. He sounds so grown up; his own man at last.

Megan nodded. 'Truce.' She handed Daisy back to Beth, who looked down at her, adoring, utterly absorbed, before returning her to Ella and Jake. Of course Daisy would come first from now on. Neither of them wanted to forfeit their part in her life.

Megan heard Jon clear his throat in the background and felt him take her hand. As she turned to him, their eyes met for a moment, then they both looked away. But when she gave the smallest squeeze imaginable to his hand, he didn't let go. Instead, he squeezed right back.

These were her friends – of the kind you marched alongside through life. She loved them. She loved them not. And they felt the same. In the end, loving and not loving became irrelevant because, at whatever stage it was, the friendship was ineradicable.

That's what friendship was. Plus, for so long now, Beth had been part of her and she part of Beth. Whatever happened, that would not change.

Megan … ?' Beth held out her hand.

Megan smiled, and took a step towards her.

Acknowledgements

Many thanks are due to:

Clare Alexander, the best agent I could ever hope for.

Susan Lamb and Kate Mills and their fantastic team, with a special shout out for Jemima Forrester and Gaby Young.

Sue James and Tessa Hilton for all their great support.

Frances Hughes who advised me on the life and work of a family lawyer (any mistakes are undoubtedly mine).

My family and friends who stick by me and help me in so many ways.